MISSING PIECES

Joy Fielding

MISSING PIECES

COMPASS PRESS
AN IMPRINT OF WHEELER PUBLISHING, INC.

Published in Large Print by arrangement with Doubleday, a division of Bantam Doubleday Dell Publishing Group, Inc. in the United States and Canada.

Wheeler Large Print Book Series.

Set in 16 pt Plantin.

Library of Congress Cataloging-in-Publication Data

Fielding, Joy.
    Missing pieces / Joy Fielding.
        p. (large print) cm.(Wheeler large print book series)
    ISBN 1-56895-491-3 (hardcover)
    1. Large type books.
I. Title.
[PR9199.3.F518M57   1997b]
813′.54—dc21   97-34306
                                                              CIP

For Carole

ACKNOWLEDGEMENTS

I wish to thank officials at Union Correctional Institution and the Florida State Prison who provided me with much needed information. I would especially like to thank the staff of the medical examiner's office of Palm Beach County who were so generous with both their time and expertise. A special thank-you to Lawrence L. Lewis, a volunteer at the Palm Beach County Courthouse, who gave me directions, pamphlets, and a much-appreciated cup of coffee at the end of a very long day.

My heartfelt gratitude to Larry Merkin and Beverley Slopen, both of whom read earlier drafts of the manuscript and offered invaluable advice and encouragement.

Thank you to Janet Tanzer and Sally Muir, two of the world's great family therapists, whose wit and wisdom changed my life. And to my daughers, Shannon and Annie—I couldn't have written this book without them.

Lastly, my thanks to my husband, Warren, for everything.

MISSING PIECES

Chapter
1

Another woman is missing.

Her name is Millie Potton and she was last seen two days ago. According to today's paper, Millie is tall and thin and walks with a slight limp. She is fifty-four years old, which isn't surprising. Only women over fifty have names like Millie anymore.

The small article on page three of the local news section of the *Palm Beach Post* states that she was last seen wandering down the street in her bathrobe by a neighbor, a woman who obviously saw nothing particularly peculiar in the incident. Millie Potton, the article continues, has a long history of mental problems, the implication being that it is these mental problems that are responsible for her disappearance and are not therefore anything the rest of us have to be concerned about.

Over two dozen women have disappeared from the Palm Beach area in the last five years. I know because I've been keeping track, not consciously, at least not at first, but after a while their numbers just started adding up, and a vague figure affixed itself to my conscious mind. The women range in age from sixteen to sixty. The police have dismissed some as runaways, especially the younger ones, girls like Amy Lokash, age seventeen, who left a friend's house at ten o'clock one evening and was never seen or heard from again. Others, and Millie Potton will undoubtedly be among them, have been dismissed for any number of indisputably logical reasons, even though the police were wrong about Amy Lokash.

Still, until a body turns up somewhere, stuffed into a garbage bin behind Burger King like Marilyn Greenwood, age twenty-four, or floating face down in a Port Everglades swamp like Christine McDermott, age thirty-three, there really isn't anything the police can do. Or so they say. Women, it seems, go missing all the time.

It's quiet in the house this morning, what with everybody gone. I have lots of time to tape my report. I call it a report, but really it isn't anything so clearly defined. It's more a series of reminiscences, although the police have asked me to be as specific and as orderly as I can, to be careful not to leave anything out, no matter how insignificant—or how personal—something may seem. They will decide what is important, they tell me.

I'm not sure I understand the point. What's done is done. It's not as if I can go back and change any of the things that have happened, much as I'd like to, much as I tried to before they occurred. But I was just hitting my head against a brick wall. I knew it at the time. I know it now. There are certain things over which we have no control—the actions of others being

2

the prime example. Much as we may not like it, we have to stand back and let people go their own way, make their own mistakes, no matter how clearly we see disaster looming. Isn't that what I'm always telling my clients?

Of course, it's much easier to give advice than it is to follow it. Maybe that's one of the reasons I became a family therapist, although that certainly wasn't the reason I gave on my college entry application. There, if memory serves me correctly, and it does so with alarmingly less frequency all the time, I listed my intense desire to help others, my reputation among friends as someone to whom they could always turn in times of trouble, my experience with my own dysfunctional family, although the term "dysfunctional" had yet to be coined at the time I entered university way back in 1966. It's so common now, so much a part of the everyday vernacular, that it's hard to imagine how we managed for so long without it, despite the fact that it's essentially meaningless. What constitutes dysfunction, after all? What family doesn't have problems? I'm certain my own daughters could give you an earful.

So, where to start? This is what my first-time clients ask all the time. They come into my office, which is on the third floor of a five-story Pepto-Bismol pink building on Royal Palm Way, their eyes wary, the fingers of one hand chipping at the wedding band on the other, as they perch on the ends of the upholstered gray-and-white chairs, their lips parting in anticipation, their mouths eager to give voice to their rage, their fears, their displeasure, and the first thing that tumbles out is always the same: Where do I start?

Usually, I ask them to describe the event that brought them to my office, the proverbial straw that broke the camel's back. They think for several seconds, then start slowly, building their case from the ground up, like a new house, piling detail upon detail, like blocks, one on top of the other, one indignity crowding against another, perceived slight over implied threat, the words spilling out so fast that they barely have time to fit them all into the space of an hour.

I've used a building analogy—Larry would be amused at this. Larry is my husband of twenty-four years, and he's a builder. A good portion of those spectacular new homes going up on golf courses across Palm Beach County are his. His profession is supposedly the reason we relocated from Pittsburgh to Florida some seven years ago, but I've always suspected that at least part of the reason Larry was so anxious to move down here was to get away from my mother and sister. He denies this, but since it was a large part of the reason *I* agreed so readily to the move, I have always found his denials suspect. It's pretty much a moot point anyway, since my mother followed us here less than a year later, and my sister several months after that.

My sister's name is Jo Lynn. Or at least, that's the name she goes by. Her real name is Joanne Linda. But our father took to calling her

4

Jo Lynn when she was just a child, and the name stuck. Actually, it suits her. She looks like a Jo Lynn, tall and blond and bosomy, with an infectious giggle that starts somewhere deep in her throat and ends up floating around her head like fairy dust. Even the deep, honey-coated Southern accent she's affected since moving to Florida seems more right, more genuine somehow, than the flat, cold tones of the North she spoke with for most of her thirty-seven years.

I said my father, but in fact he was only Jo Lynn's father, and not mine. My father died when I was eight years old. The way my mother tells it, he got up from the dinner table to get a glass of milk, remarked casually that he felt a hell of a headache coming on, and the next minute he was dead on the floor. An aneurysm, the doctor later pronounced. My mother remarried the following year, and Jo Lynn came along the year after that, just weeks after my tenth birthday.

My stepfather was a mean and manipulative man who relied more on his fists than his brains, assuming he had any. I'm sure it was from him that Jo Lynn acquired her lifelong habit of picking abusive men, although he was always very tender with her, his clear favorite. It was my mother who bore the brunt of his ill temper. Aside from a few well-placed cuffs to the back of the head, he largely ignored me. At any rate, my mother left him when Jo Lynn was thirteen and I'd already left home to marry Larry. My stepfather died the following year of pancreatic cancer. Jo Lynn was the only one of us who mourned.

And now I cry for my sister, as I have so often over the years. Technically, of course, she's only my half sister, and the ten-year age difference, coupled with her often erratic behavior, made it difficult for us to be close. But I will never forget the morning my mother first brought her home from the hospital, how she walked toward me cradling this small golden bundle in her arms and gently transferred her to mine, telling me I had a real doll to help care for now. I remember standing beside her crib for hours at a time while she slept, watching carefully for telltale signs of growth, as she moved inexorably from baby to toddler. She was such a beautiful child, so headstrong and confident, in the way small children have of knowing that they are absolutely right about everything, that it's still hard to reconcile that image with the lost soul she grew into, one of those people who wander aimlessly through life, always convinced that success and happiness are just around the corner. Except that she'd get distracted, forget what direction she was headed in, make a wrong turn, and end up on a dead-end street, no corners anywhere in sight.

I see traces of her in my older daughter, Sara, who also has to learn everything the hard way, and it scares me. Maybe that's why I'm on her back all the time, or so she says. Actually, Sara never *says* anything—she yells. She believes that the way to win an argument is to keep repeating the same thing over and

6

over, each time louder than the time before. She's probably right, because eventually you either give in or run screaming from the room. I've done both more times than I care to admit. My clients would be properly horrified.

Sara is seventeen and stands just under six feet tall. Like Jo Lynn, she has big green eyes and huge breasts. I don't know where they came from. To be honest, I'm not all that sure where *she* came from. Sometimes, I look at her when she's in the middle of one of her tirades and wonder: Did the hospital make a mistake? Could this tall, wide-eyed, big-breasted creature screaming at me at the top of her lungs really be mine? There are days when I look at her and I think that she's the most beautiful thing on the face of this earth. Then there are other days when I swear she looks just like Patricia Krenwinkel. You remember her— she was one of Charles Manson's murderous gang, the sullen-faced teenaged killer with the long brown hair parted lazily down the middle, her eyes blank yet unforgiving, the same look I occasionally see on Sara's face. Sara wears clothes I swear I threw out twenty-five years ago, those shapeless, see-through, Indian caftans I have since come to despise, unlike Michelle, my fourteen-year-old, who will only wear clothes from Club Monaco and The Gap, and who carefully monitors each family altercation from the sidelines, commenting on the action later, like some skinny, adolescent Greek chorus. Or budding family therapist.

7

Is that why I have relatively few problems with my younger child? Do I want, as my elder daughter has suggested numerous times, that everyone be exactly like me? "I'm not you," she yells. "I'm my own person!" And isn't that exactly what I've brought her up to be? But does her own person have to be so objectionable? Was I so rebellious, so rude, so downright miserable? I ask my mother, who smiles cryptically and assures me I was perfect.

Jo Lynn, she adds wearily, was another story.

"I wish on you a daughter just like you," I still hear my mother shouting at Jo Lynn in exasperation, something I've had to bite my tongue to keep from saying myself on more than one occasion. But whether out of spite or fear, my sister remained childless through three failed marriages, and I ended up with the daughter just like Jo Lynn. It doesn't seem fair. I was the one who played by the rules. If I was rebellious at all, I did so within all the prescribed parameters. I stayed in school, got my degree, didn't smoke, drink, or do drugs, and married the only man with whom I'd ever had sex. By contrast, Jo Lynn stayed in college only long enough to tune in, turn on, drop out, and was sexually active early and often. I became a family therapist; she became a family therapist's worst nightmare.

Why am I going into all this? Is this really the sort of thing the police will feel is relevant? I don't know. In truth, I don't know much of anything anymore. My whole life feels like one of those giant jigsaw puzzles, the kind that takes forever to put together, and then just when you're coming to the end, right at the point where you finally think you've got it, you discover that all the key pieces are missing.

With age comes wisdom, I distinctly remember hearing in my youth. I don't think so. With age comes wrinkles, I'm sure they meant. And bladder problems, and arthritis, and hot flashes, and memory loss. I'm not handling aging very well, which surprises me, because I always thought I'd be one of those women who grew old gracefully. But it's hard to be graceful when you're running to the bathroom every ten minutes or breaking into a sweat just after you've finished applying your makeup.

Everyone is younger than me. My dentist, my doctor, my daughters' teachers, my neighbors, the parents of my children's friends, my clients, even the police who came to question me—they're all younger than I am. It's funny because I always assume that I'm younger than everyone else, and then I find out that not only am I older, I'm *years* older. And I'm the only one who's surprised.

Actually I surprise myself sometimes. I'll be all dressed up, feeling good, thinking I look great, and then I catch my reflection unexpectedly in a store window or a pane of glass, and I think: Who is that? Who is that middle-aged woman? It can't be me. I don't have those bags under my eyes; those aren't my legs; surely that's not my rear end. It's genuinely frightening when your self-image no longer corresponds to the image you see in the mirror. It's even scarier when you realize that other people barely see you at all, that you've become invisible.

Maybe that explains what happened with Robert.

How else can I explain it?

I'm doing it again, digressing, going off on one of my famous tangents. Larry says I do it all the time. I explain that I'm working my way up to the main point; he claims I'm trying to avoid it. He's probably right. At least, in this instance.

I'm about to have a hot flash. I know because I just got that horrible feeling of anxiety that always precedes it, as though someone has emptied a glass of ice water down my throat. It fills my chest, lies like a puddle around my heart. Ice followed by fire. I'm not sure which is worse.

At first I thought these feelings of anxiety were related to the chaos that was going on around me. I blamed my mother, my sister, Robert, the trial. Anything. But gradually I realized that these feelings of dread were immediately followed by tidal waves of heat that surged upward from the pit of my stomach toward my head, leaving me perspiring and breathless, as if I were in danger of imploding. I marvel at the strength of these interludes, at how powerless I am to stop them, at how little control I have over my own life.

My body has betrayed me; it follows an invisible timetable all its own. I wear reading glasses now; my skin is losing some of its elasticity, rippling like cheap fabric; there are thin lines around my neck, like the age lines of a tree. Things grow inside me, uninvited.

I was at the doctor's recently for a check-up. During the course of a routine pelvic examination, Dr. Wong, who is tiny and delicate and looks all of eighteen, discovered several cervical polyps which she said had to be removed. "How did they get there?" I asked. She shrugged. "These things happen as we get older." She gave me the choice: she could schedule an operation in several weeks under a general anesthetic or she could snip them out right there and then in her office, no anesthetic at all. "What do you recommend?" I asked, not thrilled with either alternative. "How high is your pain tolerance?" she answered.

I opted to have the polyps out in her office. As it turned out, it was a relatively simple procedure, taking less than ten minutes, during which time the doctor explained clearly, and in more detail than I really needed, everything she was doing. "Now you might feel as if you have to go to the bathroom," I remember her saying seconds before my stomach began twisting into a series of tight little knots.

When she was finished, Dr. Wong held up a small glass jar for my inspection. Inside were two little round red balls, the size of large cranberries. "See," she said, almost proudly, "these are your polyps."

Twins, I thought giddily, then burst into tears.

I was supposed to call her office two weeks later to find out if there was a problem. I can't remember now whether I did or not. It was in the middle of all the craziness. It's quite possible I forgot.

Something is happening across the street. I can see it from the window. I'm sitting at my desk in the den, a small, book-lined room at the front of the house off the center foyer. Do the police want a description of the house? I'll include one, although surely they know it. They've been here enough times; they've taken enough photographs. But for the record, the house is a relatively large bungalow with three bedrooms and a den. The girls' bedrooms are to the right of the front door, the master bedroom to the left at the back. In between are the living and dining rooms, four bathrooms, and a large open space consisting of the kitchen, the breakfast nook, and the family room, whose back wall is a series of paneled glass windows and sliding glass doors overlooking the kidney-shaped backyard pool. The ceilings are high and dotted with overhead fans, like the one turning softly above my head right now, the floors large blocks of ceramic tile, interrupted by plush area rugs. Only the bedrooms and den have wall-to-wall broadloom. The predominant color is beige, with accents in brown, black, and teal. Larry built the house; I decorated it. It was supposed to be our sanctuary.

I think I know what's going on across the street. It's happened before. Several large boys bullying a couple of smaller boys to come over, to knock on my door. The big boys are laughing, taunting the smaller ones, pushing them and calling them cowards, daring them to cross the street. Just ring the bell and ask her, I can hear them say, although no sound reaches my ears beyond their cruel laughter. Go ring her bell, then we'll leave you alone. The two younger boys— I think I recognize one of them as six-year-old Ian McMullen, who lives at the end of the street—straighten their shoulders and stare at the house. Another push and they're off the sidewalk and on the road, creeping up the front walk, their small fingers already stretching toward the buzzer.

And then suddenly they're gone, running madly down the street, as if being chased, although the older boys have turned and run off in the opposite direction. Maybe they saw me watching them; maybe someone is calling them; maybe good sense got the better of them. Who knows? Whatever it was that made them turn and flee, I'm grateful, although I'm already half out of my chair.

The first time it happened was just after the story hit the front pages. Most people were very respectful, but you always get a few who aren't satisfied with what they read, who want to know more, who feel they're entitled. The police did a good job of keeping most of them at bay, but occasionally young boys such as these made their way to my front door.

"What can I do for you?" I hear myself say, recalling their presence, feeling it still.

"Is this where it happened?" they ask, giggling nervously.

"Where what happened?"

"You know." Pause, anxious glances, trying to peer around my stubborn bulk. "Can we see the blood?"

It's around this time that I shut the door on their curious faces, although I admit the perverse temptation to usher them graciously inside, direct them toward the back of the house, like a tour guide, my voice a melodic whisper, to point out the area on the family-room floor that was once covered in blood, and even now shows faint traces of blush, despite several professional cleanings. Probably I'll have to have those tiles replaced. It won't be easy. The company that manufactured them went bankrupt several years ago.

So, how did all this happen? When did my once steady and comfortable life begin careening out of control, like a car without brakes on a high mountain road, gaining speed and momentum until it crashes into the abyss and bursts into flames? At what precise moment did Humpty-Dumpty fall off the wall and shatter into thousands of tiny pieces, impossible to repair or replace?

Of course, no such moment exists. When one part of your life is coming apart at the seams, the rest of your life doesn't just sit back and patiently wait its turn to continue. It doesn't give you time to cope, or space to adjust and refocus. It just keeps piling one confusing event on top of the next, like a traffic cop rushing to make his quota of tickets.

Am I being overly dramatic? Maybe. Although I think I'm entitled. I, who have always been the steady one, the practical one, the one with more common sense than imagination, or so Jo Lynn once stated, am entitled to my few moments of melodrama.

Do I start at the very beginning, announce myself like a label stuck to a lapel: Hello, my name is Kate Sinclair? Do I say that I was born forty-seven years ago in Pittsburgh on an uncharacteristically warm day in April, that I'm five feet six and a half inches tall and one hundred and twenty-five pounds, that my hair is light brown and my eyes a shade darker, that I have small breasts and good legs and a slightly lopsided smile? That Larry affectionately calls me funny face, that Robert said I was beautiful?

It would be much easier to start at the end, to recite facts already known, give name to the dead, wipe away the blood once and for all, instead of trying to search for motivations, for explanations, for answers that might never be found.

But the police don't want that. They already know the basic facts. They've seen the end results. What they want are details, and I've agreed, as best I can, to provide them. I could start with Amy Lokash's disappearance, or the first time her mother came to my office. I could begin with my mother's fears she was being followed, or with the day Sara's teacher called to voice her growing concerns about my daughter's behavior. I could talk about that first phone call from Robert, or Larry's sudden trip to South Carolina. But I guess if I have to choose one moment over all the others, it would have to be that Saturday morning last October when Jo Lynn and I were sitting at the kitchen table, relaxing and enjoying our third cup of coffee, and my sister put down the morning paper and calmly announced that she was going to marry a man who was on trial for the murder of thirteen women.

Yes, I think I'll start there.

Chapter
2

I remember it was sunny, one of those perfect Florida days when the sky is so blue it seems artificial, the temperature balancing on the comfortable side of eighty, with only a warm whisper of a breeze. I swallowed the balance of coffee in my cup, inhaling it as lovingly as a chain-smoker with her last cigarette, and stared out the back window at the large coconut palm that curved from behind the pool toward the terra-cotta tile roof of the house. It was the kind of picture you see on postcards that trill, "Having a wonderful time, wish you were here." The sky, the grass, even the bark of the trees, were so vivid they seemed to vibrate. Diamondlike sparkles of air reflected from their surfaces. "What a day," I said out loud.

"Hmm," Jo Lynn grunted from somewhere behind the morning paper.

"Look at it," I persisted, not sure why I was bothering. Was I looking for confirmation or conversation? Did I need either? "Look at how blue that sky is."

Jo Lynn's eyes flashed briefly over the top corner of the local news section of the *Palm Beach Post*. "Wouldn't you just love a sweater in that shade?" she asked, her voice a lazy Southern drawl.

Somehow this wasn't quite the response I'd been hoping for, although it was typical Jo Lynn, for whom nature was merely backdrop. I lapsed back into silence, debated whether to have another cup of coffee, decided against it. Three cups was more than enough, although I do love my morning coffee—my only real vice, I used to say.

I thought of Larry, out on the golf course since before 8 A.M. with prospective clients. Larry was relatively new to golf. He'd played a bit in college, was actually quite good at it, he confided, but gave it up for lack of time and money. Now that he had substantially more of both, and clients and business acquaintances were always inviting him out for a round, he'd taken it up again, although he wasn't finding it quite as relaxing as he remembered. The night before, he'd spent almost an hour practicing in front of the full-length bathroom mirror, trying to recapture the effortless swing of his youth. "Almost there," he kept repeating, as I grew tired of waiting for him to come to bed, and allowed myself to drift off to sleep, vague stirrings of frustration teasing at my groin.

He'd already left by the time I woke up. I got out of bed, threw on a short pink cotton robe, ambled into the kitchen, made a large pot of coffee, and sat down with the newspaper that Larry had been thoughtful enough to bring inside before heading out. The girls were still asleep. Michelle had been out with her girlfriends till after midnight. I didn't even hear Sara come home.

I was reading the movie reviews and enjoying my second cup of coffee when Jo Lynn showed up. She was in a lousy mood, she announced in lieu of hello, partly because she hadn't slept very well, but mostly because she'd been stood up the night before. Apparently her date, a former football player turned sporting goods salesman, who she said looked like a weathered Brad Pitt, had begged off at the last minute, claiming a sore throat and achy limbs. So she'd gone to a bar and who should show up, looking healthy as a horse? Well, you know the rest, she told me, pouring herself a cup of coffee, settling in.

So there she was, in white shorts and revealing halter top, looking gorgeous as usual, despite her sleepless night, her shoulder-length blond curls gloriously askew—the freshly fucked look, she called it, although she hadn't been, she groused. That makes two of us, I almost confided, but didn't. I could never bring myself to discuss my sex life with Jo Lynn, partly because I didn't trust her to be discreet, mostly because there was nothing much to tell. I'd been in a monogamous relationship for almost a quarter of a century. To Jo Lynn, monogamy equaled monotony. I'd given up trying to change her mind. Lately, my words sounded hollow, even to me.

Jo Lynn, on the other hand, was always more than willing, eager even, to share the secrets of her love life with me. Details of her escapades flowed from her lips as briskly as water from a mountain stream. I tried to tell her that her love life was nobody's business but her own, but this was a concept she clearly didn't understand. I tried to remind her that discretion was the better part of valor; she looked at me as if I were crazy. I tried to warn her against disease; she scowled and looked away. I told her I really wasn't interested; she laughed loud and long. "Of course you're interested," she'd say, and of course she was right. "Just don't talk about it in front of the girls," I'd plead, to no avail. Jo Lynn loved an audience. She relished the effect she had on my daughters, who openly worshipped her, especially Sara. Sometimes they'd gang up on me, laugh at my so-called conservative ways, talk about dragging me onto one of those dreadful daytime talk shows they sometimes watched. "Girl, you need a makeover!" Jo Lynn would shout in the hyperextended voice of Rolonda or Ricki Lake, while Sara doubled over with laughter.

"He's cute," Jo Lynn was muttering now, her face buried so deep behind the morning paper that I wasn't sure I'd heard her say anything at all.

"Did you say something?"

"He sure is cute," she repeated, more clearly this time. "Just look at that face." She spread the paper across the round glass top of the kitchen table. "I'm gonna marry that man," she said.

I stared down at the front page of the local news section. Three men stared back: the President of the United States, in Florida to confer with local politicians; a Catholic priest, lending his support to a projected gay and lesbian rights march; and Colin Friendly, the ironically named accused killer of thirteen women, sitting in a courtroom in West Palm Beach. I was afraid to ask which of the three she meant.

"I'm serious," she said, the long orange nail of her index finger tapping at the photograph of the accused murderer. "Just look at that face. He looks a little like Brad Pitt, don't you think?"

"He looks like Ted Bundy," I corrected, although, in truth, I couldn't make out what he looked like. I'd taken off my reading glasses and everything about the newspaper was a soft blur.

"Put on your glasses," she instructed, reading my mind, pushing the wire-rimmed half-glasses toward my face. The grainy black and white dots of the photograph immediately snapped into place, forming a clear, cohesive whole. "What do you see?"

"I see a cold-blooded killer," I pronounced, about to remove the glasses when her hand stopped me.

"Where does it say he killed anybody?"

"Jo Lynn, do you actually read the paper or do you just look at the pictures?"

"I read the article, smarty-pants," she said, and instantly we were both ten years old, "and it doesn't say one word about him being a murderer."

"Jo Lynn, he killed at least thirteen women..."

"He's *accused* of killing them, which doesn't mean he did it. I mean, correct me if I'm wrong, but isn't that why there's a trial?"

I opened my mouth to protest, thought better of it, said nothing.

"Whatever happened to "innocent until proven guilty'?" she continued, as I'd known she would. Benign silence had never worked with Jo Lynn.

"You think he's innocent," I stated, a technique I often used with clients. Instead of arguing, instead of trying to change their minds, instead of providing them with answers that might or might not be correct, I merely repeated their own words back at them, sometimes reframing those words in a more

21

positive light, hopefully giving them time to discover the answers for themselves, sometimes just to let them know they'd been heard.

"I think there's a good chance he might be. I mean, just look at that face. He's beautiful."

Reluctantly, I studied the photograph. Colin Friendly sat between his lawyers, two faceless men conferring with each other behind his back, as the accused serial killer hunched forward, staring blankly toward the empty witness stand. What I saw was a man in his early thirties, his dark wavy hair combed neatly away from his finely chiseled features, a face that, under other circumstances, I might have regarded as handsome. I knew, from other pictures I'd seen, that he was over six feet tall and slim, almost wiry. His eyes were said to be blue, although never *just* blue, but always *piercing* blue or *intensely* blue, although today's photograph revealed nothing of the sort. But maybe it was hard for me to look at him objectively, even then.

"Don't you think he's gorgeous?"

I shook my head.

"You can't be serious. He looks just like Brad Pitt, only his hair is darker, and his nose is longer and thinner."

I stared at the thirty-seven-year-old woman sitting across from me. She'd gone from sounding like a ten-year-old to sounding like a love-struck teen. Would she ever grow up? I wondered. Did any of us? Or did we just grow old?

"Okay, so maybe he doesn't look that much

like Brad Pitt, but you've got to admit he's good-looking. Charismatic. Yeah, that's what he is—charismatic. At least, you have to admit that much."

"It's very hard for me to think of anyone who tortured and murdered thirteen women and girls as being either gorgeous or charismatic. I'm sorry, I just can't do it." I thought of Donna Lokash, a client of mine, whose daughter, Amy, had disappeared almost a year ago, a possible victim of Colin Friendly's rage, although her body had yet to be found.

"You have to separate the two issues," Jo Lynn was saying, and I almost laughed. I was the one, after all, who was always talking about separating issues. "The fact that he's good-looking has nothing to do with whether or not he killed anybody."

"It doesn't?"

"No. One thing has nothing to do with the other."

I shrugged. "What do you see when you look at him?" I asked, genuinely curious. "Aside from Brad Pitt."

"I see a little boy who's been hurt." Jo Lynn's voice was solemn, genuine.

"You see a boy who's been hurt," I parroted, recalling Jo Lynn as a child, gently rocking a stray kitten back and forth across her bare tummy. It had given her ringworm. "Where? Where do you see that?"

The bright orange nail drew a small circle around Colin Friendly's mouth. "He has a sad smile."

I studied the photograph more closely, surprised to discover she was right. "Don't you think it's odd," I asked, "that, under the circumstances, he's smiling at all?"

"It's just boyish bravado," she said, as if she'd known Colin Friendly all her life. "I find it endearing."

I stood up, shuffled over to the kitchen counter, poured myself another cup of coffee. Clearly, I was going to need it. "Can we talk about something else?"

Jo Lynn swiveled around in her chair, held out her cup for me to fill. Her long tanned legs stretched toward me, the bright orange polish on her toenails peeking out from between the crossing leather bands of her white sandals. "You don't think I'm serious, do you?"

"Jo Lynn, let's not…"

"Let's not what? Talk about something just because it's important to me?"

I stared into my coffee cup, wishing I were back in bed. "This is important to you?" I asked.

Jo Lynn sat up straight, drew her legs back beneath her chair, pushed her lips into a Bardot-like pout that men usually found appealing, but which had always annoyed the hell out of me. "Yes, it is."

"So where do you want me to send the wedding present?" I asked, straining for levity.

Jo Lynn was having none of it. "Sure, make a joke. I'm just a big joke to you."

I took a long, slow sip of my coffee, the only thing I could think to do that wouldn't get me into more trouble. "Look, Jo Lynn, what is it you want me to say?"

"I want you to stop being so damned dismissive."

"I'm sorry, I didn't realize I was being dismissive."

"That's the problem. You never do."

My shortcomings weren't something I particularly wanted to get into at this hour of the morning. "Look, can't we just agree to disagree? It's a beautiful day. I really don't want to waste it arguing about some guy you've never even met."

"I'm going to change that."

"What?"

"I'm going to meet him."

"What?"

"I'm going to meet him," she repeated stubbornly. "I'm going to go down to that courthouse next week and meet him."

My patience was all but exhausted. This was worse than dealing with Sara. "You're going to go to the courthouse..."

"That's what I just said. I'm going to the courthouse. On Monday."

"And what do you think you're going to accomplish by going to the courthouse?" I asked, ignoring the little therapist's voice in the back of my head urging me to be quiet, to let Jo Lynn sputter on until she simply ran out of steam. "They're not going to let you talk to him."

"They might."

"They won't."

"Then I'll just sit in the courtroom and watch. I'll be there for him."

"You'll be there for him," I repeated numbly.

"As support. And stop repeating everything I say. It's very annoying."

I tried another approach. "I thought you were going job-hunting Monday."

"I've been job-hunting every day for the past two weeks. I've left résumés all over town."

"Have you followed any of them up with a phone call? You know you have to be persistent." I hated the sound of my own voice as much as the look on Jo Lynn's face told me she did. "God knows you can be persistent when you want to be."

"Maybe I don't want to be," she shot back. "Maybe I'm tired of working at a bunch of stupid low-paying jobs for a bunch of stupid low-lifes. Maybe I'm thinking of starting my own business."

"Doing what?"

"I haven't decided yet. Maybe opening an exercise studio, or a dog-sitting service, something like that."

I struggled to keep my face calm while digesting this latest bulletin. Jo Lynn had never attended an exercise class in her life; she lived in an apartment complex that didn't allow pets.

"You don't think I can do it."

"I think you can do anything you set your mind to," I told her honestly. At the moment, it was the thing about her that worried me the most.

"But you think it's a dumb idea."

"I didn't say that."

"You don't have to. I can see it all over your face."

I turned away, caught sight of myself in the dark glass of the wall oven. She was right. Even through the smoky glass, I could see how pale my skin had turned, how slack-jawed I'd become. Of course, it didn't help that my hair hung around my face like a limp, chin-length mop, or that the bags under my eyes had yet to shrink with the light of day. "You need money to start a business," I began, once again ignoring the tiny therapist pummeling her fists against the inside of my brain.

"I'll have money."

"You will? How? When?"

"When Mom dies," she said, and smiled, the same sad twisting of her lips as the killer in the morning paper.

For an instant, it felt as if my heart had stopped. I quickly lowered my coffee cup to the counter, took one shaking hand inside the other. "How could you say such a thing?"

And suddenly she was laughing, great whoops of glee that circled the air above my head like giant lassos, threatening to drop down and take hold of my throat, to jerk me mercilessly toward the ceiling, leave me kicking frantically at the air. "Lighten up, lady. Can't you tell when someone's kidding?"

"Kidding on the square," I said, then bit down hard on my lower lip. Our mother always said that.

"I never understood what that was supposed to mean," Jo Lynn said testily.

"It means you're kidding, but you're not really kidding. You're making a joke, but really you're serious."

"I know what it means," she said.

"Anyway," I insisted, "Mom's only seventy-five, and she's in great shape. I wouldn't count on her going anywhere for a while yet."

"I never count on her for anything," Jo Lynn said.

"Where is all this coming from?" I asked.

Now it was Jo Lynn's turn to stare at me with openmouthed disbelief. "It's always been like this. Where have you been all these years?"

"Well, how long is it going to go on? You're all grown up now. How long are you going to keep blaming her for things she may or may not have done over twenty years ago?"

"Don't minimize what she did."

"What *exactly* did she do?"

Jo Lynn shook her head, brushed several blond curls away from her cheek, pulled on the long gold loop earring that dangled from her right ear. "Nothing. She did nothing wrong. She was the perfect mother. Forget I said anything." She shook her head. The blond curls fell back across her flushed cheek. "It's just PMS talking."

That didn't mollify me. "Have you ever stopped to think that there is no such thing as PMS, and that this is the way you really are?"

Jo Lynn stared at me, green eyes narrowing, orange mouth pursing, as if she were giving

28

serious thought to leaping across the table and wrestling me to the floor. Then suddenly her eyes widened, her lips parted, and she was laughing again, only this time the laughter was genuine and expansive, and I was able to join her.

"That was funny," she said, as I basked in her unexpected goodwill.

The phone rang. It was our mother. As if on cue. As if she'd been privy to our conversation. As if she knew our most secret thoughts.

"Tell her we were just talking about her," Jo Lynn whispered, loud enough to be heard.

"How are you, Mom?" I said instead, picturing her on the other end of the receiver, already showered and dressed, her short tightly curled gray hair framing her narrow face, dark brown eyes sparkling with expectation for the day ahead.

Her voice filled the room. "Magnificent," she trilled. That was what she always said. Magnificent. Jo Lynn mouthed the word along with her. "How are you, darling?"

"I'm good."

"And the girls?"

"They're fine."

"I'm good too," Jo Lynn called out.

"Oh, is Jo Lynn there?"

"She dropped by for a cup of coffee."

"Give her my love," our mother said.

"Give it back," Jo Lynn said flatly in return.

"Sweetheart," our mother continued, "I'm calling because I can't find that wonderful recipe I have for poach crumble, and I wondered if you had a copy of it."

"Poach crumble?" I repeated.

"Yes," she said. "Remember? I made it for you a few weeks ago. You said it was delicious."

"You mean the *peach* crumble?"

"Yes," she said. "Isn't that what I said?"

"You said...Never mind. It's not important. I'll look for it later and call you back. Is that okay?"

There was a moment's silence. "Well, don't wait too long." A hint of agitation crept into her voice.

"Is something wrong?" I mentally crossed my fingers. Please don't let there be anything wrong, I prayed. The day was already disintegrating around me, the sky steadily paling, leaking blue.

"No, nothing's wrong," she assured me quickly. "It's just Mr. Emerson next door. He's mad at me for something. I can't imagine what, but he's been quite unpleasant these last few days."

"Unpleasant? What do you mean?" I pictured old Mr. Emerson, charming, slightly stooped but still debonair, with a full head of thick white hair. He'd lived in the apartment next to my mother's for the two years she'd been a resident at the Palm Beach Lakes Retirement Home, a community for independent seniors. Mr. Emerson had always been an ideal neighbor, thoughtful, friendly, in possession of all his faculties. Of course, he was also closing in on ninety, so anything could happen.

"I thought I'd make him a peach crumble

as a sort of peace offering," my mother continued. "But I can't find the recipe."

"I'll look for it and call you later," I told her. "In the meantime, don't worry about it. Whatever it is, he'll get over it in time."

"How much time does he have?" my mother quipped, and I laughed.

"Tell her I'm getting married," Jo Lynn said loudly as I was about to hang up the phone.

"What's that? She's getting married again?"

"You're gonna love him," Jo Lynn said, as I whispered hurried assurances to our mother that it was all a joke.

Jo Lynn became visibly indignant, the green eyes narrowing once again, the orange lips disappearing one inside the other. "Why did you tell her that? Why are you always trying to protect her?"

"Why are you always trying to hurt her?"

We stared at each other for what seemed an eternity, our unanswered questions suspended in the air between us like particles of dust in the sunlight. What's the matter with you? I wanted to shout. Can you really be serious about Colin Friendly? Aren't you tired of being abused by selfish losers? Who exactly are you punishing here? Are you really going to keep cutting off your nose to spite your face?

"What's going on here?" a voice asked sleepily from somewhere beside us. I turned around as Sara slouched into the kitchen, her feet bare, her Amazon's body slipping in and out of a navy silk teddy and boxer shorts. *My* navy silk teddy and boxer shorts, I realized, understanding now why I hadn't been able to find them in several weeks. Her eyes barely open and all but hidden by her long tangled hair, elegant arms extended in front of her, groping for the fridge like a blind woman, she opened the fridge door and extricated the carton of freshly squeezed orange juice, raising it to her lips.

"Please don't do that," I cautioned, trying not to scream.

"Chill," she said, one of those delightful teenage expressions I'd like to wipe from the face of this earth. "Get a life" is another.

"There are glasses in the cupboard," I advised.

Sara lowered the carton and opened the cupboard, careful to make sure that I caught the disdainful roll of her eyes as she reached for a glass. "So, what were you two making such a racket about before? You were laughing so loud you woke me up."

For a minute I couldn't imagine what she was talking about. It seemed so long ago.

"Your mother actually said something funny," Jo Lynn told her, reducing me instantly to the status of humorless crone. "About PMS. What was it again?"

"Well, I can't really take the credit for it," I qualified. "I heard it on a sitcom once."

"So, what was it?" Sara filled the tall glass with orange juice, downed it in one noisy gulp, then put both the carton and the empty glass on the counter.

"Uh-uh. In the fridge." I motioned. "In the dishwasher."

Another roll of the eyes as two sets of appliance doors clumsily opened and closed. "Never mind," she said, walking across the room, glancing down at the newspaper spread out across the kitchen table. The President, the priest, and Colin Friendly stared back. "He's cute," Sara said, heading back toward her room.

"I'm gonna marry him," Jo Lynn called after her.

"Cool," Sara said, not breaking stride.

Chapter
3

Monday arrived. I had clients booked every hour from eight through six o'clock, with forty-five minutes off for lunch.

My office, in the heart of Palm Beach, only blocks from the ocean, consists of two small rooms and a smaller waiting area. The walls of each room are soft pink, the furniture predominantly gray. Stacks of recent magazines fill several large wicker baskets on either side of two padded benches that sit against the walls in the waiting room. I've made a point of keeping the magazines up to date ever since one of my clients walked tearfully into my office clutching a copy of *Newsweek*, asking if I knew that Steve McQueen had cancer. At this point, Steve McQueen had already been dead many years.

An eclectic group of pictures hang on the walls: a black-and-white photograph of a polar bear hugging a baby cub; a muted watercolor of a woman reading under the shade of a giant banyan tree; a bright reproduction of a well-known poster by Toulouse-Lautrec—Jane Avril, kicking up her leg to dance. Classical music plays in the background, not too loud, but hopefully loud enough to cover up the sometimes raised voices that emanate from behind the closed doors of my inner office.

Inside, three upholstered gray-and-white chairs sit grouped around a rectangular glass coffee table. More chairs can be brought in when required. There are some potted plants that look real but are actually replicas, since I have no talent with plants whatsoever, and I got tired of watching the real ones wither and die. Besides, on a symbolic level, dying plants seemed to reflect badly on my ability as a therapist.

On the coffee table sit a small tin of cookies, a large notepad, and a giant box of tissues. There is a video camera in one corner that I sometimes use to record sessions—always with the client's permission. A clock is on the wall behind my head, as well as several Impressionist prints: Monet's incandescent water lilies; a peaceful Pissarro village; an apple-cheeked Renoir girl standing on a swing.

There's another room at the back where I keep

my desk, my phone, my files, a small fridge, some stacking chairs, and a treadmill, or "dreadmill," as I've come to refer to it. The treadmill has always struck me as a perfect symbol of the times: people walking as fast as they can, going nowhere. Even so, I try to spend at least twenty minutes a day on this awful contraption. It's supposed to relax my mind while toning my body. In fact, it only irritates me. But then, everything irritates me these days. I blame it on my hormones, which are in a state of constant flux, the magazines all tell me. These articles irritate me as well. It doesn't help that "women of a certain age," as I believe the French call us, are always being pictured in the accompanying illustrations as dried-up bare branches on a once-flowering tree.

Anyway, it was Monday, I'd been seeing clients all morning, and my stomach was growling its way through my last session before lunch. The couple sitting across from me had come for help in dealing with their teenage son, who was as sullen and difficult a fourteen-year-old as I'd ever encountered. After two sessions, he'd refused to come back, although his parents persisted, gamely trying to find some sort of compromise that everyone could live with. Of course, compromise only works if all those involved are committed to it, and their son was committed only to wreaking havoc.

"He snuck out again after we'd gone to bed," Mrs. Mallory was saying, her husband sitting stiffly beside her. "We wouldn't even

35

have known he was gone except that I woke up to go to the bathroom and I saw a light on. I went into his room, and you wouldn't believe it, he'd stuffed his bed with pillows to make it look like he was still in it, like they do in those prison movies you see on TV. He didn't get home until almost three in the morning."

"Where did he go?" I asked.

"He wouldn't say."

"What happened then?"

"We told him how worried we'd been..."

"*She* was worried," her husband corrected tersely.

"You weren't?" I asked.

Jerry Mallory shook his balding head. He was a neat man who always wore a dark blue suit and a gold-striped tie, in contrast to his wife, who usually looked as if she'd thrown on the first thing that tumbled out of the dryer. "The only thing I worry about is the police showing up on our doorstep."

"I don't know what to do anymore." Jill Mallory looked from me to her husband, who stared resolutely ahead. "He's making me a nervous wreck. I don't sleep; I yell at everyone. I yelled at little Jenny again this morning. Although I explained to her that even though I yell at her a lot lately, it doesn't mean I don't love her."

"You also gave yourself permission to keep yelling at her," I told her, as gently as I could. She looked at me as if she'd been shot through the heart with an arrow.

Jill, Jerry, Jenny, Jason, I recited in my

mind, wondering whether the succession of J's had been deliberate. Jo Lynn, I found myself adding, picturing her in a crowded West Palm Beach courtroom, praying that common sense had kept her at home.

"Is there some way to force Jason back into counseling?" his mother asked. "Maybe a psychiatrist..."

I told her that wouldn't be a good idea. Teenagers are not great candidates for therapy, for two main reasons: one, they have no insight into why they do things, and two, they have no curiosity about why they do things.

When the hour was over and the Mallorys had gone, I went into the other room, grabbed a tuna fish sandwich from the small fridge, and checked my voice mail. There were two hang-ups and seven messages: three from clients seeking appointments; one from the guidance counselor at Sara's school asking me to call at my convenience; two from my mother asking me to call as soon as possible; and one from Jo Lynn telling me she'd spent the morning in court, that Colin Friendly was even better-looking in person than in his photographs, that she was more convinced than ever of his innocence, and that I had to go with her to see for myself on Wednesday, a day I normally don't go into the office. I closed my eyes, took a deep breath, and called my mother.

There was a frantic edge to her voice I wasn't used to hearing. "Where have you been?" she asked. "I've been calling all morning. I kept getting that stupid machine."

"What's the matter, Mom? Has something happened?"

"It's that damn Mr. Emerson."

"What happened with Mr. Emerson?"

"He accused me of trying to poison him with that peach crumble I made for him. He claims he was up all night throwing up. I'm so upset. He's telling everyone in the building that I tried to poison him."

"Oh, Mom, I'm so sorry. You must be so disappointed. Here you went to all that effort." I imagined her bent over her kitchen counter, arranging slices of peaches in the pan in neat little rows. "Try not to worry about it. No one there is going to take him seriously."

"Do you think you could talk to Mrs. Winchell?" she asked, referring to the retirement home's administrator. "I'm just too upset, and I know if you phoned her and explained..."

"I really don't think that's necessary, Mom."

"Please." Again, that unfamiliar urgency clinging to her voice.

"Sure thing. What's her number?"

"Her number?"

"Never mind." Clearly my mother was in no frame of mind for such details. "I'll find it."

"You'll call right away?"

"As soon as I can."

"Thank you, darling. I'm sorry to be such a burden."

"You're never a burden. I'll speak to you later." I replaced the receiver, took a few quick bites of my sandwich, and flipped through my address book for Mrs. Winchell's phone number, deciding first to check in with my daughter's school. The guidance counselor came on the line just as an enormous piece of tuna glued itself to the roof of my mouth.

"Sara has been missing a lot of classes," he told me without preamble. "In the last two weeks, she's missed four math classes and two Spanish classes."

Oh God, I thought. Here we go again. Hadn't we been through this last year?

"I'll talk to her," I told the guidance counselor, feeling like a total failure, although I knew this was Sara's responsibility, not mine. Still, I felt responsible. Some family therapist, I thought, swallowing the rest of my sandwich, feeling it awkward and heavy as it lurched its way down my esophagus toward my stomach.

I called Mrs. Winchell, quickly explaining the reason for my call, and asking if she could pay Mr. Emerson a visit. Maybe he'd reached a point in his life, I suggested gently, when he needed to find a place that offered more supervised care. There was a moment's silence before Mrs. Winchell spoke. I found myself holding my breath, though I wasn't sure why.

"It's not quite as simple as that," she began, then stopped. I tried to picture her on the other end of the phone, but her silence was distracting. It took several seconds for a mental image of her to take shape. When it did, she emerged as a woman about a decade older than me, ebony-skinned and pretty despite a receding chin line, with short black hair and an engaging smile. "Actually, I've been meaning to call you."

"Is there a problem?" I coached reluctantly.

"We've had a few complaints," she began, "from some of the other tenants."

"Complaints? About Mr. Emerson?"

"About your mother," she said.

"About my mother?"

A long pause followed. Then: "There have been some problems over the last couple of months."

"What kind of problems?"

Another silence. Clearly, Mrs. Winchell was not someone who spoke before she was ready, a trait I've always admired in others but never quite mastered in myself. I checked my watch, then my appointment calendar. The name Donna Lokash was scribbled through the one o'clock slot.

"I'm sure you know your mother loves to bake..."

"Yes, of course. She's a wonderful cook."

Mrs. Winchell ignored the interruption. "And she's always been very sweet, making things for her friends and neighbors..."

Get to the point, I wanted to shout, but didn't, locating an errant cookie on my desk and stuffing it into my mouth instead.

"But I'm afraid that the last few times she's baked anything for anyone, they've gotten very sick."

My eyes creased toward the bridge of my nose. What was this woman trying to say?

That my mother was deliberately poisoning her neighbors, as Mr. Emerson had accused? "I'm not sure I understand what you're getting at," I said.

There was another lengthy pause. I imagined the woman looking around her office, patting her tight dark curls, rubbing the tip of her nose. "It's probably just a case of old stomachs becoming increasingly delicate and not being able to tolerate such rich foods," she offered gently, "but I was wondering if you could suggest to your mother that she not bake anything for anyone for a while."

Already I could see the wounded look that would ambush my mother's features when I relayed Mrs. Winchell's request, and it broke my heart. "I'll talk to her," I said.

"There's something else," Mrs. Winchell continued.

I held my breath, said nothing.

"It's about the charges your mother has made with regard to one of our staff."

"I beg your pardon?"

"She's never said anything to you?"

I shook my head, then realized I would have to do more. "No, she's never said a thing."

"I think this might be too complicated for us to get into over the phone. It's probably better if we meet in person. Perhaps we could get together sometime soon, you, your mother, and I. Oh, and you have a sister, don't you?"

My mind instantly replayed Jo Lynn's message on my voice mail. *You have to see this man*

41

in person, Kate. He's even better-looking than his photographs, and I'm absolutely convinced he's innocent. "Yes, I have a sister," I said.

"I think she should probably join us as well. We can talk things through, hopefully get to the bottom of everything."

My mother, Jo Lynn, and I, I thought, picturing Jo Lynn sitting in the courtroom, a one-woman cheering section, probably skipping lunch so she could get a seat closer to the accused for when court resumed in the afternoon. She'd be wearing all white, as usual, to highlight her honeyed complexion, and a short skirt to show off her legs. Not to mention the tightest of little tank tops. There was no way Colin Friendly was not going to notice Jo Lynn Baker. She'd make sure of that.

"The only day I have free is Wednesday," I told Mrs. Winchell, wondering how I was going to persuade Jo Lynn to come along.

"How's Wednesday at two o'clock?" Mrs. Winchell offered immediately.

"Fine."

"I look forward to seeing you then."

She hung up. I sat cradling the phone against my ear, wondering what was going on. My mother wasn't a troublemaker, and she'd never been one to complain, even when she had just cause. She'd suffered years of abuse from my stepfather without saying a word, trying to protect my sister and me from things we already knew. Was that what she was doing now? Still trying to protect us?

I shook my head, inadvertently dislodging Sara from the recesses of my mind. Did a mother ever really stop trying to protect her child?

I returned the rest of my calls, then quickly exchanged my blue dress and flats for a gray sweat suit and sneakers, and stepped on the treadmill, gradually increasing its speed until I was walking a brisk four miles an hour, my arms keeping pace at my sides, my mind peacefully blank. It didn't take long, however, for my family to join me, their images attaching themselves to my arms and legs, like heavy weights, slowing my step, dragging me down.

Leave me alone, I admonished them silently, trying to shrug them off. This is my time alone, my time just for me, to unwind, to refresh, to tone and relax. I'll deal with your problems later.

But instead of fading away, their images grew bolder, more insistent. My mother appeared in front of me, like a genie escaped from a bottle, pushing her face just inches from my own, her arms clinging to me in a suffocating embrace; my daughter jumped on my back, knees circling my waist, hands clutching at my throat, riding me as if she were a small child, both women pressing so tightly against me I could barely breathe. Why was my daughter skipping classes? What was going on with my mother? And why were these things *my* problem? Why was I the one caught in the middle?

Don't expect any help from me, Jo Lynn warned, invisible hands tugging on my ankles, so that it felt as if I were trudging through deep snow. You're never there for me; why should I be there for you?

I'm always here for you, I said, kicking at her prone image, almost tripping over my own feet. Who stood by you through Andrew, through Daniel, through Peter, through all the men who repeatedly broke your bones and battered your spirit?

Yeah, but what have you done for me lately? she demanded, tightening her grip.

Don't bother with her, Sara admonished.

You'll deal with her later, my mother said.

Me first, said Sara.

No, me, my mother insisted.

Me.

Me.

Me. Me. Me. Me. Me.

I closed my eyes, anxiety tightening around my chest like a straitjacket. "This is my time," I said out loud. "I'll deal with you later."

The anxiety suddenly lifted. I smiled, took a deep breath. You see, I reminded myself, sometimes all that's necessary is to voice these thoughts aloud. Almost immediately, however, the anxiety was replaced by a wave of heat so intense it felt as if someone were aiming a blowtorch at my brain. Perspiration soaked through my sweatshirt; my forehead grew damp; wisps of hair plastered themselves to the sides of my face. "Great. Just what I needed," I pronounced, adjusting the treadmill's speed, slowing it down too quickly, so that when it stopped, I almost fell off.

Steadying myself against my desk, I grabbed a soft drink from the fridge, and held it against my forehead until the room stopped spinning and the hot flush grew tepid, then disappeared. When I next glanced at my watch, it was almost fifteen minutes after one o'clock and I was still in my sweats. I quickly peeked into the waiting area, but Donna Lokash wasn't there. I was grateful, though worried. It was unlike Donna to be late.

My sweatshirt was halfway over my head when the phone rang. I yanked it off and answered the phone, standing there in nothing but my underwear. Donna's voice on the phone was garbled, crowded with tears. "I'm so sorry. I know I'm late. I was on my way out the door when the phone rang."

"Donna, what's wrong? Has something happened? Is it Amy?" Donna's daughter, Amy, had been missing for almost a year. I had a special interest in her disappearance, since Amy had attended the same school as Sara and had been in some of the same classes. I recalled the first time Donna Lokash came to my office, several months after Amy vanished. She remembered me from several parent-teacher meetings, she'd whispered, her thin frame hugging the doorway, eyes swollen almost shut from crying, further accentuating the grief-imposed gauntness of her face. She needed help, she said. She was having trouble coping.

"The police just called. They've found a body. There's a chance it could be Amy."

"Oh God."

"They want me to go to the medical examiner's office. They're sending a car for me. They asked if I could bring a friend. I don't know what to do."

I knew that Donna had drifted away from most of her friends since Amy's disappearance, and that her ex-husband lived in New York. He'd flown in when Amy first went missing, but had gone back after several weeks when Amy hadn't been found. He had a new wife and family to look after now. Donna had no one. "Would you like me to go with you?"

"Would you?" Her gratitude was so palpable I could almost hold it in my hands. "We'd have to go right now, which would mean canceling your other appointments. Of course, I'd pay you for your time and trouble. I wouldn't dream of asking you to do this without paying you for your time."

"Please don't worry about that. It's a slow day," I lied, drawing an invisible X through the rest of the day's appointments. "Tell me where to meet you."

"At the medical examiner's office on Gun Club Road. West of Congress. In front of the jail."

"I'm on my way." I hastily rescheduled the rest of my afternoon appointments, taped a note of apology to my office door for those I hadn't been able to reach, and left the office, heading for the county morgue.

Chapter
4

Twenty minutes later I pulled into the large entranceway of the Palm Beach County Criminal Justice Complex, an impressive array of sand-colored buildings that included the sheriff's office, various administrative offices, and the jail, a towering structure at the rear, nicknamed the Gun Club Hilton. Were it not for the rows of barbed wire that ran along the top of the prison gates, the complex might be mistaken for just another series of offices, like the South Florida Water Management District buildings directly across the street.

The medical examiner's office, a squat one-story structure at the front of the complex, had the look and feel of a building that didn't quite belong, like an old portable classroom that's been tacked on to a brand-new school, necessary but vaguely unwelcome. I found a parking spot nearby, switched off the car's engine, then sat staring out at the pond that stretched along the side of the road, my mind racing ahead to a sterile room smelling vaguely of chemicals. I saw myself positioned slightly behind Donna, my eyes carefully averted, my hands on the sides of her arms, bracing her as the coroner pulled back a white sheet from a steel slab, exposing the gray face of a teenage girl, possibly her daughter. I heard her cry out, saw her sway backward, felt her collapse into my arms. The full, horrible weight of her grief fell on me, pressing against my nose and mouth like a pillow, robbing me of air, taking my breath away. I can't do this, I thought.

"If she can do it, you can do it," I admonished myself, scrambling out of the car and hurrying along the concrete walkway to the side entrance of the unimpressive building, pursued by another unwanted image, more terrible than the first: the coroner pulling down the sheet, the body of my own child staring lifelessly up at me. "Sara," I said, and gasped out loud.

A sharp quack sent the image scattering in all directions, like a bullet through a pane of glass, and I turned toward the sound. There, in a corner of the building, close to the door, a large Muscovy duck sat watch over a bunch of freshly hatched ducklings, their recently discarded eggshells lying broken and empty on the grass around them. I stared at the unexpected scene in amazement, afraid to approach too closely, lest I frighten the baby ducks and antagonize their mother. I watched them for several seconds, marveling at the fragility and resilience of life, and then I took a deep breath, and opened the door on death.

Donna Lokash was sitting in one of two steel-and-vinyl chairs along the off-white concrete-block wall of the small reception area, a uniformed police officer at her side. She was even thinner than the last time I'd seen her, and the lines under her clouded hazel eyes had deepened, forming large dark semicircles. Her brown hair was brushed back into a ponytail that spoke more of convenience than style, and the flesh around her fingernails had been picked raw, the nails themselves bitten to the quick. Donna jumped up, lunged toward me. "Did you see the baby ducks?" she asked, her voice giddy, incipient hysteria bracketing her words.

"I saw them."

"It's a good omen, don't you think?"

"I hope so," I told her. "Are you all right?"

She cast an unsteady glance around the room, dropped her voice to a whisper. "I feel a little sick to my stomach."

"Take deep breaths," I told her, then did the same.

The uniformed officer approached, extended his hand. He was of medium height with reddish-blond hair and a barrel chest. "Mrs. Sinclair, I'm Officer Gatlin. Thank you for coming."

I nodded. "What happens now?"

"I'll tell them you're here."

"And then what? Do I stay here or do I go inside with Mrs. Lokash?" I motioned toward the back room with my chin.

"Nobody's allowed back there," Officer Gatlin said.

"I don't understand."

"It's not like you see on television," Officer Gatlin explained gently. "We never allow anyone to actually see the body. A few of the more modern facilities in the country have special viewing rooms, complete with soft lighting, where you can view the body through

49

a glass window. But this is an old building, and a small one. We don't have the space or the facilities."

"Then how...?" I broke off, bit down on my lower lip.

"They'll bring out a photograph for you to look at."

"A photograph?"

"They won't let me see my baby," Donna said.

"We don't know yet that it's Amy," I told her.

"They won't let me even look at her picture," Donna continued, as if I hadn't spoken. She covered her mouth with her trembling hand, barely stifling a sharp cry.

"What do you mean?"

"We never let an immediate family member see the photograph," Officer Gatlin said. "It's too traumatic. That's why we ask them to bring a clergyman or a family friend, someone who knew the girl..."

"But I didn't know her," I said, the realization suddenly hitting me that I was the one expected to identify the body. "I mean, I only met her on a couple of occasions. I'm not sure I could..."

"I didn't know they wouldn't let me see her," Donna cried, rocking back and forth on the balls of her feet. "I don't know what to do. Oh God, I don't know what to do. I don't know who else to call. I'm so sorry I dragged you into this, Kate. Please forgive me. I didn't know they wouldn't let me see her."

"I'll look at the picture," I said quickly,

recalling the hours that Donna had spent in my office, poring over the family albums with me, pointing out Amy as a fair-haired infant, Amy as a pudgy little girl, Amy in a strapless prom dress, her light brown hair hanging in ringlets around her dimpled cheeks, Amy on her seventeenth birthday, brown eyes sparkling, just weeks before she disappeared. I grabbed Donna's hand, squeezed it tightly. "I should be able to recognize her."

Officer Gatlin nodded, walked toward the glass plate that separated the waiting room from the receptionist's office. *Push button for assistance*, a small sign read beside an imposing black button. He pushed the button, told the receptionist that I was ready to proceed.

"Why don't we sit down," I suggested to Donna, pulling out one of four chairs hovering around a round Formica table in the center of the room. She fell into it, and I lowered myself into the seat next to hers, concentrating on the details of the small room—a wine-colored mat that lay on the linoleum floor just inside the entrance, vertical blinds on the window, a water fountain in one corner of the room, two vending machines, one for soft drinks, the other for candies, against two of the walls, recessed fluorescent lights humming from the ceiling, illuminating a small, unimpressive landscape painting, a *No Smoking* sign printed in fifteen different languages, a small sign that read: *Sometimes it's the little things you do that make the big difference*—in an effort to ward off my mounting panic.

51

I'd never seen a dead body before, or even a picture of one, other than on the television news, and I didn't know how I was going to react to the sight of a teenage girl, a girl the same age as my older daughter, lying dead on a table, even if her death was presented via the distancing lens of a camera. And then another terrifying thought hit me. "Is there any trauma to the face?" I asked, struggling to keep my voice steady.

"We wouldn't show you the picture if there was," he said.

"How did the girl die?" Donna Lokash asked from her chair. She was staring at the door to the back room, although her eyes were blank, and it was unlikely she saw anything at all.

"Multiple stab wounds," Officer Gatlin answered, his voice low, as if trying to minimize the impact of his words.

"Oh God," Donna moaned.

"When?" I asked.

"Probably several days ago. A group of kids found her body this morning in a park in Stuart."

"But Amy disappeared almost a year ago," I said. "What makes you think it's her?"

"She fits the general description," he said.

"What happens if I'm not able to make a definite identification?"

"We can check the dental records, if there are any," Officer Gatlin said. "Or we might ask Mrs. Lokash to bring in Amy's hairbrush, something with her fingerprints on it, lift the prints from that, compare the two."

The door at the back of the room suddenly opened. A tall, good-looking man with salt-and-pepper hair combed straight back off his face crossed into the waiting area, a photograph in his hand.

"Oh God, oh God," wailed Donna, rocking back and forth in her seat, arms clasped around her stomach.

"This is Fred Sheridan, one of the medical examiner's assistants," Officer Gatlin said, as I rose to my feet. "Are you ready, Mrs. Sinclair?"

"I'm not sure," I replied honestly.

"Take your time," Fred Sheridan said, his voice husky, full of gravel.

Several slow steps brought me to his side. I swallowed, closed my eyes, said a silent prayer. Please let me know one way or the other, I prayed, conjuring up a quick image of the last time I'd seen Amy, enlarging it, focusing in on each facet of her face, dissecting it piece by piece: the dimples on either side of her round mouth, the freckles dotting the sides of her upturned nose, bright eyes brown and wide apart. She was a pretty girl, of average height and weight, which meant she probably thought she was too short, too fat. I shook my head, opened my eyes. If only they knew how beautiful they really are, I thought, thinking again of my daughter Sara, as I glanced down at the photograph in Fred Sheridan's outstretched hand.

"She was wearing a red barrette," Donna Lokash suddenly announced.

"What?" I turned away before the picture had a chance to register on my brain.

"When she went out that night, she was wearing a red barrette. It was just a silly plastic thing, a cupid sitting on a bunch of hearts, but she loved it. One of the kids she used to babysit for gave it to her, and she misplaced it, and was very upset, until I found it one morning when I was straightening up her room. It had fallen behind her dresser, and she was so excited when I showed it to her. She was wearing it in her hair, just above her right ear, the night she went out. She said it was her good-luck charm." Donna's voice broke off abruptly. She lapsed into silence, stared at the floor.

"Is this Amy?" Fred Sheridan asked gently, his words pulling me back toward the photograph.

The face I found myself staring at was young and round and surprisingly untroubled. No laugh lines interrupted the flat surface of her mouth; no worry lines tugged at the edges of her eyes. A blank slate, I found myself thinking. She hadn't even had a chance to live. Tears welled up in my eyes. I turned away.

"It isn't her," I whispered.

Donna emitted a strangled cry. Immediately, I returned to her side. She grabbed my hand, sobbed against it, her tears lying warm and wet on my skin.

"You're sure?" Officer Gatlin asked.

"Yes."

The girl in the photograph may have fit Amy's general description, but her nose pointed down instead of up and her lower lip was thinner, less prominent. There were no freckles on her ashen skin.

There was no red barrette.

"What happens now?" I asked.

"We keep trying to find out who she is," Officer Gatlin said, as Fred Sheridan retreated into the back room. "We keep our eyes out for Amy."

"My daughter didn't run away," Donna told him decisively.

"I'll give you a ride home, Mrs. Lokash," the officer said.

"I'll take her home," I told him.

Donna smiled gratefully. "I'm not sure I can stand up," she said.

"Take your time," I told her, as the coroner's assistant had earlier told me.

"What about you?" she asked as I helped her to her feet. "How are you doing?"

"Don't worry about me."

Officer Gatlin held the door open for us, and we stepped out into the sunlight. Into the land of the living, I thought. "Oh, look," Donna said, pointing to the spot where less than half an hour earlier the mother duck had been sitting with her newborn ducklings. All that remained now were a dozen empty and abandoned shells. Mother and children had vanished. "What happened to them?"

"The mother probably took them over to the pond," Officer Gatlin said. "There's another bunch getting ready to hatch around back, if you want to have a look."

"Can we?" Donna asked me, as if she were a small child.

"If you'd like."

We said goodbye to Officer Gatlin, and walked around to the back of the building. There, in a shaded corner, sat another large Muscovy duck, eggs fanned out around her.

"Look," Donna said, pointing. "There's a crack in that one. It must be getting ready to hatch."

"Pretty amazing."

"Can we watch for a few minutes? Would you mind?"

"We can watch." I sat down on the grass, tucking my legs underneath me, the skirt of my blue dress falling in folds around me. We sat this way for several minutes, as still as the eggs we were watching, neither of us speaking, each lost in her own private world. I thought of Sara and Michelle, how grateful I was for their well-being. I ached to hold them in my arms, to tell them how much I loved them. Had they any idea? Did I tell them often enough? "How are you feeling?" I asked finally.

"I don't know," Donna said, her voice as lifeless as the girl in the photograph. "On the one hand, I'm so relieved, relieved beyond words, that it wasn't Amy." She sighed deeply. "But on the other hand, it would have been almost a relief if it had been, because at least that way I would have known once and for all what happened to her. There would have been some sense of closure. Not this waiting, all the time waiting," she said, her voice picking up urgency. "Waiting for the phone to ring, waiting for Amy to come walking through the door, waiting for her killer to come forward. I'm not sure how much more of this waiting I can stand."

"It must be so hard," I said, wishing I could say more, say something, *anything*, that might lessen her pain.

"The trial makes it harder," she said, and I knew immediately she was referring to the trial of Colin Friendly. "Every day I read about that animal in the newspaper, what he did to those women, and I wonder: Did he do the same thing to my little girl? And it's more than I can bear."

I moved to her side, cradled her in my arms.

"Do you know that he breaks their noses?" she said.

"What?"

"He breaks their noses. It's his trademark. Apparently, he doesn't always kill them the same way, but he always breaks their noses. I read that in the paper."

I recalled Colin Friendly's photograph in the *Palm Beach Post*. ("What do you see when you look at him?" I'd asked my sister. "I see a little boy who's been hurt," she'd said.)

"There are times when I want to burst into that courtroom and confront that monster myself," Donna was saying. "Demand that he tell me if he killed Amy. 'Tell me,' I want to scream. 'Just tell me so I know one way or the other, so I can get on with my life.' And then I think: No, I couldn't bear to hear him say he'd killed her, because if I know for sure that she's dead, what life do I have?"

I said nothing. Donna and I watched the mother duck as she stood up and checked beneath her feathers, then repositioned herself slightly to the right.

"I keep thinking back to the night she disappeared," Donna said. "We had an argument before she went out. Did you know that? Did I tell you that?"

"No, I don't think you did."

"I didn't think so. I haven't told anybody. I'm too ashamed."

"Ashamed about what?"

"It was such a stupid argument. It was raining. I wanted her to take an umbrella; she said she didn't need one. I told her she was acting like a child; she said to stop treating her like one."

"Donna," I interrupted, "don't do this to yourself."

"But it was the last thing I said to her. Why did I have to make such an issue over a stupid umbrella?"

"Because you cared about her well-being. Because you loved her. And she knew that."

"Sometimes, when we'd argue, and it was always about little things, never about anything important, but everything always seemed so damned important at the time, I don't know, maybe because I was a single parent, and I always felt I had to make up for Roger's not being around, I don't know, I don't know what I thought anymore, but I remember...Oh God, do you want to hear something really awful? I remember that sometimes I thought it was just too much for me, that maybe she should go live with Roger, that it would be easier if she weren't around. Oh God, oh God, how could I think such a thing?"

"Every parent has thoughts like that from time to time," I tried to assure her, thinking of my mother and Jo Lynn, myself and Sara. "It doesn't make you a bad person. It doesn't make you a bad mother."

As if on cue, the egg we'd been watching cracked apart, and a scrawny creature, wet feathers plastered to its tiny, shaking skull, beak spread wide, eyes tightly shut, pushed itself into the open air, impatiently shucking off its protective shell, then collapsing onto its side with the effort, lying prone on the ground without moving.

"Is he dead?" Donna squealed.

"No, he's just too weak to move around yet."

Donna stared at the fallen duckling. "I have to know what happened to Amy," she said.

I said nothing. My mind was on Sara. Children drive you crazy, I was thinking, sometimes even make your life an absolute hell. But once they were part of your life, there was no life without them.

It was this thought more than anything else that persuaded me to accompany Jo Lynn to the courthouse on Wednesday.

Chapter 5

I arrived at the courthouse at just after eight o'clock Wednesday morning. Jo Lynn was already in line, near the front of the long queue that snaked its way through the lobby of the magnificent new peach-colored marble building in the downtown core of West Palm Beach. Jo Lynn had warned me to be at the courthouse at least two hours ahead of time in order to get a seat, but I'd refused to arrive before eight, and she'd agreed to hold a place for me. Cutting into the line, I got more than my share of dirty looks.

"Next week, you'll have to come early," Jo Lynn said, "or I won't save you a place."

I scoffed. "This is it for me."

Jo Lynn only smiled, lazily lacing a bright fuchsia scarf through her blond curls, then securing it with a saucy little bow at the side. The scarf matched her lipstick and slingback, high-heeled shoes. In between, she sported a clinging, low-cut white jersey dress with a thigh-high slit up the side. Standing next to her in my conservative, albeit fashionable, beige Calvin Klein suit, I felt like an old frump, the still-virginal maiden aunt who stands in judgment, showering her disapproval on everything the younger folks do. People walked by, smiled and nodded at Jo Lynn, scarcely aware of my presence.

It was the same whenever I went anywhere with Sara. Men craned their necks to get a better view of my daughter, visually pushing me out of the way. Why was I wasting my money on expensive designer fashion when it obviously didn't matter what I looked like? No one saw me anyway.

I pictured Sara, still flopped across her bed when I left the house, which meant she'd be late for school again today. Of course, her lateness yesterday had been my fault, she claimed. I was the one who started the fight, who had to butt my nose into her business. I reminded her that her business became mine when I got phone calls from the school. She told me to get a life. Despite the insights I'd received at the coroner's office, despite my best intentions and newfound resolve, the discussion went downhill from there. It ended with the front door slamming, Sara's final words reverberating down the otherwise quiet street: "Thanks for making me late for school, *Ms*. Therapist!"

A man approached, medium height, slightly scruffy in jeans and a lightweight navy sweater. He told Jo Lynn he was going across the street for a cup of coffee and asked if he could get her anything.

"Coffee would be great, Eric," she told him. "How about you, Kate?"

"Coffee," I agreed, smiling my appreciation. He didn't notice.

"Cream and two sugars, right?" he asked Jo Lynn.

"You got it."

61

"Just black for me," I said, but he was already on his way. "And who is Eric?" I asked her.

She shrugged. "Just a guy I met in line the other day. He's been coming since the beginning of the trial."

The trial was in its second week. According to news reports, it was expected to last until Christmas. I looked around, casually perusing the faces of the others waiting behind me. Just a bunch of ordinary people, I realized, awaiting their opportunity to glimpse into the heart of extraordinary evil. The young outnumbered the old; the women outnumbered the men; the young women outnumbered everybody, undoubtedly drawn here by the powerful twin magnets of revulsion and attraction. Did being here make them feel safer, I wondered, more in control? Were they confronting their own worst fears, staring down their demons? Or were they here, as was my sister, to ask for the demon's hand in marriage?

It was the first time I'd been inside the new courthouse, which had been completed in May 1995. My eyes swept the foyer, trying to see it as Larry might, with a builder's appreciation for detail, but all I saw was a lot of glass and granite. Maybe I was too nervous. Maybe I already regretted my decision to be there.

Eric returned with our coffee. Mine, like Jo Lynn's, contained cream and enough sugar to induce a diabetic coma. I smiled my thanks and held the undrinkable thing between my palms until it grew cold. At least Eric had remembered I was here.

About an hour later, a large contingent of men and women appeared, seemingly from out of nowhere, and swept past us through a set of glass doors. "Press," Jo Lynn whispered knowingly as my eyes trailed after them, my attention focusing on the profile of one man in particular, thinking he looked vaguely familiar. He was about fifty, slim, maybe five feet ten inches tall, with autumn-brown hair that matched his expensively tailored suit. My gaze accompanied him through the metal detectors and around the corner until he disappeared. "Too bad the judge won't allow TV cameras into the courtroom," Jo Lynn was saying, sounding very knowledgeable about the whole proceedings. "Of course, if there were cameras, I'd have to buy a whole new wardrobe. White doesn't photograph very good on TV. Did you know that?"

"White doesn't photograph very *well*," I corrected, trying to decide whether or not she was serious.

She looked stricken. "Well, who died and appointed you Mrs. Grundy?" We didn't speak again until we'd passed through the metal detectors ourselves and were in the crowded elevator on the way to the courtroom on the top floor.

I didn't know what to expect, and I was astonished when I stepped out of the elevator and found myself staring out an expansive wall of windows at a truly spectacular view of the city, the Intracoastal Waterway, and the ocean beyond. A dreamscape, I remember thinking, as I proceeded down the long corridor, knowing I was walking into a nightmare.

The spectacular view continued inside the courtroom itself, where the entire east wall was made up of windows. The trial was taking place in Courtroom 11A, the so-called ceremonial courtroom, and the largest courtroom in the building. I'd never been inside a courtroom before and was amazed to discover how familiar it all felt. Years of watching fictional trials in the movies and on TV, plus the relatively new experience of Court TV, had rendered the arena more accessible, if not downright cozy. There was the judge's podium, flags to either side, the witness stand, the jury box, the spectator's gallery with room for about seventy-five people, everything exactly where I'd known it would be.

"Colin sits there." Jo Lynn indicated the long, dark oak table and three black leather chairs of the defense team with a nod of her head. "In the middle." She was already sitting on the edge of her seat, straining her body forward to get a better look, although there was nothing yet to see. We were in the third row of the middle section, just behind the prosecutor's table and the two rows reserved for the families of the victims. "We get a better view of Colin from this side," she explained.

I watched the courtroom fill, wishing that she would stop referring to the accused serial killer as if he were a close personal friend. "Wait till you see how handsome he is," Jo Lynn said. The shoulders of the woman sitting directly in front of us stiffened, her back arching, like a cat's. I turned toward the back of the room, stared absently at the cloudless blue sky, my face flush with embarrassment and shame.

It was several seconds before I realized that someone was staring back. It was the man I'd noticed outside, the man with the autumn-colored hair and expensively tailored suit. In profile, he'd appeared lean and angular, intense and inaccessible; full-face, he appeared kinder, softer, less formidable. Too many years of Florida sunshine had rendered his handsome face somewhat leathery, and there were crease lines around his full mouth and hazel eyes.

How could I know his eyes were hazel? I wondered, looking away, then immediately back again, staring at him outright, watching in awe as the years fell away from his features, like layers of paint being stripped from the side of a house. The grown man vanished; a boy of eighteen took his place. He was wearing a white track suit, a bright red number 12 stamped across his chest, the sweat of victory from his final race trickling down his cheeks and into his smiling mouth, as he accepted the congratulations of the adoring crowd around him. *Way to go, Bobby! Hey, guy, great race.* "Robert?" I whispered.

Jo Lynn's elbow pierced the side of my

ribs. "That's the prosecutor, Mr. Eaves, coming through the door. I hate him. He's really out to get Colin."

Reluctantly, my focus shifted from the past back to the present, as the assistant state's attorney and his associates made their way up the left aisle of the courtroom to take their seats in front of us. They began opening and closing assorted briefcases, noisily setting up shop, ignoring our presence, as if we weren't there. Mr. Eaves was a serious-faced man with thinning hair and a gut that strained against the jacket of his dark blue suit. He undid the top button as he sat down. His associates, a man and woman who looked young enough to be his children, and enough alike to be siblings, wore similarly grave expressions. Their clothes were simple and nondescript. Rather like mine, I realized with a start, deciding I should have worn a scarf to brighten things up, wondering why I was even thinking such inane thoughts. Slowly, I let my gaze return to the back of the room.

The boy in the red-and-white track suit was gone. Back was the grown man in the expensive suit, now engaged in earnest conversation with the man beside him. I waited for him to turn back in my direction, but after a few minutes, he was still talking to the man next to him. No doubt I was mistaken, I told myself. Robert Crowe was a boy I'd dated back in high school, and hadn't seen since his family left Pittsburgh for parts unknown. I remember being so grateful they'd left the state—it made having been dumped slightly easier to bear. What would he be doing here now?

I shook my head, exhaled an angry breath of air, and stilled the foot that was tapping nervously on the floor with an impatient hand, my heart pounding unaccountably fast. It had been over thirty years since I'd last laid eyes on Robert Crowe. Could he really still have this effect on me?

"Here he comes now," Jo Lynn announced anxiously, twisting around in her aisle seat, crossing one leg over the other, maximizing the effect of the slit in her skirt.

A concentrated hush fell across the courtroom as Colin Friendly entered the court from a door at the front of the room and was directed to his seat by an armed police officer. Immediately, his attorneys rose to greet him. The accused killer was dressed in a conservative blue suit with a peach-colored shirt and paisley tie, his dark wavy hair combed neatly off his face, looking exactly as he had in the photo in the weekend paper. I watched his eyes sweep effortlessly across the room, a hunter searching for his prey, I thought with a shudder as his eyes rested briefly on Jo Lynn.

"My God, did you see that?" she whispered, grabbing my hand, her long nails cutting into my flesh. "He looked right at me."

I struggled for air but found none. Without even trying, Colin Friendly had sucked up all the oxygen in the room.

"Did you see that?" Jo Lynn pressed. "He saw me. He knows I'm here for him."

The woman seated directly in front of us spun around angrily in her seat, then turned immediately away.

"What's her problem?" Jo Lynn asked indignantly.

"Good God, Jo Lynn," I stammered. "Would you just listen to yourself? Do you hear what you're saying?"

"What's *your* problem?"

The judge entered the room a few minutes later. Dutifully, we all rose, then retook our seats. Judge Kellner was suitably gray and judicious-looking.

Next came the jury, seven women, five men, two more women who served as alternates, all of them wearing badges that identified them as jurors. Of the fourteen, eight were white, four were black, two were somewhere in between. They were neatly dressed, although surprisingly casual. At least *I* was surprised. Of course, I was also the only one in the courtroom, other than the lawyers and the defendant, who was wearing a suit. Except for Robert Crowe.

Again, my head spun toward the back of the room. This time, Robert Crowe was looking right at me. He smiled. "Kate?" he mouthed.

I felt my heart leap into my throat, my lungs filling with sudden dread, as thick as smoke. There is nothing to feel anxious about, I told myself. Just because you're in the same room with an accused murderer *and* an old high school sweetheart, this was not something to get unnecessarily worked up about.

In the next second, it was as if someone had

taken a match to my insides. I felt my inner organs shriveling and disappearing inside invisible flames. Sweat broke out across my forehead and upper lip. I pulled at the collar of my beige blouse, debated taking off my jacket. "It's very hot in here," I whispered to Jo Lynn.

"No, it's not," she said.

The clerk called the court to order and the judge directed the prosecutor to call his first witness. The temperature in the room returned to normal. Jo Lynn squirmed excitedly in her seat as a studious-looking young woman named Angela Riegert was sworn in.

"Look at her," Jo Lynn muttered under her breath. "She's dumpy and homely and just wishes she could get a man like Colin."

As if he'd heard her, Colin Friendly slowly turned his head in my sister's direction. A slight smile played at the corners of his lips.

Jo Lynn crossed, then uncrossed her legs. "We're with you, Colin," she whispered.

His smile widened, then he turned his attention back to the witness stand.

"I'm gonna give him my phone number." Jo Lynn was already fishing inside her white straw purse for a piece of paper.

"Are you crazy?" I wanted to swat her across the back of her head, physically knock some sense into her.

Just like dear old Dad, I thought with disgust, marveling at the baseness of my instincts. I'd never hit anyone in my life, wasn't about to start now, however tempting it might be.

I glared at the back of Colin Friendly's head. Obviously, he brought out the best in me.

Jo Lynn was already scribbling her name and number across a torn scrap of paper. "I'll give it to him during a break."

"If you do, I'll leave. I swear, I'll walk right out of here."

"Then I won't come with you to Mom's," she countered, bringing her fingers to her lips to quiet me.

She had me there. The only way I'd been able to persuade her to attend the afternoon's meeting was to agree to accompany her to court, although she insisted we change the time of the meeting to four o'clock so that she didn't have to "abandon Colin," as she put it, before court let out. She didn't know I'd already decided to tag along.

I still wasn't a hundred percent sure what exactly I was doing in that courtroom. Did I really think I might learn anything that might help Donna Lokash? Or was I trying to watch out for my sister, to protect her from Colin Friendly, to protect her from herself? Or was it simple curiosity? I don't know. I probably never will.

"State your name and address," the court clerk instructed the witness, a short, slightly overweight young woman, who looked nervous and uncomfortable, her small eyes refusing to look at the defense table.

"Angela Riegert," she said, barely audibly.

"You'll have to speak up," Judge Kellner said gently.

Angela Riegert cleared her throat, restated her name. It was only slightly louder the second time. The entire courtroom shifted forward, straining to hear. She gave her address as 1212 Olive Street in Lake Worth.

The prosecutor was on his feet, doing up the button of his dark blue jacket, the way you always see them doing on TV. "Miss Riegert, how old are you?" he began.

"Twenty," she replied, looking as if she weren't altogether sure.

"And how long had you known Wendy Sabatello?"

"We'd been best friends since the fourth grade."

"Who's Wendy Sabatello?" I asked.

"One of the victims," Jo Lynn said, the words sliding out of the side of her mouth.

I stared into my lap, not sure I wanted to hear more.

"And can you tell me what happened on the night of March 17, 1995?"

"We went to a party at someone's house. Her parents were away, and so there was this big party."

"What time did you get there?"

"About nine o'clock."

"And the party was in full swing?"

"It was starting to heat up. There were lots of people; the music was very loud."

"Did you know everyone?"

"No. There were a lot of people there I'd never seen before."

"Did you see the defendant?"

71

Reluctantly, Angela Riegert glanced toward the accused, then looked quickly away. "Not at first," she whispered.

"Sorry, could you repeat that?"

"I didn't see him till later."

"But you did see him?"

"Yes, he was in the backyard. I saw him when we went outside to get some air."

"Did you talk to him?"

"He talked to me."

"You wish," Jo Lynn scoffed.

"What did he say?"

"Not much. 'Nice party,' 'nice night,' that sort of thing."

"Was Wendy Sabatello with you at the time?"

"Yes. She thought he was cute."

"Objection, your honor," one of the defense lawyers protested, jumping to his feet. "Can the witness read minds?"

"She told me," Angela Riegert said clearly.

"Objection," the lawyer countered. "Hearsay."

"Overruled."

The witness looked confused, as if she weren't sure what exactly had transpired. She wasn't the only one.

"Did she say anything else about him?"

Angela Riegert nodded. "That he had incredible eyes."

"And what did you think?"

"I thought he was cute too, a little older than most of the other guys there."

"What happened then?"

The witness swallowed, bit down on her lower lip. "We went back inside."

"And did you speak to Colin Friendly again?"

"I didn't, no, but later on, Wendy said she was going back outside to talk to him."

"And?"

"It was the last time I saw her."

"She never came back in?"

"No. When I went to look for her later, to tell her I was ready to leave, she was gone."

"And the defendant?"

"He was gone too."

The prosecutor smiled. "Thank you, Miss Riegert." He nodded toward the defense. "Your witness."

The defense counsel was already on his feet, buttoning his jacket. He was an athletic-looking man, blond and thick-necked, the muscles of his arms clearly evident beneath the jacket of his gray silk suit. "Miss Riegert," he said, biting off each syllable, "was there any drinking at this party?"

Angela Riegert shrank back in her seat. "Yes."

"Drugs?"

"Drugs?" she repeated, clearly flustered.

"Marijuana? Cocaine?"

"I didn't see anyone doing cocaine."

"Were you drinking?" the attorney pressed.

"I had a few beers, yes."

"Were you drunk?"

"No."

"Did you have any marijuana?"

"Objection, your honor," Mr. Eaves protested. "The witness is not on trial."

"Goes to state of mind, Judge. It directly affects the witness's ability to identify my client."

"Objection overruled. Please answer the question, Miss Riegert."

She hesitated, looked close to tears. "I had a few tokes," she admitted.

"A few tokes off a marijuana cigarette and a few beers, is that what you're saying?" the defense attorney repeated.

"Yes."

"Were you stoned?"

"No."

"But you did go outside to get some air."

"It was hot inside, and very crowded."

"And outside?"

"It was better."

"Was it dark?"

"I guess."

"So," the defense lawyer stated, positioning himself directly in front of the jury, "it was dark, you'd been drinking and smoking marijuana..." He paused for effect. "And still you claim you can positively identify my client."

Angela Riegert pulled back her shoulders, stared directly at Colin Friendly. "Yes," she said. "I know it was him."

"Oh, Miss Riegert," the lawyer asked, almost as an afterthought, "do you wear glasses?"

"Sometimes."

"Were you wearing them that night?"

"No."

"Thank you. No further questions." The lawyer quickly returned to his seat.

"Well done," Jo Lynn said, and I was forced to agree. In less than a minute, Colin Friendly's attorney had neatly skewered Angela Riegert's testimony, introducing at least a modicum of reasonable doubt.

"You may step down," Judge Kellner instructed the witness. Angela Riegert took a deep breath, then stepped off the witness stand, Jo Lynn's eyes glaring at her as she walked past us out of the room.

"What a loser," Jo Lynn pronounced as the next witness was called.

"The state calls Marcia Layton."

I looked toward the center aisle at the same precise moment as Colin Friendly. For a fraction of a second, our eyes met. He winked boldly, then looked away.

Chapter
6

It was almost four-thirty by the time we reached our mother's apartment, located on Palm Beach Lakes Boulevard, several miles west of I-95.

"What's the big rush?" Jo Lynn asked, teetering on pencil-thin high heels behind me, as

I ran across the parking lot toward the yellow structure that resembled nothing so much as a large lemon pound cake. "It's not like she's going anywhere."

"I told Mrs. Winchell we'd be here by four o'clock," I reminded her. "She wasn't happy. She has to be out of here by five."

"So, whose fault is it we're late?"

I said nothing. Jo Lynn was right. The fact that we were almost half an hour late was at least partly my fault. And Robert's.

He'd been waiting for me when we exited the courtroom at the end of the day. "I'm sorry I missed you at lunchtime," he apologized immediately, while I tried not to notice how clear his hazel eyes were. "I had to rush off to a meeting."

"How are you? What are you doing here?" I asked, my voice an octave higher than usual. I was grateful that Jo Lynn wasn't beside me to witness my regression to adolescence, that she was still poised at the side of the courtroom doors, waiting for her chance to accost one of Colin Friendly's attorneys. She'd spent the better part of the lunch break composing a letter to the monster, having decided her phone number wasn't support enough. Colin Friendly needed to know why she was so convinced of his innocence, she told me. I told her she needed to have her head examined.

"What am I doing in Palm Beach or what am I doing in court?" The lines around Robert Crowe's eyes crinkled in a way that told me he was well aware of his effect on me, as he'd always been, and that he was amused, possibly even touched, by it. "I might ask you the same thing."

"I live here. In Palm Beach. Well, actually in Palm Beach Gardens. We moved here about seven years ago." Had he really asked for so much information? "And you?"

"My family moved to Tampa right after I graduated high school," he said easily. "I went off to Yale, then joined my folks in Florida after graduation, met a girl, got married, moved to Boca, got divorced, moved to Delray, got married again, moved to Palm Beach."

"So you're married," I said, and immediately wished the scales of justice would come crashing down on my head.

He smiled. "Four kids. And you?"

"Two girls."

"And a husband?"

"Oh yes, of course. Larry Sinclair. I met him at college. I don't think you know him," I babbled, wishing someone would stick a gag in my mouth. All my life, I've wanted to be a lady of mystery, one of those women who smile enigmatically and say little, probably because they have little to say, but everyone always assumes it's because they're so deep. At any rate, mystery has never been my strong suit. My mother always says you can see everything on my face.

Robert Crowe shook his head, revealing a number of gray hairs around his temples. They made him look more distinguished, I thought. "Just the one husband?" he asked.

"Pretty boring," I said.

"Pretty amazing," he countered. "So, what brings you to court today?"

I glanced toward my sister, still waiting anxiously by the courtroom doors. "To tell you the truth, I'm not really sure. What about you? Are you a reporter?"

"Not exactly. I own a radio station, WKEY."

"Oh, of course." I hoped I didn't sound as impressed as I felt.

"Normally I wouldn't be here. We have reporters covering the trial, of course."

"Of course," I concurred.

"But I had a lunch meeting nearby, so I thought..." He broke off. "You're very beautiful," he said.

I laughed out loud. Probably to keep from fainting.

"Why are you laughing? Don't you believe me?"

I felt my cheeks grow crimson, my knees go weak, my body temperature rise. Oh sure, I thought, great time to turn into a red, quivering mass of sweat. That should impress the hell out of him. "It's just been a long time since anyone told me I was beautiful," I heard myself say.

"Larry doesn't tell you how beautiful you are?" He smiled, curling his lips around my husband's first name. He's playing with me, I thought.

There was a slight commotion at the door. Colin Friendly's attorneys were leaving the courtroom. "Mr. Archibald," I heard my sister call out, thrusting the letter she'd spent the lunch break composing at the lawyer in the gray silk suit, "I was wondering if you could make sure that Colin receives this. It's very important."

"Pathetic," Robert Crowe pronounced.

"What is?"

"Courtroom groupies. Every trial has them. The more gruesome the crime, the more ardent the bimbos." He shook his head. "It makes you wonder."

"About what?"

"About what kind of lives these poor deluded souls live. I mean, look at that woman. She's not bad-looking; she probably wouldn't have any trouble getting a man, yet she chooses to go after a guy who gets his kicks from killing and mutilating women. I don't get it. Do you?"

I shook my head, although, in truth, I was barely aware of anything he'd said after "she's not bad-looking." Moments before he'd told me I was beautiful. Jo Lynn was merely "not bad-looking." Shallow thing that I was fast becoming, I couldn't get it out of my head.

"So, what does Larry's wife do when she's not attending sensational murder trials?" he asked.

The second mention of my husband's name snapped me out of my reveries. "I'm a therapist."

"That's right, I remember you were always interested in that sort of stuff." He managed to make it sound as if he'd actually been listening to anything I'd had to say thirty years ago. "So little Kate Latimer grew up to become the woman she always wanted to be."

Had I? I wondered. If so, then why was she such a stranger?

"Well, Kate Latimer, it's been very nice seeing you again after all these years." He leaned his face close to mine. Was he going to kiss me? Was I going to let him? Was I a total idiot?

"It's Kate Sinclair now," I reminded us both.

Cocking his head to one side, his eyes never leaving mine, he took my hand in his and brought it slowly to his mouth. His lips grazed the back of my hand. I don't even want to describe the effect this had on my body, which was already struggling to remain upright and in one piece. "Uh-oh," he said.

I froze. "What's the matter?"

"The bimbo is headed this way."

"Okay, we can go now," Jo Lynn announced, arriving at my side, eyes wandering between me and Robert Crowe.

"Jo Lynn," I said, "I'd like you to meet Robert Crowe. Robert, this is my sister, Jo Lynn Baker."

"Please shoot me now," Robert said simply, and I laughed. It felt good to be in control again.

"Am I missing something?" Jo Lynn asked. Her voice was light, but her eyes flashed a familiar combination of anger and hurt. She didn't like to feel left out. She hated being laughed at.

"Your sister and I knew each other in high school," Robert said, as if this were explanation enough.

For some reason, this seemed to satisfy her. "Really? Well, then I guess you can thank me for this mini high school reunion. I'm the one who dragged her down here, and let me tell you, it wasn't easy." She leaned forward to shake his hand, her breasts all but spilling into the air between them.

"Yes, I seem to recall that it's pretty hard to get Kate to do anything she doesn't want to do." Robert's smile grew wicked. He'd spent six months in high school trying to seduce me, then dropped me like the proverbial hot potato when it became apparent I was a lost cause.

"We should get going," Jo Lynn stated, then leaned toward Robert, conspiratorially. "Our mom is terrorizing the tenants of the old folks home she lives in. We have a meeting."

"Interesting family," Robert Crowe said, as Jo Lynn led me away.

"So, did you sleep with him?" she asked on the way to the Palm Beach Lakes Retirement Home.

"No, of course not."

"But you wanted to," she persisted.

"I was seventeen; I didn't know what I wanted."

"You wanted to sleep with him, but you were

such a goody-goody that you didn't, and you've always regretted it."

"For God's sake, Jo Lynn, I haven't thought about the man in years."

When I refused to discuss him further, Jo Lynn launched into a recap of the day's proceedings. Angela Riegert was a disaster as a witness, she pronounced; her testimony had been more helpful to the defense than to the prosecution. It didn't matter that she'd placed the defendant beside the victim shortly before the girl's disappearance; all the jury would remember was that Angela Riegert was a beer-guzzling, marijuana-smoking, half-blind half-wit.

Marcia Layton was similarly gutted, then tossed aside, as were the rest of the day's witnesses, all of whom put Colin Friendly squarely in the vicinity of the murdered girls at the time they went missing. "Inconclusive," Jo Lynn pronounced stubbornly. "Eyewitnesses are notoriously unreliable."

There was no point in arguing. Jo Lynn had always believed exactly what she wanted to believe. She saw what she wanted to see. When she looked at Colin Friendly, she saw a lonely little boy with a sad smile, and she believed him to be innocent, as much a victim as each of the women he stood accused of murdering. Possibly more.

It had been the same way with Andrew and Daniel and Peter. Andrew, whom she married at eighteen, broke first one arm, then the other; Daniel, whom she married six years later, stole

82

her money and cracked her ribs; Peter, whom she married just after her thirty-second birthday and divorced just prior to her thirty-third, threw her down a flight of stairs on their wedding night. Still, in the end, it was Andrew, Daniel, and Peter who did the walking. I tried to get her into therapy, but she would have none of it. "It's Mom's fault," she'd joke. ("Kidding on the square," our mother would say, shoulders slumping forward, accepting responsibility.)

"Would you slow down a bit," Jo Lynn whined as we reached the front door of the retirement home.

"Why'd you have to wear such high heels?" I asked, transferring my frustration from her to her fuchsia pumps.

"You don't like my shoes?"

The lobby was large and cheery, all white paint and green trees and chairs covered in bold floral prints. At least a dozen senior citizens sat in a row of white wicker rocking chairs, staring out the large front window, as if at a drive-in movie. Thinning hair, liver spots, stooped backs, and sunken faces, an old man fumbling with his fly, an old woman adjusting her teeth—I looked at them and saw the future. It scared me half to death.

Our mother was waiting for us outside Mrs. Winchell's office. "Where have you been? It's not like you to be late." She looked from me to Jo Lynn.

"Don't give me that look," Jo Lynn said immediately, her defenses, like fists, already raised.

"I was just thinking how nice it is to see you," our mother said.

Jo Lynn made a sound halfway between a laugh and a snort, and looked away.

"I'm sorry, Mom," I explained. "I met an old friend from high school."

"Who she wanted to sleep with, but didn't," Jo Lynn said.

"What?" said my mother.

"Jo Lynn..."

"It's true," Jo Lynn said, smiling at our mother. "Did she tell you I'm getting married?"

At our meeting Mrs. Winchell, whose tomato-red suit set off her velvety black skin but clashed with the rest of her predominantly canary-yellow office, made no effort to disguise repeated glances at her watch. She couldn't stay long, she'd stated before the meeting got underway; we were almost forty minutes late and, regrettably, she had a dinner engagement in Boca.

Got married. Moved to Boca. Got divorced. Moved to Delray.

"Perhaps you could tell your daughters your complaints regarding Mr. Ormsby," Mrs. Winchell began.

Our mother looked surprised, then confused. Clearly, she had no idea what Mrs. Winchell was talking about.

"Didn't you tell me that Mr. Ormsby was harassing you?" Mrs. Winchell prompted. "Fred Ormsby is part of our janitorial staff," she explained, checking her watch.

"He's a lovely man," our mother added.

"He hasn't been calling you at all hours of the night?"

"Why would he do that?"

It was Mrs. Winchell's turn to look confused. "Well, of course, he wouldn't. He didn't. I'm just repeating what you told me."

"No," my mother insisted. "Fred Ormsby is a lovely man. He would never do anything like that. You must have misunderstood."

"Then there's no problem?" my sister asked, jumping to her feet.

"Apparently not." Mrs. Winchell smiled, obviously relieved the meeting had reached such a surprisingly swift and satisfactory conclusion. If she had any other concerns, she wasn't about to get into them now.

"What did you make of that?" I asked my sister as we rode with our mother in the elevator up to the fourth floor.

Jo Lynn shrugged. "Mrs. Winchell obviously got her inmates confused."

"I don't trust that woman," our mother said.

Jo Lynn laughed. "You just don't like her because she's black."

"Jo Lynn!" I gasped.

"Mrs. Winchell is black?" our mother asked.

"How could she not know the woman is black?" I whispered as we exited the elevator and proceeded along the peach-colored corridor. "Do you think something's the matter with her eyes?"

"She just didn't notice."

"How can you not notice something like that?"

"Didn't anyone ever teach you it's not polite to whisper behind people's backs?" our mother asked pointedly, stopping in front of the door to her apartment, making no move to open it.

"What are you waiting for?" Jo Lynn said. "There's nobody home."

My mother reached into her pocket for her keys. She was elegantly dressed in a soft pink skirt and matching sweater set, highlighted by a single strand of pearls. "I was just thinking."

"About what?" I asked.

"About what I've done that would make Mrs. Winchell not like me." Her voice carried the threat of tears.

"She doesn't like you because you're Jewish," Jo Lynn said.

"I'm Jewish?" our mother asked.

"She's joking, Mom," I said quickly, glaring at Jo Lynn, feeling like Alice at the Mad Hatter's tea party.

"So was I," our mother said, smiling mischievously as we stepped into her small one-bedroom apartment. "Where's your sense of humor, Kate?"

I left it at the courthouse, I thought, my eyes taking in the room in a single glance. The living area contained a small love seat and matching chair, with a glass coffee table crowded in between, and a standing lamp cramped into one corner. Pictures of me, my daughters, and Jo Lynn covered every available surface, including the windowsill that ran along the far wall, overlooking the parking lot below.

"It's like an oven in here. How high do you have the heat?" Jo Lynn moved to the thermometer. "It's eighty-three degrees. How can you stand it?"

"Older people feel the cold more," our mother said.

I took off my jacket, threw it across the back of the beige chair.

"What are you doing?" Jo Lynn said, scooping it up again, handing it back. "We're not staying."

"We can stay a few minutes."

"Of course you'll stay," our mother insisted. "We'll have some cake."

"Not a chance," Jo Lynn said. "You trying to poison us like you did old Mr. Emerson?"

Our mother was already on her way to the tiny galley kitchen, opening the fridge, removing a slightly lopsided angel food cake. "Oh, Jo Lynn," she said. "There you go again, kidding on the square."

"What's that?" I asked, coming up behind her, spying a large bottle of dishwashing detergent on the refrigerator's top shelf. "Mom, what's this doing in the fridge?"

Jo Lynn was immediately at our side. "God, Mom, is that what you've been cooking with?"

"Of course not," our mother scoffed, removing the detergent from the fridge, putting it by the side of the sink. "Don't you ever make mistakes?"

87

"Something's very wrong," I said as we were driving home. "She's losing it."

Jo Lynn waved dismissive fingers in the air. "She got confused."

I invited Jo Lynn over for dinner and was grateful when she said no. She wanted to relax and get a good night's sleep, she said, so she'd look fresh for tomorrow's day in court. It was important that Colin have attractive people around him to boost his morale. Besides, his attorneys might try to contact her, and she didn't want to miss their call.

"Whatever," I said, dropping her off at her low-rise apartment near Blue Heron Drive, watching till she was safely through the lobby's front door. My sister was pining for a serial killer and my mother kept dishwashing detergent in the refrigerator. Interesting family is right, I thought, recalling Robert's words, squirming in my seat as I turned the car back toward I-95.

Now, I am not anything like my sister. I am mature, levelheaded, not given to flights of fancy. If anything, I am too firmly grounded in reality. I have a clear understanding of my strengths and weaknesses; I've come to terms with my foibles and insecurities. I am decidedly unsentimental; I am definitely not a romantic. So, what did it mean that I was suddenly, inexplicably, overwhelmingly, desperate for a man I hadn't seen in over thirty years, a shallow jock who'd wooed me, then dumped me when I wouldn't put out? Why couldn't I get his sly smile out of my mind? "You're very beautiful," he'd said, the facile phrase repeating itself over and over in my head, attaching itself to Dwight Yoakam's country twang. Station WKEY, I realized, wondering when I'd changed the dial.

In fact, it doesn't require a great deal of psychoanalyzing to figure out my state of mind: I was getting older; my life with Larry had settled into a comfortable groove; I'd seen flashes of my own mortality in the face of my mother; my sister was driving me nuts. Robert Crowe was a harking back to my youth, my innocence, a reminder that my whole life lay before me. Plus, of course, he was a symbol of all that was desirable but unattainable, the one who got away.

Jo Lynn was right. I'd wanted to sleep with him very badly when I was seventeen. I'd been severely tempted on more than one occasion to throw caution to the wind, along with my morals and every article of clothing on me. I'm not sure what stopped me, other than the certainty that once I gave in, he would undoubtedly lose interest and move on. Well, he'd lost interest and moved on anyway. Then he'd moved away altogether and I never even had the chance to change my mind.

I'd lied earlier when I told Jo Lynn I hadn't thought about him in years. The truth was that I thought about him more often than I cared to admit, more often than I'd even realized. His features may have faded, blurred, grown indistinct, but he was always there, lurking, a symbol of simpler times, of youthful ardor, of lost chances, of what might have been.

Dinner was already on the table when I arrived home. I was grateful to Larry, who was a better cook than I was, probably because he enjoyed cooking and I didn't. At any rate, he'd made some sort of chicken dish that Michelle didn't eat because she said it was too spicy and Sara didn't eat because she said she was getting fat. I wolfed down everything on my plate, and almost choked on a piece of chicken.

"Are you okay?" Larry asked.

"Do you need the Heimlich maneuver?" Michelle was already on her feet. She'd taken a St. John's Ambulance course the previous summer and was always asking if anyone needed the Heimlich maneuver.

"Sorry, sweetie, no," I told her.

Both Sara and Michelle left the table while Larry and I were still eating, Michelle to do homework, Sara to return to school. There was a rehearsal for an upcoming fashion show; she was in it and she couldn't be late. An interesting concept for Sara, I thought, who had no such qualms about being late for anything else.

Larry and I chatted briefly about our respective days, then lapsed into silence. I found myself studying him as he ate; he was a nice-looking man of average height and weight, growing bald with grace, his eyes a grayish blue, his complexion fair, his arms and legs on the thin side, any extra weight he'd acquired over the years having comfortably settled in around his stomach. He'd turned fifty the previous July with a minimum of fuss and even less angst. When I'd asked him how it felt to be fifty, he'd smiled and said simply, "It beats the alternative." How would Robert respond to a similar query? I wondered, trying to shake free of his memory as I cleared the table of food. But it was no use. Robert's presence pursued me into the kitchen as I cleaned up, crowded between Larry and me as we watched TV, followed me into the bedroom after I gave up waiting for Sara to come home.

Larry was already in bed. The fourteen decorative pillows that sit on top of the ivory bedspread during the day were now scattered rudely across the ivory carpeting. Larry hates the pillows. He says they're a pain in the neck, and he's right, they are. But I love organizing them in the morning, arranging them in neat little rows, and truthfully, I don't really mind taking them off and stacking them at night. Probably, it gives me the illusion of control. Larry has no such illusions. He simply throws them into the air and lets them fall where they may.

I undressed and climbed into bed beside my husband, reaching for him in the dark. He sighed and stirred, turning onto his back, taking me into his arms, welcoming my touch. "Hi, funny face," he whispered as I kissed the side of his neck, my fingers drawing a slowly swirling line through the curly hairs of his chest, edging downward. A slight groan escaped his lips as I reached lower, cradled his penis in the palm of my hand.

I don't know why I always feel a little insulted when Larry isn't already fully aroused when I touch him, but I do. I know this is irrational, that it takes men longer to become aroused as they get older, that certain body parts no longer snap to attention at the merest whiff of sex, that gentle perseverance will pay off in the end. Still, it disappoints me, even angers me, if I'm being really truthful, that my mere presence beside him in bed is no longer enough. I know we've been married almost twenty-five years; I know my body isn't the same as the body he married; I know things have become somewhat routine; I know romance takes hard work. Haven't I already confessed I'm not a romantic?

So I pushed my hurt feelings aside and stroked him delicately, turning his penis over in my hand, kneading it, like a piece of Plasticene. I thought of swatting it, thought better of it. Definitely a mood killer. Instead, I took him gently in my mouth, feeling gratified when he grew quickly hard. Then I climbed on top of him and fitted him inside me, starting slowly, then picking up the pace, riding him with increasing urgency, as if there were someone chasing me, and perhaps someone was.

As Larry drifted off to sleep, I saw Robert watching me from one of two ivory chairs by the window, his Cheshire cat smile reflected brightly against the shadows. His image floated forward, whispered in my ear. Pleasant dreams, he said.

Chapter 7

As I struggle now to understand Sara's role in everything that happened, I ask myself if I could have done anything differently earlier on, something that might have warded off the chaos and tragedy that followed. Certainly the clues were all around me. The pieces of the puzzle that is my older child were all there. I had only to arrange them in their correct positions. Or would there always have been one or two pieces missing? And would finding them have done any good?

When Sara went out that night, supposedly to rehearse for an upcoming fashion show at school, I had no idea she was lying. Or maybe I did. Past experience had taught me to view everything Sara said as suspect. But, like a wife who has chosen to stay with her faithless husband, I had made a conscious decision to believe the things she told me until presented with conclusive evidence to the contrary. Sara being Sara, this usually didn't take long.

The first time I'd caught Sara in an outright lie was soon after she turned fifteen. We'd been out for dinner, it was raining, and Sara dropped her purse in the parking lot as we raced for the car. About ten empty packages of cigarettes tumbled out of the overstuffed leather bag and onto the wet pavement.

"They're not mine," she said, quickly scooping them up and stuffing them back inside her purse as I watched in awed silence.

"They're not yours," I repeated.

"They belong to a friend. She collects them."

Now most people would immediately dismiss this for the ridiculous fabrication it was and get in out of the rain. But when it's *your* kid with the ridiculous yarn, it's a different story. "Your friend collects *empty* cigarette packages?"

"Yes, and her mother would be really mad if she found out, so she asked me to keep them for her." Sara vaulted to her feet, the empty, and now soaking-wet, cigarette packages safely back inside her bag and out of sight. "I don't smoke," she insisted. "They're not mine."

I struggled to believe her. People collected all sorts of weird things, I told myself. Why not empty cigarette packages? If her friend's mother would be upset at this, well, then it was perfectly logical for her to ask Sara to keep them for her. This is what I actually tried to convince myself. And then common sense prevailed and the therapist took control. "You say you're not smoking, and I'd love to believe you," I began. "You know how dangerous smoking is, and *I* know I can't follow you around twenty-four hours a day. If you're going to smoke, you're going to smoke. I only hope that if you *are* smoking, you're smart enough to quit before you become addicted." And I left it at that. And, of course, she *was* smoking, and she *wasn't* smart enough to quit before she became addicted. Why was I surprised?

94

The ten empty cigarette packages were followed by the five full bottles of beer which I found in her closet while searching for the white blouse she'd asked me to iron. How dare I go snooping around her closet! she screamed later, as if I should have realized that her white blouse lay in a crumpled heap on the floor along with most of her other worldly possessions. And, of course, the beer wasn't hers—she was merely keeping it for a friend.

There was the day she skipped school to go shopping in Fort Lauderdale, the weekend she snuck off to Miami to see the Grateful Dead. I'm sure I wasn't the only mother not to mourn the passing of Jerry Garcia, however much I might have enjoyed his music in my youth.

Sweaters disappeared from my drawers. Half our CDs went missing. Sara stole money from my purse and denied it outright to my face. The adoring creature who'd once looked at me with something approaching awe was replaced by a creature who glared at me with such utter contempt that it shook me to the bones. I told myself that this transformation was simply a rite of passage, that it was Sara's unconscious way of separating from me, of becoming her own person. But it still hurt. That's what the psychology texts don't prepare you for—how much it hurts.

Actually, it's the lies that hurt more than anything, because lies destroy trust, and it feels awful not to trust the people you love.

Not that the truth provided us with any

great comfort. Sara blithely informed me, a few weeks after she turned sixteen, that she was no longer a virgin. Since she had no steady boyfriend, to say I was stunned was something of an understatement. I mumbled something about hoping it had been a pleasurable experience for her, then launched into a lecture about the dangers of unprotected sex in today's society, probably because I was afraid that if I stopped talking, she'd tell me something else I didn't want to hear. She assured me that she knew all about the threat of AIDS and the necessity for condoms, and insisted she wasn't a child. Then she asked me to drive her to the record store.

It was around this time that she also admitted to having experimented with drugs. Just a little grass and acid, she said with a shrug. Nothing to worry our old-fashioned little heads about. She reminded us that our generation had practically invented hallucinogens; I reminded her that they were still illegal, that she was playing with fire, and that we would send her packing should we ever find any drugs in the house. "That's what I get for being honest with you," she huffed in response.

She started getting phone calls at all hours of the night. Since we only have one line, these phone calls woke up the whole house. I told Sara this had to stop; she said she couldn't be blamed for something over which she had no control. I told her it was her responsibility to tell people not to call after 11 P.M. She told me to mind my own business.

The argument ended with Larry storming into her room and literally tearing her phone out of the wall. That pretty much took care of that.

The phone was how we found out that Sara hadn't gone to the school for any fashion show rehearsal. A friend, I suspect more than slightly inebriated, called at 2 A.M. to tell us that Sara had left her purse at the party, could we tell her not to worry? We said we'd be only too thrilled.

As it turned out, Sara had already realized she'd forgotten her purse and gone back for it, so she knew about the phone call and she was as ready for us as we were for her. Can you imagine? she lamented even before she was through the front door. She'd gone all the way to school only to discover the rehearsal had been canceled. A bunch of the kids, knowing how important this fashion show was—the proceeds were going to the United Way— and wanting to do the best possible job, decided to have a rehearsal of their own at somebody's house. There was no party. They'd selflessly worked their butts off all night, stopping only an hour ago when they were fully satisfied this was going to be the best fashion show ever. If we didn't believe her, she finished with a flourish, then that was our problem, not hers, and she felt sorry for us. By the time she was through, she'd worked herself into a self-righteous fury of almost biblical proportions. How could we not trust her? What kind of pitiful excuse for parents were we? And what were we doing talking to her friends anyway?

We grounded her for two weeks.

"Go to hell!" she shouted, storming into her room.

"Watch it," I warned.

"Watch this, *Ms*. Therapist!" Her door slammed shut.

"Make that three weeks," Larry yelled after her. The response was the sound of a shoe crashing against her still-vibrating door.

Seconds later, Michelle tiptoed out of her bedroom, fixed her father and me with her most baleful glance. "You know that grounding never works," she intoned, the seriousness of her message undermined somewhat by the teddy bear nightgown she was wearing. "Grounding only makes kids angry."

She's right, I thought. "Go back to sleep," I said.

Not that it's all been awful as far as Sara is concerned. Aside from the sheer creativity of some of her tirades, there is also a tremendous vulnerability, a genuine sweetness to Sara. Behind those enormous breasts beats the heart of a good kid. Sara is a child trapped inside a woman's body. She still isn't ready to come out.

I remember when she got her period for the first time. She was fifteen years old, which is late, and she'd long ago forgotten the mother-daughter discussion we'd had about such things. She took the pads I gave her, and skulked from the room, as if this appalling state of affairs was something I'd wished on her. The next morning, I asked if the pads had interfered with her sleep.

She looked horrified. "You mean you have to wear them at night?!"

I still laugh about that one, as I do when I recall her disgust some four days later. "How long does this go *on*?" she demanded indignantly. I didn't have the heart to tell her another thirty-five years.

One night, Sara was reluctantly helping me stack the dinner dishes inside the dishwasher. I'd lined all the glasses along one side. There was one left over, which I placed on the other side of the dishwasher. Sara immediately took a glass from my neat row and put it beside the single one. "I don't want it to be lonely," she explained.

It was all I could do to keep from crying. Instead, I hugged her and told her I loved her. Sara tolerated my embrace, mumbled something about loving me too, then left the room.

So, how does one reconcile the sweet innocent thing who worries about the feelings of dirty dishes with the foul-mouthed hellion who doesn't seem to understand that human beings have feelings too?

"The apple doesn't fall far from the tree," I tell my clients, seeking to reassure them—and no doubt myself—that eventually life returns to normal, that teenagers such as Sara do become human beings again. Provided they live long enough.

Is it true we get the children we need?

I wonder what my mother would say to that.

So, to answer my own question, I don't know whether or not I could have prevented much of what happened later had I acted differently in the beginning. Hindsight, as they say, is twenty-twenty. You do the best you can with what you've got. Sometimes it's good enough. Sometimes it isn't.

I steadfastly refused all Jo Lynn's entreaties to accompany her back to the courthouse, insisting that neither Colin Friendly nor her designs on him held any interest for me. In truth, I'd started following the case quite closely in the paper and on television. In the last week, the prosecutor had called a long string of witnesses to the stand, all of whom had been able, in one way or another, to connect the defendant to at least eight of the dead girls. An elderly man testified to having seen one of the victims giving Colin Friendly directions on the day she disappeared; a teary-eyed woman swore she'd seen him sitting on a bench in the park where her friend regularly walked her dog. The dog had been found by a group of children as he wandered aimlessly through nearby streets, dragging his leash behind him. His owner—or rather, what was left of her—had been discovered four months later by a group of campers near Lake Okeechobee. The medical examiner had since determined that she'd been raped, beaten, then stabbed some eighty-six times.

By Wednesday, the medical examiner had already been on the stand for two full days. In meticulous detail, he'd recounted each of the victims' injuries and how they'd been caused. He offered the forensic findings in dispassionate tones, unshaded by nuance, untouched by emotion. Victim number one, Marie Postelwaite, age twenty-five, and a nurse at JFK Memorial, had been raped, beaten, stabbed, and strangled with her own white panty hose, the knot twisted around her neck so tightly, she'd been almost decapitated; victim number two, Christine McDermott, age thirty-three, an elementary school teacher and mother of two, had been raped, sodomized, beaten, stabbed, and bitten repeatedly; victim number three, Tammy Fisher, age sixteen, grade eleven honor student, was found raped, beaten, stabbed, her throat slashed from ear to ear; and on and on, through to victim number thirteen, Maureen Elfer, age twenty-seven and a newlywed, who'd been raped, sodomized, beaten, stabbed, and virtually gutted. Slight variations on the same grizzly theme.

The last thing I wanted to do, I'd told my sister when she called the night before, was to hear any of these gruesome details up close. It was enough to read about such awful things in the paper without having to listen to the muffled sobs of the victims' families as each fresh horror was recounted. Hadn't she had enough? I demanded.

"Are you kidding? This is only the beginning." The forensic evidence was highly suspect, probably tainted, she said knowingly. DNA was a notoriously inexact science. The medical examiner was in the prosecutor's pocket. Wait till the defense got a crack at him.

I thought of my visit to the squat building on Gun Club Road. I had told my sister about it, hoping it might scare some sense into her. It hadn't.

"Colin will be found innocent. You'll see," she insisted, still resolutely in his corner despite the fact that he hadn't responded to her note. At least somebody was thinking clearly, I thought, relieved.

"I wonder if they gave him my letter," she mused aloud in court that second Wednesday, as I squirmed around in my seat, my eyes drifting toward the back of the room, flitting casually across the representatives of the media.

Was that what I was doing here? Had I been hoping to see Robert again? Was that why I'd finally given in and agreed to spend another day in court?

Oh God, I thought with a shudder. I'm as bad as my sister.

"Do you think they'd do that?" Jo Lynn was asking.

"Do what?"

"Not give him my letter."

"I don't know," I said honestly, distracted by the powers of my own self-delusion.

"I think that would be illegal," she continued, "not giving someone their mail. I mean, I wrote him a letter, which I entrusted to them, and I would think that they're under a legal obligation to make sure he gets it. Wouldn't you?"

"I have no idea." My voice vibrated impatience. I heard it. So did Jo Lynn.

"What's the matter with you? Disappointed because your boyfriend didn't show?"

My head snapped toward her, my eyes flashing anger, my cheeks flushing red. "Do you ever say anything that's not ridiculous?"

"Hit a nerve, did I?"

The door at the front of the courtroom opened and the prisoner was let in. He looked around, eyes taking in the entire courtroom at a glance. Beside me, Jo Lynn waved, a small fluttering of her fingers, followed by a tiny kiss she blew toward him. The corners of Colin Friendly's mouth creased into a smile as he reached out to grab the invisible kiss, his fingers tightening around it, as if around a young girl's throat. He was wearing the same blue suit he'd been wearing the first time I saw him, although his shirt was white and his tie navy, and I wondered if he received a fresh shirt and tie every day, and if so, who supplied them. I thought of asking Jo Lynn, decided against it. She'd probably use it as an excuse to comment on my own clothes, the fact that I was wearing a delicately floral dress I normally reserved for more formal social occasions, undoubtedly something she would attribute to the fact I'd hoped to run into Robert.

Jo Lynn was wearing a plunging white sweater and black leather miniskirt. Her hair was freshly washed and draped across her shoulders in layers of blond curls, like a heavy brocade. More than once I caught sight of people craning their necks in her direction. Jo Lynn appeared oblivious to it all, her total attention seemingly focused on the accused, but I knew she was aware of the scrutiny. And I could tell by the way she tossed her head and flicked her hair away from her face that she was enjoying it.

She was something of a celebrity here in Courtroom 11A. People talked to her. They asked her opinions of the previous day's proceedings. They asked whether or not she thought Colin would testify in his own defense and whether or not she thought he should. I was amazed at how authoritative she sounded, at how much weight her answers were given. She'd always complained that I didn't take her seriously enough, and maybe she was right.

The medical examiner resumed his seat on the witness stand. He was a compact little man, standing no more than five feet four inches tall, with dark hair and an oblong face that looked as if it had been caught between the doors of a bus. His features were squished into the center of his face, his round wire-rimmed glasses propped awkwardly on the bridge of his nose. His name was Dr. Ronald Loring and he was about forty-five years old. Younger than me, I thought.

"We don't have too many more questions for you this morning, Dr. Loring," the prosecutor began, fastening the top button of his brown pinstriped jacket while approaching the witness.

Dr. Loring nodded.

"You've stated that the victims had all been raped and sometimes sodomized, is that so?"

"Yes, that's correct."

"Was there semen found in any of the victims?"

"There was semen found in the bodies that were sufficiently preserved." He listed the women's names.

"And did that semen match the sample of semen taken from Colin Friendly?"

"It did in many significant respects."

I glanced at Jo Lynn. She tossed her head, flicked her hair, pretended to be unaware I was looking at her.

There followed a lengthy discussion of the techniques used to analyze and identify sperm. It had something to do with bodily secretions and blood types and other variables I've forgotten. According to these variables, there was a seventy percent probability that Colin Friendly was the man who'd raped and sodomized these women.

"Seventy percent," Jo Lynn repeated, dismissively.

The same was true of the teeth marks that had been etched into the flesh of several of the victims. A mold had been taken of Colin Friendly's mouth. It closely—but not conclusively—matched the bite marks on the bodies. Traces of saliva left inside the wounds pointed to—but didn't pinpoint—the accused. Despite this, there was no question in his mind, Dr. Ronald Loring pronounced, but that Colin Friendly had been responsible for the bites on the bodies of the dead girls.

What of the bodies that had decomposed beyond recognition, that were mere collections of bones by the time they were unearthed? the prosecutor asked. How could the doctor tell that these unfortunates had been murdered, let alone murdered by Colin Friendly?

Dr. Loring went into a lengthy discussion of the marvels of forensic medicine, how scientific techniques had become so sophisticated, they could often precisely pinpoint the exact time and cause of a person's death. He went into considerable detail regarding the methods his department employed. His voice was steady, his delivery dry. I could tell he was losing some of the jury, who looked bleary-eyed, one man's eyes threatening to close altogether.

"Mumbo jumbo," Jo Lynn muttered.

Aside from this, there were patterns to the violence that linked the accused to each of his victims, Dr. Loring continued, as the jury and the rest of the courtroom perked up. The women had all been severely beaten, their noses shattered. Multiple stab wounds circled the breasts of the victims, forming horizontal figure eights; the women's stomachs had been sliced open; they'd been stabbed directly, and repeatedly, through the heart.

The thirteen women Colin Friendly stood

accused of killing had been murdered by the same man, the medical examiner concluded. That man was Colin Friendly

"What a crock," Jo Lynn pronounced.

I couldn't help it. Like a hungry fish, I snapped at the bait. "How can you say that? Didn't you hear anything Dr. Loring said?"

"I heard him say "seventy percent,' not "one hundred,' " she snapped back. "I heard "closely matched,' not "perfectly matched.' Just wait till Mr. Archibald gets through with him."

Mercifully, the judge called a recess for lunch. I watched as Colin Friendly stood up, spoke briefly to his lawyers, then smiled over at Jo Lynn as he was led from the room.

"Hang in there, Colin," Jo Lynn said, underlining her faith in him with a nod of her head.

"I think I've heard enough," I told Jo Lynn. "Why don't we call it a day."

She looked indignant. "What's the matter? Your boyfriend doesn't show up, so you're gonna pick up your marbles and go home?"

"Don't be ridiculous."

"That's the second time today you've called me ridiculous. I'm not ridiculous. You're the one who's ridiculous, mooning over some guy who dumped you thirty years ago."

It took every ounce of self-control I had to keep from screaming. Instead, I took several very deep breaths, and grabbed my purse, signaling my intention to leave. Jo Lynn stood back to let me pass, and I stepped into the aisle.

"Excuse me, Miss Baker."

I turned to see the muscular, fair-haired attorney for the defense approach my sister. He leaned forward, whispered something in her ear, then walked away.

Immediately, we were surrounded by reporters, their cameras clicking wildly, like a gaggle of geese. I lowered my head, kept walking to the door. Jo Lynn followed after me, but slowly enough for the cameras to keep up.

"What did Jake Archibald say to you?" a reporter asked.

"It's confidential, I'm afraid," my sister replied, smiling sweetly, lips pursing, eyes slightly downcast. The eternal coquette.

"What exactly is your connection to Colin Friendly?"

"I'm just a friend who's convinced of his innocence."

"Even in light of this morning's evidence?"

"I think evidence can be planted and lab samples can be tainted. The Palm Beach County medical examiner's office is old and rundown," she said, subverting what I'd told her to support her case. "Their equipment is hardly state-of-the-art."

Serves me right, I thought, for confiding anything in her.

"Is Colin Friendly your boyfriend?"

"Really, that's much too personal."

"Tell us what Jake Archibald said to you."

Jo Lynn stopped, smiled at each of the reporters gathered around her, wet her dark red lips for the camera. "Really, guys," she said, as if these strangers were her best buddies, "you know I'd tell you if I could. Please, bear with me."

With that, she grabbed hold of my arm and pushed me out into the corridor.

"For God's sake," I whispered under my breath, "what were you doing in there?"

"Being polite. Like Mama taught us." She backed me into a corner, smiled teasingly. "Don't you want to know what Jake Archibald said to me?"

"No," I said.

"Liar," she said. "Go on, ask me."

I tried to keep silent, but my heart wasn't in it. In truth, I was desperate to know, and we both knew it. "What did he say?"

Jo Lynn's smile exploded across her face. "It's happening," she said as my body went numb. "Colin Friendly wants to see me."

Chapter 8

Why don't you tell me what brought you here."

The dark-haired, middle-aged woman looked nervously toward her husband, whose eyes were all but glued to his brown Gucci loafers, then back at me. "I'm not sure I know where to begin." Again, she glanced anxiously at her husband.

"Don't look at me," he said without looking up. "I'm not the one who wanted to come here."

"You didn't want to come?" I repeated.

"This was her idea." A dismissive thumb jerked in the direction of his wife.

Lois and Arthur McKay sat across from me, their chairs angling toward opposite walls. They were a handsome couple—tall, immaculately groomed, almost regal in bearing. Probably they'd been breathtaking in their youth, the campus football hero and his beautiful homecoming queen. They'd been married almost thirty years and had three grown children. This was their first visit.

"Why do you think your wife wanted to come here?"

He shrugged. "You'd have to ask her."

I nodded. "Lois?"

She hesitated, looked around, eyes dropping to the floor. "I guess I'm tired of being ignored."

"You're complaining because I play golf and bridge a few times a week?"

"You play golf every day and bridge three times a week."

"I'm retired. It's why we moved to Florida."

"I thought we moved here so we could spend more time together." Lois McKay took a deep breath, reached for a tissue, said nothing for several seconds. "It's not just the bridge," she said finally. "It's not just the golf."

"What is it?" I asked.

"About a year ago," Lois McKay began

110

without further prompting, "I went for my routine yearly physical. The doctor discovered a lump in my right breast. She sent me for a mammogram. To make a long story short, the mammogram showed cancer. I had to have a mastectomy. Ask my husband what he was doing while I was in surgery."

"This isn't fair," her husband protested. "You said you didn't need me there, that there was nothing I could do at the hospital."

"Did you want him at the hospital?" I asked.

Lois McKay closed her eyes. "Of course I did."

"Did you or did you not tell me that I should go play golf?"

"Yes, that's what I told you."

"But you didn't mean it," I said gently.

"No."

"What stopped you from telling your husband that you wanted him with you?"

She shook her head. Several tears fell onto her lap, staining the skirt of her light green suit. "I shouldn't have to tell him."

"I'm supposed to read your mind?"

"I wanted him to *want* to be there," Lois McKay whispered.

"And you were hurt when he wasn't."

She nodded.

"I'm supposed to be a bloody mind reader," her husband reiterated.

"You're supposed to be there for me. You're supposed to care about whether I live or die. You're supposed to have the common decency to at least visit me in the hospital!"

"You didn't visit your wife while she was in the hospital?" I asked.

"She knows how I feel about hospitals. I hate the damn things. They make my skin crawl."

"Ask him the last time he touched me. Ask him the last time we made love." She continued without pause. "We haven't made love since before my operation. He hasn't come near me, not once."

"You were sick, for God's sake. First the surgery, then the radiation. You were exhausted. The last thing on your mind was sex."

"I'm not sick anymore. I'm not tired anymore. I'm just sick and tired of being ignored." She broke down into sobs. "It's like I don't even exist, like when they took off my breast, the rest of me disappeared as well."

For several seconds, the only movement in the room was the quiet shaking of her shoulders. I turned toward Arthur McKay. He sat absolutely rigid, the muscles in his face pulled tight against his scalp, like a death mask. "Were you scared when you found out your wife had cancer?" I asked.

He glared at me. "Why should I be scared?"

"Because cancer is a scary thing."

"I know all about cancer. My mother died of cancer when I was a little boy."

"Were you afraid your wife might die?" I asked.

His eyes flashed anger, his hands forming fists at his sides. He said nothing.

"Did you talk to your wife about how you were feeling?"

"She wasn't interested in how I was feeling."

"That's not true. I tried to talk to you many times."

"Look, what difference does any of this make?" he said. "It's all water under the bridge. There's nothing we can do to change it."

"What about now?"

"Now?"

"Are you scared now?"

Arthur McKay opened his mouth as if to speak, then closed it, said nothing.

"A mastectomy is a lot more complicated than most surgery. The loss of a breast has so many implications. For both partners. How did you feel about your wife's surgery? How *do* you feel?" I immediately corrected.

"I don't know," Arthur McKay said impatiently.

"I do," Lois McKay said, wiping at her tears with a fresh tissue. "He's repulsed by it. By me."

"Is that true?" I asked. "Are you repulsed by it?"

For one long, horrible second, Arthur McKay said nothing, then: "How am I supposed to feel?"

"How about grateful I'm alive?" Lois snapped.

"I *am* grateful you're alive."

"Grateful but repulsed."

Another interminable silence. Arthur McKay rose to his feet, began pacing back and forth in front of the window, like a caged tiger in a zoo. "This is just great. Now I'm an even bigger shit than I was before. It didn't seem possible, did it? You'd think you couldn't sink much lower than a guy who plays golf while his wife is on the operating table and then doesn't visit her in the hospital. But hey, we're just getting started. It seems this guy is actually repulsed by his wife's surgery. And he knows it's not going to change. He can't help the way he feels. And he's sick and tired of feeling guilty."

"Losing my breast didn't make me any less of a woman," Lois McKay said, tears streaming freely down her cheeks. "It just made you less of a man."

For several seconds, Arthur McKay stood absolutely still. Then he walked to the door, opened it, and stepped into the hall. The door closed behind him.

I jumped to my feet.

"Let him go," Lois said quietly, twisting the tissue in her lap.

"We can work through this," I told her, knowing only a few words were necessary to bring her husband back into the room.

She shook her head. "No. It's too late. Actually, it's a relief to finally get it all out in the open."

"He's terrified of losing you," I told her, knowing how strange those words probably sounded in light of the things her husband had said.

"Yes, interestingly enough, I think you might be right," she agreed, surprising me. "But I don't think it matters anymore."

"He may come around."

"I don't have that kind of time," Lois McKay said simply. "Besides, he's right—he can't help the way he feels."

"How do *you* feel?"

She took a deep breath, the words tumbling out of her mouth as she exhaled, like children tossed from a sled. I could almost see them hit the air. "Hurt. Angry. Afraid."

"Afraid of what?"

"The future." She shrugged. "Assuming I have one."

"You'll have one."

"A fifty-five-year-old woman with one breast?" She smiled, but it was a smile heavy with sadness, like a cloud threatening rain. Before she left, she scheduled a number of other appointments. Just for herself, she stressed. She'd be coming alone.

Moments after she'd left, I was out of my gray suit and into my sweats, marching determinedly on my treadmill. I wondered how I'd feel if faced with the loss of a breast. I wondered if Larry would react the same way as Arthur McKay.

I already knew the answer, at least as far as Larry was concerned. He wouldn't give a damn about the breast, any more than he would care whether I gained twenty pounds or lost all my hair. We'd met on a blind date in college. Some friends fixed us up. I was very reluctant—dating had never been my strong suit. At almost twenty-one, I was still a virgin, although less by choice, at this point, than by circumstance. I hadn't had a date in ages. My days were spent in classes, my nights at the library. I went home only as a last resort. I'd go to bed hearing my stepfather's rants; I'd wake up to my mother's sobs. I think that's why I finally agreed to go out with Larry: anything to get out of the house.

We went out for dinner, a small Italian restaurant close to the university campus. He told me later that he fell in love with me that very first night. "Why?" I asked, anticipating a wealth of compliments regarding my eyes, my lips, my towering intellect. "Because you ate everything on your plate," he answered.

How could I not love him?

There were no games, no pretenses. His kind eyes were an accurate reflection of his generous spirit. I felt safe around him. I knew he'd be good to me, that he'd never intentionally do anything to hurt me. After all the abuse I'd witnessed at home, that was the most important thing to me. Larry was decent and honorable, and as moral a man as I would ever meet. I knew that he would love me no matter what.

I was on my treadmill when the phone rang. Normally, I'd let my voice mail answer it, and I'm not sure why I chose to jump off the treadmill and answer it myself. Probably I thought it was Jo Lynn, who'd taken to calling every day with a breakdown of the day's events. The prosecutor had spent most of the last week trying to convince the jury of the exactitude of DNA evidence, calling witness after witness to break down and explain the complicated and often tedious procedures involved in its testing. The defense had spent an equal amount of time trying to discredit the claims. Jo Lynn was getting antsy. She still hadn't met with Colin Friendly, was becoming convinced that there was a conspiracy afoot to keep them apart.

"Family Therapy Center," I said into the phone.

"May I speak with Kate Sinclair, please?"

"Speaking."

"Kate Sinclair," the voice said, "Robert Crowe."

Immediately my heart started to race and my breathing became labored, as if I were back on the treadmill.

"Hello? Kate, are you there?"

"Yes," I said quickly, ashamed and angry at my body's automatic response to the sound of his voice. Hadn't I just been waxing rhapsodic about my husband's strong moral core? Where was my own? "How are you?"

"Great. I missed you in court this morning."

"You were there?"

"I was. You weren't."

"I can only go on Wednesdays."

"I'll keep that in mind. I saw your sister."

"She's hard to miss."

"That was an interesting mention she got in the paper the other day. 'Friendly's New Friend.' Catchy little phrase. What's the real story?"

"There isn't one." Was that why he was calling? To get the inside scoop?

"Well, you didn't miss anything today. The judge adjourned the trial until next week."

"He did? Why?"

"Apparently Colin has a touch of the flu. Poor baby wasn't feeling very well, so his lawyers asked for an adjournment. Who knows? Maybe he just needed a break."

"We could all use a break." I hoped Colin Friendly would develop pneumonia and die.

"That's exactly why I'm calling," Robert said, and I wondered for a moment whether I had missed part of the conversation. "I thought maybe I could take you out to lunch."

"Lunch?"

"How about next Wednesday? That's if you can tear yourself away from the court-house."

"You want to have lunch?" I repeated, biting down on my tongue to keep from saying it again.

"I have an interesting proposition for you."

"What kind of proposition?"

"Something I think you'll like."

"Are you going to tell me what it is?"

"I will on Wednesday. Where should we meet?"

We agreed on Charley's Crab over on South Ocean Boulevard. Twelve o'clock noon. I hung up the phone, wondering what the hell I was doing. "Oh God," I muttered, about to call Robert back, cancel our date, except it wasn't a date, I reminded myself, deciding I was being silly. It was just lunch. And an interesting proposition. What did that mean? "Guess

I'll find out on Wednesday," I said, letting go of the phone.

Immediately it rang.

"You can't make it," I said into the receiver, convinced Robert had had second thoughts.

"Can't make what?" Larry asked.

"Larry?"

"Kate, is that you?"

I laughed, a strange combination of guilt and relief. "This one patient of mine, she can't seem to make up her mind whether she wants to come in or not." I stressed the word "she." Twice.

"She'll be there. How can anyone resist you?"

I tried to laugh, ended up coughing instead.

"You okay?" I could hear the concern in his voice. "You getting a cold?"

"I'm fine," I said, feeling awful. "What can I do for you?"

"Just checking to see if we're free a week this Friday night."

"I think so. Why? What's up?"

"A satisfied customer has invited us to dinner."

"Sounds good."

"Great. I'll tell him to count us in. Love you, funny face," he said, instead of goodbye.

"Love you too."

I hung up the phone. "Okay, you're going to call Robert Crowe back right this minute and cancel lunch. Enough of this foolishness. If he has anything interesting to propose, he can do it over the phone."

The door to my waiting room opened, then

closed. I checked my watch, then my appointment calendar. Sally and Bill Peterson were early, and I was running late. Not a great combination. Hurriedly, I pulled off my sweatshirt, getting it tangled around my head. "Serves you right," I muttered, hearing the door to my inner office open, frantically tearing the sweatshirt away from my face. Who on earth would just walk into someone's office unannounced and uninvited?

"Mother!" I gasped.

She backed against the wall, her face as gray as her uncombed hair, her dark eyes wide with fear.

"Mother, what's happened? What's the matter?"

"Someone's following me."

"What?"

"Someone's following me," she repeated, glancing furtively around the room.

"Who's following you? What are you talking about?"

"A man. He's been following me for blocks. He followed me into the building."

In the next instant, I was in the outer hall, my head snapping quickly to my left, then right. There was no one there. I walked down the rose-carpeted corridor, past the elevator, approaching the stairway at the far end of the hall with caution, then flung open the door. Again, there was no one. I heard the sound of elevator doors opening, watched as an attractive young woman got out, hurrying past me with a wary eye. It was then that I realized I was wearing only sweatpants and a bra. "And I'm the therapist," I announced.

"There's no man out there," I told my mother, reentering my office and grabbing my sweatshirt, pulling it back over my head. I looked around. My mother was nowhere to be seen. "Mother?" I walked into the narrrow inner hallway. "Mother, where are you?" I pushed open the door to my second office, expecting to see her standing by the window, staring out at the magnificent palm trees along Royal Palm Way. But she wasn't there. "Mother, where did you go?" Had she been there at all? Or had my guilty conscience conjured her up to try to talk some sense into me?

And then I heard the whimpering. Halting, muffled, as if trying desperately not to be heard. It was a sound from my past I remembered only too well, despite the passage of the years. It froze me to the spot. "Mom?"

I found her sitting crouched behind the office door, her knees grazing her chin, her face wet with tears, her eyes narrow slits, her mouth a large open wound. I rushed to her side, slid down beside her, surrounded her with my arms. She was shaking so badly, I didn't know what to do. "It's okay, Mom. It's okay. There's no one out there. You're safe now. It's okay. You're safe."

"He was there. He was following me."

"Who, Mom? Do you know who he was?"

She shook her head vigorously.

"Someone from your apartment building?"

"No. It was someone I'd never seen before."

121

"You're sure he was following you? Maybe he was just walking in the same direction."

"No," she insisted. "He was following me. Every time I turned around, he stopped, pretended to be looking in a store window. When I slowed down, he slowed down. When I walked faster, so did he."

I wondered whether I should call the police. Why would someone be following my mother? "Had you just been to the bank?" I asked, thinking an old woman was probably an easy target for robbers. Except that her bank was located close to her apartment building, which was on the other side of the bridge and miles away. It would have taken her all day to walk here. "How did you get here?" I asked.

She looked at me with blank eyes.

"Mom," I repeated, growing fearful, although I wasn't sure why. "How did you get here?"

The eyes darkened, flitted anxiously about the room.

"Mom, don't you remember how you got here?"

"Of course I remember how I got here," she said, her voice suddenly calm as she climbed to her feet and straightened the folds of her flower-print skirt. "I took a cab to Worth Avenue, did some window-shopping, then decided to walk over here to say hello. Along the way, some man started following me." She took a deep breath, patted her hair into recognizable shape. "Probably just wanted to snatch my purse. Silly me—I guess I over-reacted. You'll have to forgive an old woman."

The door to my outer office opened, then closed. I looked warily in its direction, then back at my mother.

"It's just your next client," she assured me, running a calming hand across my cheek. "I'll go, let you get back to work."

I excused myself to Sally and Bill Peterson, and accompanied my mother downstairs, waiting until she was safely inside a taxi. "Mom," I ventured gently before closing the car door, "maybe you should see a doctor."

"Nonsense, dear. I'm perfectly fine." She smiled. "You're looking a little peaked, however. I think you work too hard." She kissed me on the cheek. "I'll talk to you later," she said, and seconds later, she was gone.

Chapter
9

Define sociopath."

The man on the witness stand—looking both distinguished and patriotic in a dark blue suit, white shirt, and red-striped tie—took a moment to consider his answer, although as an expert witness for the prosecution, he undoubtedly had his answer well prepared. "A sociopath is a person who is hostile to society," he began. "He feels little in the way of normal human emotions, except anger. This anger, combined with an almost total self-absorption and a complete lack of empathy for others, allows him to commit the most heinous crimes without any guilt or remorse."

"And a sexual sadist?"

Again a measured pause. "A sexual sadist derives sexual pleasure from inflicting pain."

"Do the two terms go hand in hand?" The prosecutor patted his brown paisley tie, looked toward the jury.

I followed his gaze, noted that the jury was paying strict attention. All it took was the mention of the word "sex," I thought, glancing over at Jo Lynn. She was wearing tight white jeans and a white tank top, the center of which was emblazoned with a bright pink heart.

"A sociopath is not necessarily a sexual sadist, but a sexual sadist is almost always a sociopath," came the reply from the witness stand.

"In your expert opinion, Dr. Pinsent, is Colin Friendly a sexual sadist?"

"He is."

"Is he a sociopath?"

"Most definitely."

Again, I looked at Jo Lynn, whose face was calm, even serene. Was she listening to this? Was she *hearing* it?

The prosecutor approached the defense table, stopping in front of the accused, staring at Colin Friendly as if he were seeing him for the first time. Colin Friendly smiled back pleasantly. He'd obviously recovered quite nicely from his bout with the flu. His eyes were clear; his color was good. Everything was back to normal. "But he doesn't look abnormal," Mr. Eaves observed, as if reading my mind. "In fact, Mr. Friendly seems as genial as his name would imply— handsome, polite, intelligent."

"Sociopaths are often quite intelligent," the witness explained. "And there's nothing that says they can't be good-looking. As for being polite, he's just giving you what he thinks you need to see."

The defense attorney was instantly on his feet. "Move to strike, your honor. The witness can't speak for Mr. Friendly."

"Sustained."

"Speaking in more general terms, Dr. Pinsent," the prosecutor continued, undeterred, "what do you mean when you say that sociopaths give people what they need to see?"

"Sociopaths are extremely manipulative. Their emotions run very shallow and they're intensely self-centered. But they can mimic the emotions they observe in others, and feed back the appropriate response, the appropriate response being whatever would be considered normal under the circumstances. They play on people's assumptions of basic human decency. People attribute feelings to them that simply aren't there." He paused, looked directly at Colin Friendly. "Sociopaths are often highly articulate, very charming, and glib. They'll make you laugh, then stab you through the heart."

"Can you believe *anything* they say?"

"Oh yes. They're often quite truthful. As long

as you keep in mind that their version of the truth is very self-serving."

"What produces a sociopath, Dr. Pinsent?"

Dr. Walter Pinsent rubbed his fingers across his chin and smiled. "I'm afraid that's a little like asking, 'Which came first, the chicken or the egg?' The eternal debate—are killers born or are they made?" He shook his head. "It's impossible to say conclusively one way or the other. There are many theories, of course, but they have a habit of changing with the times and the political climate. Sometimes we give more weight to the genetic theory, sometimes to the environment. We postulate about extra Y chromosomes and chemical imbalances. But lots of people have chemical imbalances; that doesn't make them murderers. And lots of people have an extra Y chromosome and they don't go around slicing up their fellow human beings."

"Does Colin Friendly have a chemical imbalance or an extra Y chromosome?"

"No, he does not."

"And what of the theory that environment is everything?"

Walter Pinsent cleared his throat, straightened his shoulders, tugged on his tie. "There's no question that our childhood is crucial in terms of our development. The seeds for everything we grow into as adults were planted when we were children. Almost all serial killers had truly appalling childhoods. They were neglected, molested, beaten, abused, abandoned, you name it."

126

"Is this true of Colin Friendly?"

"It is."

Jo Lynn leaned toward me. "Poor baby," she whispered, as I struggled to find a hint of irony in her words. There was none.

"Are there any characteristics that are common to all sociopaths?" the prosecutor asked.

"Research has shown that there is something we now refer to as the "homicidal triad,' three elements that are present in virtually all children who grow up to become serial killers: cruelty to small animals; bed-wetting beyond the normally appropriate age; and fire-starting."

"And were these elements present in Colin Friendly's childhood?"

"They were."

"And is there any doubt in your mind, after meeting with the accused and studying his background and the many psychiatric reports made available to you, that Colin Friendly is a sexual sadist and sociopath, guilty of the crimes for which he stands accused?"

"No doubt at all," Dr. Pinsent replied.

"Thank you, Dr. Pinsent. Your witness, Mr. Archibald."

Mr. Eaves sat down, unbuttoned his jacket; Mr. Archibald rose to his feet, buttoned his.

"Dr. Pinsent, are you a psychiatrist?"

"No."

"A medical doctor?"

"No."

"A doctor of psychology perhaps?"

"No. My doctorate is in the field of education."

"I see." Jake Archibald shook his head, appeared confused, as if he couldn't quite comprehend what Dr. Pinsent was doing as an expert witness. This was purely for effect. The jury had already been told that Walter Pinsent was a special agent with the National Academy of the Federal Bureau of Investigation in Quantico, Virginia, and part of the Investigative Support Unit that specialized in profiling serial killers.

"How many times did you meet with the accused?"

"Twice."

"Twice." Jake Archibald shook his head, somehow managing to look subtly amazed. A neat trick, I thought. "And how long were these meetings?"

"Several hours each session."

"Several hours each session," the defense attorney repeated, this time nodding his head up and down. "And this was enough time for you to come to the conclusion that Colin Friendly is a dangerous psychotic?"

"Sociopath," Dr. Pinsent corrected.

Jake Archibald chuckled derisively. So did Jo Lynn.

"You concluded after approximately four hours with my client that he was a dangerous sociopath and a sexual sadist?"

"I did."

"Tell me, Dr. Pinsent, would you have reached these same conclusions had you

128

encountered Mr. Friendly in another context?"

"I'm not sure I understand the question."

"Let's say you encountered Mr. Friendly at a party, or ran into him on a holiday and spent a few hours talking to him. Would you have come away with the impression that he was a dangerous sociopath and sexual sadist?"

For the first time since he took the stand, Dr. Walter Pinsent looked less than sure of himself. "Probably not. As I've already stated, sociopaths are often very charming individuals."

"You consider Colin Friendly charming?"

"He seems very affable, yes."

"Is that a crime?"

The prosecutor raised his hand. "Objection."

"Sustained."

"Is it possible, Dr. Pinsent," the defense attorney pressed, "that you were influenced in your appraisal of Mr. Friendly by the fact that he was already under arrest, that your meetings with him took place in prison?"

"I was influenced by the things he told me."

"I see. Did Colin Friendly tell you he was guilty?"

"No."

"Did he, in fact, repeatedly protest his innocence?"

"He did. But that's typical of this type of personality."

"Interesting. So, what you're saying is that if he confesses his guilt, that means he's guilty, and if he says he's innocent, well then, that means he's guilty too. Damned if you don't, damned if you do. Reminds me a bit of the witch hunts in Salem."

The prosecutor jumped to his feet. "Your honor, move to strike. Is Mr. Archibald asking a question or making a speech?"

"Sustained."

"I'll rephrase that," Jake Archibald said, a noticeable bounce to his words. "Do you see serial killers under every bed, Dr. Pinsent?"

Mr. Eaves's ample backside barely had time to graze his seat before he was back on his feet again. "Objection."

"I withdraw the question," Jake Archibald said quickly. "I have no further questions of this witness."

"The witness may step down."

The judge called a ten-minute recess.

"Tell me you weren't fooled by that," I said hopefully to Jo Lynn, as people all around us stood up and stretched.

"Fooled by what?" She was squinting into her compact mirror, applying a fresh coat of lipstick to already very pink lips.

"By the defense attorney's attempt to throw a smoke screen over the evidence."

"What's that supposed to mean?" She raised the mirror, dabbed at her mascara.

"It means that Dr. Pinsent is about as expert a witness as anyone could find," I began.

She interrupted. "He's not a psychiatrist. Or even a medical doctor."

"He's a specialist with the Federal Bureau of Investigation."

"Since when did you become such a fan of the FBI?"

"I'm just saying that he knows what he's talking about."

"His is only one opinion."

"An expert opinion," I reminded her.

"You put too much faith in experts," she said. "Just because someone has a degree doesn't mean they know everything."

I took this as a direct dig at me. Jo Lynn was always trumpeting the value of practical experience over a university education.

Don't bite, I told myself, determined to be pleasant. "So, anything new?" I asked, looking for safer ground.

"Like what?"

I shrugged. "Have you had any calls about those résumés you sent out?"

She clicked her compact closed. "You know I haven't."

Strike one, I thought.

"Have you spoken to our mother?"

She dropped the compact into her purse. "Why would I do that?"

Strike two.

"Do you have a date for the weekend?"

She snapped her purse shut tight. "I have a date for Friday." She spun toward me, her mouth forming a provocative pout.

"That's great. Someone new?"

"Sort of."

"Anyone I know?"

"Someone you *think* you know."

"What does that mean?"

"It means that you think you know him, but you don't. It means you've got him all wrong. It means you don't know him at all. It means that you've been staring at the side of his face all morning."

Strike three.

The room darkened around me. Normal courtroom sounds gave way to a loud buzzing in my ears. I felt dizzy, faint. I gripped the bench on which I was sitting, digging my fingers into the hard wood. "Please tell me this is a joke."

Jo Lynn adjusted her tank top, repositioning the large pink heart so that it sat directly in the center of her large chest. "Why would I joke about something this important?"

Stay calm, I told myself. "When exactly did this come about?"

"Colin's lawyer called me last night. I would have phoned you, but it was late and I know you guys are sound asleep by ten o'clock."

"I don't understand," I stammered, "where is this "date' taking place?"

"I'm not sure. Some holding room or something. They're gonna let me know."

"Jo Lynn, please," I said, unable to stop myself. "Don't you think this has gone far enough? It's not too late to call the whole thing off. You don't have to go through with it."

"What are you talking about?" Her voice was indignant. "Why wouldn't I go through with it?"

"Because the man we're talking about is a cold-blooded killer."

"I don't agree."

"The evidence is overwhelming."

"I don't agree."

"You don't agree," I repeated.

"No, and I don't think the jury will either. Anyway," she said, waving at one of the reporters in the back row, "I don't want to talk about it anymore. Why do you always put a damper on everything?"

"I'm just trying to inject a little common sense into this mess."

Jo Lynn looked toward the front of the courtroom. "You always had more common sense than imagination," she said.

He was already seated when I arrived at Charley's Crab at twenty minutes after twelve. "Sorry I'm late," I said, collapsing into the chair the waiter held out for me, looking slowly around the large series of adjoining rooms, studying the framed photographs of prize fish that ran along one wall, admiring the large stuffed marlin that was mounted on another, gazing at the crowded bar, tracking the busy waiters as they maneuvered between booths and tables, zeroing in on the well-heeled patrons, with their large blond bouffants and fixed tight smiles. Anywhere but at the man sitting across from me.

"Considering that court doesn't get out till noon," he was saying, "you made very good time."

133

"I left early." I signaled for the waiter. An hour and a half early, I almost said, but didn't. I'd fled the courtroom after Jo Lynn's unpleasant revelation, and had been driving around ever since, trying to figure out what my sister was trying to prove by throwing herself at a sexually sadistic sociopath who would most likely die in the electric chair. If she was trying to upset our mother, it wasn't working. Our mother had ignored all Jo Lynn's provocative pronouncements, carrying on as if there was nothing unusual or untoward about her younger daughter's recent behavior. On the other hand, if it was me Jo Lynn was trying to upset, I had to admit she was doing a damned good job.

The waiter appeared.

"Could I have a glass of white wine?" I asked.

The waiter looked confused. "You don't like the wine the gentleman ordered?"

For the first time, I looked at the man sitting across the table from me. Robert Crowe, looking suave, sophisticated, and generally drop-dead gorgeous, held up a bottle of California Chardonnay that had been cooling beside him.

"Thank you," I told the waiter, feeling like a total idiot. "This will be fine."

Robert said nothing, simply poured the wine into my glass, then clicked his glass against mine in a toast. "To the past," he said.

"The past," I agreed. It sounded safe enough.

"And the future."

I downed half the glass.

"Someone's either very thirsty or very uptight," he said.

"It wasn't an easy morning."

"You want to talk about it?"

"I want to talk about anything but."

"Talk about why you won't look at me."

I laughed, one of those awful, self-conscious barks that die upon contact with the air. "I'm looking at you."

"You're looking at my left ear," he said.

"And a very nice ear it is." I laughed, looked directly into his rich hazel eyes. Oh God, I thought, struggling to maintain eye contact, not to be the first to blink or turn away. Was there no end to my sophomoric musings?

I shouldn't have come. I should have followed my instincts and headed for home after leaving the courthouse. Instead I'd driven around aimlessly for half an hour, then turned the car loose on I-95. I was almost at Pompano when I realized it was closing in on twelve o'clock, and I turned the car around, telling myself I was going home, but knowing the car was pointed toward the ocean and Charley's Crab.

Charley's Crab and Robert Crowe, I thought, and must have smiled because he picked right up on it.

"That's better," Robert said. "You have a beautiful smile."

"It's lopsided," I corrected.

"That's what makes it beautiful."

I blinked, looked away.

We ordered—grilled salmon for him, blackened swordfish for me. "And gazpacho," I said. Lots of garlic, I thought.

"So, tell me about the therapy business," he said.

I shrugged. "What can I say? Lots of people, lots of problems."

"What sort of problems?"

"Problems with parents, problems with children, marital problems, extramarital..." I broke off, took another long sip of my drink.

"And you solve these problems?"

"I do the best I can."

"How long have you been practicing?"

"Over twenty years," I said, feeling more secure now that we were on firm professional ground. "I started out as a social worker with the Pittsburgh Board of Education, then I left and opened up a family therapy clinic with a few other women. Eventually, we moved to Florida, and I set up shop on my own."

"Can't hold a job, huh?"

I thought of my sister, who'd flitted from one dead-end job to another all her life, from one dead-end relationship to another.

"Uh-oh," Robert said. "Storm clouds on the horizon. What are you thinking about?"

I really didn't want to talk about Jo Lynn. She'd taken up enough of my day as it was. "Just about how quickly time passes," I lied. It was easier. "What about you? How did you wind up owning a radio station?"

"I married it," he said simply.

I didn't know what to say, so I said nothing.

"Brandi's father owns a number of radio stations across the country." He smiled. "Beware of women whose first names are potable."

"I'll keep that in mind."

"Actually, her real name is Brenda. She was named after Brenda Marshall, who was an actress in the forties. Apparently, my father-in-law was a huge fan."

"She was married to William Holden," I said.

Robert Crowe regarded me with bemused admiration. "How did you know that?"

I shook my head. "The mind is a strange and wondrous thing. I can barely remember my telephone number, but I know Brenda Marshall was once married to William Holden."

"You're an interesting woman, Kate Latimer," he said.

I was about to correct him, decided not to bother. He knew what my name was. So did I. "So what does your wife do?"

"She shops, she lunches, she goes to exercise class."

"And looks after the kids," I added. "Four, I believe you said."

"Ages twelve through nineteen. Two boys, two girls."

"I'm sure she has her hands full."

"The oldest is away at college. The others are in school all day. We have two housekeepers. Trust me, Brandi's not overtaxed."

"Problems?" I asked, despite my best efforts not to.

"The usual, I guess."

"Is that why you asked me to lunch?"

He smiled, traced the rim of his glass with his fingers. "No. If it was therapy I wanted, I'd come to your office. I have something else in mind for you."

"Sounds interesting."

"I'm hoping you'll think so."

The waiter brought our lunch, refilled our glasses. For several minutes, we did nothing but eat and drink. "So," I began, fortified by my second glass of wine, "just what is it you have in mind for me?"

"Your own radio show," he said.

I dropped my fork. It bounced off my lap and onto the floor. A passing waiter immediately replaced it. "I don't understand."

"I haven't thought this through yet," Robert continued. "In fact, it wasn't until I saw you in court and you told me what you were doing that I thought about it at all."

"Thought about what exactly?"

"About you doing some sort of therapy show on the radio."

"You mean like on *Frasier*? A nightly phone-in show?"

"I'm not sure. Like I said, I haven't thought it through yet. That's one of the reasons I suggested lunch. I wanted your input."

"But I have no experience with radio."

"You know how to talk. You know how to give advice. And you have a great speaking voice."

"I don't have that kind of time. I have a job; I have a family."

"It doesn't have to be every night. It could be once or twice a week. And it doesn't have to be at night. It could be during the day. Wednesday." He smiled. "Your day off."

"But what would I do?"

"Be yourself. Answer questions. Help people with their problems."

"Why me?"

"Why not you? You're smart. You're beautiful. You're local. Look, I realize this is coming at you out of left field. Why don't you toss some ideas around in your head for a while. See what you come up with. Decide what kind of show might intrigue you, the kind of format you'd feel comfortable with. In the meantime, I'll mention the idea to a few of our producers, see if they can come up with anything. Think about it. That's all I'm asking."

"I'll think about it," I heard myself say.

"Good." He lifted his glass in another toast. "To interesting propositions," he said.

Chapter 10

Friday started out normally enough. Sara was still in bed when Larry, Michelle, and I left the house. I'd given up trying to wake her. Being on time for school was Sara's responsibility, not mine.

I knew to expect a phone call from the school informing me of Sara's lateness, so I wasn't surprised when I checked my messages during a five-minute break between sessions, and learned that the school had, indeed, called. I saw no point in calling back right away, reasoning that they weren't about to tell me something I didn't already know. Instead, I called home, trying to convince myself that the fact that no one answered the line was a sign that Sara was by now safely ensconced in her classroom. Or at least on her way. Or still sound asleep, a pesky voice whispered. I shushed it, as one shushes a small child, then ushered in my next clients. Outwardly, I was calm. Inside, I was screaming.

I wasn't the only one. Everyone who came into my office that day was hollering about something. No one spoke softly. No one struggled to maintain composure. Everybody yelled—at one another, at themselves, at me. Perhaps it was a case of simple transference, my mood into their mouths; more likely it was the literally breathtaking humidity that had descended upon the Palm Beach area over the last twenty-four hours like a giant tarpaulin, threatening instantaneous combustion to anyone who ventured outside. Or maybe it was just one of those days.

By six o'clock that evening, I was exhausted. All I wanted to do was go home and crawl into bed, but I knew this was impossible. Larry had already committed us to a dinner party with "satisfied customers." I smiled. It was nice to know that someone, somewhere, was satisfied about something.

Before leaving my office, I again checked my voice mail for messages, and was dismayed to find that there were two more calls from Sara's school, one just after lunch, informing me that Sara had yet to show up at school, and another at the end of the school day to inform me that Sara had skipped a whole day of classes and was risking suspension. I checked my watch, knew it was too late to return the school's calls. Besides, what could I say? Maybe being suspended was just what Sara needed, some real consequences for her actions, but I wasn't convinced. Sara would shrug off the suspension as she did everything else. It was my life that would be placed on hold, not hers.

As I drove north along I-95, weaving restlessly through the Friday night traffic, worse now that the snowbirds had started their annual winter migration, I promised myself that I was going to remain calm when I confronted Sara. I would simply inform her that the school had called repeatedly about her truancy and that an explanation from her was neither wanted nor required. The school would deal with her on Monday. In the meantime, she was grounded. I knew that Sara would scream, swear, slam doors, the usual, trying to suck me into a fight. Whatever happened, I decided, exiting the highway at PGA Boulevard and heading west, I wasn't going to raise my voice. I was going to remain calm.

"What do you mean, she's not here?" I demanded loudly of my younger child not two seconds after I walked through the front door.

"Why are you yelling at me?" Michelle asked. She was standing in the middle of the living room, to the right of the large glass-topped coffee table and between the two oversized tan-colored sofas, a cherry Popsicle at her mouth, coloring her lips blood red.

She looked like a beautiful porcelain doll, I thought, but didn't say. Instead I said, "Could you get off the carpet with that?" and proceeded into my bedroom. She followed me.

"Tough day?"

I smiled. Sara would have yelled at me; Michelle was worried about my day. "The worst." I looked toward the closed doors of the master bathroom, suddenly cognizant of the shower running. "When did Daddy get home?"

"A few minutes ago. He broke a hundred."

"A hundred what?"

"In golf. He broke a hundred. That's supposed to be good," she assured me, glancing at the carpeting beneath her feet and quickly stuffing the balance of the cherry Popsicle into her mouth. A thin line of red liquid dribbled down her chin, disappearing into her neck, as if she'd cut herself shaving.

I said, "It's nice someone had a good day."

"He said it was really hot, but that he thought it helped his concentration."

I undid the top buttons of my white blouse, flipped off my shoes, lay back against the army of decorative pillows. "Did he say anything about Sara?"

"Like what?"

Like where she's been all day, I wanted to shout, but didn't. Calm, I repeated silently. Calm was the answer. "Has she phoned?" I asked instead.

"What's the big deal about Sara?" A slight pout found its way to Michelle's mouth, further exaggerating the ruby outline of her lips. "Why are you always asking about Sara? Aren't you interested in *my* day?"

"Your day?"

"Yes, my day. I'm a person too, just like Sara, and I have days, just like everyone else."

I edged my back away from the pillows, my body on instant alert. I had been prepared for a scene with Sara, not Michelle. "Of course you do."

"Nobody ever asks about my day," she continued, as if she were a windup toy that someone had wound too tight and was now spinning out of control, unable to stop. "I asked Daddy how his day went, I asked you if you had a tough day, I always ask everybody, but does anybody ever ask about me?"

"Michelle..."

"No. You tell me to get off the carpet with my Popsicle..."

"Michelle..."

"You ask about Sara..."

"Honey, please..."

"Does anybody care that I got eighty-five percent in my math test? That I stood first in the class? No! Nobody cares!" She fled the room.

I was instantly on my feet. "Michelle, wait. Of course we care." Tripping over my shoes, a heel digging painfully into the sole of my right foot, I limped after her, watching the door to her bedroom slam shut. "Honey, please, let me in." I tapped lightly on her door, then more insistently. "Michelle, please let me in."

Slowly, the door to her room fell open. Michelle stood tearfully on the other side. I swayed toward her, my arms aching to encircle her skinny frame.

"Don't," she said softly, and I teetered momentarily on my toes before falling back on my heels, regaining my balance.

"You got eighty-five on your math test?" I repeated, my eyes welling with tears. "That's wonderful."

She didn't look at me. "It was the highest mark in the class."

"You should be very proud."

She backed into her room, plopped down in the middle of her queen-size bed, stared straight ahead. Unlike Sara's room, which was decorated in various shades of chaos, Michelle's predominantly pink-and-ivory room was as neat as the proverbial pin. Her bed was expertly made, pale pink-and-white-flowered pillows resting comfortably atop a matching quilted spread; the top of her wicker dresser was clear, save for a pearl-encrusted jewelry box in the shape of a treasure chest; her clothes were hung in the closet and not strewn thoughtlessly on the floor. I winced. Even in the privacy of

Michelle's own bedroom, Sara had a way of taking over, pushing her younger sister aside.

Gingerly, I approached the bed, sitting down only after I'd received the silent signal, a subtle nodding of Michelle's head that told me it was all right. "I'm sorry."

The nodding became more pronounced as one bright red lip disappeared inside the other, quivering. She turned away.

"Sometimes adults get so caught up in their own little worlds that they forget about the worlds of those around them," I began. "Especially when those around them are as capable and well adjusted as you are." I reached up, gently stroked the wavy brown hair that fell around her shoulders. She didn't pull away, for which I was very grateful. "We tend to concentrate all our energy on those who give us the hardest time, and that's not fair, because you deserve more. Lots more. And I'm sorry, honey. I'm really sorry. You're my sweet angel, and I love you so much. Please," I whispered, "can't I hug you?"

Silently, she fell against me. My nose immediately buried itself inside the folds of her soft brown hair, her smell as sweet to me as a newborn baby's. The heat from her slender body burned into my side, as fierce as a branding iron, welding us together. "I love you," I repeated, kissing the top of her head, once, twice, as many times as she would allow.

Michelle swiped a few errant tears away from her face, but she made no attempt to disengage. "I love you too."

We sat this way for some time, enjoying the intimacy, neither wishing to be the first to break away. For the first time all day, I was truly calm.

The peace was shattered with the sound of Larry's voice. "Kate?" he was calling. "Kate, where are you?"

"It's okay," Michelle said, squirming out of my arms, taking all tranquillity with her. Immediately, I felt my anger returning. What was Larry yelling about? Why did we have to go out tonight when all I wanted to do was stay home? Where was Sara? What was she trying to pull this time?

"What's the problem?" I asked, greeting Larry at the doorway to Michelle's room. He was wearing a large beige towel around his waist and rubbing his wet hair with another.

"No problem." His deep voice filled the space between us, spilled over into Michelle's room. "Did Michelle tell you I broke a hundred?"

"She did."

"It was hot as hell out there, I tell you," he continued enthusiastically, following me back to our bedroom, an overgrown puppy at my heels. "But I don't know, all that humidity seemed to work for me. It made me really focus or something, I'm not sure. Whatever it was, it worked. I hit a ninety-eight. I would have gotten even lower if I hadn't blown up on the last two holes." He laughed. "I guess that's golf. It's a game of could-have's. How was your day?"

"Terrible. Do we have to go out tonight?"

He looked at his watch, still wet from the shower. "Sure do. In fact, we should be leaving in about ten minutes."

"Ten minutes? I have to take a shower, get dinner ready for Michelle."

"You don't have time for a shower, and Michelle can order a pizza."

"I'm not going anywhere without a shower," I said stubbornly, "and what about Sara?"

"You can take a long, leisurely bath when we get home from dinner, and what *about* Sara?"

"Do you know where she is?"

"Should I?"

"Somebody should," I said testily, knowing I was being unfair. "Apparently she didn't show up for school today."

Resignation replaced the elation on Larry's face. "Did you check the answering service to see if she called?" he asked.

I walked around the bed to the white phone that sat on the large, curved end table, quickly pressing the appropriate numbers to retrieve my messages. There was only one message. It was from Jo Lynn. "Call me," was all it said.

Calling my sister was the last thing I wanted to do. Today was the day, after all, when Beauty was scheduled to meet the Beast, and I had no desire to hear the blow-by-blow. Already I knew more details than I cared to, that the meeting was to take place directly after court recessed for the weekend, that the place of assignation was to be the Palm Beach

County Correctional Center on Gun Club Road, and that Romeo and Juliet would be separated by a wall of glass, speaking to each other through specially constructed phones. Just like in the movies, I thought, shaking my head at the irony of situating a penitentiary on a street named Gun Club Road. I closed my eyes, trying not to picture my sister and Colin Friendly, their hands pressed together against the glass of the partition that divided them.

"Well?" Larry was asking.

"No messages," I said. It was easier that way.

"Better start getting ready," he advised, already in his underwear and black knee-high socks.

"How can we go out without knowing where she is?"

"Easy." He slid his arms into a blue-and-white-striped shirt. "We just go. I am not about to let an inconsiderate child control my life. We'll deal with Sara when we get back."

He was right and I knew it, but I was in no mood for rational thought. "But we don't even know where she is."

"Even if we did," Larry said, "we don't have time to deal with her now. So, let's just get ready. This dinner is in Jupiter, and you know what the traffic's going to be like."

"Jupiter?!"

"Jupiter," he repeated, his lips curling into a smile. "Not Mars. It'll only take twenty minutes."

"Then I have time for a shower," I insisted, already on my way to the bathroom, pulling off my clothes as I walked, leaving them in a careless heap where they fell. Just like Sara, I thought, quickly locking the door behind me, and turning on the shower, welcoming the onslaught of hot water as it rained down, like tiny hailstones, on my head. "Excuse me, can I use your phone?" The words were out of my mouth as soon as we walked through the door of our host's brand-new home in the gated golfing community of Windfall Village in Jupiter.

"Of course." The startled hostess, a plump brunette in toreador pants, pointed the way through her cavernous living room toward the kitchen. Deliberately ignoring Larry and the look I knew was taking root on his already unhappy face, I walked briskly across the marble-tiled floor, briefly nodding at the half dozen guests assembled around the grand piano and hurrying around the sweeping spiral staircase—one of two on either side of the house—to the marble-and-steel kitchen at the back. Two uniformed maids were preparing canapés and looked startled to see me. No more startled than Michelle was at the sound of my voice.

"Sara's not here," she told me, petulantly. I'd dragged her away from the umpteenth rerun of *Roseanne*. "Don't worry about her, Mom," she advised before hanging up. "You know she's fine. Don't let her ruin your evening."

It was already ruined, I almost confided, returning the phone to the waiting palm of one of the maids, who replaced it in its carriage, as if I couldn't be trusted to do it myself. And maybe I couldn't, I thought, catching sight of myself in the steel trim of the double oven, looking like a slightly deranged matron, my face distorted with aggravation, my hair still slightly damp from the shower, and not properly combed out. Who is that? I wondered.

Larry had stood over me like an impatient father while I applied my makeup, pointedly checking his watch as I fussed with the side zipper of my black cocktail dress. "It'll dry in the car," he'd protested when I reached for the hair dryer, taking it out of my hand and returning it to the drawer, ignoring my shrieks of protest. "You look fine," he insisted then, and again, repeatedly, in the car on the drive over, "fine" not being a word given to inspiring great confidence.

Not like "beautiful," I thought, thinking of Robert, knowing that he'd think nothing of being a little late for a dinner party, deciding that he would have given me all the time I needed to get ready, probably even jumped in the shower with me, delaying us further. Or maybe we wouldn't have gone at all, I fantasized, reluctantly returning to Larry's side, allowing myself to be introduced to the general gathering, to be taken on the obligatory tour of the house that Larry built. "Beautiful," I said, then again: "Beautiful. Just beautiful."

We'd fought all the way to the party and we fought all the way home. "I can't believe how rude you were," he said as we raced along

Donald Ross Road.

"I wasn't rude," I insisted.

"You don't call excusing yourself to use the phone every ten minutes rude?"

"I used the phone exactly three times."

"Four."

"All right, four. I used the phone four times. Guilty as charged." I thought immediately of Colin Friendly and Jo Lynn. According to Michelle, my sister had called a second time. I knew I'd have to call her in the morning, get the gory details of her jailhouse tryst whether I wanted to hear them or not.

"And what did it accomplish?" Larry persisted. "Nothing. Sara still isn't home, and you know what? She isn't going to be home when we get back, which is probably a good thing, since if she's there, I'm likely to kill her."

"I don't know how you can be so indifferent," I said, deliberately misinterpreting what Larry was saying. But I was angry, and it was easier to pick a fight with Larry—one I felt I stood a chance of winning—than to wait and have it out with Sara, where there was no chance at all.

He wouldn't rise to the bait. No matter how low I descended, and I descended pretty low, at one point accusing him of being more concerned about his clients than his daughter, he wouldn't bite. He wouldn't engage. The more he withdrew, the more I pushed. The tighter his hands gripped the steering wheel, the looser my tongue became. I yelled, I cried, I carried on. He said nothing.

151

What I wanted him to do, of course, was to stop the car and take me in his arms. Just pull over to the side of the road and hold me, tell me that I was a wonderful mother, that I hadn't failed Sara, that everything was going to be all right, that I was beautiful. But of course he didn't do this. It's hard to tell someone she's beautiful when she's insulting your manhood, your profession, your fitness as a father.

When we got home, Larry went straight to our bedroom, not even bothering to check on Sara. He knew she wasn't home, as did I, though I insisted on checking anyway.

"She didn't phone," Michelle said from her bed. It was almost midnight and sleep was curled around her voice, like a kitten in a basket.

I approached Michelle's bedside, leaned over, and kissed her forehead, smoothing some hair away from her delicate face. She sighed and turned over. "Sleep well," I whispered, closing her door behind me as I left the room. If there were fireworks later, I didn't want Michelle to be disturbed.

Larry was already in bed, feigning sleep. My anger was spent; depression was settling in. "I'm sorry," I said, and I was, and he knew it, although that wasn't much consolation. What difference does it make that you don't mean the hurtful things you say? The fact remains that someone else hears them. And words hurt more than sticks and stones after all. They echo in the stillness of the mind long after other bruises have healed.

I lay down beside Larry on top of the covers, fully clothed for when I heard Sara come home. I wanted our confrontation to be on an even footing. Since Sara already had youth on her side, I didn't want to compound my disadvantage by being dressed in a nightgown.

Sara's curfew was two o'clock, although I'm not sure why I expected her to be on time. Does someone who skips a whole day of classes worry about being late for their curfew? Did Sara ever stop to weigh the consequences of any of her actions?

At this point, I wasn't really worried. I was angry, depressed, and disappointed, at her, by her, and in her, but not really worried. It wasn't the first time, after all, that she'd pulled this sort of stunt.

When the hour of her curfew came and went, I got out of bed and went back to her room, staring through the darkness toward her unmade queen-size bed. "Where are you?" I whispered, still fighting off worry, trying desperately not to think of all the awful things that could have happened to her. I tried not seeing her lying bleeding in a ditch, the victim of a drunk driver who'd hit, then run; I tried not imagining her lying broken in an alley, the victim of a mugger's angry fists; I tried not hearing her screams as she was attacked by some sadistic rapist. I tried not seeing a photograph of her beautiful face, ashen and still, as she lay on a cold steel slab in the back room of the medical examiner's office. I tried, and I failed.

I stretched out across her sheets, the odor

of stale cigarettes settling quickly on my skin. What was the matter with her? Didn't Sara know how many lunatics were out there just waiting for innocent young girls who thought they were invincible? Men like Colin Friendly, I thought with a shudder, obliterating his image by burying my face in the soft darkness of her pillow.

Surprisingly, I fell asleep. I dreamed of a girl I'd known in high school. She'd come down to Florida a year ago on holiday and I'd run into her at the Gardens mall. It was the first time I'd seen her since our graduation, but she still looked startlingly young. Full of energy and enthusiasm and proud stories about her family. Six weeks later, I heard she'd been killed in a traffic accident shortly after returning to Pittsburgh. Apparently she'd lost control of her car on an icy stretch of highway and hit a guardrail. The car had flipped over, killing her instantly. In my dream, she was waving at me across the frozen foods section at Publix. I'd lost my grocery list and she was laughing, telling me to stay calm, it would all work out.

When I woke up, Larry was sitting at the side of the bed, staring down at me. "I think we should call the police," he said.

Chapter
11

We decided to try Sara's friends first.

This wasn't as easy as it should have been. The people in Sara's life kept changing. Every year brought with it a fresh set of names. Old faces disappeared; new faces popped into view. No one seemed to stay around very long.

This was a pattern that had been established early in Sara's life. I remember her nursery school teacher taking me aside one afternoon during a get-acquainted tea and confiding that she'd never seen a child attack a classroom quite the way Sara did. Apparently, every afternoon Sara would climb off the little yellow bus that transported her from home to school and announce, "Today I'm going to play with so-and-so." Every day she chose a new playmate, and every day she was successful in winning that child over. The next day, she moved on to someone new. Sara never formed a lasting bond with anyone in particular, although these temporary attachments were intense and heartfelt. But when each new day came, she moved forward, without ever looking back.

The move from Pittsburgh to Palm Beach hadn't affected her in any noticeable way. Sara, unlike Michelle, left no real friends behind. Several classmates wrote letters; Sara never answered them. She threw herself into her new life with typical enthusiasm and abandon, quickly making a new set of acquaintances, and sliding from one year into the next without the unnecessary encumbrances that lasting friendship often brings.

And so it was difficult to even think of whom Sara might be with. "Jennifer," I offered, mentioning a name I'd heard Sara mutter from time to time.

"Jennifer who?" Larry asked, a not unreasonable question.

I shook my head. I had no idea. Just as I had no idea what names went with Carrie, Brooke, or Matt. "I know Carrie's last name," I insisted, conjuring up the image of a young girl with waist-length blond hair and black jeans pulled tight across an ample backside. "She was here a few weeks ago. You remember her. Carrie...Carrie...Carrie Rogers or Rollins or something with an R." The fact that I couldn't recall the last name of even one of our daughter's so-called friends made me feel guiltier than ever. How can you call yourself a good mother, I could already hear the police declaim, when you don't even know who your daughter's friends are?

"Does she have an address book?" Larry asked finally, and we began searching through Sara's scattered belongings, as one might search through the rubble of a bombed-out building. We gathered up clothes from the floor, some dirty, some freshly laundered, picked up discarded tapes and closed open books. We found pencils and pennies and scrap pieces of paper, not to mention a half-eaten bran muffin under the bed.

"Look," I said, hearing a strange note of wistfulness creep into my voice as I held up four empty packages of cigarettes. "She's still collecting."

"Here it is." Larry pulled a tattered, black leather-bound book in the shape of a motorcycle jacket out from underneath several tubes of makeup. He opened the book, and we watched as flecks of baby powder drifted toward the carpet, like snow. "There's nothing under R," he said.

"Try C," I offered.

Sure enough, there was Carrie, scrawled across the page in dark green ink. No last name accompanied it. Maybe, I thought, Sara didn't know it either.

We returned to our bedroom and phoned Carrie. The voice that finally answered was heavy with sleep and smoke. It mumbled something unintelligible, more a prolonged sigh than an actual hello.

"Carrie?" I asked, my voice loud, demanding, the auditory equivalent of hands on her shoulders, shaking her awake. "Carrie, this is Sara's mother. Is Sara there?"

A long pause, then: "What?"

"Is Sara there?"

"Who?"

"Sara Sinclair," I shouted angrily. Clearly, this was a waste of time.

"Sara's not here."

"Do you know where she is?"

"What time is it?"

"Eight o'clock."

"In the morning?"

I dropped the receiver into its carriage. "Sara's not there."

We tried six other names before giving up. My hand was on the receiver, about to call the police, when the phone rang. "Sara?" I all but shrieked.

"Jo Lynn," came the unwelcome response.

My shoulders slumped forward; my head dropped to my chest. My sister was the last person on earth I wanted to deal with. "Jo Lynn, I'm sorry, I can't talk to you now. Sara didn't come home last night..."

"Of course she didn't come home," Jo Lynn said. "She's with me."

"What?" I barked. "Sara's with Jo Lynn," I told Larry quickly. He shook his head and collapsed on the bed.

"You'd know that if you bothered to return your messages."

"What?"

"I called you twice last night."

"You didn't say anything about Sara."

"I assumed you'd call me back."

I was about to protest, decided not to. The important thing was that we knew where Sara was and that she was safe. I was so grateful that I almost forgot that Sara had skipped a whole day of school. How long had she been with my sister? I wondered, seized by a different fear. "What's she doing with you?" The words emerged slowly, almost reluctantly, as if they had to be pushed from my throat.

"Promise you won't get angry," Jo Lynn began, as every muscle in my body began twisting into spasms.

"Please don't tell me she was with you all day."

"It was very educational for her. She's never been inside a courtroom before. Which is shameful, when you think about it. I mean, she's going to be eighteen on her next birthday."

Assuming she lives that long, I almost said, but didn't. It was Jo Lynn, after all, whom I wanted to kill. "You took her to court with you," I said, as Larry gazed up at the ceiling, his eyes frozen in disbelief, as if he'd been shot.

"Well, you wouldn't go with me."

So it was my fault, I thought, almost afraid to say another word. "Tell me you didn't take her with you to the jail."

"Of course I took her with me. What did you expect me to do—leave her alone in the middle of North Dixie Highway? That's not the greatest area, you know."

"You took her to meet Colin Friendly?"

"No, of course not. She waited in the waiting room. Wait till you hear about this visit, Kate. It was incredible."

"You took my daughter to the county jail," I repeated numbly.

"That is some amazing place," Jo Lynn babbled, oblivious to my hands reaching through the phone wires for her throat. "I was really nervous, but Sara was great. She was my navigator, directing me to the visitors' parking, and telling me to relax, that I looked beautiful, all that stuff that girlfriends are supposed to say."

"Sara isn't your girlfriend," I reminded her. "She's your niece, and she's half your age."

"What's age got to do with it?" Jo Lynn demanded testily. "Really, Kate, you don't give your daughter enough credit. She says you treat her like a child, and she's right."

"I treat her like a child because she acts like one."

"You sound just like our mother."

"Someone has to sound like an adult."

"Anyway," Jo Lynn continued, "we had to walk across a bridge to get to the inmate visitation area. It was like a moat, you know, like around a castle. Actually, it's quite a pretty building," she said, one word running into the next, as if she were afraid I might hang up were she to take a breath.

I'd been considering doing just that, and I'm not sure why I didn't. I tried telling myself that I was waiting to speak to Sara, which necessitated wading through the rest of Jo Lynn's story, but I'm not sure that's the truth. Listening to Jo Lynn was akin to driving by the site of a bad accident. No matter how hard you tried not to look, you couldn't turn away.

"You go in the front entrance, and there are all these signs. *Stop! Read! The following personal items will not be allowed into the facility past the metal detector!* And then it lists fourteen things, fourteen! And you wouldn't believe

160

what some of them are—cell phones, diaper bags, hats. Hats!" she shrieked with obvious disbelief. "And then you get to security, and there are these other signs, the usual ones about no smoking, stuff like that, but then this really funny one that says, *No Firearms, Ammunition, or Weapons of any kind beyond this point.* We had a good laugh about that one. I mean, who would be stupid enough to bring a weapon to a jailhouse?"

Probably someone stupid enough to bring their seventeen-year-old niece, I thought but didn't say.

"I told them my name and who I was there to see, and they looked at me like, I don't know, like with new respect or something, because I wasn't there to see some nobody who's robbed the local 7-Eleven. And I had to sign in and everything, and we sat down in this waiting area, which wasn't the greatest place in the world. Just a bunch of uncomfortable blue chairs, and the rest of the room was this icky shade of gray. But there were vending machines, so I bought us some Cokes, but I only got to have a couple of sips before they called my name, and I had to leave my Coke behind because they won't allow any food or beverages into the visitors' rooms. Not even gum. Can you believe that?"

"So you left Sara in the waiting room by herself."

"There were other people there. It's not like I abandoned her. She was fine. She was enjoying herself."

"Can I speak to her?"

"She's still asleep."

"Then wake her up. And bring her home. Now."

"Why? So you can yell at her? She didn't do anything wrong."

"She skipped school," I reminded my sister. "She didn't come home last night."

"She was with me. And I tried to reach you. Several times. Trust me, she learned more yesterday out in the real world than she would have at school. She'll write an essay about it, get an A."

"You had no right..."

"Lighten up," Jo Lynn said. "It's over, and the kid had a great time. Don't ruin it for her."

"Just wake her up and bring her home," I instructed.

"Soon," Jo Lynn said stubbornly.

"Not soon. Now."

Jo Lynn's response was to hang up the phone. I turned toward Larry. He shook his head and walked from the room.

It was almost four o'clock when I heard Jo Lynn's car pull into the driveway. Larry had left the house at two for the driving range, afraid that if he waited one more minute for my sister to show up with our daughter, he would explode. I encouraged him to go. I was way past anger by this time.

Michelle was off with her girlfriends, and I was alone in the house. I moved from room to room, compartmentalizing my anger, tucking it away, like knickknacks into a drawer, rationalizing it out of reach. Sara was safe, I told myself, and I knew where she was. No harm had befallen her. Missing one day of school wasn't the end of the world. She'd easily make it up. She'd spent the night with my sister, and my sister had called twice. It was my fault that I hadn't returned her calls. I couldn't be angry with my daughter for my sister's lack of judgment. And what was the point in being angry with Jo Lynn? Had it ever done me any good?

By four o'clock, I'd settled into an eerie calm. I would greet them at the door, thank my sister for bringing Sara home, get rid of her as quickly and as painlessly as possible, then wait till Larry got home to talk to Sara. We'd already agreed the best way to deal with her was without the fireworks she'd be expecting, and possibly even counting on. We would give her nothing to rage at. The less said, the better. Sara wasn't stupid; she knew what she'd done wrong. There would be consequences for her actions; it remained only for Larry and me to decide what those consequences might be.

Jo Lynn pushed past me as soon as I opened the front door.

"Where's Sara?" I asked, staring toward the old red Toyota leaking oil on my driveway.

"She's in the car."

I strained to see her through the glass of the car's dirty front window. "Where? I don't see anybody."

"She's hiding."

"Hiding? That's ridiculous. What does she think I'm going to do?" I was about to step outside.

"Don't go out there," she warned, her voice stopping me. "I promised her I'd talk to you first."

"I think we've talked enough," I said, calm giving way to anxiety.

Jo Lynn reached over and closed the front door. "I promised her," she repeated. "You don't want to make a liar out of me, do you?"

I'd like to make mincemeat out of you, I wanted to say, taking note of her white T-shirt and short shorts, her newly trimmed hair. I restrained myself, forced a smile onto my lips.

"You're angry," she said. Obviously my smile lacked a certain degree of sincerity, and besides, Jo Lynn had always been very good at stating the obvious.

"You got your hair cut," I said.

She fluffed at the sides of her blond curls. "This afternoon. You like it? It's only a few inches."

"It looks very nice."

"Look, I know I shouldn't have asked Sara to go with me without first clearing it with you," she said, catching me by surprise. Jo Lynn was not one who apologized easily. "But I was really nervous, and I didn't want to go alone, and I really needed someone to go with me, and I knew you wouldn't come."

"You're saying it's my fault?"

"No, of course it's not your fault. It's

nobody's fault. There is no fault. I'm just saying that if you'd been a little more understanding, a little more sympathetic..."

"I would have gone with you, and you wouldn't have had to drag my daughter down with you," I said, completing her sentence. This was more the sort of apology from Jo Lynn that I was used to.

"Well, yes," she said. "I really needed you. And you weren't there for me."

I nodded, took a deep breath. I was no longer anxious. I was on fire. Beads of sweat broke out across my forehead and upper lip. Jo Lynn didn't notice.

"It was so incredible, Kate," she was saying. "It was the most amazing thing being there in that jail with Colin."

I opened my mouth to protest, then instantly thought better of it. The more I protested, the longer this scene would drag out. So I said nothing, wiped the perspiration from my lip, and waited for her to finish.

"I was wearing this new white dress I bought that I thought he would like, and I was right, he loved it. It's very classy, not too short, not too low-cut. Subtle, you know."

I nodded. My definition of subtle and Jo Lynn's definition of subtle were not to be found in the same dictionary.

"Anyway, I was a nervous wreck all afternoon. But Colin was really great, he kept looking over at me in the courtroom, giving me his little smile, like he was telling me not to worry, that it was all going to work out fine. And, of course,

165

Sara was so sweet. She was holding my hand, and telling me how cute he was, and how romantic the whole thing was, kind of like Robin Hood and Maid Marian, and making me feel better. And I was telling her not to believe all the awful things people were saying about him on the witness stand."

"So you went to the jail," I said, trying to hurry her along.

"We went to the jail, and I told you about the moat and the signs and everything."

"You told me."

"Well, the room where you visit with the prisoners is on the second floor. Longest walk of my life, I tell you." She giggled. "I was so nervous. It was this long room with a glass partition, and you sit on one side of the partition and the prisoner sits on the other and you talk into these phones. It's really silly. I mean, they've already made us leave everything behind, our cell phones, our diaper bags, our hats, for God's sake, so why do we have to be behind glass? They don't even let you touch. I mean, I think that's cruel and unusual punishment, don't you?"

I said nothing. *This* is cruel and unusual punishment, I thought.

"So, I'm waiting there behind the glass. There are a few other people in there too, talking to their husbands or whatever, but everybody stops and looks up when they bring Colin into the room. I mean, he's really a celebrity. He has this aura, you know." She paused. I assumed this was for effect, and I tried to look suitably impressed. "So, the guard directs him over to his chair, and all the while he's looking at me and smiling that sad little smile of his, and I'm thinking that he is so gorgeous, I'm about to wet my pants, and then he sits down and he picks up his receiver and I pick up mine, and we just start talking, like we've known each other all our lives. He has a little bit of a stutter that's just so endearing. He tells me how grateful he is for my support, how he loves coming to court every day because he knows he's going to see me, and how much he appreciates my faith in his innocence. He's so polite, Kate. He's a real gentleman. And he has a great sense of humor. I think you'd like him."

I cleared my throat to keep from screaming. I stared hard at the floor.

"He wanted to know all about me, the kinds of things I like, what I like to do. Oh, and he asked about you."

My head snapped up sharply, as if I were a puppet whose strings had been yanked. "What?"

"He remembers you from court," she said, her voice growing instantly defensive.

"And what did you tell him?"

"That you were my sister, that you were a therapist. He laughed about that, said he'd have to meet you one of these days."

I shuddered, felt my body grow cold.

"And he thought Sara was absolutely beautiful."

"Good God."

"He said that…"

"I'm not interested in anything else that monster had to say." I moved briskly to the front door and yelled toward the shadowy figure in the car. "Sara, get in here this minute."

"Don't get angry when you see what she's done," Jo Lynn began. "I think it looks spectacular."

"What looks spectacular? What are you talking about now?"

"It wasn't my idea."

If I hadn't already known that it was Sara in the front seat of the car, I probably wouldn't have recognized her. The creature who emerged from the red Toyota was familiar to me only by height and the size of her bosom. Her long brown tresses had been trimmed to shoulder length and bleached ash blond. The flowered-print Indian blouse and blue jeans had been replaced by a tight white T-shirt and red-and-white-checkered miniskirt.

"The clothes are mine," Jo Lynn offered unnecessarily. "That hippie stuff didn't exactly go with the new hair."

She looks like a hooker, I thought, too stunned to say anything out loud. Actually, I realized as Sara walked past me and straight into her bedroom, she looked just like Jo Lynn.

C h a p t e r
12

We tried not to make too big a deal about Sara's hair, reasoning that anything negative we might say would only encourage her further, and anything positive would only be misinterpreted. I went so far as a meek "So, how does it feel to be blond?" Larry mumbled something about everybody needing a change now and then. It was left to Michelle, as usual, to state what was obvious: "My God, what did you do to your hair?" she screamed as soon as she saw her sister. "It looks awful!"

Actually, it didn't look awful. It just took some getting used to, and over the course of the next few weeks, we all sincerely tried. But Sara never makes things easy, and she was, by turns, remote, nasty, defensive, and hostile. Everything but contrite. Anything but sorry. We never got an apology for our night of anguish; we received no assurances she wouldn't put us through it again. For a while I tried pretending that she was a character in a play, dropped temporarily into our world to provide some much-needed comic relief. But in the long run, it was hard to find her funny. Interestingly, she did write an essay for her English class about her day in court, as Jo Lynn had suggested. Naturally, she received an A. So much for consequences.

It was around this time that Larry started his

gradual retreat from the rest of the family. At first, it was just Sara he avoided, reasoning that the less contact he had with her, the less chance of conflict, the less chance of heartache. So whenever possible, when Sara was at home, Larry wasn't. His workdays got longer, his golf games more frequent. The result of this, of course, was that Michelle and I saw that much less of him too, but in those weeks before Thanksgiving, this subtle shifting away from us went largely unnoticed. I was pretty busy myself. The holiday season, contrary to popular myth, is not a time of unrestrained joy and merriment. It does not bring out the best in people. In fact, just the opposite is true. My office calendar was booked solid through Christmas and into the new year.

And then there was the little matter of my mother and sister, both of whom I decided were, in their own unique ways, completely looney tunes. My sister continued her public vigil at the courthouse and her private visits to the jail. My mother expanded her list of complaints: if strange men weren't following her, they were banging on her door at all hours of the night, and whispering obscene messages over the phone; certain women on her floor were plotting to have her thrown out of the building; she was receiving smaller portions at mealtimes than any of the other residents; Mrs. Winchell was trying to starve her out.

She began calling me, both at the office and at home, at least fifteen times a day. Hers was the first call I received in the morning and the last one I took at night. One minute, she'd be hollering; two minutes later, she'd be as pleasant as could be. Often, she'd be crying.

I didn't blame my husband for not wanting any part of either my mother or my sister at this point. They weren't his family, after all. His family was quiet and sweet and had never given us any trouble. His mother, widowed a decade earlier, lived in South Carolina, two blocks from Larry's older brother, and next door to a lovely widower she'd been seeing for the last five years. We made occasional forays into each other's territory, and such visits were always unfailingly pleasant. No, it was only my family that was ever, and increasingly, problematic. Had I been able to escape them, I would have. Hadn't I already tried?

So, I honestly didn't mind that in those weeks surrounding Thanksgiving, Larry was rarely at home. In a perverse way, I was probably even grateful. It was one less person to worry about.

Thanksgiving itself was strangely calm. The proverbial lull before the storm. We celebrated at our house, and everyone was on their best behavior. Larry was a genial host, expertly carving the turkey and making small talk with my mother, who was pleasant and talkative and minus her recent paranoia. Jo Lynn came conservatively dressed in a white silk shirt and black crepe pants, and refrained from mentioning either Colin Friendly or his trial, which was on a week's hiatus. Sara, whose dark brown roots were beginning to intrude rudely on her otherwise ashen mane, was helpful with the dishes and attentive to her grandmother. "Who is that sweet thing?" my mother whispered at one point during the evening, and I laughed, thinking she was making a joke, realizing only later that she really didn't know. At its conclusion, Michelle pronounced the evening a resounding success. "Almost like a normal family," she said, proffering her cheek for me to kiss good night.

As for Robert, we'd been communicating through our voice mail, never quite connecting. He'd call; I'd be tied up with clients. I'd return his call; he'd be in a meeting. He was thinking about me, he left word on my machine; I was thinking about his offer, I responded on his.

The Monday after Thanksgiving, there was a message waiting when I arrived at the office. "Enough of this nonsense," Robert's voice announced. "I'll see you at my office this Wednesday at noon. I'll take you around, introduce you to the gang, show you how we operate, then take you out for lunch. Have those ideas ready." He then left the station's address and directions on how to get there. There was no mention of my calling back to confirm. Since he already knew I didn't go into the office on Wednesdays, it was simply assumed I'd be available. That I might have made other plans was obviously not part of the equation.

As it happened, I'd already promised to take my mother shopping on Wednesday. We'll make a day of it, I'd offered after

Thanksgiving dinner, almost giddy with relief at how well the evening had gone. First we'd go Christmas shopping, then have lunch, I'd suggested. No way was I going to call her now and cancel just because I'd had a better offer. This wasn't high school, after all. Although it *was* business, I reminded myself, my hand already on the phone. "We can still go shopping in the morning," I told my mother.

"What a nice idea," she said, as if it was the first time she was hearing it.

I picked her up at ten o'clock Wednesday morning. She was already downstairs in the lobby, standing by herself just inside the front doors, casting furtive glances over each shoulder, anxiously clutching her purse. I waved. She looked startled, as if surprised to see me, then hurried outside. "Are you all right?" I asked, helping her into the front seat of my white Lexus, watching as her upper torso curved around her purse, as if protecting it from would-be thieves. "Mother?" I asked again, positioning myself behind the wheel. "Is something wrong? Are you okay?"

"I have something to show you," she whispered. Then: "Drive."

Slowly, reluctantly, I pulled out of the driveway onto Palm Beach Lakes Boulevard. "What is it?" I asked. "What do you want me to see?"

"I'll show you when we get there."

I was about to protest when I realized she was no longer listening, all her attention devoted to watching the road ahead. Quickly, my eyes absorbed her profile for any outward signs of disturbance, but her gray hair was freshly washed and neatly styled, her deep brown eyes were clear and focused, her small mouth was curled upward into a smile. Everything seemed normal. Only her posture, the way her body folded protectively over her purse, seemed out of place. Then I noticed her hands.

"What happened to your nails?" I asked, noting the dark purple smudges across her fingernails.

She glanced toward her long, slightly arthritic fingers, then displayed them proudly, as if surprised by what she saw. "Do you like them? The salesgirl at Saks assured me this polish is all the rage."

I reached over and rubbed the top of one thin nail. The so-called polish came off on my fingers. "This isn't polish, Mom," I told her, wondering what the salesclerk had been trying to pull.

"It isn't?"

"It's lipstick." I rubbed at her other fingers. "You've put lipstick on your nails."

She shook her head. "No," she said adamantly. "You're quite mistaken. And now you've ruined it," she said, her eyes threatening tears.

"But, Mom," I began, then stopped, driving on in confused silence. Clearly, something was very wrong with my mother. Although she'd been just fine over the weekend, I quickly assured myself. Maybe the weekend had been too much for her. Older people didn't adjust as quickly to a break in their routine. Was seventy-five really all that old? What was happening to her?

We didn't speak again until I pulled the car into the Marshalls plaza on Military Trail. As soon as I turned the engine off, my mother spun around in her seat, her eyes flashing excitement, her fingers fluttering nervously in the air, like a child's. "Wait till you see this." She reached inside her purse, cradling something gingerly in the palm of her hand.

"What is it?" I could hear the nervousness in my voice.

My mother smiled proudly, then slowly opened her fist, revealing a small white egg. "Have you ever seen anything like it?" she marveled, as my breath constricted in my chest. She looked nervously around, as if afraid someone might be standing just outside the window, spying in on her. "They had some of these on the table at breakfast," she continued, "and I couldn't get over them. So, when no one was looking, I slipped one into my purse to show you. Just look at how perfectly it's shaped. Have you ever seen anything like it?"

"It's an egg, Mom," I said gently, staring at the small ovate object in disbelief. "Don't you know that?"

"An egg?"

"You eat them every day."

My mother stared at me for several long seconds. "Well, of course I do," she said, with-

175

out changing her expression. She tucked the egg back inside her purse.

"Mom," I began, not sure what I was going to say, but terrified of the silence.

"Don't you look lovely," she exclaimed, as if seeing me for the first time. "Is that a new dress? Very fancy just to go shopping."

My hand automatically smoothed the folds of my newly purchased red-and-white-flowered print dress. "I have a luncheon meeting," I reminded her. "About doing a possible radio show. Remember, I told you about it."

"Of course I remember," she said. "Have you got Michelle's Christmas list?"

I suppose I should have realized at this point that there was something terribly wrong with my mother. Looking back, it seems incredible that I failed to recognize the obvious signs of Alzheimer's disease. Had she been the mother of one of my clients, no doubt I would have seen this much earlier, or at least considered the possibility, but this was *my* mother, and she was only seventy-five. And besides, usually she was fine. Usually she didn't go around stealing eggs from the breakfast table and applying lipstick to her fingernails. Usually she didn't accuse her neighbors of harassment or bake with dishwashing detergent. Usually she was fine, a little forgetful maybe, but then weren't we all? And it wasn't as if she didn't remember most things. Hadn't she been fine all weekend? Hadn't she just mentioned Michelle's famous Christmas list?

"I have it right here," I said, extricating the list from my black leather bag.

"She's such a funny girl," my mother said, and I laughed, although I wasn't sure why.

Normally, I received tremendous pleasure from Michelle's yearly list, which came complete with drawings of each requested item, their correct sizes, prices, and the stores where they could be purchased, along with an accompanying chart indicating preference. Items highlighted in yellow were deemed *nice*; those with an asterisk beside them were *nicer*, an arrow indicated *very nice*, and those marked with both an asterisk *and* an arrow were *the nicest*.

You always knew exactly where you stood with Michelle, I thought gratefully, clutching the list as if it were a lifeline.

Sara, it goes without saying, refused to make any list at all.

The morning progressed reasonably well. My mother snapped back into seeming normalcy; we managed to locate several of the items on Michelle's list with a minimum of difficulty; I was feeling more comfortable about my upcoming meeting with Robert. I even had a few ideas for what I'd now started to think of as "my radio show." So today's lunch was legitimate after all, I rationalized, leading my mother across the parking lot toward a small shop that specialized in golfing equipment.

Of course, I was as delusional about Robert as I was with regard to my mother.

"What's the best line of men's clubs you carry?" I asked the Greg Norman look-alike who offered his assistance. Guilt had nothing to do with my decision to buy my husband the best set of clubs currently on the market, I told myself, following the young man to the back of the store.

"Well, of course, that depends on your needs," he said as he walked. "But there's this new line of clubs called Titans that's just fabulous." He grabbed a long club with a large wooden head from its bag and began waxing rhapsodic about its particular virtues, his hand sliding up and down its smooth surface as lovingly as if it were a woman's body. "It's the perfect combination of titanium and graphite. For my money," he concluded, replacing the wood with an iron, assuming I knew the difference, "it's the best there is."

"How much is it?" I asked. It was, after all, *not* his money, but mine.

"Well, let's see," he began, scanning the store as if he didn't already have a price worked out in his head. His eyes suddenly widened, then froze, as if he'd been shot. "My God, watch out!" he yelled.

I heard the *whoosh* of the golf club before I actually saw it, felt the air beside me stir as it swept past me, the club missing my head by no more than six inches. Several young men suddenly appeared, seemingly from out of nowhere, and all but wrestled my mother to the floor, tearing the golf club she was wielding, as if it were a baseball bat, from her hands.

"Kate!" she cried, a look of pure terror distorting her delicate features as strange hands seized her. "Help me! Help me!"

"It's all right," I yelled. "She's my mother." Looks of astonishment crossed the faces of the young men as they reluctantly released her. "It's all right," I repeated, as confused as everyone else. "She wasn't trying to hurt me."

"Hurt you?" My mother was whimpering now, her head bobbing up and down, as if attached to her body by wires, the bobbing accentuating the skin that hung in folds around her neck, like loose-fitting socks. "What are you talking about? I would never hurt you. I just wanted to try out that bat. Remember in high school, I was such a good hitter. The best on the team."

"It's okay, everything's fine," I assured the small crowd gathered around us. "She gets a little confused at times, that's all. Are you all right?" I asked her.

"You know I would never do anything to hurt you," my mother said as I led her from the store.

"I know," I told her. It wasn't until I was behind the wheel of my car that my knees stopped knocking together. And it wasn't until I'd dropped her safely back at her apartment that I could breathe.

"You look a little flushed," Robert was saying, his hand reaching over to touch my cheek. "Are you coming down with something?"

The touch of his hand on my cheek was almost more than I could bear. I closed my eyes, imagined us on a shimmering white beach, far away from mothers and daughters and husbands and wives. And sisters, I reminded myself, forcing my eyes open, firmly relocating us in his impressive suite of offices in the heart of Delray. "My mother thinks she's Babe Ruth," I said.

"Why do I think there's an interesting story there?" he asked, eyes twinkling.

"Because you're the media," I told him. "Everything's a story to you."

"Ah," he said, "but not always an interesting one. Why is it I find everything about you so interesting?"

"Because you haven't seen me in thirty years," I replied dryly. "Because you don't know me very well."

"Something I'd like to change."

For the second time that morning, I was finding it hard to breathe. I looked around his office, forced my eyes to absorb a host of inconsequential details: the walls were pale blue, the broadloom thick and silver, the top of his large desk a black marble slab, dominated by a large-screen computer. There were two blue-and-gray tub chairs in fashionable ultrasuede positioned in front of the desk, and several more in front of a full-size sofa that sat at the far end of the rectangular room. We were on the top floor of a twelve-story building; floor-to-ceiling windows faced east toward the ocean. It was the spectacular view that was responsible for my shortness of breath, I told myself, almost laughing out loud at this feeble attempt at self-denial.

A row of framed photographs graced the top of the oak credenza behind Robert's desk. I walked toward the pictures, casually perusing the happy family smiling back at me: a woman, dark-haired, petite, pretty enough without being beautiful, a slightly startled look about her eyes that indicated either surprise or plastic surgery; four children, two boys, two girls, their growth captured inside silver frames as they advanced from childhood through adolescence to young adulthood. "You have a lovely family," I said, although, without my reading glasses, the more minute details of their faces were lost on me.

"Thank you," he acknowledged. "And what about you? Any pictures of your girls?"

I fished around inside my purse, grateful for something to do with my hands. Immediately, I pictured my mother reaching inside her handbag and proudly proffering forth her wondrous new discovery. An egg. Maybe she was right, I found myself thinking. There *was* something pretty wondrous about an egg.

"What are you thinking about?" I heard Robert ask, his eyes crinkling into a smile.

"Eggs," I told him, quickly resuming my search.

"Eggs," he repeated, shaking his head. "You're a woman of mystery, Kate Latimer."

I smiled. It was something I'd always wanted to be. "Kate Sinclair," I corrected softly, almost hopeful he wouldn't hear, finally locating a small red leather folder that contained pictures of Sara and Michelle, and extending it toward him. "These are at least a year old. Michelle hasn't changed that much, except she's even thinner now."

"She's lovely."

I studied the small photograph of my younger child: heart-shaped face and huge navy eyes; light shoulder-length brown hair and slightly sad little mouth. Of my two girls, Sara was the more striking, Michelle the more conventionally pretty.

"And this...?"

"Is Sara," I said. "Her hair's different now. It's shorter, and blond."

"And you don't approve?"

I returned the red leather folder to my purse. Was I that transparent? "I like the cut," I qualified. "I'm not wild about the color."

"No pictures of your husband?" A mischievous twinkle danced in Robert's hazel eyes.

I moved to the window, stared out at the ocean, although I wasn't able to distinguish where the sky ended and the water began. What did it matter? It was all a miraculous shade of blue. "No," I said, wondering what I was really doing in Robert's office, feeling slightly guilty. "No pictures of Larry."

The intercom on his desk buzzed and his secretary informed him that a Mr. Jack Peterson was on the phone from New York. Robert excused himself to take the call, and I excused myself to go to the ladies' room.

I leaned against the large bathroom mirror. "What are you getting yourself into?" I asked my reflection, applying some fresh blush to my cheeks, fluffing the sides of my hair. Do you need this in your life right now? Even if this whole thing is really about a job in radio, is that what you really want?

In truth, all I wanted was a semblance of normalcy back. I wanted a daughter with brown hair and a good report card, a sister with a steady job and no love life, a mother who wasn't acting like a visitor from another planet.

At least I'd been able to persuade her to see a doctor, I consoled myself, smoothing on a fresh coat of lipstick, recalling the magenta lipstick smudged across my mother's fingernails. At first, she refused to see a doctor, said she'd seen enough doctors, so I made it seem as if I was the one who required the appointment and wanted her along for moral support. "Of course, dear," she'd readily agreed. Unfortunately, the earliest appointment I could schedule was two months away.

Maybe by then the problem, whatever it was, would have sorted itself out, I told myself. Maybe in two months' time my daughter's hair would have returned to its brown roots, Colin Friendly would be on his way to the electric chair, and my mother would be herself again.

I had no way of knowing that things were only going to get worse.

Although maybe I suspected as much. Maybe that's why I decided not to let Robert introduce me to the station brass, not to join him for lunch, not to pursue some half-baked notion of radio stardom. Instead, I splashed some cold water on my face, in what was decidedly a symbolic cleansing gesture, returned my makeup to my handbag, and marched from the ladies' room.

Robert was waiting for me in front of the elevators. "Sorry about the interruption," he began, taking me by the elbow and leading me across the hall to the office of his station manager. "I can't wait to show you off," he said.

I allowed myself to be led through the labyrinth of offices that made up the twelfth floor, shaking hands with the various managers and office workers, touring the recording studios below, meeting the announcers and producers, those who worked on-air and behind the scenes. I have to admit I loved everything about it, the atmosphere, the people, the lingo, the buzz. Mostly, I loved the feel of Robert's arm on my elbow as he guided me from one room to the next, from one unfamiliar situation to another, from new face to new face. It wasn't his touch so much as what that touch represented: the feeling of being gently led, of not having to do for myself, the knowledge that someone else was in charge, was making the decisions, was leading the way. That I was no longer responsible.

So I allowed myself to be seduced, as one

always consents to a seduction, still insisting to myself as we left the station for the restaurant that Robert's interest in me was strictly professional and that my interest in him was strictly the same, a way of branching out, of spreading my professional wings.

Of course, that was before we had our lunch.

Self-delusion, rationalization, outright denial—they'll only take you so far.

Chapter
13

So, tell me, what are the secrets of a happy marriage?"

I stared across the table at Robert Crowe, searching for signs of irony in his bright hazel eyes. There weren't any. I tried to laugh, but the intensity of his gaze caused the laugh to stick in my throat. My hand fluttered to my face, returned to my lap, stretched across the table for another roll—my third.

He reached over, his palm covering the top of my hand. "You seem a little nervous."

Was he playing with me? "I guess I'm not sure how seriously to take you," I answered truthfully.

"And that makes you nervous?"

"I like to know where I stand."

"Take me very seriously," he said, removing his hand.

I was more confused than ever. I hadn't engaged in this kind of elliptical banter in over twenty-five years. One of the things I'd always liked about my husband was that I'd known where I stood with him right from the very beginning of our relationship. There'd been no anxious nights by the telephone waiting for him to call. No emotional roller-coaster rides. So why wasn't it my husband I was flirting with across the table of a cozy little restaurant in Delray Beach?

"The secrets of a happy marriage," I repeated, trying not to think of how handsome Robert looked in his dark green suit. "There are no secrets. You know that."

"You've been married almost a quarter of a century," he reminded me.

"You've been married over twenty years yourself," I reminded him back.

"Who said I was happy?"

My mouth went suddenly dry. I looked around the dimly lit restaurant, decorated in shades of burgundy and pink, and wondered what was taking our food so long. We'd been sitting here, in a corner table at the back, for almost half an hour. We'd already tossed around a host of ideas for my so-called show: Was a daily hour-long format preferable to a weekly two-hour show? Would I interview various experts or go it alone? Should we concentrate on one topic at a time or should we open the phone lines and let the topics fall where they may? What about conducting real-life therapy sessions on the air? How about dramatizations? Was there a way to combine the two?

We'd reached no conclusions. Clearly, we had a long way to go in our discussions. It was obvious more such lunches would be necessary.

"You're not happy?" I asked, the question out of my mouth before I could stop it.

"I'm not *un*happy," he qualified. "My wife is a very nice woman; she's given me four beautiful children and a very successful career. I owe her a great deal. I know that."

"Do you love her?" I knew the question sounded naive, maybe even trite. But in the end, it was the only question that really mattered.

"Define love."

I shook my head. "Love means different things to different people. I couldn't presume to speak for you."

"Speak for me," he said. "Go ahead—presume."

I smiled, wishing I wasn't such a sucker for his easy charm. Get up now, I told myself. Get up out of your seat, and tell him you're not hungry, that this whole radio show idea is a bad one, that you're not fooled by his newfound interest in your therapeutic capabilities, and that you have no more intention of sleeping with him now than you did thirty years ago. Go ahead, tell him. Instead I stayed put, twisted restlessly in my seat, said, "I can only tell you what love means to me."

"Please do."

I swallowed. "I think that love is a combination of many factors—respect and tolerance and acceptance of the other person for who they are." My eyes shifted inexorably toward his. "And, of course, physical attraction."

"So, what happens when you have respect and tolerance and you accept the other person for who she is, but the physical attraction is no longer there?"

"You work hard to get it back," I said, somewhat stuffily, grateful beyond words when the waiter approached with our food.

"Be careful," the waiter warned, prophetically. "It's very hot."

I tore into my seafood pasta as if I hadn't seen food in weeks. It burned my tongue, seared the roof of my mouth. Still, as long as my mouth was full, I couldn't get into trouble, I reasoned, barely taking a breath between forkfuls. My tongue grew numb. The food lost all taste. I kept shoveling it in regardless, aware that Robert was smiling at me from across the table, that he was enjoying my discomfort.

"You're suggesting that I fake it?" he asked after a long pause.

"Why not? Women do it all the time."

"Are you speaking from personal experience?"

"I didn't say that."

"You didn't deny it."

"I'm not suggesting you fake anything," I said, my mouth on fire.

"That's good, because it's not always possible. From a strictly physical point of view," he added unnecessarily, as I struggled unsuccessfully not to imagine him naked. "The male body doesn't always cooperate with its best resolve."

"I don't think we should get into this," I said finally, swallowing, the pasta sitting like a lump of burning coal in the middle of my stomach.

"What are we getting into?" he asked.

"I'm not sure." I put down my fork, stared him straight in the eyes. "Why are you telling me these things?"

"I guess I was hoping you'd have some easy answers for me," he said, and laughed sadly. "The McDonald's School of Psychiatry. Quick and effortless. Over eight billion cured."

"McTherapy." I laughed. "Sounds like a good name for a radio show."

We lapsed into silence. I finished the balance of my pasta, felt it burn a trail through my esophagus, razing various internal organs on its way to my intestines, where it wrapped itself into a series of tight little knots.

"So, how do you do it?" he asked calmly, sipping on his wine.

"Do what?"

"Keep your relationship...what's the word they use?...vital?"

I sighed, more deeply than I'd intended. I understood that "vital" was a euphemism for "sexy."

"Do you love your husband?" he pressed.

"Yes," I answered quickly.

"You have the right combination of respect

and tolerance and acceptance of one another?"

"Yes." One-word answers were about all I was capable of at the moment.

"And you still find each other physically attractive?"

"My husband is a very handsome man."

"And my wife's a very lovely woman. That's not what I asked."

"I still find my husband physically attractive, yes."

"And he, you?"

Did he? I wondered. "He says he does." Really? I asked myself. When was the last time he said that?

"You still make love?"

I reached for my water, took a long gulp, half hoped I would choke, have to be carried out of the restaurant. I glanced around the room, hoping for a diversion of some sort—a waiter dropping a tray, a couple breaking into a loud argument at a nearby table, someone's mother swinging a golf club at her head. "I really don't think that's any of your business."

"For sure it's none of my business," he agreed. "I'm asking anyway."

I tried not to smile, felt my lips wobbling all over my face. "We still make love," I answered.

"How often?"

"What?"

"You heard me."

"Yes, I did, and I have no intention of answering you."

"Not as often as you used to, I'll bet."

"Pretty safe bet after twenty-five years of marriage."

"And are you happy about that?"

"I'm not *un*happy about it," I replied, echoing his earlier phrase. Was that true?

He smiled.

Did he still have to look as handsome as he had so long ago? Couldn't he have grown fat or bald or dim-witted? Did he still have to move with an athlete's grace? Did his hips have to be so impossibly slim, his chest so impressively expansive? Did he have to look so damned... vital?

"My wife and I haven't made love in three years," he said.

"What?"

"You heard me."

"Yes, I did." Hadn't we already had this exchange? "I'm not sure what you want me to say."

"What would you say if I were your client?"

"I thought you once told me that if you wanted my professional advice, you'd make an appointment," I said, trying to shift the conversation to another level, one I could deal with safely in the professional confines of my office.

"Is that what you think I should do?" he asked.

"Is that what you need?" I asked in return.

"You're the therapist. You tell me."

"I think if you're unhappy with your situation, you should change it."

"I'm trying to," he said, provocatively.

I shifted uncomfortably in my chair, crossed one leg over the other. "You should talk to your wife about this. Tell her how you feel."

"You don't think I've done that?"

"I have no idea."

"My wife insists that part of her life is over. She's done her bit for posterity. She's gone forth and multiplied. Now all she wants is companionship and a good night's sleep."

"Maybe it's physical," I offered. "Some women going through menopause experience a decrease in their level of sexual desire."

"Has that happened to you?"

"We're not talking about me."

"I prefer talking about you."

"Have you tried courting your wife? Taking her out for dinner?" I persisted. Or lunch, I thought, but didn't say. "Sometimes all it takes is a few kind words. Try saying at least one nice thing to her every day. You'll see, it'll change your life."

"You used to drive me crazy," he said, sidestepping my advice, as if I hadn't spoken. "I'd come home from a date with you and head straight for the cold shower."

"You'd head straight for Sandra Lyons," I said, remembering how hurt I'd been when my girlfriend first informed me of his extracurricular activities, experiencing a slight twinge even now.

He looked surprised.

"Didn't think I knew about her, did you?"

"Everybody knew about Sandra," he said easily, recovering nicely, taking a long sip of his wine. "She was the girl everybody knew."

"She killed herself shortly after you left town."

The wineglass almost slipped through his fingers. "What?"

I started to laugh, at first only a slight giggle, soon a great hearty guffaw. "I'm sorry," I said, then laughed even louder.

"You're laughing?!"

"I made it up. I'm sorry. I couldn't help myself."

"You made what up?"

"Sandra Lyons—she didn't kill herself." I tried to stop laughing, couldn't. "She's fine. At least she was fine the last time I saw her. I don't know—she could be dead by now." My laughter was verging on hysteria.

He looked horrified. "Why did you say she'd killed herself?"

"I'm not sure," I told him, still laughing, but that was only partly true. I'd been trying to shake him up. It wasn't fair that only one of us was a quivering mess.

He shook his head. "You're a strange woman, Kate Latimer."

"Sinclair," I corrected, the laughter suddenly freezing in my throat. Back to square one, I thought.

"Sinclair, right. Tell me, does your husband often see this side of you?"

"What side is that?"

"This twisted, rather sadistic side that, for some perverse reason, I'm finding extremely attractive."

I tried to laugh, couldn't. "I'm sure he sees it more often than he'd like."

Robert finished his wine, poured himself some more, studying me all the while. "Your husband's the only man you've ever been with, isn't he?" he said.

I felt suddenly exposed, as if he'd reached over and unbuttoned the front of my dress, laid bare all that was private and untouchable. Probably I should have slapped his face. I definitely should have gotten up and left. At the very least, I should have told him to shut the hell up, enough was enough. Instead I said, "What makes you say that?"

"I was always pretty good at reading people."

"My mother says my face is an open book."

"Your mother's right."

"Where is it written that my husband has been my only lover?"

Robert reached across the table, traced the line of my lips with his index finger. "Right here," he said, as a shiver raced through me, as strong as an electrical charge. "Aren't you ever curious," he asked, "what it would be like with somebody else?"

Oh God, I thought, I'm lost. If I didn't stop this and stop it now, I'd never find my way back. "No," I lied, pushing my chair back, just slightly out of his reach. His hand remained where it was, absently caressing the space between us. His touch lingered on my lips. I felt it as one supposedly feels the presence of a recently amputated limb. "I'm not curious."

"You've never been tempted?"

"I'm a married woman."

"Does that matter?"

"It matters to me."

"Has your husband ever been unfaithful?"

"No."

"You sound very sure."

"I *am* very sure," I said, and I was. There weren't many things I was sure of anymore, but I was sure of this: Larry would never cheat on me. It was something I'd never doubted in all our time together. "This is a very dangerous conversation," I finally acknowledged.

"What is?"

"This is. This—what we're doing."

"We're not doing anything."

"Yes, we are."

"What are we doing?"

"We're laying a foundation," I said, thinking of Larry.

"A foundation for what?"

"You know for what. Please don't be coy."

"Tell me."

"I'm not interested in an affair," I told him, pushing the words out of my mouth, hoping I sounded more convincing than I felt.

"An affair? That's what you think I want?"

"Isn't it?" Had I misinterpreted everything?

"I've never gotten over you, Kate," he was saying, his voice a soft blanket, inviting me inside. "I look at you, and I still feel the same sparks I did when I was a pimply-faced teenager."

"You never had a pimple in your life," I said.

"You're missing the point."

"I'm trying to."

"I want you, Kate," he said simply. "I've always wanted you. I think you want me too."

"I want a lot of things. It doesn't mean I'm going to get them. It doesn't mean those things are good for me."

"How do you know if you don't try?"

"And what would be the point of trying?"

"I don't know." He reached for my hands. I quickly put them in my lap. "I just know that something is missing from my life, and has been for a very long time. I thought I'd gotten used to it. I told myself that my life was full, that romance was for teenagers, all the stuff people tell themselves to get them through the night. But all that went out the window the day I saw you in the courthouse. There you were, every bit as beautiful as I remembered. And not only beautiful, but funny and smart and sexy as hell. It was like discovering my youth all over again, only better. I look at you and I feel that anything's possible. It's a feeling I'd forgotten. And I don't want to lose it. I don't want to lose *you*. I want you. Is that so wrong?"

"Oh God," I said, trying not to be overwhelmed. "That was quite a speech."

"I meant every word."

"I don't know what to say."

"You don't have to say anything right now. Just think about it."

"It'll be hard not to," I told him.

He smiled, then frowned, then smiled again,

196

his hands retreating to his sides. And suddenly he was on his feet, his arms extended, and I realized we were no longer alone, that someone else had joined us. "What are you doing here?" Robert was asking, sounding pleased by this unexpected interruption. I was amazed at how quickly he could shift gears. I was still locked in first, and slipping down that mountain road. "How did you know where to find me?"

The next voice was soft and unmistakably feminine. "I called the office; your secretary told me you'd probably still be here. I hope I'm not interrupting anything too important."

Of course I knew it was Robert's wife even before I turned around. "Actually, it's perfect timing. We were just finishing up," I told her, feeling dizzy and light-headed as Robert made the necessary introductions.

Brandi Crowe was an attractive woman approximately my own age. She was on the short side, maybe five feet three inches tall, and she wore a lot of makeup, especially around her eyes, which were small and gray and untroubled by lines. She had that vaguely surprised look I recognized from her photograph. I found myself checking her hairline for signs of recent surgery, but her hair—a shade too black, a touch too long—provided suitable camouflage. Her Chanel suit was the same shade of pink as the tablecloth.

"You're just in time for dessert," Robert said easily, pulling out a chair for his wife and signaling for the waiter.

"Well, I'll join you for some coffee, if you don't mind." His wife smiled in my direction. "I haven't had dessert in years. It's not fair, is it? I mean, look at Robert. He eats whatever he wants, and he never puts on a pound. I so much as look at a rich dessert..." Her voice trailed off. "Is that a new suit?" she asked her husband.

He shook his head, but the slight blush that appeared unexpectedly on his cheek told me otherwise. So, he'd bought a new suit for our lunch, I thought, twisting the buttons of my newly purchased red-and-white-floral dress.

"Do you work at the station?" Brandi Crowe asked as the waiter cleared away the dishes from our main course and passed around the dessert menus.

"Kate's a therapist," Robert explained. "I've been trying to talk her into doing a little something for us."

Brandi Crowe looked confused. "Really? In what capacity?"

We ordered coffee and several slices of Key lime pie, and Robert explained the general concept of what he had in mind. "McTherapy," he announced finally, and I smiled in spite of myself.

"Sounds great," she enthused. "I'd certainly listen."

"Well, the idea's still in its infancy," Robert said.

"It's by no means a sure thing," I said.

Robert smiled and looked away.

A slight chuckle escaped Brandi Crowe's carefully outlined lips. Her upper lip was very full, I noticed, wondering whether she'd had collagen injections, then wondering what she was chuckling about. "When my husband decides he wants something, absolutely nothing gets in his way." She chuckled again, an increasingly irritating sound. "This is a done deal." She reached over, patted her husband's hand. I felt a jolt through mine.

My gaze dropped to the pink linen tablecloth, and stayed there until the aroma of freshly brewed coffee forced my head back up. The waiter slid a slice of Key lime pie under my nose. The pie was tall and yellow and topped by a great lather of whipped cream.

"You're skinny," Brandi Crowe was saying. "You can eat that. If I were to eat it, it would go straight to my hips. I have to work like the devil to keep the pounds off."

"You look great," I told her, and meant it. Despite what the media tries to tell us, not everyone has to be six feet tall and a hundred and twenty pounds. Immediately, I pictured Sara, wondered whether she was in school, what she was doing. Couldn't be any worse than what her mother was doing, I realized.

"That looks delicious," Brandi said, eyeing her husband's piece of pie. "Let me just steal a forkful."

"What about your diet?"

"You're right. I'll hate myself in the morning." She sat back in her chair, watched me shoveling the Key lime pie into my mouth with the same abandon with which I'd earlier attacked my seafood pasta. In seconds, the whole thing was gone. Brandi Crowe looked vaguely stunned. "So, how did this whole idea come about?" she asked. The look on her face told me she was beginning to doubt my credentials.

"Actually, I knew Kate from high school," Robert said. I couldn't help but admire his cool. He was sipping his coffee and eating his Key lime pie just like normal people do.

"Really? You mean in Pittsburgh?"

I listened to Robert's account of our accidental reunion at the courthouse, watching his wife's reactions, searching for any signs of intimacy between them, for telltale clues as to whether or not they were sleeping together, subtle glances, furtive touches. But aside from that first pat on the hand, the jolt of which I still felt in my palm, there was nothing to give them away. They might be sleeping together; they might not.

What difference did it make? I asked myself angrily, swallowing my coffee in one prolonged rush and jumping to my feet. "I'm sorry, but I really have to get going. I'm supposed to meet my husband," I lied, glancing at my watch for added authenticity.

"Maybe the four of us could get together one night for dinner," Robert's wife suggested.

I must have mumbled something positive, because she said she'd call and we'd set something up. Then I went out and bought my husband the most expensive set of golf clubs I could find.

Chapter
14

For the next few weeks, Colin Friendly was everywhere: on television, on the front pages of the newspapers, on the covers of both local and national magazines. The trial was winding down and there was much speculation as to whether Colin Friendly would take the stand in his own defense. The rumors were contradictory and many. According to the *Fort Lauderdale Sun-Sentinel*, he would most assuredly take the stand; according to the *Miami Herald*, his lawyers would never allow it. The *Palm Beach Post* came down solidly in the middle: Colin Friendly would take the stand, and it would be against his lawyers' advice.

About one thing, almost everyone was certain—Colin Friendly would be found guilty. The only real question was how many minutes it would take the jury to arrive at its guilty verdict. Of course, my sister remained unshakable in her belief not only that Colin Friendly would be found not guilty but that he *was* not guilty.

"Did you see the profile in the *Post* this morning?" she asked me, her voice on the phone low and threatening tears. The trial had adjourned for lunch, and she'd caught me in between clients. "They had so many things wrong. Really, half their information was incorrect. And it makes me so mad because they think they can just get away with it, and of course, they can, because what's Colin gonna do—sue them?"

I said nothing, knowing no response was required.

"They said he's six feet two inches tall. Since when? The fact is he barely tops six feet. They say he weighs a hundred eighty pounds. Well, maybe he weighed that before he was arrested. He's lost at least fifteen pounds in that awful jail because the food's so bad. But the newspapers like to paint a picture of this big, threatening guy, so they add an inch here, a few pounds there, and pretty soon he's Hulk Hogan. Well, you saw him, he's not threatening-looking at all."

"I don't think his height and weight are really major issues," I ventured.

"They're deliberately misleading. And, what's more important," she countered, "they're indicative of the kind of shoddy reporting that passes for journalism in this country these days. They said his mother's name was Ruth. It wasn't. It was Ruta. At first, I thought maybe it was a typo, but they kept repeating it, so, obviously, it was just carelessness. They said he came from poverty, but his great-grandparents were really rich. They lost it all in the Depression, of course, but still, they could have mentioned it. I mean, if they can't get the simplest of facts right, then how can you believe anything they print? How can you take anything they say seriously?"

"I thought the reporters were your friends."

"Oh, please, you tell them one thing, they print something completely different. They're always getting their quotes wrong or taking things out of context. They have their own agenda."

"And what is that?"

"To see Colin Friendly in the electric chair. But it isn't going to happen. You'll see. He'll be acquitted. And when he is, I'll be right there waiting for him."

"I have to go now," I told her, not wanting to hear the familiar litany again.

"The only thing they got right," she continued, as if I hadn't spoken, "is that he had a terrible childhood. You couldn't help but cry when you read it. Wasn't it sad? Didn't you cry?"

"I didn't read it," I lied. A mistake. Jo Lynn now felt compelled to provide me with all the details I'd supposedly missed.

"Well, his mother was crazy. I mean really crazy. She got kicked out of the house when she was fifteen, got pregnant at sixteen, and was already a drunk and a doper by the time Colin was born. She'd shoot up right in front of him, have men back to her room, and have sex with them while Colin was watching. She didn't even know for sure who Colin's father was.

"When he was really little, she used to lock him in the closet whenever she went out. Sometimes she'd disappear for days at a time, and Colin wouldn't have anything to eat. And if he had to go to the bathroom, well, he'd just have to go in his pants. Isn't that pathetic? No wonder he was a bed-wetter until he was eleven. Of course, she'd punish him whenever he wet the bed, do awful things like rub his nose in it, like a dog. And she kept moving all the time, so Colin never got a chance to make any friends, and he was really shy. He started to stutter, and his mother would make fun of him and beat him. She was really awful."

"No wonder he hates women," I said.

"Oh, but he doesn't hate women," Jo Lynn exclaimed. "Which is really an amazing thing, when you think about it. He loves women."

"He loves women," I repeated, my voice as dull as a matte finish on a photograph.

"He had this great neighbor, Mrs. Rita Ketchum, and she was really nice to him. She taught him that most women weren't like his mother."

"I thought you said they moved around all the time."

"This was later, when he was a teenager, living on his own in Brooksville."

"I don't remember the article mentioning her."

"You said you didn't read it."

"I glanced at it," I qualified.

"You read every word. Why won't you admit it?"

"How does he explain the kittens he tortured as a child?"

"Colin never tortured anything. Some other kids had been at those kittens. Colin just put them out of their misery."

"And the fires he started?"

"Kid stuff. Nobody ever got hurt."

She had all the answers. There was no point trying to argue. For whatever her reasons, my sister had decided that Colin Friendly was nothing more than a sadly misunderstood young man, and no amount of logic or evidence to the contrary was going to convince her otherwise.

"Is he going to testify?" I asked.

"He wants to, but his lawyers don't think it's a good idea. Not because they think he's guilty," she added quickly. "It's because when Colin gets nervous, he stutters, and his lawyers don't want to put him through the ordeal of a cross-examination."

"Probably a good idea."

"I think the stutter's kind of sweet. And I think it would show the jury how vulnerable he is, that he's a human being, not this awful monster they keep hearing about."

"So you've advised him to testify?"

"I said I'd support him no matter what his decision. But I think it's really important to him that he makes people understand."

"Understand what?"

"That he didn't kill those women." Jo Lynn's voice was filled with exasperation. "That he could never do the awful things they say he did."

"When do they think the trial will be over?" I didn't think I could take too many more conversations like this one.

"Two weeks tops. The prosecution should

205

wrap things up tomorrow, and then it'll be the defense's turn. If all goes according to plan, Colin will be out by Christmas."

"And if he isn't?"

"He will be."

"And then what?"

"Then we can get on with our lives."

"Sounds good to me."

"Will you come with me to court on Wednesday?"

"Not a chance."

"Please. It would mean a lot to me."

"Why?" I asked. "You know I don't share your high opinion of the man."

"I want you to hear what Colin has to say firsthand. I honestly think if you just listen to him, I mean *really* listen to him, like you do with your clients, then you'll change your mind about him."

"I doubt that."

"It's really important to me, Kate."

"Why is it important?"

There was a second's silence. "Because I love him."

"Oh, please..."

"I do, Kate. I really love him."

"You don't even know him, for God's sake."

"That's not true. I've been sitting in that courtroom for almost two months. I know everything about him."

"You know nothing."

"I've been visiting him every week."

"You talk to him through a glass partition."

"That's right, I do. And he talks to me. And we really understand each other. He says I know him better than anybody."

"That's because he's killed everybody else!" I shouted in total frustration.

There was another, longer pause. "That was beneath you," Jo Lynn pronounced. "I would have thought that with your professional training, you'd have a little more compassion."

"Look, Jo Lynn," I said, trying another approach, "you're the only one that matters to me in this equation. I don't want to see you get hurt again."

Her voice softened. I could almost see the relief in her face through the phone lines. "But I'm not going to get hurt. He loves me, Kate. He says I'm the best thing that ever happened to him."

"I'm sure you are," I told her honestly.

"You know what he told me when I went to see him on Friday?"

I shook my head, said nothing.

"He said I looked as sweet as the first strawberry in spring."

I smiled despite myself.

"You're smiling. I can tell you're smiling. Isn't that just the most darling thing you ever heard? I mean, when was the last time that Larry ever said anything that romantic to you?"

It's been a while, I thought, but didn't say. I felt a sudden twinge as my thoughts shifted from Larry to Robert.

"So, you can stop worrying about me. I'm

gonna be fine. If Colin and I can get through this, then we can survive anything. I want you to be happy for us, Kate. And I need you to be there for me. Can you do this for me just this one last time? I'll even go visit Mom with you this weekend. How's that for a deal?"

I closed my eyes, lowered my forehead into the palm of my hand. "Okay, you got me," I said softly.

"Thank you, Kate," she said. "You won't regret it."

"I'll see you Wednesday," I told her, knowing she was wrong.

Some interesting facts about the Palm Beach County Courthouse: With almost 700,000 square feet of floor space, it is the largest such structure in the state of Florida and one of the largest in the nation; it was designed by Michael A. Shiff and Associates and Hansen Lind Meyer, Engineers, and built by the George Hyman Construction Company; the exterior portico arch is 52 feet high and the interior waterfall is 30 feet tall; the vaulted roofs atop the building were designed to echo the twin towers of the Breakers Resort Hotel directly to the east in Palm Beach proper.

I gleaned this knowledge from a brochure I'd taken from the information desk in the lobby, while waiting to get into court on Wednesday morning. I also learned that the courthouse was designed with 44 courtrooms and the potential to expand to 60 when two empty floors are built out, and that a central recording studio handles audio from all the courtrooms piped to the studio and put on long-playing tapes. To review a portion of testimony in a courtroom, the judge merely phones the studio and asks for a playback. Amazing, I thought, smiling at the gray-haired old man standing behind the information desk. He was wearing a bright red vest emblazoned with the words "Clerk of the Court, Volunteer." He winked. I felt ancient.

Some other interesting data: There are now 3,780 attorneys practicing in Palm Beach County; the county's courts handled 311,072 cases filed the previous year, two-thirds of them traffic-related; more than 3 miles of shelves are needed to house the 3.6 million court files; there are 55 miles of telephone cable and 40 miles of computer cable; there are 56 holding cells for prisoners standing trial.

According to the brochure, the prisoners enter the building via jail buses that park in their own garage. They reach the courtrooms through a maze of holding cells, electronic lockdowns, special elevators and corridors. The deputies guarding the prisoners are outfitted with special infrared sensors that sound an alarm and automatically seal off an area if a deputy is knocked down. The state-of-the-art security system includes 274 video cameras, more than 200 infrared detectors, 200 intercoms, and more than 300 card-key doors.

At eight o'clock that morning, we were permitted entry into the main corridor. We stepped through the tall, heavy glass doors and through the metal detector, heading toward the bank of elevators to our right. The crowd was bigger than usual, although I recognized numerous faces from my previous visits. Eric was still supplying my sister with her morning cup of coffee. According to Jo Lynn, he hadn't missed a day. There were several others, and she pointed out each one, who showed up faithfully every morning. I wondered what these people would do once the trial was over. Did they have jobs or families to return to? Or would they simply find a new courtroom to visit, a new prisoner to focus their attentions on? In a way, the trial was a kind of drug, I understood, glancing across the wide corridor at the large auditorium-like room where potential jurors waited to hear if their names would be called. Would these judicial groupies experience a kind of withdrawal when it was all over? Would I? I wondered, realizing how much of my own life this trial had absorbed.

A well-stacked law library was located beside the jury office and across from the cafeteria. The cafeteria was open between eight and five, and always smelled of Javex. Two large escalators ran up and down on opposite sides of the corridor. There were more guards and another metal detector at the Quadrille Street entrance. I'm not sure when I became aware of such details. Perhaps they passed through me by osmosis as I waited for the elevator to take us to the eleventh floor. But such unnecessary facts were now a part of my life, and I was likely to retain them, in much the same way I would always know that Brenda Marshall had once been William Holden's wife.

"Do you ever worry about things?" Jo Lynn asked as we stepped out of the elevator and began the long march to the courtroom at the far end of the hall.

"What kind of things?" I asked.

"Silly things, things you shouldn't be worried about."

"Like what?"

"I don't know." Jo Lynn stared out the long windows as we walked down the hallway, the heels of her brown sandals clicking against the gray and black squares of the marble floor. She was wearing a white sweater and a long brown linen skirt, with buttons up the front, although the buttons were undone to her thighs. Tanned bare legs flashed briefly, then disappeared, with each step.

"Tell me," I said, genuinely curious. It was unlike Jo Lynn to be overly introspective.

"You'll think I'm crazy."

"I already think you're crazy."

She made a face. "You're 'kidding on the square,' " she said, her voice an exact duplicate of our mother's.

"What do you worry about?" I asked.

We passed through the large double doors and into the small, dark anteroom that preceded Courtroom 11A. "Like here," she said, stopping unexpectedly. "It's so dark. I sometimes worry about what it would be like if it

211

were always this dark. Sometimes, I close my eyes and pretend that I'm blind, like we used to do when we were kids, and I think: What would happen if when I opened my eyes, I still couldn't see? I mean, don't you think that would be awful? Not to be able to see anything, to be a prisoner of the darkness?"

"It would be awful not to see," I agreed, not sure where this was coming from. We stepped into the courtroom, were greeted immediately by a wall of sunlight. Jo Lynn walked directly to our seats, unmindful of the spectacular view. "What else do you worry about?" I asked, taking my seat beside her.

"I worry about getting cancer," she said.

"That's a pretty normal fear," I told her.

"Ovarian cancer, like Gilda Radner," she said.

"There's no history of ovarian cancer in our family," I assured her.

"Cancer's just so sneaky, don't you think? I mean, here's Gilda Radner, she's a famous TV star with a movie star husband, she has everything, and then one day maybe she gets a pain in her lower back or something, and she goes to the doctor and discovers that she has ovarian cancer, and a few months later, she's dead. Or that friend of yours from Pittsburgh, the one who was killed in that awful car accident? Here she was, driving along, probably listening to the radio, maybe even singing along, and one minute she's fine, and the next minute she's dead. And I hate that. I really hate that."

"It's a reminder of our own mortality."

"What?"

"We all worry about things like that occasionally," I said instead.

"You don't," she stated.

"Of course I do."

Her eyes searched mine for signs I might be mocking her. "You never seem like you worry about anything."

"I have the same worries as everybody else. Don't you think I'm human?"

She fidgeted uncomfortably in her seat. "It's just that you always seem to have everything under control. You know everything..."

"I don't know everything."

"Yes, you do. Or at least, that's the impression you give. Kate Sinclair, the woman who has everything, knows everything."

I listened to her voice for signs of bitterness, but there were none. She was just stating the facts as she believed them.

"But it's not true."

"Of course it is. Kate, face it. You're hopelessly put-together. You have the perfect life—a husband who adores you, two terrific kids, a great career, a gorgeous house, a designer wardrobe."

I stared guiltily down at my navy Donna Karan pantsuit.

"You have it all," she said. "No wonder it's so hard for Sara."

"Sara? What are you talking about?"

"You're a tough act to follow, Kate," she explained. "It's hard enough being your sister."

I was having trouble keeping up with the sudden shifts in the conversation. Hadn't we started out talking about Jo Lynn? How did we end up talking about me? And what did Sara have to do with anything? "What do you mean, it's hard for Sara? What is?"

"Being your daughter, knowing how high your expectations are, knowing that she'll never measure up."

"Did Sara tell you this?"

"Not in so many words, but we've talked about you a lot. I understand the sort of things she's going through."

I felt a stab of anxiety, like an ice pick to the heart. "The only expectations I have for Sara are that she go to school and be reasonably pleasant to live with."

"That's not true. You want her to be just like you."

"No, I don't."

"That's what she thinks."

"But it's not true. I just want her..."

"To be happy?" Jo Lynn said, our mother's voice resurfacing. "No—you want *you* to be happy *with* her. Michelle makes you happy because she's just like you. She has the same style as you. She wants the same things. But Sara's different, and you have to let her live her own life."

"Why are we talking about Sara?" I demanded testily.

Jo Lynn shrugged, looked away.

The courtroom was filling up. It was becoming uncomfortably warm. I undid the buttons of my jacket, fanned my face with the brochure I'd taken from the information desk in the lobby.

"So, what do you worry about?" Jo Lynn asked, as if daring me to prove I was human.

"I worry about the kids," I told her. "And about our mother."

"She'll outlive us all," Jo Lynn said dismissively. "Besides, that's too ordinary. Tell me something crazy that you worry about, something that doesn't make any sense."

"I worry about words losing their meaning," I heard myself say, surprised to be voicing these thoughts out loud. "That I'll be reading a book or the newspaper or something, and it'll be like reading a foreign language, the words won't make any sense."

"That's pretty crazy," Jo Lynn agreed, seemingly satisfied.

"And I worry about losing pieces of myself," I continued, even as I felt her interest waning, her attention drifting away. "That as I keep giving pieces of myself to everyone else, there won't be anything left over at the end of the day for me, that there won't be anything left *of* me." That I'll look in the mirror one morning, I continued silently, and there won't be anyone looking back.

"Oh God, there he is," Jo Lynn said, rising in her seat, waving toward the front of the courtroom.

Like a vampire, I thought, snapping out of my reverie, directing my attention to the real-life vampire coming through the door beside the judge's podium, a handsome man in a conservative blue suit, not unlike my own, a man whose greatest pleasure was sucking the life's blood from defenseless women and girls. And this man was smiling at my sister.

The clerk quickly called the court to order and we all rose as the judge assumed his seat at the podium. "Is the defense ready to proceed?" Judge Kellner asked.

Jake Archibald was on his feet, doing up the top button of his tan jacket. "We're ready, your honor."

"Call your first witness."

There was a collective intake of breath from the gallery of spectators as we waited to see who that witness would be.

The lawyer paused, took a deep breath of his own. "The defense calls Colin Friendly to the stand."

Chapter
15

State your name, please."

The accused killer leaned toward the slender black microphone in front of the witness stand and spoke softly into it, his eyes sweeping across the room before settling on the jury box. "Colin Friendly."

"And do you normally reside at 1500 Tenth Street in Lantana, Florida?"

"Yes, sir. I had an apartment there before

I was arrested." His voice was pleasant, his accent subtle and melodious. He spoke slowly, carefully enunciating each word.

"What's your occupation, Mr. Friendly?"

"I worked for a waterproofing company."

"In what capacity?"

"I was a foreman."

"And what sort of hours did you work?"

"Whatever hours the job required. Usually from eight till four. Sometimes later."

"Five days a week?"

"Sometimes seven," Colin Friendly stated. "It all depended on how busy we were."

"How old are you, Mr. Friendly?"

"Thirty-two."

"And what is your level of education?"

"I have two years of college."

"What college is that?"

"Florida State University."

"Have you ever been married?"

"Not yet." He smiled directly at Jo Lynn.

Jo Lynn squeezed my hand. My stomach turned over.

"Mr. Friendly," his lawyer began, "you're well aware of the charges against you?"

"I am."

"Is there any truth to those charges?"

"None."

"Did you rape and murder Marie Postelwaite?"

"No, sir."

"Did you rape and murder Christine McDermott?"

"No, sir."

"Did you rape and murder Tammy Fisher?"

"No, sir."

"Did you rape and murder Cathy Doran?"

"No, sir."

"Did you rape and murder Janet McMillan?"

"No, sir."

I found myself counting off each successive name on my fingers, my body growing increasingly numb.

"Did you rape and murder Susan Arnold?"

"No, sir."

"Did you rape and murder Marilyn Greenwood?"

"No, sir."

"Did you rape and murder Marni Smith?"

"No, sir."

"Did you rape and murder Judy Renquist?"

"No, sir."

Jo Lynn leaned toward me, whispered in my ear. "Look at his eyes. You just know he's telling the truth."

I looked at his eyes, saw only evil.

"Did you rape and murder Tracey Secord?" Jake Archibald continued.

"No, sir."

"Did you rape and murder Barbara Weston?"

"No, sir."

I stared at the jury. All eyes were riveted on the accused, all ears hanging on the defense's heartbreaking litany. Could there possibly be one among them who agreed with my sister? And if there was one, could there be more? Was there any chance that Colin Friendly might be acquitted, that he could walk from this courtroom a free man?

"Did you rape and murder Wendy Sabatello?" the defense attorney asked, almost at the end.

"No, sir."

"Did you rape and murder Maureen Elfer?" he concluded, the last of the thirteen unfortunate women.

"No, sir," came the automatic response.

Did you rape and murder Amy Lokash? I added silently. Did you smash her nose, stab her repeatedly, and leave her to die in some hostile swamp? Will we ever learn the truth about what happened to her?

"I could never hurt anybody," Colin Friendly said, as if speaking directly to me.

"Thank you, Mr. Friendly," his lawyer said. "No further questions." Jake Archibald returned to his seat, unbuttoned his jacket, nodded toward Howard Eaves, who rose to his feet, buttoning his.

"You could never hurt anybody," Howard Eaves repeated, speaking before he was fully out of his chair.

"No, sir."

"What about your mother?"

"My m-mother?" Colin Friendly stuttered briefly.

"Oh, see what that miserable man's done," Jo Lynn whispered. "He's upset him. It's okay, baby," she coached. "It'll be all right."

"Didn't you break your mother's nose, send her to the hospital?"

"Objection, your honor," the defense counsel stated, rising reluctantly to his feet. "Irrelevant and prejudicial."

Howard Eaves smiled, patted his thinning hair. "Colin Friendly opened the door to this line of questioning when he stated under direct examination that he would never hurt anybody. The state can prove otherwise. Goes to credibility, your honor."

"I'll allow it," Judge Kellner pronounced.

"Did you break your mother's nose and send her to the hospital?"

Colin Friendly lowered his head. "That was a l-long time ago, sir. I didn't mean to hurt her."

"Didn't you beat her so badly that she had to be hospitalized for almost a week?"

My sister squirmed indignantly in her seat. "The witch. She deserved it after the things she did to Colin."

Colin Friendly looked embarrassed, even ashamed. "I don't know how long she was in the hospital. I felt so terrible about what happened, I left t-town."

"Where is your mother now, Mr. Friendly?"

"I don't know, sir."

"Isn't it true that she went missing about six years ago?"

"Not to my knowledge, no."

"Well, let me ask you this: When was the last time you saw your mother?"

Colin Friendly shook his head, spoke with measured slowness. "It's been a long time."

"Six years?"

"Maybe."

"Did you have anything to do with her disappearance?"

Again, Jake Archibald was on his feet. "Objection, your honor. We have no proof that anything untoward has happened to Mr. Friendly's mother, nor is he on trial for anything concerning her."

"Sustained."

"Well done," my sister said, as Jake Archibald resumed his seat.

Howard Eaves was undaunted. He faced the jury while directing his questions at the accused. "Tell me, Mr. Friendly, did you know any of the murdered women?"

"No, sir."

"You'd never met any of them?"

"Not to my knowledge. I was p-pretty busy working," he continued, then swallowed, as if trying to swallow his stutter. "You don't meet a lot of women in the waterproofing business." He flashed one of his patented little half-smiles toward the jury. Several responded with little half-smiles of their own.

"What about the testimony of the witnesses who placed you near some of the victims at around the time of their disappearances?"

"They're m-mistaken, sir."

"You never attended a party at 426 Lakeview Drive in Boynton Beach?"

"No, sir."

"You never spoke to a young woman named Angela Riegert?"

"No, sir."

"And yet she positively identified you."

"She m-must be confusing me with s-somebody else."

"You never left the party with Wendy Sabatello?"

"I wasn't at the party, sir," Colin Friendly replied clearly. "Why would I be there? I'm a l-lot older than those kids."

"And what about Marcia Layton, who testified having seen you in Flagler Park on several occasions?"

"It's p-possible she saw me," he admitted. "Sometimes when I'd be working, I'd go to a nearby p-park to have my lunch."

"Did you meet Marni Smith in the park?"

"No, sir."

"Did you ask directions from Janet McMillan?"

"No, sir. I've l-lived in Florida all my life. I pretty much know where everything is."

"So, you're saying that, to the best of your knowledge, you've never had any contact with any of the murdered women?"

"None, sir."

"And all the witnesses who have positively identified you are mistaken," Howard Eaves stated rather than asked.

"Yes, sir."

"Seems strange, doesn't it? That so many people would have identified you incorrectly."

"A l-lot of people look the way I do," Colin Friendly volunteered.

"You think so?"

"There's nothing very special about me."

"Unfortunately, that's all too true," the prosecutor said.

Jake Archibald immediately objected, and Howard Eaves retracted his comment.

"How do you explain the seventy percent probability that it was your semen found in many of the victims' bodies?"

Colin Friendly shook his head, his lips a cruel snarl. "Seventy percent's barely a passing grade."

"Are you disputing the conclusions of the medical examiner?"

"If he says it's my semen, then he's wrong."

"And the bite marks on several of the victims? How do you explain how closely they match the mold taken of your mouth?"

"Close only counts in horseshoes," Colin Friendly said without a trace of stammer. The snarl twisted into a smirk. He winked boldly at my sister, then settled back in his chair, as if he'd somehow gained the upper hand.

"How do you explain the close matchup with your saliva?"

"It's not my job to explain it, Mr. Eaves."

"But if you had to make a guess..."

"I'd say that someone obviously made a mistake."

"I suggest that someone is you, Mr. Friendly."

"I suggest that someone is you, Mr. Eaves," came the immediate retort.

A slight gasp rippled through the courtroom.

"You think you're smarter than I am, don't you, Mr. Friendly?"

"I can't say I've given the matter much thought, Mr. Eaves."

"In fact, you think you're smarter than most people, isn't that correct?"

"Most people aren't very smart," Colin agreed, clearly starting to enjoy himself.

"And it's fun tricking them, isn't it?"

"You tell me, Mr. Eaves. Seems like you're the one interested in tricking people."

"It's a great feeling having the power of life and death over people, isn't it, Mr. Friendly?"

"You're the one here with that kind of power, sir, not me."

"No. That power rests with the members of the jury."

"Then I can only hope they'll be more interested in the truth than you are," Colin stated coolly.

"And the truth is?"

"That I'm not guilty, sir."

Jo Lynn leaned toward me. "He's very polite, don't you think?"

The prosecutor thrust a large color photograph of one of the dead girls into Colin Friendly's face. "You didn't do this?"

Jake Archibald was immediately on his feet. "Objection, your honor. This is unnecessary. The witness has already answered the question."

"Overruled."

"Your honor," Jake Archibald said, "may we approach?"

The two adversaries approached the bench.

"Damn that Mr. Eaves," Jo Lynn whispered. "He'll stop at nothing to get a conviction." She crossed, uncrossed, then recrossed her legs, her skirt flipping back and forth, exposing first one thigh, then the other, then the first again. "But I don't think the jury's buying it. See that woman, the one in the middle in the second row, I think she's on our side."

I looked toward the middle juror in the second row. She was younger than the other members of the jury, maybe thirty years old, with pale skin and badly styled blond hair that did nothing to enhance her generally nondescript features. I realized that I'd never noticed her before, and wondered if not being noticed was something she'd grown used to. Would she be the type to be charmed by the likes of Colin Friendly? Was this trial her chance to step into the spotlight, to grab for her fifteen minutes of fame, to force a nation's attention her way by being the lone hold-out for an acquittal? Would her obstinacy force a retrial?

I shuddered, not having considered the possibility of a hung jury until now. Anxiety tugged at my heart. Why couldn't the forensic evidence have been more conclusive? "Close only counts in horseshoes," I heard Colin repeat. All it took was one not-guilty vote, I realized. And then what? Another trial? More months of anguish for the victims' families and friends? More months of headlines and depressing news reports? More months of my sister haunting courtooms and visiting jails? I sighed deeply. I didn't think I could go through it again.

"Something the matter?" Jo Lynn asked, eyes scanning the room.

"It's hot in here."

"No, it's not. You're just warm because your boyfriend's here."

"What?" I spun around. Robert smiled at me from his seat at the back. Oh God, I thought, perspiration breaking out across my forehead. When had he come in?

"Relax, Kate. Nobody's going to spill your little secret."

"I don't have any secrets," I hissed between clenched teeth.

Jo Lynn smiled. "Tell it to the judge," she said.

"The objection is overruled," the judge was saying, sending the lawyers back to their battle stations. "The witness may answer the question."

"This isn't your handiwork?" Howard Eaves repeated immediately, handing the photo to the defendant.

"No, sir."

"What about this?" The prosecutor pushed a series of pictures into Colin's hands. "You didn't leave those bite marks on Christine McDermott's buttocks? You didn't slit little Tammy Fisher's throat?"

"No, sir. I c-certainly did not."

"And yet, I notice that you have no trouble looking at the photographs."

"Objection, your honor," Jake Archibald protested.

"Sustained."

"I c-could never do anything like that." Colin Friendly looked directly at my sister. "You have to believe me, Jo Lynn."

"I believe you, Colin." Heads snapped toward us as my sister rose to her feet.

"Sit down, young lady," the judge ordered, banging on his gavel, as excited whispers spun circles around us.

"It doesn't matter what anybody else thinks," Colin continued, "as long as I know you believe in me."

The entire courtroom now pivoted in our direction. I found myself holding my breath. Oh God, I thought, please let this be all a bad dream.

"I love you, Jo Lynn," Colin Friendly was saying over the mounting din. "I want to marry you."

"Order in the court," Judge Kellner bellowed.

"I love you too," my sister cried. "There's nothing I want more than to be your wife."

The courtroom erupted, people laughing, hooting with surprise, reporters scrambling for the door, everyone on their feet at once.

"Sit down," the judge ordered my sister, "or I'll hold you in contempt."

"Please, no," I muttered, feeling sick to my stomach.

In the next instant, I was pushing past my sister into the aisle and out of the courtroom.

"We'll take a half-hour recess," I heard

the judge shout as I reached the darkness of the small anteroom.

"Kate, hurry," a voice beckoned. "This way." An arm pulled me into the corridor, guided me into the sanctuary of the empty courtroom next door.

"Oh God," I cried, my body heaving, my breath coming in short, angry bursts. "Were you there? Did you see what happened?"

"I was there," Robert said.

"Did you see what they did? Did you hear what they said?"

His arms reached for me. "Kate, try to calm down."

"She told that monster she'd marry him. Right out in open court, my sister stood up and told the world she loves a crazy man, that she wants to marry him."

"Kate, it's all right, it'll be all right."

I was sobbing now. "Why is she doing this, Robert? What is she trying to prove? Does she want the publicity, is that it? Does she want to be a star on *Hard Copy*? Does she want to make the front page of the *National Enquirer*? What is the matter with her?"

His arms were around me. "I don't know what her problem is, but you can't let it get to you."

"You don't think that she'll really marry that monster, do you? I mean, you don't think that the jury will actually find him not guilty, that there's any chance they'll let him go."

"I don't think there's a chance in hell of that happening."

"I want him to die," I cried. "I want him to die and get out of our lives."

"Ssh," Robert said gently as I buried my face against his chest. "Don't worry. It'll all be over soon."

He held me tight against him, one hand stroking the back of my hair, as if I were a small child who'd scraped her knee and needed comforting. My own arms reached around him, clung to him as if I were drowning, as if he were the only thing keeping me afloat. His lips grazed the sides of my cheeks, kissing away my tears, assuring me without words that everything would be all right, that he was there to ensure that nothing bad could ever happen to me again.

And then he was kissing me, really kissing me, full on the lips, and I was kissing him back, with a passion that astounded me. Suddenly, I was a sophomore in high school and he was a senior, and our lives were just beginning and everything was right with the world.

Except that we were no longer in high school, our lives were half over, and my world was quickly disintegrating into dust. "This is the last thing I need," I told Robert, breaking free of his embrace, trying to make sense of what was happening.

But even as I regained my composure and walked from the room, past the throng of reporters who crowded the corridors clamoring for my sister's attention, and toward the bank of waiting elevators, I knew it was too late, that there was a very good chance my world would never make sense again.

Chapter
16

I tried burying myself in my work. It wasn't easy. Everywhere I looked, there were my sister and her "fiance," as she had taken to referring to him on television and in print. Their pictures tormented me from the front pages of every newspaper and tabloid in town; Jo Lynn gave interviews to *Hard Copy* and appeared twice on *Inside Edition,* although on both broadcasts she mercifully refrained from mentioning she had a sister. Since our last names were different—she went by her second husband's name because she liked the sound of it with Jo Lynn—no one made the connection between us. Because we never traveled in the same circles, her newfound notoriety was not a problem to me either socially or professionally. Still, I was embarrassed—I like to think more for her sake than for mine, but truthfully, I'm not sure—and deeply concerned about both my sister's mental state and her well-being.

Sara, of course, pronounced the situation "cool"; Larry, as usual, ignored the whole business; Michelle asked simply, "What's *wrong* with her?" As for my mother, she seemed oblivious to the commotion raging around her younger child. She never commented on the many stories in the newspapers or the ubiquitous interviews on TV. When I asked if she'd seen Jo Lynn's picture on the front page of the *Palm Beach Post*, she said only that I should save her a copy, then never mentioned it again. Only Mrs. Winchell called to voice her concerns, her main worry being that all the publicity might adversely impact on the Palm Beach Lakes Retirement Home should it become known that Jo Lynn's mother was a resident, and perhaps we might consider moving her someplace else. She needn't have worried. Jo Lynn showed no inclination to share the spotlight.

Robert phoned on an almost daily basis, but I was afraid to return his calls. Surely my life was chaotic enough without the addition of an extramarital affair, although his messages made no mention of what had happened between us. He asked only if I'd come up with any ideas, professionally speaking, and said nothing about the decidedly unprofessional kiss we had shared. Actually, I did have an idea I thought was pretty good, but I was growing increasingly fearful of both him and the media, and was no longer sure I wanted any part of either. Besides, if I were to have my own show, then surely, at some point, some ambitious reporter would discover the connection between my sister and me. Indeed, Jo Lynn would probably be my first caller.

"My sister's always criticizing me," I could hear her shout across the airwaves. "She doesn't approve of my choice of clothes or my choice

231

of men. She doesn't think I'm capable of making an adult decision without her input. Just because she's a professional, she thinks she knows everything. She's always telling me what to do and I'm sick of it. What do you advise?"

"I'm sorry, what did you say?" It was almost six o'clock one evening, and Ellie and Richard Lifeson, a young couple in their late twenties, were staring at me expectantly across the coffee table in my office, obviously awaiting some inspired words of wisdom to tumble from my lips. I realized that I had no idea what we'd been discussing, and silently cursed Jo Lynn, blaming her for my inability to concentrate. Immediately, I was back in the courtroom, watching as the accused serial killer proclaimed his love for my sister for all to hear. What had Colin Friendly hoped to prove with his little stunt? What had he been trying to gain? Sympathy? Support? What? "What?" I asked again, as Ellie and Richard Lifeson exchanged worried glances. "I'm sorry, could you repeat what you just said?"

"She's always telling me what to do, and I'm sick of it," Richard Lifeson repeated.

"I don't tell him what to do," his wife protested.

They were a nice-looking couple, fresh-faced and well scrubbed. They'd been married three years; it was the first marriage for both; they had no children; they were contemplating divorce. I checked my notes to reacquaint myself with the particulars of their situation, then my watch to determine how much of the session I'd already missed.

"Are you kidding?" Richard Lifeson asked. "Tell her what happened right before we got here."

"Why don't *you* tell me," I suggested, concentrating on his wide forehead, his square jaw, in a concerted effort to keep Colin Friendly out of my office, out of my thoughts.

"I wanted to buy some potato chips," he began, "and she tells me to get that new low-fat kind. I don't like the low-fat kind, they have no taste, and why should she care, she doesn't eat them anyway. But, of course, what kind do I end up having to buy? Guess."

"I never said you had to buy them. I just made a suggestion."

"Her Majesty never suggests anything. She issues proclamations."

"There he goes again, putting me down. He's always putting me down. I can't say one thing to him without his putting me down."

"Like what?" Richard Lifeson asked. "When do I put you down?"

"Try last night when we went to my niece's ballet recital," Ellie Lifeson answered before I could step in. "After it was over, he asked me which dance I liked best and I told him I liked the one with the swans, and he said, 'That just shows how little you know about ballet.' And we end up in this huge fight, so, of course, we go to bed angry, and we don't make love. Again," she added pointedly.

"You going to order me to make love to you now?" Richard Lifeson demanded.

"Okay, wait, wait," I said calmly. "There are a lot of issues here. Let's try to take them one at a time. First, with regard to the potato chips: Ellie, you think you're being helpful; Richard, you think she's being dictatorial. This is a gender issue. Women think they're making suggestions. Men hear them as orders."

"I'm not allowed to make suggestions?"

"I know it won't be easy, Ellie, but try to curb your desire to help out. And, Richard, you have to learn to stand your ground. If you don't want low-fat potato chips, you have to say so."

"And get into a huge argument?"

"You get into a huge argument anyway," I told him. "Maybe not about the potato chips, but all that repressed anger is going to come out somewhere."

"She's the one who's always angry."

"Because you're always putting me down."

"Try to avoid words like 'always' and 'never.' They're counterproductive and inflammatory. And, Ellie, remember that nobody can put you down unless you allow it. Let me show you how the conversation after the ballet recital could have gone. Ellie, I'll be you; you be Richard. 'So, Richard,' " I began, addressing my comments to Ellie, " 'which dance did you like best?' "

Ellie automatically deepened her voice, speaking as if she were Richard. " 'I liked the modern one at the end. What about you?' "

" 'I liked the one with the swans,' " I told her.

" 'That just shows how little you know about ballet,' " Ellie huffed.

" 'You didn't like it?' "

" 'I thought it was terrible.' "

" 'That's very interesting,' " I said. " 'I liked it. I guess we have different tastes.' "

Ellie and Richard stared at me in silence.

"You see?" I said. "Nobody gets put down; nobody fights."

"It's that simple?" Richard asked.

"Nothing's simple," I told him. "It's a whole new way of relating, a brand-new vocabulary. It'll take time to learn, even more time to put into practice. But eventually, it gets a little easier."

They looked skeptical.

"I promise," I said.

At home, Larry and I were at each other's throats.

"Sara's teacher called today," I announced one evening as Larry sat, feet comfortably up on the ottoman, watching a hockey game on TV. The girls were in their rooms, supposedly doing homework.

"What did she have to say?"

"Who said her teacher is a woman?"

"Sorry, I just assumed."

"Are all teachers necessarily female?"

"Of course not. What did this teacher have to say?"

"She said that Sara has been…"

"*She?*" Larry asked. "So, her teacher *is* a woman?"

"This one is, yes."

"The one who called."

"Yes. What's the big deal?"

"You're the one who made it a big deal," he said.

"Are you interested in what she had to say or not?"

"Yes, I said I was."

"I don't remember you saying any such thing."

"Maybe if you paid attention."

"You're saying you don't get enough attention?"

"Just tell me what Sara's teacher had to say," he said.

"She said that Sara has been acting very strangely."

"She just noticed?" He smiled.

I refused the chance to smile back. "Stranger than usual," I said.

"How so?"

"Nothing she could put her finger on."

"That's helpful."

"Are you going to treat this whole conversation as a joke?"

"I'm certainly not going to get all worked up about it."

"You never do."

"What's that supposed to mean?"

"It means that I'm starting to feel like a single parent around here."

"Excuse me? You want to clarify that statement?"

"It means you're never here."

"I'm *never* here?"

"You're always on the golf course."

"I'm *always* on the golf course?"

"When you're not at work," I qualified.

"Oh, so I work. Well, thanks for noticing."

"It really doesn't bother you that our daughter is failing?"

"She's failing?"

"She failed her last two English tests."

"Have you talked to her about it?"

"Why should I be the one who talks to her about it?"

"All right. Do you want me to talk to her about it?"

"And just what would you say?"

He was on his feet. "I don't know. I guess I'll find out when I get there."

"I don't think you should put her on the defensive."

"I wasn't planning to put her on the defensive."

"Just tell her that her teacher called and that she's very concerned about Sara's recent behavior."

"If you're going to tell me what to say, why don't you talk to her yourself?"

"Because I always talk to her, and I'm tired of being the one who takes care of everybody's problems. I do it all day at work, and when I come home, I'd like somebody else to shoulder a little bit of the responsibility. Is that too much to ask?"

"Apparently, since you won't let me do it."

"I'm just trying to help you. Is your ego so frail that you can't take a few simple suggestions?"

"Is your ego so inflated that you can't imagine I might not need them?"

"You're really a bastard sometimes, you know that?"

He flipped off the television, walked out of the family room.

"Where are you going?"

"To bed."

"I thought we were having a discussion."

"The discussion is over."

"Why? Because you say it is?"

"That's right."

I followed him into our bedroom. "That's very mature."

"I thought one of us should be."

"Meaning?"

He reached the bed, started throwing pillows into the air. "I don't want to fight with you, Kate. I don't have the strength. I'm tired. You've been on my back all week."

"I've been on your back?"

"Yes."

"How could I be on your back when you're never here?"

"I don't know, but you manage." He tossed the remaining pillows on the floor. One landed close to my feet.

"Watch that!" I yelped, as if I'd been injured.

He looked startled. "Watch what?"

"You almost hit me with that."

"What are you talking about? It's nowhere near you." He pulled down the covers of the bed, started undressing.

"Don't you dare go to sleep," I told him.

"Kate, it's been a long day. You're obviously all worked up about something, and I don't think it has anything to do with either Sara or me."

"Oh, really? And when did you earn your psychology degree?"

"Let's stop before we say things we'll regret."

"I don't want to stop. I want to know what you think I'm so worked up about."

"I don't know. Maybe your sister, maybe your mother, maybe something happened at work that I don't know about."

"Or maybe it's you," I shot back.

"Maybe it is," he agreed. "Maybe you're right, and I'm the problem. I accept it. You've made your point. You win. I'm a rotten human being."

"I never said you were a rotten human being."

"I'm sure you were getting to it."

"Don't put words in my mouth."

"I'd like to put a gag in your mouth."

"What?" I gasped. "Are you threatening me?"

Anger flushed his cheeks bright red. "I'm suggesting that we both shut up and try to get some sleep."

"You're telling me to shut up?"

"I'm telling you to get some sleep."

"I don't want to get some sleep."

"Then shut the fuck up!" he shouted, and climbed into bed.

And then he didn't say another word. No matter what I said or did, how much I tried to provoke him, how hard I tried to pull him back into the fray, he wouldn't bite. Instead, he withdrew, burying himself inside his covers as if inside a cocoon. The harder I tried to drag him out, the farther he retreated.

I accused him of being a poor husband, a bad father, an indifferent son.

He sighed and turned over.

I accused him of caring more for his golf game than his family.

He put a pillow over his ears.

I said he was selfish, childish, and mean.

He brought the comforter up over his head.

I told him he was being passive-aggressive.

He feigned sleep.

I told him to go to hell.

He pretended to snore.

I stormed from the room.

We didn't speak for three days.

It didn't help that I knew Larry was right. He wasn't the problem. Maybe I would have liked it had he spent more time at home on the weekends, but, truthfully, I didn't begrudge him his golf games. Maybe I was even a little jealous. At least Larry had somewhere to go, a place to escape the insanity that seemed everywhere around us. I had nowhere. Work didn't help—it only compounded my confusion. I was so busy being in control at the office that I was losing it at home. Larry was my scapegoat, and for a while, he seemed to understand this, but there's only so much understanding a person can have.

What I really wanted was for Larry to take me in his arms, as Robert had done that morning in the courthouse, and to tell me that everything was going to be okay: Sara would get out of high school and into the college of her choice; my mother would slough off her alien skin and become the woman I'd known and loved all my life; my sister would get off the front pages and back to her senses; Colin Friendly would die and we'd get on with our lives. Was that too much to ask?

But even when Larry did just that, it wasn't enough.

"It's okay," he said one evening as I cried softly against his shoulder. The trial had concluded that afternoon, and despite predictions of a speedy verdict, the jury had been out for over five hours. Reporters were now speculating that if a verdict wasn't returned within the hour, the jury would be dismissed for the weekend.

"What could possibly be taking them so long?" I asked.

"I think they're just going over all the evidence, and that by this time on Monday, it'll all be over," Larry said, telling me what he knew I needed to hear. "Colin Friendly will be on death row; your sister will be back to normal. Well, normal is a relative concept when it comes to your sister," he said, and I laughed gratefully. And then we were kissing, softly at first, and then with greater urgency.

It had been several weeks, I realized, since we'd made love. In fact, the last time a man had kissed me this way, it hadn't been Larry at all, but Robert. "Oh God," I said guiltily.

Of course, Larry misinterpreted my guilt for passion, and suggested we go into the bedroom. It was Friday night and the girls were both out for the evening.

"Do you think this is a good idea?" I asked between kisses, as he led me into our room, stopping beside our bed.

"Best idea I've had in weeks," he said, sending the fourteen decorative pillows to the floor with one wide sweep of his arm.

"What if the kids come home?"

"They won't."

"What if they do?"

"I'll close the door," he said, leaving my side to close the door. In the next instant, his lips were back on mine, and his hands were at my breasts, undoing my blouse. "I've missed you," he said, slipping the blouse off my shoulders and onto the carpet.

"I've missed you too," I told him, as his fingers gently teased my nipples through the lace of my bra. "That tickles," I said, feeling mildly irritated, though I wasn't sure why.

His fingers fidgeted with the hooks of my bra.

"I'll do it," I said.

"No, let me," he urged softly. "I'm just a

little out of practice, that's all." He struggled for several more seconds before I ran out of patience and reached behind me to unsnap the recalcitrant hooks.

"I wanted to do that," he said.

"Don't whine," I started to say, but he covered my mouth with his kisses, and pushed me down on the bed, his lips moving to my bare breasts, fastening themselves on my nipples.

In the past, this was always something I enjoyed. Now it annoyed me. As Larry sucked on first one breast, then the other, I found myself growing increasingly angry. "That tickles," I said again, squirming away from his insistent mouth.

He moved on, undoing the zipper of my gray trousers and sliding them easily off my hips.

"Careful with those," I admonished as he tossed them aside, his fingers tracing the outline of my lace panties, his lips returning to my nipples. I felt nothing, no sexual stirring of any kind. Just growing irritability. I tried fantasizing: I was a slave girl being auctioned off to the highest bidder. There were perhaps a dozen men pawing me, lifting my skirt to inspect the merchandise, exposing me to their hungry eyes...

It didn't work. I tried another. I was a college student whose professor had given her a failing grade. What could I do? I begged him. I'd already told my parents I was getting straight A's. I could come to him after class, he told me, wearing nothing but a garter belt and stockings...

I shook my head, pushed Larry's head away from my breasts. Nothing was working.

Larry pulled my panties down, buried his head between my thighs. I waited anxiously to feel some release, felt nothing but frustration.

"That hurts," I told him after several minutes.

"Just relax," he said. "You're so uptight."

"I'm uptight because you're hurting me."

"How am I hurting you?"

"You're applying too much pressure."

He shifted his weight, adjusted his position. "How's this? Better?"

"You're not in the right place," I said, my voice testy.

"Show me."

"I don't want to show you."

He raised himself on his elbows. "What's wrong, honey?"

"You're not in the right place," I repeated stubbornly, knowing I was being unfair, knowing the right place was anywhere away from me. "Let's just forget it. It's not going to work."

"Let me try again," he said.

"No," I said loudly, drawing my legs together, staring toward the window. I didn't have to see his face to feel the hurt on it.

The phone rang.

"Don't answer it," Larry pleaded softly.

I reached over, grateful for the interruption, and lifted the receiver to my ear. "Hello," I said as Larry turned away.

"Kate, oh God, Kate." It was Jo Lynn. She was sobbing.

"What is it? What's happened?"

"The jury came back. They just announced their verdict."

I held my breath. Was she sobbing from disappointment or relief?

"I can't believe it, Kate. They found him guilty. Guilty!"

I closed my eyes. Thank God, I uttered silently.

"Are you all right?" I asked my sister as Larry edged his body off the bed.

"I can't believe it," she repeated. "How could they do that when he didn't do it? It's so unfair."

"Do you want to come over?" I asked as Larry walked from the room.

I could feel her shaking her head. "No. I don't know what to do."

"I think you should go home, get a good night's sleep..."

"They found him guilty," she cried, not listening to me. "He's my whole life. Oh God, Kate, what am I going to do now?"

Chapter
17

Two days before Christmas, my mother disappeared.

I was in the middle of an argument with Sara when the phone rang. "Could you get that?" I asked. We were in the family room, and I was on my knees, stacking the last of the Christmas presents around the tall, ornament-laden spruce tree.

Sara remained where she was, in the middle of the room, impossibly long legs planted firmly apart on the tile floor, stubborn hands poised on improbably slim hips. She was wearing elasticized black leggings, a cherry-red, too short, too tight tank top, and ankle-length black boots with three-inch heels that exaggerated her already considerable height. Her hair, like parchment paper, had yellowed from continual exposure to the sun, except for the dark roots that framed her oval face like a wide headband. To say she was a formidable-looking opponent would be something of an understatement. In fact, she was terrifying. "The answering machine will pick it up," she said, not budging. "Why won't you give me any money?"

"Because I don't feel like paying for my own Christmas presents again this year," I told her truthfully, as the phone fell mercifully silent. "I think you're old enough now to be buying gifts for people with your own money."

"What money?"

"Money you're supposed to have saved. Christmas isn't exactly a surprise. You've had lots of time to prepare. Michelle's been saving her money for months." I knew it was a mistake the minute the words were out of my mouth.

"Sure, compare me with Michelle, why don't you?" Sara threw her arms into the air, in a gesture that was simultaneously threatening and full of defeat.

"I didn't mean to compare you with Michelle."

"You're always comparing us. Little Miss Perfect, she can't do anything wrong. Little Miss Bitch," she sneered.

"Sara! Stop it right now. Leave your sister out of this."

"You're the one who brought her in."

"Yes, and I'm sorry."

"So nobody will get any presents from me this year because I don't have any money," she repeated.

I shrugged. "That's too bad."

"Yeah, you sound really broken up about it."

The phone rang again.

"You're determined to embarrass me, aren't you?" Sara continued, trying a new approach. "Just because I'm not organized like Michelle, because I'm different than you guys, you're trying to punish me."

God help me, I thought, clambering to my feet, heading for the phone on the counter that separated the kitchen from the family room. "Hello."

"Mrs. Sinclair?"

"Yes."

"Thank God. I tried you a few minutes ago and got your machine."

"Mrs. Winchell?" I asked, connecting a face to the harried voice on the other end of the line. "What's wrong? Has something happened to my mother?"

There was an ominous silence. "Then she's not with you?"

247

"If I were Michelle, I bet you'd give me the money," Sara raged, pacing back and forth in front of the counter.

"What do you mean?" I asked Mrs. Winchell.

"I mean, if I were Michelle, there wouldn't be any problem," Sara said.

"We can't find your mother," Mrs. Winchell said.

"What do you mean, you can't find my mother?" I demanded. "Would you stop that!" I shouted at my daughter, whose pacing came to an abrupt halt.

"I beg your pardon?" Mrs. Winchell asked sheepishly.

"Don't yell at me," Sara snapped.

"Please tell me what happened," I urged Mrs. Winchell.

Mrs. Winchell cleared her throat, paused, cleared it again. "Your mother didn't come down for breakfast this morning, and when we went to check on her, we discovered she wasn't in her apartment, and her bed hadn't been slept in. I was hoping that she was with you, what with Christmas and everything, and that you'd just forgotten to inform us."

"She isn't here." My eyes shot aimlessly around the room, as if my mother might be hiding behind the large silk palm tree in the corner.

"Is there any chance she's with your sister?"

"None," I said, then promised to check with her anyway. "Have you searched the building?"

"Who's missing?" Sara asked. "Is Grandma missing?"

248

"We're searching it now."

"I'll be there as soon as I can."

"I'm sure we'll find her," Mrs. Winchell said, although the quiver in her voice told me otherwise. "If she's wandered off somewhere, she can't have gotten very far."

If she's been walking all night, she could be halfway to Georgia by now, I thought as I punched in my sister's number, picturing my mother walking along the center line of the freeway, falling off a bridge into the Intracoastal Waterway, or wading fully clothed into the ocean.

"Jo Lynn, is Mom with you?" I asked as soon as I heard my sister's voice.

"Is this a joke?" she asked in return.

"She's missing. I'll pick you up in five minutes," I said, hanging up before she could object, grabbing my purse, and running for the door.

"I'm coming with you," Sara said, right behind me.

I didn't object. Truthfully, I was grateful for the company.

"Have you found her?" I demanded as my sister, my daughter, and I stormed into Mrs. Winchell's office. We must have been quite a sight—my yellow-haired Amazonian daughter with her black roots, three-inch heels, and forty-inch bosom, my similarly endowed sister, her hair wild and uncombed, with her white mini-dress barely grazing the top of her thighs, and me with no makeup, blue

249

jeans, and crazed visage, all of us towering above poor, petite Mrs. Winchell, who took several instinctive steps back when she saw us.

"Not yet," she said, her dark face pinched with worry, "but I'm sure we will."

"How can you be sure," Jo Lynn said, "when you have no idea where she is?"

"Have you notified the police?" I asked.

"Of course. They're keeping their eyes open for her. So far, they haven't found..."

"...any bodies," Jo Lynn said.

"Anyone matching her description," Mrs. Winchell corrected.

"Half of Florida matches her description," my sister told her.

"And in the meantime," I interrupted, "what's being done?"

"We've searched all the common rooms, and the kitchen, and the garage. So far, nothing. We have staff checking all the floors."

"I don't understand, how could this have happened?" I knew the question was pointless, but asked it anyway.

"It's hard to keep track of everyone twenty-four hours a day. This isn't a hospital. It's strictly a facility for assisted living," Mrs. Winchell reminded me, as I marveled over the phrase "assisted living." 'The residents are free to come and go as they please. We check on them every morning, of course. If someone doesn't come down for breakfast and they haven't previously informed us, then well..." Her voice drifted off. "I'm sure she'll turn up."

"Bad pennies always do," Jo Lynn said, only half under her breath.

I almost smiled. Despite the circumstances, it was nice to know that my sister seemed to have snapped out of her self-imposed mourning and was back to her usual caustic self. Our mother always managed to bring out the best in her, I thought, wondering where on earth she could be.

It was almost two hours before they found her.

A janitor discovered her hiding behind the central air-conditioning unit in the main utility room. She'd somehow managed to squeeze between the unit and the wall, a not inconsiderable feat, considering the tiny amount of space, and it took three workers almost half an hour to extricate her. When they finally brought her to Mrs. Winchell's office, she was bruised and whimpering, and the front of her mint-green dress was dirty and torn.

"My turn to hide now?" Jo Lynn asked when she saw her.

I rushed to my mother's side, took her in my arms, hugged her gently to me. "Are you all right?"

"Hello, dear," she said. "What are you doing here?"

"What happened, Grandma?" Sara asked, laying a gentle hand on her grandmother's back. "Why were you hiding behind the air conditioner?"

"Someone was after me," my mother confided with a wink. "But I tricked them."

"Were you there all night?" I asked.

"I don't know," she answered, rubbing her arms. "Maybe. I'm a little stiff."

"You must be hungry," Mrs. Winchell said. "I'll arrange to have some breakfast sent to your room, and of course we'll get you all cleaned up and have a doctor look at you."

"Who was after you?" Sara asked.

"I don't know." My mother's unsteady hands reached over to stroke Sara's hair. "You're a pretty thing, aren't you?" she said. "Are you new here?"

I watched Sara's features crumple even as her eyes grew wide. "Don't you recognize me, Grandma?" she asked, her voice as small as a child's. "It's me, Sara, your granddaughter."

"Sara?"

"I've changed my hair color," Sara explained.

"So you have," my mother said, and smiled. "I think I'd like to lie down now." Watery eyes swept across the room. "Would you mind? I seem to be very tired."

"Of course not," I told her. "You rest for a while. We'll see you later."

"It was the hair color," Sara said as we crossed the parking lot to my car. "That's why she didn't recognize me. It's my hair."

"Time to get those roots done, kid," my sister said.

"My mother won't give me any money."

I unlocked the car door. We climbed inside, Sara beside me, Jo Lynn in the back. Jo Lynn's hand instantly flopped over the front seat, waved five twenty-dollar bills beside Sara's head. "Here. My treat. Christmas comes a day early."

"Wow. This is so cool."

"You're in a good mood," I said, deciding not to be angry with Jo Lynn's impromptu generosity.

"Our mother is safe," she said sarcastically, flopping back in her seat. "All is right with the world."

"Who do you think was after her?" Sara asked.

"Her conscience," Jo Lynn said.

"Her conscience?" Sara repeated.

"What's that supposed to mean?" I asked.

"It means I'm hungry," Jo Lynn said. "It means we stop for lunch. My treat."

"I don't have time," I began.

"Everybody has time to eat," Jo Lynn pronounced. "What kind of example are you setting for your daughter? You want her to turn into one of those scrawny anorexics?"

I didn't think there was much chance of that, but I agreed to stop for lunch.

"We'll go to the mall," Jo Lynn said as I turned onto I-95. "That way, we can eat, Sara can get her hair done, and we can do some last-minute Christmas shopping."

"Not me," Sara said. "Mom won't give me any money to buy presents."

"Mean Mommy," Jo Lynn said, and laughed. "Don't worry, kid, I have lots of money. You can buy whatever you want."

"And where is all this money coming from?" I asked. "Did you get a job?"

Jo Lynn made a sound halfway between a laugh and a snort. "You don't want to know," she said.

I decided she was probably right, so I said nothing further.

Sara, however, had no such qualms. "Where'd you get the money?" she asked.

Jo Lynn required no further prompting. She lurched forward, leaned her elbows on the back of the front seat, rested her head on her hands. "I promised the *Enquirer* an exclusive. They paid me half the money in advance."

"An exclusive what?" Sara asked as I tried to block my ears to the inevitable.

I could feel Jo Lynn's smile burning a hole in the back of my neck. "An exclusive on my wedding," she said.

"What is it going to take to convince you that the man you're so intent on marrying is a homicidal maniac?" I asked Jo Lynn as soon as Sara took off to get her hair done. We were sitting in the crowded food court on the second level of the Gardens Mall, Jo Lynn taking her time with a piece of apple pie, me on my fourth cup of coffee.

"Nothing you could say would ever convince me, so you might as well stop wasting your breath."

"Don't you understand that the man would just as soon kill you as look at you?"

"Don't *you* understand that I really don't appreciate these kinds of comments?"

"And *I* don't appreciate you undermining my authority."

"What authority do you have where Colin is concerned?"

"I'm not talking about Colin. I'm talking about Sara."

"Whoa! Hold on a minute." Jo Lynn made a sweeping gesture with her hands, elegant magenta nails fluttering before my face. "When did we make the switch?"

"I told Sara I wasn't giving her any money this Christmas…"

"How can you not give the kid money to buy Christmas presents?" Jo Lynn interrupted.

"That's not the point."

"The point is it's my money," Jo Lynn said, "and if I want to give money to my niece so she won't be embarrassed on Christmas morning, then that's what I'll do. Don't be such a grinch. She'll probably buy you something fabulous."

"I don't need anything fabulous."

"You need something, that's for sure."

"Some sane relatives might be nice."

Jo Lynn swallowed another piece of pie. "So, what do you think is the matter with the old girl anyway?"

"I don't know."

"What's your educated guess?"

She underlined the word "educated," making it sound vaguely obscene. I closed my eyes, took a deep breath, and released it slowly. When I opened them, I noticed several teenage boys looking our way, snickering behind closed fingers.

"You don't think it could be Alzheimer's, do you?" Jo Lynn asked.

It was a possibility I'd deliberately refused to consider, and one that, even now, I admitted to my vocabulary with only the greatest of reluctance.

"She has all the symptoms," Jo Lynn continued. "She's disoriented; she's paranoid; she's forgetful."

"That doesn't necessarily mean..."

"You said yourself she was losing it when we found the dishwashing detergent in her fridge."

"Still..."

"She didn't recognize Sara."

"It was her hair."

"It wasn't her hair."

"I know," I said, admitting defeat.

"So, you think it's Alzheimer's?"

"I think there's a good chance."

"Damn!" Jo Lynn snapped, pushing what was left of her apple pie halfway across the table with an angry flip of her fingers. "Damn it to hell. That makes me so mad."

I was surprised by the ferocity of Jo Lynn's reaction. I'd expected her to treat this latest development regarding our mother with her usual degree of casual disinterest.

"There's no point in getting angry about it," I told her. "If it's Alzheimer's, then, unfortunately, there's not much we can do. We just have to make sure she's as comfortable as possible."

"Why would I want to do that?"

Now I was really confused. "You don't want her to be comfortable?"

"I want her to get exactly what she deserves."

"Meaning?"

"Why couldn't she get cancer like everybody else?"

"Jo Lynn!"

"A little suffering is good for the soul. Isn't that what they say?"

"You want her to suffer?"

"Why shouldn't she? What makes her so damn special that she should get off scot-free?"

"She's your mother."

"So, what does that mean? That I'm just supposed to forgive and forget? That the past gets wiped clean? She won't remember it, so I might as well pretend it never happened? Is that what you're telling me?"

"What is it you want her to remember? I don't understand."

"Of course you don't." Jo Lynn shook her head, dislodging several angry tears. "You never have."

"I'd like to try," I said honestly.

Jo Lynn jumped to her feet. "What's the point? You said it yourself. We can't change anything."

"That's not true. Some things can be changed."

"The past?"

"No, not the past."

Jo Lynn nodded her head vigorously up and down, her mouth a bitter pout. "So she just gets away with it."

"Gets away with what? What are you talking about?"

"Excuse me, miss," a voice said from somewhere beside us, and we turned to see a brown-haired boy of about fifteen, wearing cut-off jeans at least four sizes too large and a baseball cap worn back to front and pulled low across his forehead. "Are you Jo Lynn Baker?"

"Yes." Jo Lynn swiped at her tears with the back of her hand, forced a smile onto her lips.

The teenager looked back at his buddies. "It's her," he yelled excitedly. "I told you." He grabbed a napkin off our table and thrust it toward her. "Could you autograph this for me? I don't have a pen."

Jo Lynn fished inside her purse for a pen, then quickly scribbled her signature on the crumpled serviette. "Have a good Christmas," she called after him, her smile now wide and genuine. "Wasn't that sweet?"

"Gets away with what?" I pressed.

But Jo Lynn was already weaving her way between the tables of the extended food court toward the escalator. "Forget it," she called back. "Everybody else has."

It was almost midnight by the time I got to bed, and it took several hours for me to fall asleep, the events of the day ringing in my brain, like a malfunctioning alarm. I'd finally lapsed into merciful unconsciousness when I felt something sweep across my face, soft and gentle, like a chiffon scarf. My hand extended lazily to brush it aside, my eyes still firmly closed. Seconds later, it happened again, only this time it was more a tapping against my skin, like water dripping from a leaky faucet. My fingers brushed the air in front of my face, finding nothing. I turned over, refusing to wake up. Something tickled the back of my neck. I swatted it, felt the sting of my fingers as they connected with my skin, jolting me awake. Reluctantly, I opened my eyes, sat up in bed, stared impatiently through the darkness, saw nothing. "Great," I muttered, glancing over at Larry, wrapped peacefully inside the covers. He hadn't touched me since our last disaster. I knew he was waiting for me to make the first move, to be the one to take him in my arms, to coax him into passion, but I couldn't seem to work up the necessary enthusiasm. I lay back against the pillow, exhaled a deep breath of troubled air, reclosed my eyes.

Almost immediately, something danced lightly across my closed lids. A spider? I wondered, shaking my head in an effort to dislodge it. Possibly a mosquito, I thought, as once again I forced my eyes open.

He was leaning over me, smiling through the darkness, the knife dancing in his fingers as it played with the air around my face. I opened my mouth to scream but he shook his head no, and the scream died in my throat. "I thought we should get better acquainted," Colin Friendly said. "Seeing as we're going to be family."

"How did you get out of jail?" I heard myself ask, amazed at my ability to speak.

His smile stretched eerily across his face, his pale skin almost translucent. "You really think that a bunch of video cameras and infrared sensors are gonna be enough to keep me away from you?"

"I don't understand. What do you want with me?"

He brought the knife to the tip of my chin. "Brought you a little Christmas present." He grabbed my hand, brought it to the front of his pants.

"No!" I screamed, pulling my hand away as he climbed onto the bed. I looked helplessly toward Larry. What was the matter with him? Why didn't he wake up?

"He can't help you," Colin Friendly stated, blue eyes slicing through the darkness, as deadly as the knife in his hand.

"What do you mean?"

"Take a look," Colin Friendly instructed, his free arm reaching across the bed to tear the blanket away from my sleeping husband. I saw Larry's open eyes, his parted lips, the deep red line that slashed across the center of his throat.

"No!" I screamed as Colin Friendly pushed himself on top of me. "No!"

I bolted up in bed, my screams bouncing off the walls.

Miraculously, Larry didn't wake up. "It was a dream," I marveled, my hands on my heart, as if to contain its wild beating. "It felt so real."

Larry stirred, groaned, refused to wake up.

"I'm going to check on the girls," I said to the darkness, climbing out of bed.

The house was dark and quiet. I walked toward the girls' bedrooms, knowing I was being silly, but needing to see them sleeping soundly in their beds. You can't protect them forever, I told myself, peeking in on Michelle, kissing her warm forehead, her hand reaching up in sleep to brush my kiss aside. Just as I had done moments ago in my nightmare, I realized with a shudder, pushing open the door to Sara's room, approaching her bed, leaning forward to touch her cheek.

It took me a moment to realize that Sara's bed was empty. "Sara?" I called, checking her bathroom. "Sara?" I flipped on the overhead light. Her bed hadn't been slept in.

I was racing back through the living room toward my bedroom, about to rouse Larry, when I saw a tiny light coming from the back patio, and thought I heard voices. I stopped, stood absolutely still, listened as the soft voices floated to my ears. "Sara?" I hurried toward the sliding glass door at the back of the family room, pushed it open, stepped outside.

Sara, still wearing the clothes she'd had on earlier in the day, was sitting in one of two chaise longues, a lit cigarette dangling from her fingers. She stared at me defiantly, almost daring me to object.

"What are you doing out here?" I asked instead.

"What does it look like?"

"I don't understand. It's late. You know you're not supposed to smoke anywhere on the property."

"Oh, give the kid a break," my sister said, leaning forward on the other chaise longue.

"Jo Lynn! What's going on?"

"You haven't heard the news?"

I shook my head, too dazed to speak.

"A juror at Colin's trial announced she's been having an affair with one of the prosecutors. The whole case has been thrown out of court. Colin's a free man."

"What?!"

"You heard me. He'll be out by morning. I came by to celebrate." She lifted a champagne glass into the air. "You don't mind," she said. "I helped myself."

I stumbled back inside the house. "No, this can't be. It can't be." I ran into the bed-room. "Larry, wake up. Something terrible's happened." I reached his side, prodded his shoulder beneath the blanket. "Larry, please wake up. Colin Friendly is a free man. He'll be out of jail by morning."

Larry's body shifted beneath the covers. He breathed deeply, pushed the blanket aside, sat up in bed. "Well, don't you look as sweet as the first strawberry in spring," Colin

Friendly said, his hand reaching for my throat.

I screamed. Or at least I thought I did. Probably the scream was silent, because Larry didn't wake up. He lay there, his sleep undisturbed, as I sat crying beside him, my breathing labored and painful, perspiration soaking my skin, my mind trying frantically to distinguish between the nightmares of my sleep and those of my daily existence.

"Larry, are you awake?" I whispered, needing the comfort of his arms.

But he either didn't hear me or pretended not to. I lay back against the damp pillow, as cold and alone as if I were lying in my grave, and waited for morning.

Chapter
18

Tell me again who these people are and why we're having dinner with them," Larry said as we pulled the car into the large parking lot in front of Prezzo's, a trendy Italian restaurant located in a long strip plaza at the corner of PGA Boulevard and Prosperity Farms.

The parking lot was crowded and there were no spaces close to the restaurant. We drove slowly, looking down each successive aisle, our eyes peeled for an empty spot. A light rain was falling. "Robert and Brandi Crowe," I reminded him. "I knew him in Pittsburgh."

"Right." Larry nodded, but his voice was flat,

disinterested. "And you ran into him at the courthouse."

"Right," I agreed. "There's one." I pointed toward a car that was just pulling out of a space at the side of the enormous Barnes & Noble bookstore that occupied one corner of the lot.

"And the reason for this dinner?"

"Does there have to be a reason?"

Larry pulled the car into the space just vacated and turned off the engine. The rain was falling harder now. We hadn't brought an umbrella. "I guess I should have let you off in front of the restaurant," he said.

"Too late now."

"I can go back." He restarted the engine.

"Don't be silly," I said. "A little rain won't kill me."

"If you're sure," he said.

"I'm sure."

Which was pretty much the extent of most of our conversations in the past weeks. Excessive, forced politeness over the minutest of inconsequential things. A careful treading of the waters. Saying just enough to be understood, not risking the one word that might lend itself to misinterpretation.

"We should probably wait a few minutes," he advised.

"Sure." I stared out the front window at the rain. It wouldn't last long, I decided. The rain in Florida was often ferocious and brief. Like a doomed love affair, I thought, picturing Robert, wondering if he and his wife were similarly trapped, if they sat staring wordlessly out the front window of their car, waiting for a lull in the weather so that they could escape the confines of their car, of their life together.

There's nothing lonelier than an unhappy marriage, I thought, then wondered when I had started to consider my marriage an unhappy one. I glanced at my husband, hoping to catch the flicker of a smile in his face, some sign of reassurance, a ray of hope regarding our future, but his head was pressed back against his headrest and his eyes were closed.

We'd endured rough patches before, I reminded myself: the months following Sara's birth, when she was colicky and kept us up all night (and we were too tired and confused to make love); the months preceding our move to Palm Beach, when we were trying to convince our families and ourselves of the rightness of our decision (and we were too tired and confused to make love); the weeks that followed first my mother's move down here and then my sister's, when we wore ourselves out trying to accommodate them (and were too tired and confused to make love).

Was there a pattern here? And were we not making love because we were tired and confused, or had we grown tired and confused because we'd stopped making love? Did everything ultimately come down to sex? No matter how old we were?

Nothing ever really changes, I thought. We are who we were. Our pasts are always with us, our personalities chronic, like a lingering illness. No need to look over our shoulders.

The past is right in front of our eyes, setting up roadblocks, blocking the way to a happy future.

My mind raced back through more than thirty years. Another parked car in the rain. A deserted strip of country road instead of a crowded parking lot. Robert and I in the front seat of his father's black Buick, his lips on mine, his tongue halfway down my throat, his hands reaching for my breasts. "Let me," he whispered, and again, more urgently, "Let me."

And I might have. I was so close. Why not? I screamed silently at my conscience. Robert was the boy all the girls wanted, and he wanted me. I'd heard the rumors about Sandra Lyons, the girl he sometimes went to see after he drove me home. Was I driving him into her arms? Was I prepared to lose him? All my friends were doing it. What would be so wrong?

I let his hand sneak higher, held my breath. It felt so good. I was so close. "Let me," he said again.

And then that awful knocking on the window. A flashlight shining on our faces, two strangers peering in. We scrambled to fix our clothing, regain our composure. We'd heard all the apocryphal stories of young couples ambushed in lovers' lanes. By thieves, by killers, by monsters with deadly hooks in place of arms. Was that to be our fate?

"You all right?" a uniformed police officer asked me as Robert rolled down the car window.

I nodded, too frightened to speak.

"Would you like a ride home with us, miss?"

I shook my head.

"This isn't a good spot to be," the second policeman said to Robert.

"No, sir," Robert agreed.

"I'd get this girl home right now if I were you."

"Right away," Robert said, starting the car engine.

"Drive carefully," the officer said, slapping the top of the car with the flat of his hand, sending us on our way.

"What do you think?" Larry was asking now, his voice snapping me back into the present, as if I were wrapped inside an elastic band.

"What?"

"I said, it doesn't look like it's going to stop."

I stared at the rain beating down on the front window, aware of my heart pounding wildly in my chest. He was right. The rain was coming down as strongly as before. I checked my watch. It was ten minutes after eight.

"Do you think we should make a run for it?"

"Let's give it another few seconds," I said. What were we doing here anyway? *This isn't a good spot to be.* How had I allowed myself to be talked into having dinner with my prospective lover and his wife? Had I had any choice? "Pick a day, any day," Brandi had chirped over the phone the previous week. What could I say? And when had I started thinking of Robert as my prospective lover?

Probably around the same time I decided my marriage was unhappy, I told myself, understanding how one such decision necessarily impacts on the next. The last time I'd thought of going too far with Robert, the police had intervened. This time, I doubted there would be any cavalry riding to my rescue.

Larry restarted the car. "I'm going to drop you off."

"We'll lose our spot."

"Maybe we'll find something closer."

We did. Right in front of the restaurant.

"Tell me again these people's names," Larry said as we pushed open Prezzo's heavy glass doors, shaking the rain from our heads.

"Robert and Brandi Crowe." My eyes darted skittishly around the noisy, crowded room.

"And you knew her from high school."

"I knew *him*," I shouted over the noise, spotting Robert in a corner booth on the other side of the room. He was on his feet, waving. "There they are."

We began snaking our way through the crowd in front of the bar, which was normally the focal point of the large, well-lit room, but which tonight was all but hidden by the crush of well-toned, well-tanned bodies milling ten deep around it, vying for one another's attention. There were a trio of blondes in coordinating tight red dresses, a brunette in an emerald-green sweater, a redhead in a black plunging neckline and white thigh-high boots. The men wore expensive gold jewelry under open-necked silk shirts in a variety of hues, and black trousers, as if they were students at the same exclusive private school. "Do you have a license to carry that smile?" I heard one man ask as I passed by, but I didn't bother to turn around. I knew he wasn't talking to me.

Robert was waiting for us with his hand extended. Behind him was a large red poster of white noodles wrapped lovingly around a fork. "You must be Larry. It's a pleasure to meet you. Kate speaks very highly of you," he said, shouting in order to be heard.

Larry smiled, shook Robert's hand, shouted back, "I understand you knew each other from high school."

"That we did." Larry and I slid into one side of the booth, upholstered in subtle green and beige stripes, opposite Robert and his wife. "Larry, this is my wife, Brandi."

"Nice to meet you," Larry said.

"A pleasure," Brandi agreed, then looked over at me. "That's quite the deluge out there."

For a moment I thought she was referring to the crowd, then I realized she meant the weather, and self-consciously swept my hair free of any possible remaining raindrops. "We've been waiting in the car, hoping it would let up."

"I think this is an all-nighter," Brandi said.

We were actually talking about the weather, I thought, avoiding Robert's eyes by concentrating on his wife. Yellow Valentino had replaced pink Chanel, although her eyes were still heavy with blue shadow, obviously a personal trademark. Her black hair was brushed away from her face and secured with a beaded black headband. She was trying to look ten years younger than she was, and as a result, looked ten years older. It was sad, I thought, hoping I wasn't making the same mistake.

"You're looking very lovely," Robert said, as if reading my mind, and I buried my face in the menu, thanking him without looking up. I'd already taken in every detail of his appearance when I first spotted him across the room: the brown slacks, the tan shirt, the hair falling carelessly across his forehead, the wondrous smile. *Tell me, do you have a license to carry that smile?*

I realized, in that instant, that I had no idea how my husband was dressed, and glanced guiltily beside me. Larry was wearing an old dark green floral shirt that had always been one of my favorites, but which now seemed rather dull, even a trifle shabby. His thinning hair seemed sparser than usual, and his forehead was red and peeling slightly from too much golf and too little sunscreen. Still, he was a handsome man. I wished that he would look over at me and smile, give me some indication that he was still on my side, that he wouldn't let me do anything foolish.

Was my foolishness his responsibility?

I should have told him how nice he looked before we left the house. *Say something nice to your spouse every day*, I always advise clients.

It'll change your life. But I was too busy thinking of other ways to change my life.

"You look very glamorous in black," Robert
continued.

"Thank you," I muttered as the waiter
approached to take our drink order.

"That's quite the scene, isn't it?" Brandi
Crowe pointed with her chin toward the bar.
"You should have seen what it was like before
you got here. There was this young guy with
a little girl. She was about three years old, and
I heard him tell these two women that he was
her uncle, and of course they were oohing and
aahing, and making a huge fuss over her."

"The better to show off their qualifications
for motherhood," Robert quipped.

"And next thing you know, he's got both
women's phone numbers, and they're taking
care of his niece while he supposedly uses
the men's room, but is actually off trysting with
bachelorette number three. It was amazing."

"It was quite a display," Robert agreed.

"The kid's probably not even his niece."
Brandi laughed. "He probably borrows her from
a neighbor to meet girls."

"Sounds like something I might have done,"
Robert said.

"I doubt that would have been necessary,"
I heard myself say, then bit down hard on my
tongue.

Brandi reached over and patted her husband's
hand, the gesture unleashing the same kind
of havoc in my body as the first time I'd seen
it several weeks earlier. "Yes, I understand my

husband was quite the ladykiller back in his high school days. You have to tell us all about him."

"I'm afraid I didn't know your husband that well," I lied, doubting that Robert would have said much about our past relationship to his wife.

"Well, you obviously made quite an impression if he remembered you thirty years later."

"I'm the one who remembered him," I told her.

"Amazing, running into each other in court like that," Brandi said.

"So, what do you think of our boy getting the chair?" Robert asked, deftly switching the subject.

"I couldn't be more thrilled," I said, truthfully.

"How's your sister taking it?"

"As you might expect."

"Your sister?" Brandi asked.

"Jo Lynn Baker," I said, assuming this was explanation enough.

It was. "Oh my God," she whispered, then glared accusingly at her husband. "You didn't tell me that."

The waiter returned with our drinks and a list of the night's specials, the conversation drifting back to the weather, the sports pages, and the joys of life in southern Florida. I cocked my head, feigned interest in the small talk, probably even contributed to it, but my mind was elsewhere, back in Jo Lynn's messy one-bedroom apartment, where I'd spent most of the morning listening to her rail hysterically against a justice system that could so heartlessly condemn a man to die for crimes he didn't commit.

"How could they do it?" she sobbed repeatedly, yesterday's mascara streaking her swollen, unwashed face. She'd been crying since the previous afternoon's sentencing hearing, when the judge had dispatched Colin Friendly off to the Florida State Prison in Starke to await execution without so much as a by-your-leave. "Of course, his lawyers are planning an appeal."

I held her while she cried, said little. I wasn't there to gloat. Colin Friendly had been found guilty and sentenced to die, and my sister, probably the only person in the world who hadn't been prepared for this eventuality, was in torment. Why she'd put herself in this position, how she could love such a man, why she did any of the crazy things she did, all this was now irrelevant. Out of sight, out of mind, as the saying goes, and my sister's attention span was limited at the best of times. She would weep for him, maybe even make the trip up to Starke to visit him once or twice, but eventually, Jo Lynn would grow tired of the long drive, the longer wait, the lack of a normal life. Eventually, she'd accept the inevitable, proceed with her life, forget about the man on death row.

Colin Friendly, I assured myself, tuning back in to the conversation around the restaurant table, was now safely out of our lives.

"I find the names of the streets so fascinating," Robert was saying. "Military Trail, Worth Avenue, Gun Club Road."

"Prosperity Farms," I chimed in.

"Exactly," Robert said.

"I don't think there's anything particularly fascinating about any of those names," Brandi Crowe said. "Military Trail was probably just that a long time ago; the same is likely true of Gun Club Road. Worth Avenue was undoubtedly named after somebody important, and has nothing to do with all the expensive stores on it, and this part of Palm Beach was all farmland at one point, and the largest one was probably called…"

"Prosperity Farms," Robert concluded with a shake of his head. "You're right. Nothing very interesting there, I guess."

Brandi Crowe slipped her arm around her husband's shoulder and laughed as my fists formed tight little balls in my lap. "In case you hadn't realized it, my husband is the last of the romantics." She laughed again, withdrew her arm. My hands relaxed. "So, what do you think of your wife becoming a big radio star?" she asked Larry.

"A big radio star?" Larry repeated.

"You mean she hasn't told you?"

"I guess not." Larry turned to me, waited for an explanation.

"Well, nothing has been decided yet," I stammered.

"I thought you had it all worked out," Brandi said to her husband.

"I've made your wife an offer," Robert said

274

to Larry. "I think she's waiting to see it in writing before she makes any announcements."

"What kind of offer?"

"To host her own phone-in show," Brandi Crowe explained.

"My wife is a therapist," Larry said.

"Exactly," Robert told him. "She'd be giving advice."

"Like on *Frasier*?" my husband asked.

"We haven't decided on a format," Robert said.

"Well, actually, I do have an idea I think is pretty good." A wide smile stretched across my face for the first time that evening.

"What's your idea?" Robert's smile was almost as big as mine.

"A weekly two-hour spot which would combine love songs with advice to the lovelorn." I spoke rapidly, nervous excitement creating a slight wobble in my voice. Until then, I hadn't realized how excited I was about the idea, how eager I was to throw myself into something new. "Every week, we pick a different topic, choose some appropriate songs, and intersperse the songs with the live phone-ins asking for my advice. The music can be used to illustrate a point, or underline it, or the song can be the advice itself, like *Stand by Your Man* or *Take This Job and Shove It*, depending on what the show's about. The list of topics is endless—drinking, loneliness, marriage, cheating..." I broke off, coughed into the palm of my hand. "What do you think?"

Larry shrugged. "It's different."

Brandi smiled. "It's interesting."

"It's great," Robert said.

"When would you have time to do this?" Larry's voice was a glass of cold water, dampening our enthusiasm.

"Well, naturally, we'd have to work around Kate's schedule," Robert began.

"You've never done anything like this before," Larry said.

"That's the whole point," I told him. "It would be a challenge."

"You don't think you have enough challenges in your life at the moment?"

I fell silent. What was the matter with him? Had he always been such a wet blanket?

"Ideas like this take months to develop," Robert said. "We're in the very beginning stages. And we haven't even started contract negotiations."

"Should I be hiring an agent?" I joked. Kidding on the square, as my mother would say.

"Uh-oh," Brandi said, and laughed, once again snaking her arm across her husband's shoulders. "Something tells me you're going to have your hands full with this one."

"Don't fuck this guy," Larry said, his voice measured and calm, his anger restrained and simple.

"What? What are you talking about?"

"You tell me," Larry said as we climbed into the car. The downpour had ceased, but a light drizzle persisted.

"I don't know what you're talking about."

"Are you sleeping with him?"

"What?"

"You heard me."

"You can't be serious."

"Do I sound as if I'm joking?"

"You think I'm sleeping with Robert Crowe?"

"Are you?"

"No, of course not. Where is this coming from?"

"You tell me."

"There's nothing to tell."

"This is just some guy you knew from high school," Larry said.

"Yes."

"Who you just happened to run into one day at the courthouse."

"Yes."

"And he just happens to own a radio station."

"His wife's father..."

"And he offers you your very own show. Just like that. Out of the blue," he continued, not interested in my clarification.

"More or less," I conceded.

"How much more?"

"What?"

"Why would he offer you your own show? You have no experience. He hasn't seen you in thirty years. What's he really after, Kate?"

"This is very insulting," I said, and actually managed to be offended.

"I'm not an idiot," Larry said.

"Then stop acting like one." My voice was shaking, although whether it was shaking more with indignation or guilt, I'm not altogether sure. Was I really so transparent? And did just thinking about having an affair make me guilty as charged? Maybe I should be on my way to the state prison in Starke along with Colin Friendly.

Larry started the car and we drove home without speaking. I flipped on the radio, tried to make my mind a blank, to lose myself in the music. "Here's an old favorite," I suddenly heard my voice crackle across the airwaves. "*Your Cheatin' Heart* by Hank Williams. Callers, the phone lines are now open. Have your questions ready."

Chapter
19

It was around this time that I started having recurring dreams. There were two of them, different in content, though equally disturbing. In the first one, I'm lying face down on my bedroom floor, my hands tied with a rope behind me, my sister sitting on the small of my back, bouncing up and down, riding me as if I were a pony, as a faceless stranger ransacks my drawers, throwing a seemingly endless supply of bras and panties into the air, letting them fall where they may.

In the second dream, I'm walking alone along a sunny strip of sidewalk, my steps propelled by a feeling of buoyancy, of being almost lighter than air. In the next instant, I am absolutely convinced that with a little effort, I can actually take flight, and so I start flapping my arms wildly up and down, angling my body to forty-five degrees, my chin thrust forward and leading the way, my neck and shoulders following, as if skiing off a high jump. And suddenly my legs actually leave the ground, and I am suspended in the air, maybe a foot or two off the sidewalk, and I flap my arms even more furiously, trying to sustain the momentum, to increase my speed, to gain greater height, to fly through the air. I'm so close. "Let me," I cry, even as I feel my feet returning to the ground, my flight aborted, my energy spent.

It's not hard to figure out what these dreams mean: the perceived loss of control, the outside forces keeping me down, my desire to break free, to escape the underpinnings of my life, the oblique references to Larry and Robert, the not so oblique reference to my sister. Even my dreams are transparent, it would seem.

The dreams became a constant, alternating with one another on a nightly basis, occasionally doubling up, like an old-fashioned double bill at the movies. They interrupted my sleep, woke me at three in the morning, like a colicky infant, and hung on till it was time to get up. Occasionally, I awoke from one of these dreams dripping with perspiration, the skin between my breasts glistening with sweat, the sheets around me damp and cold. I forgot what it was like to sleep through the night.

Interestingly enough, it was during this time that Larry and I started making love again. I woke up one night, sweaty and breathless from my attempts to take flight, and he was sitting up in bed beside me. My thrashing had awakened him, he said matter-of-factly, and I apologized, which he said wasn't necessary. I smiled gratefully, and told him I loved him. And he took me in his arms and told me he loved me too, that he was sorry for his part in our recent estrangement, and I apologized for mine. And we made love. And it was nice and familiar and comforting, and I hoped that would put an end to the dreams, but it didn't.

The subconscious, it would appear, is not so easy to fool as our waking selves, and the truth was that I didn't want lovemaking that was nice and familiar and comforting. I wanted lovemaking that was furious and unfamiliar and exciting. The kind of lovemaking that transports you, makes you think that anything is possible, the kind of lovemaking that can save your life. Or destroy it.

I wanted Robert.

Don't fuck this guy, I heard Larry say, even as I fucked him daily in my mind. Robert was everywhere around me, his voice in my ear, telling me what to say, his eyes behind mine, showing me where to look, what to see, his hands at my breasts, dictating the beat of my heart. I made love to my husband, but it was Robert who slept inside me at night, who guided my hands when I showered in the morning, and if I tried scrubbing myself free of him, which I did only rarely, he clung to me stubbornly, coating my body, like a soapy residue, refusing to give way.

As for Robert himself, he was mercifully out of town, first at a media convention in Las Vegas, then reluctantly, on some sort of cruise, organized on behalf of one of his wife's pet charities. He'd be gone just over three weeks, he told me over the phone before he left. He'd call as soon as he got back. By which time, I assured myself repeatedly in the interim, I would have returned to my senses.

I kept hoping the same would hold true for Jo Lynn, who, during the month of January, made weekly treks to Starke, driving up on Friday and staying at a motel not far from the penitentiary, then spending the allotted six hours with her "fiancé" on Saturday, before making the five-hour drive back home. She had few kind words to say about how the state prison operated. What could possibly be the harm, she demanded indignantly, in allowing the inmates visitors on both Saturday and Sunday, and not forcing them to choose either one day or the other? And talk about cruel and unusual punishment, did we know that the state of Florida didn't allow conjugal visits? Not that this would stop her from going ahead with her wedding plans, she insisted.

Probably it was that blind, stubborn insistence that propelled me into action, although I had no idea what I was doing, or what I thought I could accomplish. One afternoon,

I simply picked up the phone, punched in 411, and waited for the recorded voice to come on the line.

"Southern Bell," the cheery voice obliged. "For what city?"

"Brooksville," I heard myself say.

"For what name?"

"Ketchum," I answered, spelling the name of Colin Friendly's neighbor, the one who'd tried to help him, who'd supposedly taught him that all women weren't like his mother. "Rita Ketchum." Why did I want to speak to her? What good did I think talking to her would do?

Seconds later, a human voice replaced the recorded message. "I show no listing for a Rita Ketchum," the woman said, her voice decidedly less cheerful than the recording she replaced. "Do you have an address?"

"No, but how big is Brooksville? There can't be very many Ketchums."

"I have a listing for a Thomas Ketchum on Clifford Road."

"Fine," I told her.

The recorded voice returned, relayed the phone number, offered to dial it directly for a nominal charge. I accepted, not trusting my fingers to do the job.

The phone rang once, twice. Assuming I had the right number, what was I planning on saying to Rita Ketchum? *Hello, I understand you taught Colin Friendly all he knows about love?*

The phone was answered on its fourth ring. "Hello," a young woman said, a baby crying in the background.

"Is this Rita Ketchum?" I asked.

The voice grew suddenly wary. "Who is this?"

"My name is Kate Sinclair. I'm calling from Palm Beach. I need to speak to Rita Ketchum." Except for the baby crying in the background, there was silence. "Hello? Are you still there?"

"My mother-in-law isn't here. May I ask why you want to speak to her?"

"There are some questions I'd like to ask her," I said, growing uneasy.

"Are you with the police?"

"The police? No."

"What kind of questions do you want to ask her?"

"I'd rather discuss this directly with Mrs. Ketchum."

"I'm afraid that won't be possible."

"Why is that?"

"Because nobody's seen or heard from her in almost twelve years." In the background, the baby began screaming.

"She disappeared?"

"Twelve years ago this May. Look, I really have to go. If you want to call back this evening, you can speak to my husband."

"Thank you," I said, too stunned to say anything else. "That won't be necessary."

"So what are you saying?" Jo Lynn demanded over the phone only minutes later. "That just because some woman ran away from home, Colin had something to do with it?"

"For God's sake, Jo Lynn, what is it going

to take to get through to you?" I said angrily. "The woman didn't just run away from home. She disappeared. Of course Colin had something to do with it."

"Colin would never hurt Mrs. Ketchum. He loved her."

"The man is incapable of love. He makes no distinctions between feelings, between people. If he could kill the one woman who tried to help him, what makes you think you'll be any different?"

Her answer was to hang up the phone. I lowered my head into the palms of my hands and cried.

On February 5, I took my mother to our scheduled doctor's appointment. Dr. Caffery's office, located on Brazilian Avenue in Palm Beach proper, is a small series of examination rooms off a larger waiting room, the whole area decorated in gradations of pink. Like the womb, I thought, ushering my mother inside and pushing her toward the receptionist's desk.

"Hi, I'm Kate Sinclair," I announced. "This is my mother, Helen Latimer."

"Hello, dear," my mother said to the receptionist, who was about twenty-five, with short black hair cut on the diagonal and half a dozen assorted gold loops and studs running up each earlobe. Her nameplate identified her as Becky Sokoloff.

"We have an appointment," I said.

"Have you been here before?" Becky asked.

"No, this is our first visit."

"You'll have to fill out these forms." Becky pushed several sheets of paper across her blond-wood desk. "Why don't you have a seat for a few minutes. The doctor is a little behind schedule."

I took the forms and directed my mother to the row of bright pink chairs that ran along the pale pink wall. Several women were already waiting, and one glanced up from her magazine with a weary smile, her eyes indicating that the doctor was more than a *little* behind schedule. "Would you like a magazine, Mother?" I didn't wait for her reply, just grabbed a handful of magazines from the long, rectangular coffee table that sat in the middle of the room, and plopped them into her lap.

My mother promptly folded her hands on top of them, like a human paperweight, making no move to open them. I studied her for several seconds, deciding that she looked well. Her skin color was good, her dark eyes bright, her gray hair combed and curled. She seemed in good spirits. No one was plotting against her, nobody was following her, everything was "magnificent," she'd trilled on the drive over from her apartment, then lapsed into silence, other than to ask how the girls were getting along, a question she repeated at least five times.

"Mom, don't you want to read a magazine?" I reached under her hands and extricated the latest edition of *Elle*, opening it to a page of naked breasts in quite an astonishing assortment of shapes and sizes.

"Oh my," my mother and I both said, almost as one. Immediately, I flipped to another page. More breasts. Some barely covered, some simply bare. And still more: here a breast, there a breast, everywhere a breast-breast, I sang silently, flipping quickly through the entire magazine. A seemingly inexhaustible supply.

What every well-dressed woman is wearing, I thought, turning my attention to the forms the receptionist had handed me, starting to fill in the blanks. Name, address, phone number, place and date of birth. "Mom, what year were you born?" I asked without thinking, then bit down on my tongue. She had trouble remembering what she had for breakfast. How was she going to remember what year she was born?

"May 18," she said easily, "1921."

I felt strangely elated by the fact my mother knew the date of her birth. Maybe she wasn't in such bad shape after all, I rationalized, even though I knew that Alzheimer sufferers often had no trouble recalling even the minutest details of their distant pasts. It was their short-term memory that deserted them. I tried another question, deciding that short-term memory was vastly overrated. "Are you allergic to any medications?"

"No, but I'm allergic to surgical tape."

"Surgical tape?"

She leaned against me, as if about to confide

something highly confidential. "We didn't find that out until after my cesarean with Jo Lynn." She laughed. "The doctors put regular surgical tape across my stomach to hold the stitches from the operation in place, and of course, nobody thought a thing about it until a few days later, when I started to itch something terrible, and they took off the bandages, and discovered that my stomach was covered in these horrible, angry red welts. Oh, it was terrible. I thought I'd die, I was so itchy. And there wasn't much the doctors could do for me, except to lather my skin in cortisone cream. It was months before those welts went down. I looked terribly ugly, what with this big scar and those angry red welts covering my stomach. Your father hated it."

It was the most I'd heard my mother say in months, and I couldn't help but smile, despite the mention of my stepfather. "Do you think much about him?" I heard myself ask.

"I think about him all the time," she answered, surprising me, although I'm not sure why. She'd been married to the man for fourteen years, had a child with him, been regularly beaten to a bloody pulp by him—why wouldn't he still be part of her thoughts? Hadn't I held on to my memories of Robert all these years?

"He was such a handsome man," she continued, without prompting. "Tall and dashing and very funny. You inherited your sense of humor from him, Kate."

It was then that I realized she was talking

about *my* father, and not Jo Lynn's. "Tell me about him," I said, partly to find out how much she recalled, but mostly because I was suddenly hungry to hear news of him, as if I were a small child waiting for word of her handsome and brave father, off fighting a distant war.

"We met at the end of World War II," she said, repeating a story I'd heard many times before. "My father gave him a job in his textile factory, and Martin eventually worked his way up to foreman. He was so smart and ambitious, he would have become foreman even if he hadn't married the boss's daughter." Her eyes suddenly clouded over. "But then my father lost the business, and my parents had to sell their house, and my mother never forgave him. Do you remember your grandmother?" she asked.

An image of a heavyset old woman with strawlike hair and thick ankles flashed before my eyes. "Vaguely," I said. I was only five years old when she died.

"She was a very strong woman, your grandmother. There was no gray in her world, only black and white. Something was right, or it wasn't. If you made your bed, you had to lie in it."

"That couldn't have been very easy for you," I heard the therapist in me reply.

"We learned. If you made a mistake, you had to accept the consequences. You couldn't just pack up your things and run away."

"Is that why you stayed with my stepfather even after he started beating you?" I knew the question was too simplistic, but I asked it anyway.

"Your father never beat me," she said.

"My stepfather," I repeated.

"Your father was a wonderful man. He was a foreman at my father's textile plant until my father lost the business, then he took a job with General Motors during the day and went to law school at night. He'd always wanted to be a lawyer. Isn't that interesting? We've never had a lawyer in the family. But he died before he could graduate." She smiled sadly at the receptionist.

"It shouldn't be too much longer," Becky Sokoloff automatically replied.

"We were finishing our dinner," my mother continued, as I watched the scene play out in my mind. "You were in your room, getting ready for bed. Your father and I were still at the dining-room table, taking our time over dessert. It was so rare, you see, that we got to spend a whole evening together, and so we were lingering over our dessert, just talking and laughing. And your father got up to get a glass of milk, and suddenly he said that he felt a hell of a headache coming on. Those were his exact words, 'I feel a hell of a headache coming on.' I remember because it was very unusual for him to swear, even a simple word like 'hell.' And I was about to suggest that he take a few aspirin, even though he didn't like pills, but I never got the chance. He stood up, took two steps, then collapsed onto the floor."

I said nothing, watching as her eyes flickered with the passage of time, as if she were watching an old newsreel.

"Do you know what I did?" she asked, not waiting for an answer. "I laughed!"

"Laughed?"

"I thought it was some sort of joke. Even after I called for an ambulance, even on the ride to the hospital, I kept expecting him to open his eyes. But he didn't. The doctor told me later that he was dead before he hit the floor."

I reached over and hugged her, felt the outline of her skeleton beneath the soft cotton of her blue dress. When had she become so frail? I wondered, as her body bent to my embrace. And how long before these memories, now so strong, ultimately faded, then disappeared?

So the past gets wiped clean? Jo Lynn had demanded in the mall the day before Christmas. *She won't remember it, so I might as well pretend it never happened?*

Pretend what never happened?

She just gets away with it.

Gets away with what? I wondered, as I'd been wondering ever since that afternoon.

"Mom," I began.

"Yes, dear."

"Can I ask you something?"

"You can ask me anything, dear."

I paused, not sure how to pose the question, deciding finally that the most direct approach was probably the best. "What exactly happened between you and Jo Lynn?"

"Something's happened to Jo Lynn?" Her eyes flashed immediate concern.

"No, she's fine."

"Oh, I'm so glad."

"I mean, what happened between the two of you a long time ago?"

"I don't understand." My mother's eyes grew restive, flitting fearfully around the room.

"You two have never really gotten along," I began again, trying a different approach.

"She was always such a headstrong little girl. You could never tell Jo Lynn anything."

"Tell me about her."

"Don't get me started," my mother said, and laughed, the fear in her eyes vanishing as quickly as it had appeared.

"She was a cesarean delivery," I coaxed, waiting.

"That's right," my mother marveled. "I had a terrible time after she was born because I had an allergic reaction to the surgical tape."

"And she was headstrong and you could never tell her anything..."

"She had a mind of her own, that's for certain. I couldn't get her to wear a dress for love or money. I'd put her in all these pretty, frilly little things, the kind you always loved, and she'd rip them off, wouldn't have anything to do with them. No, she only wanted to wear pants. She was such a handful. Not like you. You were such a good baby. You loved your little dresses, but not our Joanne Linda. No, she had to wear the pants in the family." She laughed. "That's what your father used to say anyway."

"My stepfather," I qualified.

"Jo Lynn could do no wrong as far as he was concerned. He let her get away with murder. Whatever she wanted, he made sure she got. Spoiled her terribly. Always took her side whenever there was an argument." She shook her head. "She never got over my leaving him. I know she blames me for his death."

"He died of pancreatic cancer. How can she blame you for that?"

"She blames me for everything."

I looked toward the receptionist, then over at the two women waiting in the chairs across from us. "What else does she blame you for?" I asked.

My mother smiled and said nothing, her eyes drifting back to the bare bosoms on the pages of *Elle*. "Oh my," she said.

"That's what she told you?" Jo Lynn asked over the phone later that afternoon.

"She says you blame her for his death."

"She would say that."

"Do you?"

"He died of cancer."

"That's beside the point."

"There is no point. Not to this conversation, anyway. What did the doctor say?"

"Not much. She's going to run a bunch of tests. Apparently, Alzheimer's is one of those diseases that they identify more by a process of elimination than anything else."

"What kind of tests?"

"EKG, CAT scan, MRI, mammogram."

"Mammogram? Where'd that come from?"

"Dr. Caffery feels we might as well do a complete physical. She wants me to have one too," I added.

"You? Why? Aren't you feeling all right?"

"She thinks I might be starting menopause," I admitted.

"What?"

"It's no big deal," I lied.

"So, are you coming up to Starke with me this weekend?" The question was deceptively casual in its delivery, as if we'd been discussing this for some time and were simply tying up a few loose ends.

"You must be kidding," I answered.

"I thought you might find it interesting."

"Not a chance." There was an awkward silence. "You could do me a favor, though," I said, surprising myself.

She waited, said nothing. I could almost feel her body tense.

"You could ask your boyfriend what he did with Rita Ketchum."

There was another pause, this one redolent with silent fury. "You know what?" Jo Lynn asked, her voice edgy and cold, like chipped glass. "If you have anything you want to ask my *fiancé*, I suggest you ask him yourself."

Chapter
20

Which may, or may not, explain what I was doing sitting beside my sister as she raced her old red Toyota up the Florida Turnpike toward the state prison outside Starke the following Friday night.

"Don't you think you should slow down a bit?" I fidgeted in my seat, eyes darting through the darkness for state troopers along the side of the highway. "I thought the police had this area pretty well covered."

"They never stop me," Jo Lynn said confidently, as if surrounded by an aura of invincibility. "Besides, I'm not going that fast."

"You're doing almost eighty."

"You call that fast?"

"I think you should slow down."

"I think you should relax. I'm the driver, remember?" She lifted both hands off the wheel, cracked her knuckles, stretched.

"Get your hands on the wheel," I said.

"Will you please calm down. You'll make me so nervous, I'll have an accident."

"Look, you've been driving for almost three hours," I said, watching the speedometer stubbornly climb, trying a different approach. "Why don't you let me take over for a while."

She shrugged. "Sure. Next time we stop for gas, it's all yours."

I stared out the front window at the battery

of signs that regularly interrupted the flat stretch of road along the ink-blue sky, most of them announcing the imminent arrival of Disney World, located just outside the city of Kissimmee, twenty miles southwest of Orlando.

"You want to go there?" Jo Lynn asked.

"Where?"

"Disney World. We could go on Sunday."

I shook my head in amazement. The state penitentiary one day, Disney World the next.

"Or we could do Universal Studios. I've always wanted to go there, and it's around here somewhere."

"I think I'll pass."

"What about Busch Gardens? It's supposed to be terrific."

"We were there about five years ago," I reminded her. "Remember? You went with the kids on that water ride and everybody got drenched."

Jo Lynn squealed with delight. " 'The Congo River Rapids' ride! I remember. That's the place with all the animals. It was great. Let's go there." Her head snapped toward me, her eyes appealing longingly to mine.

"Would you please keep your eyes on the road."

"Party pooper." Her eyes returned to the highway stretching monotonously before us. "How about one of those alligator farms? You know, the ones you hear about where some poor kid always falls off the bridge and gets eaten?"

"You're not serious."

"Of course I'm serious. I love that sort of stuff."

"I can't," I told her, watching the enthusiasm drain from her face, like liquid from a straw. "I promised Larry I'd be home tomorrow night." Actually I hadn't promised him any such thing. In fact, Larry had encouraged me to wait until Sunday to make the long drive home. But I knew my tolerance level for my sister would take me only so far.

"You're such a wet blanket," Jo Lynn said, her mouth a pronounced pout.

"I'm here, aren't I?"

She scoffed. "Colin doesn't know anything about what happened to Rita Ketchum. You'll see."

What about Amy Lokash? I thought, but didn't say. What about the scores of other women who crossed his path and disappeared? "Where is this place anyway?"

"It's either in Raiford or Starke, depending on who you talk to," Jo Lynn explained. "Between Gainesville and Jacksonville, in Bradford County. Another couple of hours and we should be at the motel."

"I don't think I've ever been to Bradford County," I said.

"Well, it's one of the state's smallest counties," Jo Lynn pronounced with the authority of a tour director. "Its early settlers were farmers from South Carolina and Georgia. The main businesses are truck crops, tobacco, timber, and livestock. The largest private employers include manufacturers of work

296

clothing, wood products, and mineral sand. Population around 23,000, about 4,000 of whom live in Starke, which is also the county seat. Raiford's even smaller."

"My God, where'd you learn that?"

"Are you impressed?"

"Yes," I said honestly.

"Would you still be impressed if I told you I made it all up?"

"You made it up?"

"No," she said grudgingly. "But I kind of wish I had. Actually, the manager of the motel we're staying at supplied me with the details."

"What else do you know?"

"About this area?"

I nodded, though it was my sister who fascinated me far more than the data she was reciting.

"Well, Starke is twenty-four miles away from the nearest airport, which is in Gainesville, and there are three colleges and universities within fifty miles of the county, as well as three community colleges and two vocational schools."

"Not to mention the state penitentiary," I added.

"Actually, there are five prisons between Starke and Raiford," she said, her voice adopting a world-weary tone. "There's the North Florida Reception Center, for newly arriving prisoners from the north, the Central Florida Reception Center, the South Florida Reception Center, as well as the Union Correctional Institution, which is just across the river from

Florida State Prison. Colin will probably be transferred there when there's a vacancy."

"I thought he was on death row."

Even in profile, I could feel the glare in Jo Lynn's eyes. "They have death rows in both places," she said slowly, between newly clenched teeth. "The executions, however, take place in Florida State Prison. If Colin were to be executed, and he won't be, then he'd have to be transferred back again."

"What's happening with his appeal?" The Florida Supreme Court, which automatically reviews all death sentence convictions, had already upheld Colin's sentence.

"His lawyers are appealing to the U.S. Supreme Court."

"And if they refuse to hear the case?"

"Then there's a hearing before the governor and his cabinet. If the hearing is denied and the death warrant is signed by the governor, then we petition the Florida Supreme Court a second time with briefs stating that new evidence is available."

"Even if there isn't?"

"If that petition is rejected," Jo Lynn continued, ignoring my question, and continuing on as if she were a recorded message, "then Colin's lawyers go to the trial court and insist that the defendant didn't get a fair trial the first time and that he should get a new one. If that fails, we go back to the Florida Supreme Court for a third time with a request to stay the execution."

"And if that fails?"

"You needn't sound so hopeful." Jo Lynn straightened her shoulders, tightened her grip on the steering wheel. "If that fails, we go to the federal district court, where we say that the defendant deserves a stay of execution or that the sentence is unfair. If this court refuses to do anything, then we go to the U.S. Eleventh Court of Appeals in Atlanta, requesting that the execution be stopped. And if that doesn't work," she said softly, "there's a final appeal to the U.S. Supreme Court. If that fails, Colin gets the chair. Would you like to hear about that?" she asked, continuing before I had a chance to object.

"Florida began using the electric chair in 1924. Prior to that, hanging was the execution of choice. Between 1924 and 1964, when executions were temporarily halted because of court battles challenging their constitutionality, Florida electrocuted 196 people. The oldest was fifty-nine; the youngest three were sixteen. Two-thirds of the total were black. Electrocutions resumed in September of 1977, and today there are more than 340 residents living on death row.

"The executioner, a private citizen whose identity is never disclosed, is hired from a host of applicants for the job. He wears a mask when he throws the switch, and makes the princely sum of 150 dollars per execution.

"As for the death chamber itself, it's pretty basic. A twelve-by-fifteen-foot room whose only furniture is this massive oak chair bolted down to a rubber mat. The source of power for this chair is a diesel generator capable of producing 3,000 volts and 20 amps, although I'm not sure I understand the distinction. At any rate, it's irrelevant because a transformer behind the chair turns those 3,000 volts and 20 amps into 40,000 watts, which is enough to shoot the body temperature of the person in the chair up to 150 degrees."

"My God."

"Once in the chair, the prisoner faces a glass partition behind which is a small room with twenty-two seats, twelve of which are for official witnesses picked by the warden, and the rest of which are for reporters. Just before the execution, the prisoner is taken to a so-called prep room, where his head and right leg are shaved for electrical attachments, just like you see in the movies. What you don't see is that his head is also soaked with salty water to assure good contact. Of course, when he's in the chair, his head is covered with a rubber hood. There are also rumors that a tight rubber band has been fitted around the inmate's penis and a pack of cotton wadding stuffed up his ass. Oh, and did I mention that behind Old Sparky, as the chair is affectionately known, are two telephones, one for the institution and the other for the governor in case he changes his mind at the last minute?"

"Unbelievable," I said, trying to rid my mind of the graphic images that were filling it.

"Less than four minutes after the prisoner enters the death chamber, he's toast. The body is then slipped into a dark coat, ready for burial. The state of Florida is nothing if not efficient."

"I don't believe it," I said.

"I'm not making any of this up," she said.

"That's not what I mean."

"What *do* you mean?"

"I mean you're amazing," I told her.

"What's *that* supposed to mean?"

"It means I think you're amazing. I can't believe you know all this stuff."

She shrugged. "I've been doing a little reading, that's all. I can read, you know."

"But you actually *remember* everything. That's the amazing part."

"What's so amazing? I have a photographic memory. No big deal. Besides, I have kind of a vested interest in all this."

"Have you ever thought about going back to school, becoming a lawyer?" The idea was forming as I spoke.

"Are you nuts?"

"No, I'm serious," I said, warming to the idea. "I think you'd make a terrific lawyer. You have a great mind. You have all these facts and figures at your fingertips. God knows, you know how to argue. I bet you wouldn't have any trouble at all swaying a jury to your point of view."

"I flunked out of college, remember?"

"Only because you never tried. You could go back, get your degree."

"Degrees aren't everything," she said defensively.

"No, of course they're not," I agreed quickly. "But you'd be a natural. I mean, you should have heard yourself. You're really good at this stuff. I bet you'd do great. You could go back to school, get your law degree, then defend Colin yourself. If anyone can keep him out of the electric chair, it's you." My sister, the lawyer, I thought. My brother-in-law, the serial killer.

A slow smile crept onto Jo Lynn's face. "I probably would make a good lawyer."

"You'd be great."

She took a deep breath, held the smile for several seconds, then allowed it to tumble from her lips, like a baby's drool. "No," she said quietly. "It's too late."

"No, it's not," I insisted, even as I knew it was. "We could make some inquiries when we get back home, find out what you'd have to do, how much it would cost. Larry and I could loan you the money. You'd pay us back as soon as you started raking in the dough." *Raking in the dough?* I asked myself, knowing I'd traveled beyond the realm of reason into the territory of giddy.

"I bet Mom would give me the money," Jo Lynn stated, and I held my breath. She'd made me promise not to discuss our mother during the trip, and I'd reluctantly agreed. Now she was the one bringing her up. Was she opening the door, beckoning me to step through?

"I bet she'd be happy to."

"She owes me," Jo Lynn said. "Oh, good, there's a service station." She quickly transferred lanes and pulled off at the next exit.

The brightly lit service station contained both a gas station and a Burger King. "I'll take care of the gas if you go get us something to eat," Jo Lynn said as we opened the car doors and climbed out.

I arched my back, stretched my legs. "Oh, that feels so good."

"You stupid idiot," a girl's voice screamed, and for an instant, I thought it was Jo Lynn screaming at me. But when I looked across the top of the car at Jo Lynn, I saw that her attention was directed at the young couple standing by the car in the next aisle, a blue Firebird as bruised as the young girl's arms.

The girl couldn't have been more than sixteen, her boyfriend only marginally older. Both were pale-skinned, fair-haired, and painfully thin, although the boy's arms were muscular and veined, as if he'd been pumping iron. His cheeks were flushed with anger; his fists clenched at his sides. "Who are you calling an idiot?" he raged.

"Who do you think?" the girl challenged, emboldened perhaps by those of us watching nearby.

"I don't need this kind of crap from you," the boy said, opening the car door. "Now, get in the goddamn car. We're outta here."

"No."

"You want me to just leave you here? Is that what you want? 'Cause I'll do it. I'll drive off and leave you in the middle of goddamn nowhere."

I was debating with myself whether or not there was anything I could say or do that might defuse the situation when my sister came up behind me and whispered in my ear. "Stay out of it," she said.

"Maybe we should call the police," I said.

"Maybe we should mind our own business," she countered, directing my attention to the Burger King. "I'll have a cheeseburger, large fries, and a jumbo Coke."

I went to the bathroom, splashed water on my face, stared at my tired reflection in the mirror, noting the deep bags tugging at my eyes. "Turning into an old crone," I whispered.

There was a line at the Burger King counter and it took almost ten minutes for my order to be placed and delivered. "What kept you?" Jo Lynn asked as I handed her the cheeseburger, fries, and soft drink. She slid into the passenger seat while I walked around the car to the driver's side. If I saw the thin wisps of dishwasher blond hair in the back seat, my subconscious refused to acknowledge it until I was behind the wheel of the car and halfway out of the lot. "Where's your food?" Jo Lynn asked, unwrapping hers.

"I didn't get anything."

"Want some?"

I shook my head. "I'm not very hungry."

"I wasn't talking to you," she said, and I screamed as a thin hand reached across the front seat from the back.

I spun around, saw the young girl with the

bruised arms staring back at me, pale green eyes wide and frightened.

"For God's sake, watch where you're going," Jo Lynn admonished with a sly smile. "You want to get us killed?"

I clutched the wheel as tightly as I could, more to keep from strangling my sister than for safety's sake. Hadn't she told me, just moments ago, to mind my own business? What was she doing inviting a stranger into our car? Didn't she know how dangerous it was to pick up hitchhikers?

"This is Patsy," my sister said by way of introduction. "Patsy, this is my sister, Kate."

"Hi, Kate," the girl said, taking a large bite out of my sister's burger and a long sip of her Coke, before handing them back. "Thanks for the ride."

"Where exactly are we taking you?" I managed to ask, wincing as my sister fastened her lips around the same straw the young stranger had just relinquished.

"Wherever," Patsy said, her voice a low growl. "It doesn't much matter."

"Patsy's boyfriend took off without her," Jo Lynn explained.

"Stupid idiot," Patsy said.

"Where do you live?" I asked.

She shrugged. "I'm not sure," she said. "Nowhere now, I guess."

This answer was somewhat less than satisfactory. "Where are you from?"

"Fort Worth."

"Fort Worth? Fort Worth, Texas?"

"Way to go, Katie," my sister said. "Give that girl a silver star."

"How'd you get all the way over here?" I asked, trying to push my voice back into its normal register.

"Drove," came the disinterested reply. Patsy reached forward, grabbed a handful of fries from the container that my sister was stretching over her shoulder.

I watched through the rearview mirror as Patsy flopped back against her seat, stuffing the fries into her mouth, then rubbing her bruised arms, closing her eyes, heavily outlined in black pencil. "With your boyfriend?" I asked, despite the look on my sister's face that told me to be quiet.

"Yeah, the stupid idiot."

"What about your parents?"

"Kate, this is none of our business," Jo Lynn interjected.

"Do your parents know where you are?" I persisted.

"They don't care where I am."

"You're sure of that?"

Patsy laughed, but the sound was hollow, and echoed pain. "I haven't seen my dad since I was a little kid, and my mother has a new boyfriend and a new baby. She probably doesn't even realize I'm gone."

"How long ago did you leave?"

"Two weeks."

I thought immediately of Amy Lokash, pictured her mother, Donna, cowering tearfully at my office door on the day of her first visit. "Have you called her? Does she know you're all right?" Even without looking at Patsy, I could see the confused mixture of defiance, loneliness, and stubborn pride playing havoc with her delicate features.

"I haven't called her."

Don't you think you should? I wanted to scream, but didn't, knowing it would only put the girl on the defensive. "Do you want to?" I asked instead.

Patsy said nothing for several seconds. "I don't know." She leaned her forehead against the glass of the rear side window.

"What's stopping you from just picking up the phone and calling home, telling your mother that you're safe?" I asked.

"What's the point?" Patsy countered sullenly. "She'll only yell at me, tell me she was right about Tyler all along."

"That's what's stopping you?"

"I don't want to hear it again."

"*Was* she right about Tyler?"

"Yes," came the barely audible mumble from the back seat.

"So, are you going to let Tyler call the shots here or what?" I asked, after a slight pause.

"Tyler's the stupid idiot, right?" Jo Lynn asked, and I smiled gratefully for her subtle support.

"Maybe I'll call her," Patsy said, reaching for a few more fries. "I'll think about it."

"Just a phone call to let her know you're okay," I continued, thinking again of Donna

Lokash, how easily this could be her child, praying that a similar insanity had overtaken Amy, that she was even now hitchhiking across the country, unmindful of the pain she was causing, the anguish she'd left behind. But alive.

I fought back the sudden threat of tears as I realized how alien our children were becoming to us. E.T., phone home, I thought.

We said nothing for the next few minutes, Jo Lynn slurping up the balance of her Coke to the rhythm of Garth Brooks and Shania Twain, occasionally passing her drink to the back seat, along with what was left of her cheeseburger and fries. The odor of fast food permeated the car, sinking into the seats like water into soil, lingering long after the food was gone, reminding me that I hadn't eaten since lunch. Probably I should have eaten something when I had the chance. It would be close to midnight before we got to the motel in Starke.

"Hey," Patsy suddenly shouted, her hand extending over the top of the front seat, her finger pointing excitedly toward the side of the road. "The next exit is for Disney World."

"We're not going to Disney World," I told her.

"Where *are* you going?" That there might be other options had obviously never occurred to her.

"We're on our way to Starke," I said.

"Starke? Where's that?"

"Bradford County, between Gainesville and Jacksonville," my sister clarified.

"I don't want to go to Starke," Patsy said, sounding in that instant very much like Sara. "I want to go to Disney World. That's where Tyler and I were headed when we got into that stupid fight."

"Why don't you come with us instead," I suggested. "Then you can call your mother from the motel."

"I want to go to Disney World," Patsy insisted. "It's the whole reason I came to Florida in the first place. Just pull the car over and let me off. I can hitchhike the rest of the way."

"Don't you know how dangerous it is to hitchhike?" I began, then stopped. Was there really any point in arguing with her, trying to make her see reason, to change her mind? I signaled, pulled the car over to the side of the road, and stopped.

"I don't think this is such a good idea," Jo Lynn said suddenly. "I mean, there are lots of looney tunes out there, just waiting to pick up young girls." If Jo Lynn was aware of the irony inherent in her advice, she gave no sign.

"I'll be fine," Patsy insisted, with all the arrogance of youth. "Thanks for the ride and the food and everything." She opened the door, climbed out. "I'll call my mother after I ride "The Pirates of the Caribbean.' "

"You do that," I said, watching Patsy in the rearview mirror as she proffered her thumb into the air. I drove off before I could see anyone stop to pick her up.

"How could you let her do that?" my sister demanded angrily, assuming the mantle of motherly worry I normally wore. "How could you just let her get out of the car like that?"

"Are you suggesting that we should have held her against her will? I believe that constitutes kidnapping."

"She's a minor, for God's sake. How could you just let her go like that? Aren't you worried what might happen to her?"

I thought of Amy Lokash, of Sara, Michelle, my mother, even Jo Lynn. All the women in my life passed quickly before my eyes, like the last images of someone who is drowning. "Can't save everyone," I said.

Chapter
21

We left the motel for the prison at precisely eight-thirty the following morning. Visiting hours were from nine till three, and Jo Lynn was determined to be there for every minute of those six hours. Although the prison was only eleven miles west of Starke on State Road 16, she'd already warned me that it would take about twenty minutes to pass through all the gates and various security checks, which made leaving the motel by eight-thirty an absolute necessity.

When Jo Lynn awakened me at seven-thirty that morning, she was already showered and dressed in the white miniskirt and tank top that had become something of her trademark, her makeup meticulously applied, her hair gloriously askew. I stumbled around the garishly appointed room, with its heavy red curtains and deep purple bedspreads, amazed I'd slept so soundly. For the first time in months, I'd actually slept through the night—no dreams, no pesky trips to the bathroom. Was it because I was so exhausted, both mentally and physically, from the long drive up from Palm Beach? Or was it because I was almost afraid of opening my eyes to face this new day? I stepped into the shower, allowing the surprisingly satisfying torrent of hot water to envelop me.

"Hurry," Jo Lynn prompted later, as I zipped up the fly of my navy slacks and reached into my overnight bag for my orange blouse. "Is that what you're wearing?" she asked, then laughed.

"Something wrong with this?"

"No, it's perfect." She laughed again, watching as I did up the buttons, then quickly ran a brush through my hair. I thought of applying a bit of blush, a stroke of lipstick, then decided against it. Jo Lynn was in a hurry, and besides, there was nobody I wanted to impress. "We'll stop for an Egg McMuffin on the way," she said, picking up the cooler stuffed with the various cheeses and chicken salad sandwiches she'd made herself—Colin's favorite—and pushing me out the motel room door toward the car.

Probably because we'd driven at night, I'd failed to notice how drastically the scenery had changed once we'd transferred off the turnpike onto Highway 301. I saw now that here, in the heart of rural north-central Florida, truck farms and scraggly pines had replaced the orange groves and majestic palm trees of the southeast coast. "I didn't realize the area was so poor," I said, perhaps disingenuously, as we made our way along the state road toward the prison, Jo Lynn behind the wheel.

"Looks a bit like the backwaters of Georgia," Jo Lynn agreed, and I wondered when she'd last seen the backwaters of Georgia.

"It's so hot," I marveled, trying to find a radio station that was broadcasting something other than the latest farm reports, the air hanging fetid and bloated around me, like a drowned man draped across my shoulders. I heard a huge roar and turned my head, half expecting to see an enormous tidal wave gathering force behind me; instead I saw a massive tractor-trailer riding up our tail, then drawing precipitously close to the side of our car.

Jo Lynn looked up and waved to the driver and his male passenger, both of whom were practically hanging out their window to get a better look at my sister's bare legs. "I like to give 'em a flash of thigh," she confided as they sped past.

"You think that's such a good idea?" I asked, not expecting, nor particularly wanting, any reply. The road opened onto a broad plain. Cattle grazed along the roadside, some standing up, others lying down.

"It might rain," Jo Lynn pronounced.

I stared through the window at the cloudless blue sky, as waves of heat bounced, like pebbles, from the road across the hood of the car. "Rain?"

"If the cows are all standing up, it means it's going to be sunny. If they're all lying down, it's going to rain. If some are up and some are down, then the weather's going to be change-able."

"Something else you picked up from the motel manager?" I asked.

"No," she said. "From Daddy."

I tried not to look surprised by the sudden intrusion of my stepfather into the conversation.

"He used to take me for drives in the country sometimes, and we'd see all these cows grazing, just like these guys are doing, and he'd say that if all the cows were standing up, it was going to be sunny, and if they were all lying down, well, you know the rest. These cows are owned by the prison, by the way."

"Are those prisoners?" I asked, suddenly cog-nizant of small gangs of men working along the side of the road, supervised by uniformed guards wearing sunglasses and carrying shot-guns.

"This ain't Oz," Jo Lynn said, chuckling at my discomfort.

And suddenly the prison stretched before us, actually two prisons, one to either side of the stream, ambitiously named New River, that divided Union and Bradford counties. The Union Correctional Institution was situated to the right, Florida State Prison to the left, each identified by huge signs in front of dou-ble rows of chain-link fences topped with razor ribbon, and differentiated by color: Union Correctional was a series of concrete block buildings painted an indifferent beige; Florida State Prison was a sickly pastel lime green.

Jo Lynn pulled the car into the designated parking area, turned the engine off, and dropped the keys into her straw purse. "We have arrived," she said solemnly, throwing open her door. "Everybody into the pool."

I followed Jo Lynn toward the main gate, our pace brisk in order to keep the horde of insistent insects at bay, mindful of the guard watching us, rifle in hand, from the watchtower high above our heads. As we approached, the gate opened, and we stepped through. Immediately, it closed behind us, and I instantly felt sick to my stomach. Another gate sputtered noisily open, beckoning us further inside. We're entering hell, I thought, hearing the second gate clang shut behind us as I followed my sister down the concrete walkway to the double doors of the prison itself.

I don't remember pushing open the doors, or even stepping across the wide threshold. All I remember is standing in a small waiting area, staring at a large man in a tiny glass-enclosed booth, who sat in front of a crowded control panel, smiling at Jo Lynn as she strode purposefully toward him. "Hi, Tom," she said easily.

"Hi, Jo Lynn, how're you all doing today?"

"Just fine, Tom," Jo Lynn answered. "Want you to meet my sister, Kate."

"Hello there, Kate," Tom said.

"Hello there, Tom," I said in return, marveling that people actually talked this way, that *I* was talking this way.

"You know the routine," Tom said to Jo Lynn.

"Sure do," Jo Lynn said, offering him both her purse and the cooler.

Tom spent the next ten minutes going through each and every item in our bags. He inspected the contents of the cooler, actually unwrapping the cheeses and breaking them into smaller chunks and opening the halves of the chicken salad sandwiches to peer inside, before moving on to our purses, studying our driver's licenses as if committing each detail to memory, checking us both carefully against our photographs, even though he'd obviously recognized my sister from her past visits. "He does this every week," Jo Lynn whispered over the constant clanging of prison doors.

"Nice seeing you again," Tom said to my sister, motioning us toward a third barred gate and a metal detector. "A pleasure to meet you, Kate."

We had to rid ourselves of our shoes, our belts, our keys, our sunglasses, and any pens and loose change we might be carrying, and once through the metal detector, a guard accompanied us through yet another loudly clanging gate and down a long yellowy-beige corridor with a shiny linoleum floor. "The prisoners wax and polish this floor every day," Jo Lynn confided.

There were some steps and still another gate controlled by a guard in a glass-enclosed booth, and suddenly we were in the heart of the prison, a four-way intersection called Grand Central. To our right were floor-to-ceiling bars, beyond which were the cellblocks of the prisoners. "That's where they keep the electric chair." Jo Lynn pointed through the bars toward a closed door at the very end of the long, wide hall.

Several prisoners walked past us on their way to work at the prison laundry, wearing blue prison-issue dungarees and blue work shirts. "We go this way," Jo Lynn motioned, and we followed another guard into the so-called visiting park off the main corridor.

A variety of cooking smells assaulted my nose, one blending into the next, rendering them indistinguishable. "We're in the same wing as the kitchen and the mess hall," Jo Lynn said. "In fact, this visiting park *was* the old mess hall. You'll see, it looks just like a high school cafeteria."

She was right. The room was large, nondescript, filled with maybe thirty or forty stainless-steel tables and chairs. The only thing that distinguished it from a school cafeteria was the fact that these tables and chairs were bolted to the floor. "See that watercooler over there?" Jo Lynn pointed toward the large glass watercooler in one corner of the room.

I nodded.

"Keep your eye on it," she advised.

"Why? Does it do something?"

"Wait till the prisoners get here. You'll see." She checked her watch, pointed to her left. "They'll be bringing them in anytime now. I gotta use the facilities," she announced abruptly, placing the cooler on one of the tables and marching quickly to the rest room just outside the door.

I looked around, pretending to casually peruse my surroundings, but actually concentrating my attention on the other men and women waiting for the arrival of their friends and loved ones. There were about a dozen of us, the women outnumbering the men by a ratio of three to one, the blacks outnumbering the whites by perhaps the same ratio. All the younger women wore dresses, as opposed to slacks, although none were quite as provocatively attired as my sister. One older black woman, wearing black from head to toe, so that it was hard to distinguish where her skin left off and her clothing began, was crying softly against her husband's shoulder; another woman, whose lips were pierced by a series of small gold loops and whose arms were covered by a series of ink-blue tattoos, paced anxiously back and forth behind a nearby table.

"You okay?" I asked my sister when she returned, looking slightly flushed.

"Oh sure."

"You rushed out of here so fast, I was afraid something might be wrong."

She waved away my concern with a sharp

flick of her wrist. "I just had to get something."

"Get something?"

She slid into one of the chairs and leaned both elbows on the stainless-steel top of the table, nodding toward the seat across from her for me to sit down. "I brought Colin a little present," she said out of the side of her mouth, eyes on the guard at the doorway.

"A present?"

"Ssh! Lower your voice."

"What kind of present?" Images of guns stuffed inside bras and knives secreted inside lush layer cakes danced before my eyes, although I knew this was absurd. We'd passed through two metal detectors, and there was nothing other than cheese and chicken salad sandwiches inside Jo Lynn's cooler. Nor had I noticed any gifts when Tom went through her purse. "What kind of present?" I asked again.

She slipped her hand inside her straw bag and pulled something out, which she was careful to conceal from the guard. When she was confident no one was looking, she opened the palm of her hand, showing me a smooth oblong container filled with about six hand-rolled cigarettes.

"Marijuana?!"

"Ssh!" She immediately returned the container to her bag. "Do you have to yell everything?"

"Are you crazy?" I demanded. "Bringing that stuff in here."

"Will you lower your voice and stop acting

318

like some silly schoolgirl. Everybody does it."

I looked anxiously around me, at the black woman crying on her husband's shoulder, the girl with the lip rings and tattoos pacing nervously behind the next table. "But how did you sneak it past the guards? Tom went through our bags with a magnifying glass."

"I stuffed it up my snatch," she said, and giggled. "Close your mouth. Flies will get in."

"Your vagina?"

"Vagina," she echoed, her mouth twisting with disdain. "God, Kate, who but you uses words like vagina anymore?"

"I don't believe this."

"You'd be amazed to find out what goes on in places like these."

"But how does Colin get them back to his cell?"

"Trust me, you don't want to know."

"I think I'm going to be sick."

"You can't be sick now. Here they come. Remember to keep your eyes on the water-cooler."

I looked quickly from the door to the water-cooler and back again to the door as several guards—tall, burly, vaguely menacing—escorted a coterie of about ten men into the room. All were dressed in the same blue prison garb, with one notable exception—Colin Friendly. Like me, he was wearing blue pants and an orange top.

Now I understood why Jo Lynn had laughed

at my choice of clothes. Orange T-shirts were what distinguished the prisoners on death row from the other inmates.

My fingers went self-consciously to the neck of my orange blouse, as I watched my sister leap from her seat to embrace the convicted serial killer, his hands sliding down to cup her rear end, his palms catching the hem of her short skirt, momentarily exposing the rounded bare flesh of her buttocks. I realized, in that instant, that when Jo Lynn had rid her body of its hidden contraband, she'd also removed her panties. "Oh God," I moaned as they broke from their embrace and walked toward me.

Colin Friendly seemed taller than I remembered him from court, and while somewhat thinner, he was definitely more muscular. Probably he'd been working out, I thought as I rose unsteadily to my feet, my hands resolutely at my sides, trying to decide how I would react were he to offer his hand in greeting.

He didn't.

"Colin," Jo Lynn said, hanging on to his arm, "I'd like you to meet my sister, Kate. Kate, this is Colin, the love of my life."

"Nice to meet you, Kate," he said easily. "Your sister talks about you all the time."

Or words to that effect. Truthfully, I'm not exactly sure what was said that morning, or during most of our time together in that so-called visiting park. The hours pass through my brain with the swiftness and cruelty of an ambush. I remember our conversation in fits

320

and starts, a few choice words here, a chilling phrase there, most topics blending one into the other, one hour disappearing inside the next.

"You don't look much like sisters," Colin was saying as we took our seats, Colin beside Jo Lynn, their hands in each other's laps, despite the rules against touching. Prisoners were permitted opening and closing embraces, nothing in between, but the three guards who were present often looked the other way, and a wide variety of indiscretions were taking place, all of which I tried hard not to notice.

"Different fathers," I told him.

"So Jo Lynn tells me."

"Isn't he the most gorgeous thing you've ever seen?" Jo Lynn said, and giggled, like an adolescent. She leaned toward him, her bosom grazing the side of his arm, and wiped a dark curl away from his high forehead.

He laughed with her. "You're the most gorgeous thing I've ever seen, that's for sure," he told her without a trace of self-consciousness, as if I weren't privy to their conversation, as if they were the only two people in the room. "You have no idea how jealous everybody is of me back on the row. They know I have the most beautiful, sexy woman in the world waiting for me every Saturday."

"I'm wearing your favorite underwear," she told him, and I drew a huge intake of breath as I saw his hand sneak beneath her short skirt, and the laughter spread to his cold blue eyes.

"I hope you're taking real good care of

your baby sister," he said without looking at me, "until I get out of here."

I said nothing, tried to look elsewhere, saw similar gropings at other tables.

"You gotta make sure she's eating right and getting plenty of exercise and sleep."

"You shouldn't be worrying about me," Jo Lynn said. "You've got enough to worry about in here with all these perverts."

He laughed. "Yeah, we got 'em all in here. Sodomites, pederasts, necrophiliacs, faggots. We even have guys that drink their own urine and eat their own shit. One guy likes to smear the stuff all over his body. Disgusting son of a bitch if there ever was one. I stay away from him, I tell you."

"Colin is in R Wing now," Jo Lynn said, glancing briefly in my direction, "but when he first got here, they put him in Q Wing, which is where they house all the nut cases. Colin's lawyers got him out of there pretty damn quick."

"It was a scary place," Colin agreed, shaking his head, his hand disappearing farther under my sister's skirt. "Here they pretty much leave me alone."

"Colin lets them think he's guilty," my sister explained.

"Smart move," I mumbled.

"One of the perks of being on death row is that we get our own cells."

"You're a lucky man," I said.

Colin's head slowly turned from my sister to me, his eyes piercing through mine like a pin through a butterfly. "Your sister told me you had kind of a sarcastic sense of humor. I see what she means."

I said nothing, surprised and dismayed that my sister had discussed me in any kind of detail at all.

"You don't approve of me, do you?" he asked some time later, and it took me a moment to realize he was serious.

"Does that surprise you?" I asked in return.

"Disappoints me," he answered.

"You're a convicted murderer," I reminded him.

"He's innocent," Jo Lynn said.

"I'm innocent," he repeated, eyes twinkling.

I nodded, fell silent.

"I brought you a present," Jo Lynn said as we were eating our sandwiches, her voice a singsong. She indicated her purse with a nod of her head.

"Brought you something too," Colin told her, reaching into the pocket of his blue pants.

Jo Lynn squealed with delight as he produced a handful of letters. "Oh good, fan mail," she trilled, laughing as she opened the first letter. " 'Dear Colin,' " she read aloud, " 'you are the handsomest man I have ever seen. Your eyes are like sapphires, your face the visage of a Greek god.' Visage? That's one of your words, Kate." She laughed. "Don't you just love this stuff?" She tore into the next one. " 'Dear Colin, do not despair. As long as you accept Jesus and take Him to your heart, God will forgive you your sins and evil deeds.' Stupid woman," Jo Lynn proclaimed. "Colin didn't commit any evil deeds." She opened another letter, read silently for several seconds. "Oh, this is the best one yet. Listen to this, Kate. I bet you can identify with this one. "Dear Colin, I am fifty years old with brown hair and hazel eyes, and friends tell me I still have a pretty good figure.' " She glanced knowingly in my direction. " 'I know I'm a married woman with a husband who loves me, but the truth is, the only man I want is you. I think about you night and day. I long to suckle you to my breast, to cradle you in my arms, to give you all the love your mother denied you.' What do you think, Kate?"

"I think the woman wants a baby, not a man," I answered, embarrassment staining my cheeks, like the blush I hadn't bothered to apply.

Jo Lynn handed the letters back to Colin. "Thanks for showing them to me, sweet buns."

"You know I don't keep any secrets from you," Colin said.

"Just don't go writing any of these crazies back," Jo Lynn cautioned.

"You don't have to worry about a thing from me, babe," he told her. "You know that."

"I know I love you."

"Not half as much as I love you."

"Now!" Jo Lynn suddenly hissed across the table, motioning with her chin toward the watercooler in the far corner of the room. I watched as one of the inmates snuck in behind it with his wife, another inmate and his wife positioned in front of it, perhaps blocking, perhaps guarding, perhaps simply waiting their turn. Seconds later, the cooler began shaking, the water inside it sloshing from side to side, like waves in a turbulent sea.

"What happens if they get caught?" I asked.

"You worry too much about consequences," Jo Lynn said. "Besides, it's the state's fault for not allowing conjugal visits."

"A guy's gotta do what a guy's gotta do," Colin Friendly said, squeezing my sister's thigh.

"You haven't..." I started, then stopped, deciding I didn't want to know.

"Gone for a drink of water?" Jo Lynn teased. "No, we haven't. Not yet, anyway."

"We're saving ourselves for our wedding night," Colin said, and they laughed.

I jumped to my feet, although I'm not sure what I was planning to do. One of the guards looked over, his eyes an inquisitive squint. I smiled, pretended to stretch, then sat back down. "Have you set the date?"

"Not yet. There's still a lot of things that have to be arranged. Blood tests, shit like that. But it'll be soon," Jo Lynn assured me.

"A simple thing like getting married, and they make it so difficult." Colin shook his head in dismay. "Have you asked your sister yet?"

"Asked me what?"

"To be my matron of honor," Jo Lynn said hopefully.

I swallowed hard, looked away, tried not to

burst into tears. She couldn't be serious, I thought, knowing she was. "I don't think that would be a very good idea."

"Why don't you give yourself some time to think about it," Colin advised, eyes boring into mine. "We'd sure appreciate your support."

"I'd sure appreciate knowing what happened to Amy Lokash," I said, shocking not only my sister and her so-called fiancé but myself as well. I'd been planning to ask about Rita Ketchum, not Amy. Obviously, my subconscious had other plans.

"Amy L-lokash?" Colin stuttered for the first time all day.

Jo Lynn rolled her eyes in disgust. "What are you trying to pull, Kate? Who the hell is Amy Lokash?"

"She's a seventeen-year-old girl who disappeared about a year ago. I thought you might know something about it."

"This is ridiculous," my sister raged. "Colin, you don't have to answer any of her stupid questions." In the next instant, Jo Lynn was out of her seat and on her way to the rest room, adjusting her skirt across her bottom as she walked.

"Isn't she the juiciest thing you ever saw?" Colin marveled, eyes trailing after Jo Lynn until she disappeared.

"Why don't you just leave my sister alone."

"Say 'please,' " he said, casually, almost as if he hadn't spoken.

"What?" Maybe I hadn't heard him correctly.

He swiveled toward me. "You heard me. Say

'please.' " A sneer tugged at the corner of his lips. "Make that 'pretty please.' "

I said nothing.

"You want me to leave your sister alone, you gotta do something for me. Say 'pretty please.' Go on, say it."

"Fuck you," I said instead.

He laughed, ran his tongue across his upper lip. "Maybe in time."

My body went instantly cold as I recalled my earlier nightmares. My heart beat wildly, its errant pulse reaching inside my brain, as noisy and relentless as a massive tractor-trailer, so loud against the inside of my ear that I could barely hear the sound of my own voice. "This is all a sick game to you, isn't it?"

"I don't play games. I play for keeps."

"Did you kill Amy Lokash?" I asked, struggling to regain control.

Colin Friendly leaned closer, rested his elbows on the table. "Cute kid, dimples, wore a little red plastic barrette in her hair?"

I grabbed the side of the table for support, felt it cold against the palms of my hands. "Oh God." I thought of Donna Lokash, wondered if I'd have the courage to confide in her the certainty of her daughter's fate. "She was just a baby, for God's sake. How could you hurt her?"

"Well, you know what they say," Colin said lazily. "Old enough to bleed, old enough to butcher." He paused, allowing several seconds for this latest obscenity to sink in. "You familiar with John Prince Park?" he asked.

I shook my head, too numb to do anything else.

"Real pretty park. Just east of Congress between Lake Worth and Lantana roads. You should go there sometime. There's barbecues and picnic benches, and a bicycle path, even a playground. Real pretty sight. Right on Lake Osborne. You know Lake Osborne?"

"No."

"Too bad. It's a pretty big lake, one of those long and winding numbers. A couple of little bridges. Real scenic. Lots of people fishing from the shore. Or you can rent boats. You should do that sometime, Kate. Rent a boat, take a little ride out to about the middle of the lake, where it's deepest."

"What are you saying?"

"Your daughters would really like it," he said, smiling widely. "You've got a daughter Amy's age, don't you? Real attractive girl, if I remember correctly."

I held my breath.

"And a younger one too. Michelle, right? Maybe one day, you, me, Sara, and Michelle, we could all get together, have some fun. I've never had a mother-daughter act before."

"Bastard," I muttered.

"So they say."

"I hope you rot in hell."

He smiled. "Does that mean you won't be coming to the wedding?"

I'm not sure what I said next, if, in fact, I said anything at all. I wanted to lash out, to slap that stupid smirk off his face, to pummel him lifeless. Instead I fled the room, as helpless as any of his victims, crying as I raced toward the parking lot, bugs swarming around my face, seagulls screeching overhead, a slight rain starting to fall. By the time Jo Lynn appeared, at just after three o'clock, I was soaking wet, my orange blouse clinging to my arms, like Saran Wrap, my hair plastered against my head, like seaweed.

"The cows were right," my sister said, unlocking the car door. Neither one of us said another word for the duration of the long ride home.

Chapter
22

Four days later, I stood on the shore of Lake Osborne, watching the police drag the area from small, flat-bottomed boats. A dive team, complete with scuba gear, had been in the water for the better part of the morning.

"What are they looking for?" a woman asked, coming up beside me.

"I'm not sure," I said, truthfully. Amy Lokash had been missing, and presumably in her watery grave, for almost a year. What could the police hope to find?

Unless Colin Friendly had weighted down her body, or encased it in cement, Amy's body would have floated to the surface within days of its disposal. No such body had been found, the police were quick to assure me when I reported my conversation with the convicted serial killer.

"He's just playing with you," one police officer told me. But they agreed to search the area anyway.

Generally speaking, spectators aren't allowed close to such a scene, but John Prince Park is a large public area, and easily accessible from a variety of spots. It's impossible to close off the area entirely. In any event, it wouldn't have been necessary. It was the middle of the week in the middle of February. There were only a smattering of people in the park: a young mother pushing her toddler on a nearby swing, oblivious to everything but each other; two men strolling arm in arm, who took off as soon as they saw the police; a man drinking from a paper bag, too far gone to care if anyone saw him or not; several joggers, pausing briefly in their run to ask what was going on, then be on their way.

I wasn't sure why I'd come. Maybe I was hoping for some concrete evidence that I could present to my sister before it was too late. Maybe I was looking for some closure for Donna Lokash. Or maybe I was just putting off getting on with my own life, which today meant picking up my mother for our scheduled mammograms.

By noon, the divers had returned to the surface shaking their heads, and it was becoming obvious that the police were about to call it quits, not having turned up anything but an old tire and several stray pairs of men's shoes. Colin Friendly might have killed Amy Lokash, but he hadn't thrown her body into Lake Osborne. The police were right—he'd been playing with me.

An hour later, I was standing naked from the waist up, watching as expert, but indifferent, fingers placed first my right breast, then my left, between two cold surfaces, and squished them flat as a pancake. Smile for the camera, I thought, as I listened to the buzz of the large X-ray machine.

"Okay, we're done," the technician said, releasing my breast as I restarted my breathing. "Have a seat in the waiting room. Please don't get dressed until I make sure the X-rays are all right."

I slipped my arms back through the blue hospital gown that hung around my waist, and shuffled into the hallway, over to the waiting area, where my mother sat among four other women, all dressed in similar smocks, waiting for either their turn to be photographed or their permission to get dressed.

"How're you doing, Mom?" I asked, sliding into the seat beside her, leaning my head back against the cool blue wall, breathing deeply.

She smiled pleasantly, eyes unfocused, staring toward the Matisse print on the wall across from us. "Magnificent."

I released a deep breath of air. "You've

had mammograms before, haven't you?" I stated more than asked.

"Of course," she said.

"Be sure to let the technician know if she hurts you."

"Of course, dear."

"They don't really hurt."

"Of course not."

Such was the extent of most of my mother's discourse these days. Still, it was more than my sister had said to me since our return from Raiford. I'd tried to tell her what had transpired while she was out of the room, carefully repeating the things Colin had said, then had to sit and listen while she rushed to his defense, as I'd known she would—I'd provoked him, deliberately misunderstood him, put words into his mouth. I told her she was crazy; she told me I was jealous. We hadn't spoken since.

The technician appeared, clipboard in hand. She was tall and thin, with long, stringy red hair pulled into a ponytail, and she looked no older than Sara. I realized I hadn't really noticed her before, despite the intimate nature of our encounter. To me, she was just a pair of hands, as no doubt, to her, I was just a pair of breasts. We took from each other only what we needed, no more, no less. So easy, I thought, to separate the part from the whole.

"Mrs. Latimer?" The technician looked around the room, which was small and windowless, though not unpleasant. My mother said nothing, continued staring dreamily into space.

"Mrs. Latimer," the technician repeated.

"Mom," I said, nudging her arm. "She's calling you."

"Of course." My mother rose quickly to her feet, didn't move.

"Follow me, please," the technician told her, then looked at me. "You can get dressed now, Mrs. Sinclair."

"The tests were negative?" I asked hopefully.

"Your doctor will discuss the results with you," she said, as I'd known she would. "But the X-rays are fine. I don't have to redo them."

Thank God, I thought, watching as my mother followed the technician to the door.

"I'll wait here, Mom," I said.

"Of course, dear," she answered.

I changed back into my street clothes, a white cotton sweater over gray pants, fixed my hair, reapplied my lipstick, returned to my seat in the waiting area, and closed my eyes. Immediately, I pictured Colin Friendly's mocking smile, and opened my eyes again, grabbing the latest issue of *Cosmopolitan* from a nearby end table, and concentrating all my attention on the latest Cosmo girl. She was wearing a royal blue negligee against a royal blue background; her hair was long and dark, her eyes brown and sultry, her cleavage deep and bountiful.

I remembered when Sara was about ten years old, and I found her standing in front of the bathroom mirror studying her naked chest. "When I grow up," she asked seriously, "am I going to have big breasts or nice little ones like yours?"

I told her the odds favored the little ones, not the last time I've seriously misjudged my older daughter, whose breasts have been known to enter a room a full five seconds before she does. I used to joke that had I had big breasts, I could have ruled the world. Kidding on the square, my mother would say, and she'd be right.

When my mother reentered the waiting area, she immediately began removing her hospital gown, exposing herself to the startled women in the room. The women looked away, pretended to be coughing, reading, elsewhere.

"Mom, wait," I said, rushing to her side, tugging the gown back up across her shoulders. "Didn't the technician tell you to wait until she was sure the X-rays came out?"

My mother smiled. "Yes, I believe she did."

"Then why don't we sit down for a few minutes." I led her to the row of upholstered navy chairs. "How'd it go?"

"I didn't much care for it," she stated, and I laughed.

"Did it hurt?"

"I didn't much care for it," she repeated, and I laughed again, because she seemed to be expecting it.

"I didn't much care for it," she said a third time, and we lapsed into silence until the technician appeared and told my mother her X-rays were fine and that she could get dressed.

"You can get dressed now, Mom," I repeated when she failed to respond.

She immediately began pulling the gown from her shoulders.

"Not here, Mom. In the changing room."

"Of course, dear."

I led her toward the small changing room, my heart heavy, as if I'd swallowed something undigestible and it was sitting there in my chest, refusing to go down. I knew what was happening. By this point, I'd done quite a bit of reading about Alzheimer's disease, and my reading had told me roughly what to expect. The long and the short of it was that my mother was becoming my child. She was regressing, gradually losing pieces of herself, shedding her identity as a snake sheds its skin. Soon there would be nothing left of the woman she once was. She would forget everything—how to read, how to write, how to speak. Her children would become strangers to her, as she would become a stranger to herself. One day, her brain would simply forget to tell her heart to breathe, and she would die. It would remain for the rest of us to try to salvage the pieces of her she'd discarded, to fit them back together, to make her whole again, at least in our memories.

At the time, it felt as if my mother's deterioration had occurred very suddenly, but, looking back, the signs had been there for years. She'd often seemed vague, occasionally confused, her conversations cheery but essentially empty. She forgot things, mispronounced words, occasionally forgot them altogether.

Didn't we all? I'd told myself, not paying particularly close attention. And if talking to her was sometimes like talking to the woman on the weather channel, well, so what? Weather, food, constipation—these were probably hot topics in assisted living communities. She'd had enough turmoil in her life, I rationalized. If she wanted to speculate endlessly about the weather, she was entitled.

And, of course, there were times that she was rational, witty, and seemingly normal, when flashes of her old self would appear to remind us that she hadn't disappeared completely, that part of her was still hanging on, fighting to get through. A piece of her here, a piece of her there. She tossed them toward me, like bread crumbs to a hungry bird. Maybe, like Hansel and Gretel, she was trying to leave a path, a way to trace her steps back home, back to the self she had lost.

"Are you ready?" I asked after several minutes, knocking on the door to the changing room.

There was no answer, so I knocked again, gently pushing the door open. My mother was standing in the middle of the tiny cubicle, totally nude, arms protectively covering her sagging breasts, her ribs clearly delineated, her flesh mottled, heavily veined, her skin the color and consistency of skim milk. "I'm cold," she said, looking at me as if it were my fault.

"Oh God, Mom, here, let me help you." I stepped into the tiny changing area, closing the door behind me, tried to gather up her clothes from the floor.

"What are you doing?" Her voice was edgy, on the verge of panic.

"I'm trying to find your underwear."

"What are you doing to me?" she demanded again.

"Ssh, Mom," I cautioned. "It's all right. I'm just trying to help."

"Where are my clothes?" she shouted, spinning around in the cramped space, knocking me against the wall.

"They're right here, Mom. Try to calm down. Here are your panties." I held out a pair of voluminous pink underpants. She stared at them as if they were a foreign object. "You just step into them," I said, directing first one foot, then the other, inside the legs of the panties, then pulling them up over her hips.

Fitting her inside her brassiere took another five minutes, as did getting her into her ivory-colored dress. When we finally emerged from the cramped cubicle, I was soaking wet and breathing hard. "Are you all right, dear?" my mother asked as we exited the building. "You look a little peaked."

I laughed. What else could I do?

"You look a little peaked," she repeated, then waited for me to laugh again, and so I obliged, although the joy was gone, another piece lost.

"Jo Lynn called me last night," my mother said as I was driving her back to her apartment.

I tried not to sound too surprised. Time had become a relative concept to my mother. Last night could mean anything—last night, last week, even last year. "She did?"

"Said she was getting married next week."

"She said that?" This time there was no disguising my surprise. Or my dismay.

"I thought she was already married."

"She's divorced."

"Yes, of course, she's divorced. How could I have forgotten?"

"Jo Lynn's been married three times," I reminded her. "It's hard to keep track."

"Yes, of course."

"She told you she was getting married next week?"

"I think that's what she said. Daniel Baker, she said. A nice boy."

My shoulders slumped. I tightened my grip on the steering wheel. "Dan Baker was her second husband, Mom."

"Is she marrying him again?"

"Are you sure she told you she was getting married next week?" I pressed.

"Well, now, maybe I'm not. I thought that's what she said, but now I don't know. Whatever happened to Daniel?"

"They got divorced."

"Divorced? Why? He was such a nice boy."

"He beat her up, Mom."

"He beat her?"

"Yes, Mom."

Tears filled my mother's eyes. "We let him beat her?"

"We didn't have much choice. We urged her to leave him. She wouldn't."

"I don't remember," my mother said, pounding her fists against her lap in obvious frustration. "Why don't I remember?"

"It's over, Mom. It happened a long time ago. They got divorced. She's all right now."

My mother stared anxiously out the car window, her fingers twisting the fabric of her dress. "What's happening to me?" She asked, her voice high, birdlike. "What's happening to me?"

I swallowed, not sure what to say. Dr. Caffery had discussed the various possibilities with her, including Alzheimer's disease, a conversation my mother had seemingly forgotten. Was there really any point in going over it again?

"We're not sure, Mom," I told her. "That's why you're going for all these tests. It could be something physical, some blockage somewhere, maybe a tumor of some kind that they can remove, or maybe you're just starting to forget things. It happens when people get older. It doesn't necessarily mean it's Alzheimer's," I qualified, more for my benefit than for hers. "I know how frustrating it must be for you, but we'll get to the bottom of all this soon, and hopefully there will be something we can do about it. You know medical science. It moves so quickly, they could find a cure before they even know what you have."

My mother smiled and I patted her hand reassuringly. She closed her eyes, drifted off to sleep, and I drove the rest of the way with only my thoughts for company. My mother would be all right, I told myself. This was just a temporary problem, not a permanent condition, and certainly not irreversible. Before long, one of these X-rays would turn up something, and it would be small and entirely treatable, and my mother would be her old self again, all the pieces neatly back in place.

I pulled into the parking lot of the Palm Beach Lakes Retirement Home, turned off the ignition, gently nudged my mother awake. She opened her eyes, smiled lovingly. "Jo Lynn called last night," she said. "She's getting married next week."

"Relax," Larry was saying, as I paced back and forth behind the kitchen counter.

"Please don't tell me to relax."

"I'm sure Mrs. Winchell will reconsider."

"I'm sure she won't."

"Kate, stop pacing. Let's sit down, talk this out."

"What's there to talk about?" I plopped down on the family-room sofa, jumping immediately back up again, resuming my pacing, this time in front of the TV. "You didn't see her. You didn't hear her. She was very adamant. She said that she has a responsibility to the other residents, that the whole building could have burned to the ground."

"She's exaggerating."

"She doesn't think so. She says that if old Mr. Emerson hadn't smelled something burning in my mother's apartment, then they wouldn't have discovered the pot she left on the burner, and the whole building would have gone up in flames."

"Everyone forgets to turn a burner off now and then," Larry argued, the same words I'd used earlier in the afternoon with Mrs. Winchell.

"Palm Beach Lakes Retirement Home is an assisted living community," I said, repeating Mrs. Winchell's words verbatim. "It is not a nursing home. It is not equipped to deal with Alzheimer sufferers."

"Grandma has Alzheimer's?" Sara asked, bringing a stack of old papers into the kitchen, dropping them into the garbage can under the sink.

"We don't know that yet," Larry told her.

"What are you doing?" I asked.

"Cleaning my room," Sara said.

"You're cleaning your room?"

"It's a mess. There was nowhere to study."

"You're studying?"

"We have a big test in a few weeks."

"You're studying for a test?"

"I thought I'd give it a try," Sara said, and smiled. "Will Grandma be all right?"

"I hope so," I told her. "Meanwhile, I have to find her a new place to live."

To my shock, Sara walked to my side and drew me into a warm, comforting embrace. "It'll be all right, Mom," she reassured me, as I had reassured my mother earlier. I hugged her tightly to me, relishing the feel of her skin against mine, burying my face into the elegant bend of her neck. How long had it been since she'd allowed me to hold her this way? I wondered, realizing how much I'd missed it.

"I love you," I whispered.

"I love you too," she said.

For a few minutes, it seemed that everything would be all right.

Chapter
23

Wednesday morning found me lingering over my second cup of coffee and looking forward to a day of total self-indulgence: a much-needed, long-anticipated massage at ten, a facial at eleven-thirty, followed by a hairdresser's appointment, a manicure and a pedicure. I thought of my mother, putting lipstick on her nails, then pushed her out of my mind. Wednesday was *my* day, my oasis in the desert, my day to unwind and regroup. It seemed I hadn't had such a day in an eternity.

The phone rang.

I debated answering it, almost didn't, gave in after the third ring. "Hello." I crossed my fingers, praying it wasn't the masseuse calling to cancel our appointment.

"Just wanted to tell you how nice it was seeing you the other day," the male voice said.

"Who is this?" The muscles across my back contracted painfully. I already knew who it was.

"How was L-lake Osborne?" Colin Friendly asked.

I said nothing, my eyes shooting instinctively to the windows, to the sliding glass door.

"And how are my lovely nieces-to-be?"

I slammed down the receiver, my hands shaking. "Damn you!" I screamed. "Damn you to hell, Colin Friendly! You leave my daughters out of your sick fantasies." I began pacing, turning around in a series of increasingly small circles, until I felt my head spin and my knees grow weak. "Don't let him get to you," I said aloud, collapsing into a waiting chair, hating his newfound power over me. "There's no way I'm going to let you torment me," I said, reaching for the phone, about to call the prison officials in Starke, when the phone rang again.

I stared at it without moving. Slowly, I plucked it from its carriage, brought it gingerly to my ear, bracing myself for the familiar stutter, said nothing.

"Hello?" a woman asked. "Hello, is someone there?"

"Hello?" I asked in return. "Mrs. Winchell?"

"Mrs. Sinclair, is that you?"

For an instant, I considered telling her that I was the cleaning lady, that Mrs. Sinclair wasn't home, and wouldn't be back till the end of the day. "What can I do for you?" I asked instead.

"I was just wondering if you'd been able to find other accommodations for your mother," she began without further preamble.

I informed her politely that I'd made inquiries into several upscale nursing homes in the area, but that there were no current vacancies. In a sympathetic, yet firm voice, Mrs. Winchell told me that I'd have to look farther afield, and recommended several nursing homes I hadn't tried, one in Boca, another in Delray. Boca, I told her immediately, was out of the question. It was too far away. I might consider having a look at the one in Delray.

"Please do," she said. She didn't need to add "as soon as possible." The tone of her voice said it all.

I poured myself another cup of coffee, took my time drinking it, refusing to think about either Mrs. Winchell or Colin Friendly, then made my bed, arranging, then rearranging, the fourteen decorative pillows that graced it, trying out new groupings, ultimately returning the pillows to their original configuration. It was only then, when there was no more coffee to drink, no more pillows to disturb, and nothing left to straighten, that I phoned the nursing home in Delray, and, much to my chagrin, was able to get an immediate appointment.

There goes my day, I thought, reluctantly canceling my various appointments. Why did it always have to be me? I groused. Why couldn't Jo Lynn assume at least some of the responsibility as far as our mother was concerned? Did she have anything better to do with her time? If she could spend between ten and twelve hours every weekend driving up to north-central Florida and back, surely she could spend thirty minutes driving to a nursing home in Delray. And she could damn well tell her psychotic boyfriend to leave me and my daughters alone. On a sudden impulse, I picked up the phone and called my sister, although I hadn't spoken to her since our ill-fated excursion to the state pen.

"Your fiancé called me this morning," I said, instead of hello.

"Yes, I know."

"You know?"

"He told me he was planning to apologize for any misunderstanding there might have been..."

"Misunderstanding?" I repeated incredulously.

"I told him it would be a waste of time."

"If he ever calls me again, I'll complain to the warden. They'll cancel his phone privileges altogether," I warned, discovering how easy it was to threaten the already vulnerable.

"Thanks for your call," Jo Lynn said icily.

"I'm not finished."

She waited. I could see her eyes rolling toward the ceiling with disgust.

"Mrs. Winchell says Mom can't live at Palm Beach Lakes anymore."

"So?"

"So we have to find her somewhere else to live."

Silence.

"I've made an appointment with this nursing facility in Delray. It's called the Atrium."

"Fine."

"It's for eleven o'clock this morning. I thought you should be there."

"Not a chance."

"I just thought you might like to have a look at where Mom might have to go," I persisted.

"She can go to hell as far as I'm concerned."

"Jo Lynn!"

"So can you." She hung up.

"Jo Lynn..." Once again, I slammed the receiver down, only to watch it bounce off its carriage and tumble toward the floor, where it jerked to a sudden stop mere inches from the carpet, hanging by its white cord, like some misguided bungee jumper. "What the hell is the matter with you?" I scooped up the receiver, dropped it into its carriage, plopped down on the side of my bed, and stared out the window at the curving coconut palm. "Why couldn't I have a normal sister?" I shouted.

I was still screaming as I drove down to Delray. Screaming and speeding, for which I was duly pulled over by a waiting police officer and ticketed. "Any idea how fast you were going?" he asked. Not fast enough, I thought.

Mrs. Sullivan was a moon-faced, pleasant-voiced woman of around sixty. She had brown hair, brown eyes, and legs the size of toothpicks under an otherwise sturdy frame. She graciously showed me around the grounds, which were well manicured and attractively landscaped, then the building itself, a relatively new structure that was low and white and Mediterranean in feel. It didn't look like a nursing home, I tried to convince myself, refusing to allow the vaguely medicinal scent permeating the halls to penetrate my nostrils, ignoring the low wails I heard emanating from behind the closed doors of several of the spacious rooms, pretending not to notice the empty eyes and slack jaws of the residents lined up in wheelchairs against the walls. "Hello there, Mr. Perpich," Mrs. Sullivan said gaily, receiving no response from the white-haired, toothless old man whose body was twisted and gnarled, like the trunk of a long-dead tree.

How could I abandon my mother to a place like this? I asked myself as I raced to my car. "Don't be silly," I said out loud, fumbling with my keys. "There's nothing wrong with this place. It's a perfectly acceptable place, nicer than the ones you looked at in Palm Beach." What was I always telling clients in similar positions? You have to think about yourselves. Your mother will be happier there. She'll have people to look after her. You won't have to worry about her falling down the stairs or getting enough to eat. You can get on with your life.

Sure. Easy for you to say.

How could I get on with my life when the woman who gave me that life was losing her own? How could I abandon her to clean but sterile hallways, leave her sitting in a wheel-chair for hours at a time, staring into space, into a past she could no longer connect with, into a future that held no hope. She could last for years this way, I reminded myself, her life effectively over, death a slow tease away. I couldn't put my life on hold indefinitely. Yet she was my mother and I loved her, no matter how many pieces of her former self were missing. I wasn't ready to let go.

Still, it was clear she could no longer stay

where she was. If I wasn't prepared to put her in a nursing home, that left only one other alternative. "I was wondering how you'd feel about my mother moving in with us for a while," I rehearsed into the rearview mirror, seeing my husband's eyes widen in alarm. "It would only be temporary. A few weeks, maybe a few months. No longer than that, I promise."

"But you're gone all day. Who's going to look after her while you're at work?"

"We could hire someone to come in. Please, would you do it for me?"

I knew he would. No matter what his reservations, I knew that ultimately Larry would do whatever he thought would make me happy.

So, what was I going to do? I asked myself repeatedly as I drove aimlessly through the streets of Delray. The office building that housed radio station WKEY suddenly appeared before me like a mirage in the desert. Had I been heading here all along?

"This is a pleasant surprise," Robert said as I stepped inside his office. I heard him close the door behind me.

I turned around and into his arms, his face a handsome blur as his lips fastened on mine, my body collapsing into his with an eagerness I hadn't anticipated. "I can't believe I'm doing this," I heard myself say, but the words never made it past my mouth as I swayed, ever closer, against him.

He pulled back, just slightly, pulling me with him, like a magnet. "Why didn't you tell me you were coming?"

"I didn't know myself."

"I have a lunch appointment in a few minutes."

"I can't stay."

He kissed the side of my mouth, the tip of my nose. "I would have kept my schedule free."

"Next time."

"When?"

"What?"

"Next time—when will it be?"

He kissed my forehead, my cheek, the side of my neck. "When?" he repeated.

"I don't know. My life is such a mess right now."

"Messes become you. You look sexy as hell."

"I look sexy or I look like hell?"

"You're driving me crazy, you know that."

And then he was kissing me again, this time full on the lips, our mouths open, his tongue circling mine, and suddenly I was seventeen years old, and he was pressing my body against the hard bricks of the high school we attended, his knee pushing my legs apart as his hand tried to sneak underneath my blouse. "No, I can't," I said, pulling back, hitting my head against the window of his twelfth-floor office, snapping rudely back into the present tense. "You have a lunch appointment," I said quickly, trying to catch my breath, tucking my blouse back inside my skirt. "And I really should get going."

"We have a few minutes," he said, pinning

me against the glass. "Tell me what you want," he whispered.

"I don't know what I want."

"I think you do."

"Then you tell me."

He kissed me, one of those soft, lingering kisses that leave you limp. "No, you tell me. Tell me what you like."

"I like it when you kiss me," I managed to say.

His tongue grazed the outline of my lips. "What else do you like?" His tongue grew more insistent, pushed its way between my teeth. "Tell me what else you like."

"I don't know."

"Tell me what you want me to do."

"I don't know."

"Tell me when we can be together."

"I don't know."

"How about next week? I'll arrange to take next Wednesday off. We'll go somewhere special, spend the day making love."

"I can't next Wednesday."

"Yes, you can."

"I can't. I have a doctor's appointment."

"Cancel it."

"I can't. It was the only way I could get my mother to go." His lips muffled the last of my words.

"When, then?"

"I don't know."

"I'm not finished."

She waited. I could see her eyes rolling toward the ceiling with disgust.

"Mrs. Winchell says Mom can't live at Palm Beach Lakes anymore."

"So?"

"So we have to find her somewhere else to live."

Silence.

"I've made an appointment with this nursing facility in Delray. It's called the Atrium."

"Fine."

"It's for eleven o'clock ," he reminded me, and I smiled. "Look," he said, walking to his black marble desk, leaning against it, "I don't want to pressure you into doing anything you don't want to do..."

"I don't know what I want," I interrupted.

"I think you do." The intercom on his desk buzzed. Robert reached over, pressed the necessary button. "Yes?"

His secretary's voice filled the room, ricocheted off the floor-to-ceiling windows. "Melanie Rogers is here."

"Send her in," he said easily, eyes glued to mine. "The next move is up to you, Kate." The door to his office opened and in walked a beautiful woman with dark red hair and a wide, full mouth. "Melanie," he said, kissing the side of her cheek, as he had mine only moments ago.

I raised my hand to my face, stroked the place where his lips had lingered, felt it burn.

"I'm sorry I'm late." Her voice was soft, hypnotic.

"Don't be sorry. It worked out perfectly. Let me introduce you to an old friend. Melanie

Rogers, this is Kate Sinclair. We go back a very long way."

I don't remember Melanie's reply. I only remember thinking she had the greenest eyes I'd ever seen, and wondering what she was doing having lunch with Robert.

I muttered something like "I won't keep you," then headed to the door.

"I look forward to hearing from you again soon," Robert said as I stepped into the reception area. Seconds later, the door to his office closed behind me.

My mother moved in with us that Friday night.

She'd had another run-in with poor Mr. Emerson, this time attacking him with his own cane, whacking him against the side of his head and actually knocking him to the floor. Both Mr. Emerson's family and Mrs. Winchell were now demanding that my mother be removed from the Palm Beach Lakes Retirement Home. Mr. Emerson's family actually threatened to press charges if this wasn't done immediately.

There was no question as to where to move her. We had no choice. She had to stay with us. "She can have my room for the weekend," Sara offered, having made plans to spend the time studying for her history test with a friend from school. Without my prompting, she'd even supplied me with the name, address, and phone number of that friend, and granted me permission to check with the girl's mother to make sure it was all right.

"How long do you think this will last?" Larry marveled.

"I'll take whatever I can get," I said.

My mother appeared disoriented by the move. She kept asking when it was time to go home. I told her she'd be spending some time with us. She said, "That's fine, dear," then five minutes later asked if it was time to go home.

"She's going to drive you nuts," Larry whispered, carrying his new set of clubs to the front door.

"Who's that?" my mother asked, her head swiveling after him.

"That's Larry, Mom. My husband."

"Where's he going?"

"Not going anywhere, Mom," he answered. "I'm just getting everything ready for tomorrow."

"Good idea," she said, although the blank expression in her eyes indicated she had no idea what the idea was, let alone whether it was good or bad. "Is it time to go home yet?"

I tucked her into Sara's bed at around ten o'clock that night, and she fell asleep almost instantly. "Sleep tight," I told her, as I used to tell Sara.

"Think she'll sleep through the night?" Larry asked as I crawled into bed beside him.

"I hope so."

"Did you call Mrs. Sperling?"

"I said I was just checking to make sure that Sara wasn't an imposition, and she said that Sara is a joy to have around."

"Are you sure you called the right number?"

I laughed, settled into the crook of his arm, drifted off to sleep. At three-thirty, I awoke to find my mother wandering the house. I returned her to Sara's bed, went back to my own. This was repeated every hour until, at six-thirty, I decided I might as well get dressed. Larry left for his golf game at seven. My mother asked who that nice man was and where he was going.

When Michelle woke up, she offered to take my mother for a walk, and they left the house hand in hand. I finished making my bed and moved into Sara's room, picking up the covers my mother had kicked to the floor and straightening the tousled sheets. Sara had done a great job tidying up. "You can actually see the floor," I marveled, picking up my mother's housecoat and heading for the small walk-in closet.

I almost didn't see the books. They were hidden behind some clothes in the far corner, and I was half out of the closet before I realized they were there. I'm not sure what made me look closer. Maybe it was just the novelty of finding books in a closet, or maybe it was my suspicious nature as far as Sara was concerned. At any rate, I picked up the books, opening them to confirm what I already knew: they were a history text and a world atlas. Didn't Sara need these for her test?

I walked to the kitchen and quickly called the Sperlings. The line was busy. I hung up and tried again. Still busy, as it was five minutes later when I tried a third time. "You're

354

being silly," I told myself. "Her friend has the same books; what do they need with two sets of texts?" But even as I found reasons to reassure myself, my fingers continued punching in the Sperlings' phone number. "Damnit," I said, giving up when I heard the front door open and close.

"Something wrong?" Michelle asked from the foyer.

"I have to go out for a few minutes," I told her, returning to Sara's room and gathering up the history books. If she didn't need them, fine. That would be just fine, I told myself, asking Michelle to look after my mother, assuring my mother I'd be back before she knew I was gone. "You're being silly," I repeated as I drove to the Sperlings'. "This is not the same thing as finding those empty packages of cigarettes. This is not like finding those bottles of beer. This isn't the same thing at all. Sara has no reason to lie to you. She's turned over a new leaf." And if she hadn't? "You spoke to Mrs. Sperling. She was expecting Sara. Sara's a joy to have around. Remember?"

The Sperlings lived in the gated community of Admiral's Cove off PGA Boulevard. I pulled my car up to the front gate, gave my name to the serious-faced security guard in the access booth. He peered at his clipboard. "I'm afraid your name's not on the list."

"Mrs. Sperling's not expecting me. But my daughter is visiting for the weekend, and she forgot her books." I indicated the books on the seat beside me.

"Just a minute, please." The guard retreated to his station and used the phone. "I'm afraid the line is busy. If you'd like to pull your car over to the side there, I can try again in a few minutes."

I pulled my car into the designated spot and waited, wondering who was on the phone for so long and would they ever get off. A minute stretched to five, then ten. "Just go home," I told myself. "Sara obviously doesn't need the books. What are you trying to prove?" She's going to think you're checking up on her, I continued silently, and that's going to make her very angry. Is that what you want? Especially now when everything has been going so well? I looked toward the guard, watching his lips move as he talked on the phone.

As I was about to signal the guard my intention to leave, he hung up the phone and stepped out of the booth.

"Mrs. Sperling says your daughter isn't here," he announced, approaching my car.

"I don't understand," Mrs. Sperling said to me over the phone in the guardhouse a few seconds later. "Soon after Sara arrived, she got a phone call. She said it was from you, and that something was wrong with her grandmother, and you needed her back home. She said she'd meet you at the front gate."

I listened in silence, too numb to speak.

"I'm so sorry. I don't know what to say," Mrs. Sperling continued. "You don't think anything's happened to her, do you?"

"I'm sure she's fine," I said, my voice

expressionless, as if someone had sat on it, flattened the life right out of it.

"Do you have any idea where she is?"

"I know exactly where she is," I said, returning the phone to the guard's waiting hand and climbing back into my car, staring at my lifeless eyes in the rearview mirror. "She's at a wedding."

Chapter
24

The scene unfolds as if in a nightmare—in fits and starts, images fading in and out, no conjunctives to connect one event with the next, to provide context. I see my sister, dressed in a short, yet surprisingly traditional white wedding dress, a shoulder-length veil covering, but not hiding, her radiant smile. I see Colin Friendly, dressed in blue dungarees and death row orange T-shirt, laughing as my sister walks to his side, his eyes looking past her to the beautiful young girl who follows behind. The girl is wearing layers of black and white, much like her hair, whose dark roots are encroaching ever further into her blond curls. Her forest-green eyes are huge and curious; her mouth quivers uncertainly into a smile.

Close-ups of body parts: eyes, mouths, breasts, hands, fists, teeth.

Men in standard blue prison garb stand to either side of the spectacled prison chaplain, who cradles the Bible between steady palms.

More close-ups—stainless-steel tables and chairs, their legs bolted to the linoleum floor. Human legs mingle—white high heels, black Doc Martens, brown loafers, scuffed prison sneakers.

I watch helplessly as the chaplain opens his mouth to speak.

Do you take this woman?

Can't somebody stop this?

Do you take this man?

Run. Now—while you still can.

If anyone knows just cause why this man and this woman...

Is everybody crazy? Why am I the only one to object?

Let him speak now or forever hold his peace.

I'm screaming. Why can't anybody hear me?

He hears me. Colin hears me.

Fists clench beside blue prison dungarees. Piercing blue eyes narrow with hatred.

Long manicured fingers, nails painted bubble-gum pink stretch into the air. Fists unclench, slip a thin gold band on the third finger of the outstretched hand. The hand proudly displays the ring for all to see.

Sound effects: oohing and aahing, laughter. Someone breaks into song. *She'll Be Coming 'Round the Mountain.*

And now by the power vested in me by the state of Florida...

Don't do it. There's still time to get away.

I now pronounce that you are husband and wife.

A clock clicks noiselessly on the wall behind them. It has no face.

Colin, you may kiss your bride.

Lips connect, bodies sway together.

More laughter, cheering, congratulations all around.

Whoopee! Colin exclaims as Jo Lynn laughs, draws Sara happily into her arms.

I guess that makes us family, Colin says to Sara, beckoning her forward.

I guess so, Sara says, rough arms surrounding her as I press my hands against my temples, trying to squeeze such images from my brain.

Of course, I don't know exactly what happened that afternoon, because I wasn't there, and I've never asked for the specifics. I know only that a wedding took place, that my sister married the man of her dreams and my nightmares, that my daughter acted as maid of honor, that several inmates served as witnesses, that one broke into song, that it was all perfectly legal, that my sister was once again legally wed.

The tabloids made much of the wedding. A picture of Jo Lynn in her wedding dress graced the front page of the *Enquirer*. Another inside photo showed her proudly displaying her wedding band, a ring she'd purchased, and paid for herself. "As soon as Colin gets out," she was quoted as saying, "he's going to buy me a diamond eternity band. This marriage," she went on to say, "is forever."

Till death do us part.

Mercifully, the tabloids hadn't been allowed inside the prison, and so there were no pictures of Sara, although it was reported that Jo Lynn's niece served as her maid of honor, an indication, the paper surmised, of her family's support.

"It was everything I've always wanted in a wedding," my sister babbled. "Low-key and beautiful. There was just so much love in that room."

The paper then gave a brief description of Jo Lynn's three previous marriages, and even carried an interview with Andrew MacInnes, husband number one, who opined that Jo Lynn had always been a little wild and reckless, and a handful for any man. He didn't bother mentioning that his way of dealing with her wild and reckless nature was to beat her senseless.

My sister's courtship with Colin Friendly was rehashed and reprinted: her steadfast loyalty, her continuing support, her unwavering belief in his innocence. If you didn't know the man had been convicted of torturing and killing thirteen women and girls and was suspected in the disappearance of scores of others, you'd swear they were writing about a modern-day Romeo and Juliet, a pair of star-crossed lovers whose misguided enemies were intent on keeping them apart.

Not that Colin's history was ignored. Gruesome and lurid details of his killing spree filled page after page. Under a profile of Jo Lynn, Colin's penchant for breaking the noses

360

of his victims was duly noted, something the psychologists who'd testified at his trial had traced back to his boyhood, when his mother had held his nose in his own waste. These same psychologists now speculated on Colin's motives for marrying my sister, and hers for marrying him. Stability, image, friendship, they postulated on Colin's behalf. Publicity, loneliness, a martyr complex, they proffered with regard to Jo Lynn. They gave conflicting opinions as to whether or not they thought the marriage would last. "It stands as good a chance as any," one proclaimed.

The Saturday afternoon I found out that Sara wasn't at the Sperlings', I called the prison, hoping to prevent the marriage from taking place. But the wedding was already over. My sister had left the premises. Colin was back in his cell.

I sat up all night waiting for Sara to come home, even though I knew she wouldn't be back till the following day. She was at the Sperlings', after all, studying hard for a test. She wasn't due back till Sunday evening.

"Come to bed," Larry urged on several occasions. "You were up all night last night. You need your sleep."

"I can't sleep."

"You could try."

"She might come home."

"She won't."

"She might."

"What are you going to say to her when she does?"

"I don't know."

That much, at least, was the truth. I didn't have a clue what I was going to say to my older daughter. Was there any point in reminding her, yet again, that lies destroy trust, and that, despite the fact I would always love her, with every lie I liked her less? Would she care that she was making it harder and harder for us to believe anything she said, that she was wiping out whatever goodwill she'd managed to acquire?

Was there any point in asking her why she did these things, why she would deliberately go against our explicit instructions that she have nothing further to do with my sister and Colin Friendly? Had she learned nothing from the last episode except to make her lies more elaborate?

I shuddered with the knowledge that she'd been setting me up for weeks: cleaning her room, helping around the house, doing her homework, actually being pleasant to be around. I remembered the feel of her body in my arms when she'd comforted me about my mother, the overwhelming tenderness I'd felt toward her. I'd feasted for days on that feeling. I have my little girl back, I told myself.

But it was all a ruse. A way to soften me up, get me to drop my defenses, leave my suspicions at the door. Of course, you can stay the weekend with your friend. I know how hard you've been working for this test. I know how much you want to do well. Take care of yourself, darling. Don't study too hard.

I heard the rustle of pajamas, turned to see Michelle walking toward me, eyes half closed in sleep. "Is everything all right?" she asked.

"Fine, sweetie," I told her. "I just can't sleep."

"Are you worried about Grandma?"

"A little."

"I just looked in on her. She's sound asleep."

"Thank you, doll."

"Her blanket was on the floor, so I picked it up."

"You're a good thing."

She sat down on the sofa beside me, burrowed deep into my side. "I think I've decided what I want to be when I grow up," she said, as if this were the most logical thing to be discussing at almost three o'clock in the morning.

"Really? What's that?"

"A writer," she said.

"A writer? Really? What kind of writer?"

"A novelist, I think. Maybe a playwright."

"That's a great idea," I told her. "I think you'd make a wonderful writer."

"You do? Why?"

"Because you're sensitive, and observant, and beautiful."

She groaned. "You don't have to be beautiful to be a writer."

"You have a beautiful soul," I told her.

"Of course, I'd finish my education first," she reassured me.

"I think that's a smart move."

"I was thinking of Brown, or even Yale.

Do you think I'm smart enough to get into an Ivy League college?"

"I think they'd be lucky to have you."

I brushed some soft hairs away from her face, planted a gent thing to be discussing at almost three o'clock in the morning.

"Really? What's that?"

"A writer," she said.

"A writer? Really? What kind of writer?"

"A novelist, I think. Maybe a playwright."

"That's a great idea," I told her. "I think you'd make a wonderful writer."

"You do? Why?"

"Because you're sensitive, and observant, and beautiful."

She groaned. "You don't have to be beautiful to be a writer."

"You have a beautiful soul," I told her.

"Of course, I'd finish my education first," she reassured me.

"I think that's a smart move."

"I was thinking of Brown, or even Yale. Do you think I'm smart enough to get into an Ivy League college?"

"I think they'd be lucky to have you."

I brushed some soft hairs away from her face, planted a gentle kiss on her forehead, stared toward the front door. How could I have two children so completely unalike? How could two children raised in the same household by the same two parents, in essentially the same way, be so totally different?

It had been that way right from the beginning,

I realized, thinking back. Sara had been a difficult baby, demanding of my total attention. Michelle had been the easiest baby in the world, happy just to be included. Sara demanded to be fed every few hours; Michelle waited patiently until I was ready. Sara refused all efforts at toilet training, peeing in her pants until she was almost seven years old; Michelle trained herself at thirteen months. So, what else was new? Had anything really changed?

"You're thinking about Sara, aren't you?" Michelle said.

I closed my eyes, shook my head. Even in the dark, I was transparent. "Sorry, sweetie."

"Don't worry about her, Mom. She's all right."

I patted her hand. "I guess so."

"She's not at Robin's house, is she?"

"No."

"I didn't think so."

"Why? Did she say anything to you about where she was going?"

Michelle's head shook from side to side. "No, she just asked if she could borrow my black-and-white top—you know, the one with the matching sweater."

"How could she borrow your top? It would be way too small."

"She likes them that way."

"What did you tell her?"

"I told her no. I said, why would she need to borrow my top just to go study?"

"What did she say?"

"She said I was a stupid bitch."

"What?"

"It's all right. I'm used to it."

"Used to what?"

"She always calls me a stupid bitch. Sometimes worse."

I was horrified. "Why haven't you told me this before?"

"Because I have to learn to deal with these things myself. Isn't that what you would have told me? That deep down, my sister loves me very much, and that I'm a smart girl, I'd figure out how to deal with her?"

I smiled sadly. That was exactly what I would have told her. But that was before my daughter had run off to serve as maid of honor for my sister's marriage to a serial killer. Now I wasn't sure what I knew about anything. "I'm so sorry, sweetie. You don't deserve that. She has no right to call you names."

"She had no right to take my top and matching sweater, but she did anyway."

"She took your top after you said no?"

"I looked everywhere. They're gone. So are three of my tapes."

"Your tapes?"

"Nine Inch Nails, Alanis Morissette, Mariah Carey."

"Oh God."

"She'll bring them back. Of course, the tapes'll be ruined, and my clothes will be all stretched out and reek of cigarettes."

"I'll get you new ones," I told her.

"I don't want new ones. I just want her to stop taking my things."

"I'll talk to her."

"That won't do any good."

"Maybe it will."

"Has it ever?"

"I don't know what else to do," I admitted after a pause.

"Can I have a lock put on my closet?"

I stared through the darkness at my younger child, amazed at how innately practical she was. "Yes, we can do that."

"Good."

"How'd you get to be so smart?"

Michelle smiled. "Can I tell you something terrible?" she asked.

I held my breath. "How terrible?"

"Pretty terrible."

"About Sara?"

"About me."

I felt a strange combination of fear and relief. What could Michelle possibly tell me about herself that could be so terrible? And if there was something truly terrible about her that I didn't know, did I really want to hear it? Now? "What is it?" I asked.

For a second, she was silent, as if debating with herself whether or not to proceed.

"You don't have to tell me," I said hopefully.

"Sometimes I hate her," she confided.

"What?"

"Sara," Michelle clarified. "Sometimes I hate her."

That's it? I thought, with great relief. That's what's so terrible? "You hate your sister?"

"Sometimes. Does that make me an awful

person?"

"It makes you pretty normal."

"Is it normal to hate your sister?"

"It's normal to be angry at somone who steals from you and calls you names," I said.

"It's more than that. Sometimes, I really, really hate her."

"Sometimes I hate her too," I said.

Michelle's arms reached around my waist, hugged me tightly. Two wounded comrades-in-arms, I remember thinking, kissing the top of her head.

"Can I tell you something else?" she asked, her voice shaking with the threat of tears.

"You can tell me anything," I told her.

"You remember when I was in grade five?" she asked.

I nodded. "Yes."

"And Mr. Fisher gave me the butterfly's cocoon to take care of over the Christmas break?"

"I remember."

Michelle had brought home a glass jar that contained a butterfly's cocoon that was attached to the side of a small stick. Every day, she watched over that jar, checking the cocoon for signs of growth, fretting over it the way a mother worries about her newborn baby. "I don't think it's right," she announced one day. "I think the cocoon's supposed to be higher."

"I think you should leave it alone," Sara advised.

"I think it should be higher." Michelle

reached inside the jar, adjusted the cocoon with her fingers. "That's better."

When Michelle proudly returned the jar to the teacher, he told her that something had dislodged the cocoon and that the butterfly inside had died. "These things happen," he told her. "Don't blame yourself."

"It was my fault," Michelle said now, crying softly. "I moved the cocoon and so the butterfly died. Sara was right."

"Oh, my sweet baby."

"She said to leave it alone. I didn't listen."

"You've been worrying about this all these years?"

"I never told Mr. Fisher I moved it."

I rocked her back and forth, as I had when she was small, more for my benefit than for hers, even then. "It would be wonderful if we could go back and change things, correct all our mistakes, make everything right."

Michelle sniffed loudly. "But we can't."

"No, we can't. If we did, we'd be so busy rewriting the past, we'd have no time left for the present."

"What things would *you* rewrite?" she asked.

"Oh my. That's much too big a question for this hour of the night," I told her. "Besides, you only torture yourself when you start asking questions like that. We all make mistakes. The trick is to do the best you can."

"I think you've done really well," Michelle offered graciously.

"Thank you, sweetie. Have I ever told you that when I grow up I want to be exactly like you?"

She laughed through her tears, gave another loud sniff, hugged me tighter.

We heard footsteps, turned as one toward the sound, watched as my mother emerged from the shadows, clad in a white flannel nightgown, the dim light of the quarter-moon dancing across her face. "Hello, dear," she said, coming over and sitting on my other side. "Is it time to get up?"

"It's three o'clock in the morning, Grandma," Michelle told her.

"Of course it is," my mother said.

"We should all be in bed."

"Where's your father?" my mother asked, looking around.

"He's asleep," Michelle answered.

"Where's your father?" my mother repeated, and I realized it was me she was addressing.

"He's dead," I reminded her gently.

"Yes," she said, her gray head nodding up and down. "I remember that. We were having dinner one night, finishing our dessert, and he stood up to get a glass of milk, and said he felt a hell of a headache coming on. Those were his exact words—a hell of a headache. I remember because he almost never used profanity."

"Hell isn't a profanity," Michelle said.

"It isn't?"

"No. Not now."

"Well, it was. It was then," my mother told her with a certainty that surprised me.

Three generations of women lapsed into silence. Past, present, and future, together in the darkness before dawn. I remember thinking that I'd never felt so helpless.

God grant me the serenity to accept the things I cannot change, I found myself praying, the strength to change the things I can, and the wisdom to know the difference.

Chapter
25

Needless to say, I didn't sleep at all that night. When Larry woke up at eight o'clock the next morning, he found me still sitting on the living-room sofa, my eyes open and glazed over, staring blankly toward the front door. I was alone. I had a vague recollection of Michelle guiding my mother back to bed at some point during the night, then coming back to kiss my forehead before retreating to her room. I remembered little else. My mind was mercifully blank. One hour had drifted seemlessly into the next. The sky had gone from black to gray to blue without any input from me. I was alive to face another day.

"Have you been up all night, funny face?" Larry asked, sitting down beside me, the pillows of the sofa shifting to accommodate him, his terry-cloth bathrobe grazing my bare arms.

I turned away, trying to escape the sound

of his voice, the weight of his concern falling heavy into my lap, like an unwanted child.

"Sara's fine, you know," he continued. "You can bet that *she* didn't lose any sleep."

"I know that."

"Why don't you get back into bed for a few hours. You might surprise yourself and fall asleep."

"I don't like surprises," I told him stubbornly, deliberately missing the point.

"You know what I mean," he said.

I nodded, but didn't move.

"How can you even think of confronting Sara when you haven't slept in two days?"

"I'll be fine."

"Have you reached any conclusions about how to deal with her?"

"Other than shooting her, you mean?" I asked, and he smiled.

"Shooting's good," he said. My turn to smile. "I have some thoughts on the matter," he continued. "If you're interested," he added, waiting.

"Can we talk about them later?"

"Can you promise not to do anything until I get home?"

"Where are you going?"

"Golf game, remember? I'm teeing off at nine twenty-one."

"Nine twenty-*one*?"

"Tee-off times are scheduled every seven minutes."

I shook my head in seeming wonder, although the truth was that I really didn't care. Still, it was easier—and far less dangerous—to talk about golf than about our older daughter.

"I don't have to go," he volunteered.

"Why wouldn't you go?"

"If you'd rather I stayed home..."

"No. What's the point in that?"

"If you wanted company. If you didn't want to be alone."

"I'm not alone."

"If you wanted *my* company," Larry qualified.

I turned to him, tried to smile. "I'll be fine. You go. Break a hundred."

He rose to his feet, swayed unsteadily, his body a reflection of his state of mind. "I should be back by two. Maybe we could go to a movie."

"Maybe," I said.

He excused himself to get dressed. I went into the kitchen and made a large pot of coffee. An hour later, I was on my fourth cup, and Larry was on his way to the golf course. I checked on my mother and Michelle, relieved to find them both still sleeping soundly. Maybe Larry was right, I decided, climbing into my bed, crawling between the sheets, and pulling the covers up around my chin. Maybe a few hours' sleep would be enough to restore my perspective, if not my faith.

But the four cups of coffee had done their work, and there was no way I was going to fall asleep. After about half an hour, during which time I twisted my tired body into every conceivable position, and counted enough sheep to stock herds on both sides of the Atlantic, I finally gave up and headed for the shower, from which I emerged, some twenty minutes later, wetter but none the wiser.

Larry returned home at just after two o'clock—his score a disappointing 104—to find me sitting in basically the same position in which he'd left me. "I know you moved, because you're wearing different clothes," he noted with a sad smile. "Did you check the paper?"

"The paper?"

"To see what movies are playing."

"I can't go to a movie."

"Why not?"

"What am I supposed to do with Michelle and my mother?"

"They'll come with."

"And Sara?"

"She's not invited. Come on," he cajoled. "We'll take in a movie, then grab some fajitas at Chili's. You know how much Michelle loves Chili's."

"What if Sara gets home while we're out?"

"Then she'll wait for us for a change."

"I don't think that's a good idea."

"What's not a good idea?" Michelle asked, coming into the room, plopping down into the opposite sofa, long skinny arms dangling between long skinny legs.

"I thought we'd go to a movie around four o'clock, then have something to eat."

"Chili's?" Michelle's voice literally chirped with anticipation.

"One fajita combo coming up," Larry said.

"Why don't you check the paper and talk to Grandma and decide what movie you want to see."

Michelle was instantly on her feet. "Grandma," she called in the direction of Sara's room. "We're going to the movies."

"I can't go," I told Larry.

"Of course you can," he insisted.

"All right, then, I don't *want* to go."

"You *want* to sit here and stew until Sara comes home?"

"I need some time to think."

"You've been thinking for the past twenty-four hours. Has it done any good?"

"That's not the point."

"What *is* the point?"

"The point is that going to a movie is not high on my list of priorities right now."

"Maybe you should reexamine your priorities."

"What?"

"You heard me."

"Our daughter deceives us, defies us, and disappears for the weekend, and you want me to go to the movies instead of being here when she gets home. Those are your priorities?"

"There'll be plenty of time to confront Sara later. Right now you're wound so tight..."

"I'm not wound so tight. Please don't tell me I'm wound so tight. You have no idea what I'm feeling."

"Tell me." He sat down beside me. Immediately, I jumped to my feet.

"I'm frustrated," I said, the words flying from

my mouth, like spit. "I'm frustrated and angry and hurt." I began pacing back and forth between the two living-room sofas, anxiety gnawing at my chest, like a rat on a rope. "I trusted her, damnit! I believed her. I fell for all the lies. She got me—again! What? Am I stupid? All she has to do is smile at me and I'm ready to buy her the store?"

"You're her mother," Larry said simply.

"I'm an idiot," I raged. "And she's nothing but a goddamn liar."

"And you think this is the right frame of mind for you to be dealing with her?" Larry asked logically.

"You'd rather not deal with her at all, is that it?"

"I didn't say that."

"What are you saying?"

"I'm saying that you need a breather. You've been sitting here stewing in your own juices all day. You need to get out of this house for a few hours, get your mind on something else. You're not going to accomplish anything with Sara when you're this angry."

"And then what?" I demanded. "After the movie and the fajitas. What happens then?"

"We come home. Hopefully Sara will be here. We'll listen to what she has to say…"

"More lies."

"Then we'll decide—calmly—what we're going to do."

"Such as?"

There was a minute's silence. The anxiety curled around my heart like a snake, beginning its slow squeeze.

"I think Sara has to understand the seriousness of what she's done," Larry began, "the fact that this kind of behavior can no longer be tolerated."

I shook my head. Hadn't we been through all this before? Sara understood exactly what she was doing. It was Larry and I who had yet to come to terms with our level of tolerance.

"I think we should cancel all her privileges for the remainder of the school year," Larry continued. "That includes her allowance and any extracurricular activities. When she's not at school, she's at home, it's as simple as that."

"You really think she's going to go along with that?"

"If she doesn't, she'll have to find somewhere else to live."

The simple statement took my breath away. "What?"

Larry got to his feet, walked to my side, put his hands on my arms, forced my eyes to his. "What other choice is there, ultimately?" he asked.

"You're suggesting we kick our daughter out of the house?"

"I'm suggesting we give her the choice—either she chooses to live by the rules of this household or she chooses to live elsewhere. It's as simple as that."

"Stop saying that," I shouted, pushing his arms away, resuming my angry pacing. "Nothing is simple where Sara is concerned."

"Then, at the very least, we have to make

377

it less complicated where *we're* concerned." He looked toward the ceiling, then back at me. "Who calls the shots here, Kate? Who sets the limits? You're the therapist. You know this is exactly how you'd advise a client."

"This is our seventeen-year-old daughter we're talking about. You're saying we should just throw her out on the street?" I pictured Sara huddled around an open fire on some deserted corner. The flames from the fire reached out for me, searing the lining of my lungs.

"That's not what I'm saying."

"You know what she'll do if we kick her out, don't you? She'll just move in with Jo Lynn. That's what she'll do. God, it's so hot in here." I pulled roughly at the collar of my beige cotton sweater.

"Did you say that Jo Lynn is coming to live with us?" my mother asked, walking sprightly into the room, Michelle at her side.

"Oh God," I muttered.

"We picked a movie," Michelle announced. "It starts at three-fifty."

"I don't think I can take too much more of this." My voice emerged as a thin wail, scratching the air like nails on a blackboard.

"Mom, what's wrong?"

"Something the matter, dear?" my mother asked.

"There's nothing the matter," I snapped, the heat sweeping through my insides with the unrestrained fury of a brush fire. "It's just so fucking hot in here!" In the next instant, I ripped my sweater up over my head, threw it angrily to the floor, then stomped on it, before kicking it halfway across the room. I looked up to find my husband, my mother, and my daughter staring at me as if I were nuts.

"It *is* a little warm in here," my mother said.

"Mother!" Michelle's eyes had grown so large they threatened to overtake her face. "You said the F-word."

"You know what," Larry said, clearly flustered by my outburst. "I think we need to clear out of here and give your mother some space."

"Oh, that's just great," I said. "Rats deserting the sinking ship."

Larry raised his hands into the air, then dropped them lifelessly to his sides. "I thought that's what you wanted," he said.

"There are rats?" my mother asked. Wary eyes skirted the tile floor.

"Of course, that's what you do best, isn't it?" I said, looking directly at my husband.

"What are you talking about?" Larry asked.

"When the going gets tough, the tough go golfing. Or to the movies. Isn't that what they say?"

Larry turned toward my mother and Michelle. "Michelle, honey, we still have some time before we have to leave. Why don't you take your grandmother out for a little walk."

Michelle's eyes moved from me to her father and back again, as if she were courtside at a tennis match. "Come on, Grandma," she said finally, leading my mother toward the front door.

"Are we going to the movies?" my mother asked as the door closed behind them.

"You have something you want to say to me?" Larry said after they were gone.

I retrieved my sweater from the floor, used it to wipe the sweat from between my breasts. "Are you sure you have time? I mean, you don't want to be late for the movie."

"You have something to say, say it."

"It's just so easy for you, isn't it?"

"What is?"

"To pick up and leave."

"It's just a movie, Kate. Not everything has to be such a big deal."

"No, I recognize that our daughter isn't as big a deal as breaking a hundred..."

"Okay, let's stop this right now," Larry warned.

"I thought you said if I had something to say, I should say it."

"I changed my mind."

"Too late."

"It will be if you don't stop this right now."

"What—you're threatening me? If I don't conform to the rules of the household, you're going to throw me out too?"

"Kate, this is crazy. Listen to yourself."

"No, you listen. For the last few months, my life has been steadily falling apart. And where have you been? On the golf course."

"That's not fair."

"Maybe not, but it's true. I've been deal-

380

ing with my mother, my sister, the kids, these goddamn hot flashes," I continued, "and meanwhile you've been making yourself scarcer and scarcer. Oh, you say all the right things, you make all the right sounds, but you're never actually here when I need you."

"I'm here now," he offered softly.

"Only long enough to shower and change your clothes, then it's off to the movies, off to Chili's."

"What do you want from me, Kate?" he asked. "What do you want me to do? Tell me, because I honestly don't know anymore. I feel like, no matter what I say or do, it's gonna be wrong. It's like I'm always walking around on eggshells. I'm afraid to open my mouth, in case I say the wrong thing; I'm afraid to touch you, in case I touch you in the wrong spot, and you fly off the handle. You say I'm never here. Maybe you're right. Maybe my way of dealing with all that's been going on is to just get away from it. Is there really that much to be gained by confronting everything head-on?"

"I don't know," I admitted, pressing my sweater against me, feeling the sudden chill from the air-conditioning system creeping along my bare arms. "I don't know anything anymore."

"You know that I'm not suggesting that we throw Sara out on her ear," Larry continued softly.

"I know that."

"I guess I'm just looking for a little peace. God knows, it's been a long time since she's given us any joy."

"She's not here to give us joy," I reminded him.

"Not part of her job description, I guess," Larry agreed sadly. "Come to the movie with us, Kate. Please. It'll be good for us."

"I can't," I heard myself say as tears dropped down my cheeks. "I just can't. But you go. Really. It's all right. You go."

I left him standing in the middle of the room and went into the washroom, splashed water on my face, then pulled my sweater back over my head. I stared at my reflection in the mirror over the sink, studying the lines beneath my eyes, like the tiny but persistent river lines on a map, I thought, standing there until I heard the front door open and close. When I returned to the living room moments later, Larry was gone, and I was alone. I sat back down on the sofa and waited for Sara to come home.

She walked through the door at exactly three minutes after six o'clock, her battered brown leather knapsack draped carelessly across one shoulder. She was wearing the same tight jeans and bosom-hugging striped jersey she'd been wearing when she left two days earlier, and her hair hung loosely around her face in several shades of careless blond. "Oh, hi," she said, stopping when she saw me, a hint of blush flashing across her pale cheeks. "You scared me. I almost didn't see you sitting there. Why don't you turn on some lights?"

"I've been waiting for you," I said, my voice surprisingly, eerily, calm.

She glanced slowly from side to side. "Is everything okay? Grandma...?"

"She's fine."

"Good." She took several steps toward her room.

"Did you bring Michelle's sweaters back?"

"What?"

"And her tapes?"

"I don't have any of Michelle's tapes, and why would I take her sweaters? They don't fit me." Sara managed just the right degree of indignation. For a split second, I thought maybe Michelle might be mistaken.

"Then you wouldn't mind showing me the contents of your knapsack," I pressed.

"Of course I'd mind. I said I don't have any of Michelle's things, and I don't. What—you don't believe me?"

"Apparently not."

She shook her head, as if my suspicions were beyond belief, as if I myself were beneath contempt. "Well, that's your problem."

Oh, she's good, I thought, rising to my feet. She's very good. "No, I'm afraid it's *your* problem."

"There's nothing in my knapsack but a lot of books," Sara protested.

"History books?" I asked.

"I have a big test tomorrow. Remember?"

"Oh, I remember."

"And I still have a few things I want to go over, so if you'll excuse me..."

"Don't you think you've studied enough? I mean, you've been at it all weekend." My voice was soft, conciliatory.

"I just want to go over everything one more time." Sara punctuated her lie with a modest laugh for extra authenticity, took several more steps toward her bedroom.

"When are you going to stop lying to me, Sara?"

The simple question stopped her cold. Her back arched, stiffened, like a cat's when threatened. "I don't have Michelle's stupid sweater or her dumb tapes," she enunciated carefully, as if each word were an effort, her back still to me.

"And you were at the Sperlings' house all weekend, studying for a test."

"You know that. You spoke to Mrs. Sperling."

"Yes, I did. Several times, in fact."

Slowly, Sara spun around to face me. When she stopped, I could see her eyes still moving, trying to process this latest bit of information, readying a fresh line of defense. "When did you speak to her?"

"Yesterday afternoon."

"You were checking up on me?"

I laughed. Her indignation was truly inspirational.

"Don't laugh at me," she warned.

"Don't lie to me," I said in return.

"I didn't lie to you. I did go to the Sperlings'."

"Yes, but you didn't stay there very long, did you?"

A pause, but only a slight one. "I couldn't.

Something came up."

"Yes, I know," I sympathized. "Your grandmother. You were needed back home."

Sara rolled her eyes, glanced from side to side, as if searching for the proper alibi. "Something came up," she repeated. "It was important."

"I bet it was. Why don't you tell me about it."

Sara shifted her weight from one foot to the other. "I can't," she said.

"Why not?"

"I can't betray a confidence."

Again, I almost laughed, this time managing to keep it in check. "You can betray my trust but you can't betray a confidence?"

"I didn't mean to betray your trust."

"You just didn't care."

"Of course I care."

"Where did you go?" I asked.

Sara lowered her gaze to the floor, then slowly lifted her face back to mine. Even in the fading light, I could see the tears glistening in her eyes. She's in pain, I thought, aching to take her in my arms. Despite everything, it was all I could do to keep my feet still, my hands at my sides. "A friend of mine is in trouble," she began, and my hands instantly lost their desire to comfort, clenching into tight, angry fists. More lies, I thought, fury spreading like a cancer through my brain, all but blocking out her words. "She's been seeing this guy her parents don't like, and they want her to break up with him, and she wants to, but she's afraid she

385

might be pregnant." A pause. A gulp. The threat of more tears. "She really needed someone to talk to. What could I do, Mom? It was pathetic. She was almost suicidal. She turned to me because she knows you're a therapist, and I guess she thought that maybe some of your wisdom might have rubbed off on me, that I'd be able to help her."

I gasped at the sheer wonder of how her mind worked, the speed with which it concocted these convoluted stories, her effortless ability to suck me into each elaborate scenario, flatter me into becoming at least partly responsible. After all, if I weren't a therapist, none of this would have happened. If it hadn't been for my profession, my expertise, my *wisdom*, Sara wouldn't have been dragged into this mess, she wouldn't have had to skip out on the Sperlings, she wouldn't have had to lie. "And were you able to help her?" I asked, continuing the charade.

"I think so." She smiled, relaxed her guard. "Anyway, I'm really sorry I had to lie. But I did manage to get some studying done anyway. I think I'm going to do really well on this test."

"You studied?" I asked. "Without any books?"

"What do you mean, without books? I had my books with me." She patted her knapsack in confirmation.

"Your books are in your closet," I said, tired of the charade.

"What?"

"Your books—they're in your closet. You want me to get them?"

"No, I don't want you to get them." Sara's voice swept across the house like a broom. "Who said you could go into my room?"

"Your grandmother has been using that room," I began, but she didn't let me finish.

"What were you doing snooping around in my closet?"

"I wasn't snooping."

"God, Mom, how can you expect me to respect you when you don't show me any respect?"

"I show you plenty of respect."

"How? By sneaking into my room? By rifling through my things?"

"I did not sneak into your room. I did not rifle through your things."

"What were you doing in my closet?"

"This is not about me," I reminded her, trying to regain control.

"The minute I leave this house, you're in my room, snooping around, calling the Sperlings, checking up on me. You call that trust? You call that being honest? You're such a hypocrite."

"Watch it," I warned.

"What do you want from me?" she demanded, as Larry had demanded earlier. "I've told you the truth. I didn't want to. It meant betraying a confidence, but I told you anyway."

"You told me nothing."

"I was with my girlfriend."

"The same girlfriend who collects empty cigarette packages?"

"What? What are you talking about?" Concern softened the angry lines around her eyes and mouth. "Mom, are you all right?"

"I know where you were, Sara," I said, my voice filled with so much rage, humiliation, and disappointment, it wobbled. "I know you weren't with any pregnant suicidal girlfriend. I know you were with my sister. I know you went to her goddamn wedding."

The room fell suddenly silent. If I expected more tears, apologies, pleas for forgiveness, I had the wrong child. Sara stared at me with undisguised contempt. "If you knew all along where I was," she said, her voice low, firm, resolutely unapologetic, "then why this stupid charade? Who's really the liar here, Ms. Therapist?"

"Don't you dare talk to me that way."

"Then stop all these stupid games."

Frustration froze my tongue. It lay fat, heavy in my mouth. I should have listened to Larry, gone with him to the movies, dealt with Sara after we got home, Larry at my side. I was too tired to deal with her alone, and Sara was much too wily an opponent. Everything Larry said had been right.

"I'm going to my room," Sara said.

"You're sleeping in the den," I told her, surprising both of us.

"What?"

"Grandma has your room. I don't think it would be wise to move her. She's confused enough." This was probably true, although I hadn't given the matter any previous thought.

"Fine," Sara said. She swayed toward the den.

"And while you're there," I continued, unable to stop myself despite my best intentions, despite my years of professional training and *wisdom*, "you might give some thought as to whether you really want to be a part of this family anymore."

"What?" The look on Sara's face told me she thought I'd lost my mind. "What on earth are you jabbering about now?"

"As of this moment, all privileges are suspended."

"What?"

"You heard me. No more privileges."

"You give a dog privileges," Sara shot back. "People have rights."

We have rights too, I heard Larry say.

"No more allowance," I continued, fueled by her protest. "No more going out on weekends. For the rest of the school year, you're either at school or at home," I said, repeating Larry's words.

"Go to hell," Sara said succinctly.

"No," I said. "You're the one who'll be looking for new accommodations. You either play by the rules of this household or you find somewhere else to live. It's as simple as that."

Sara looked me straight in the eye. "Fuck you," she said.

In the next instant, I watched myself literally fly across the room at Sara, my feet off the floor, my arms outstretched. I landed almost on top of her, my fists falling like hammers across the back of her head, her neck, her shoulders, any part of her they could find. Sara screamed, tried to escape, her hands reaching up to protect herself from my blows. We were both screaming and crying, as my fists continued to pummel her flesh.

"Stop it, Mom!" she was screaming. "Stop!"

I pulled back in absolute horror, stared into Sara's startled, tear-stained face. "Sara, I'm so sorry," I began.

"Fucking bitch," she said.

Without thinking, I hauled back and slapped her hard across the face, so hard the palm of my hand stung, and the sound echoed throughout the house. I watched a torrent of angry wet tears wash the years from Sara's face. The teenager became the adolescent, then the child, then the infant at my breast. My baby, I thought, as she pulled herself up to her full Amazonian height and slapped me right back.

I stared at my older daughter in astonishment, my cheek, my insides, on fire. "If you ever hit me again," I told her slowly, my voice surprisingly calm, "then you're out of here."

"You hit me first," she protested.

"If *I* ever hit you again," I continued without missing a beat, "then you're out of here."

"What? That's not fair."

"Maybe not, but it's *my* house."

"You're crazy," Sara started screaming. "You know that? You're crazy."

It was around this time that Larry brought my mother and Michelle home.

"She's crazy," Sara was yelling, as Michelle cradled my mother in the front foyer. "I'm going to call the police. I'm going to call Children's Aid."

"What happened?" Michelle asked, temporarily abandoning my mother to come to my aid, eyes shooting daggers at her sister.

"Oh, here she is," Sara intoned. "Little Miss Perfect."

Somehow, Larry managed to settle us all in our rooms, as a referee manages to restore order in the ring, returning the combatants to their respective corners. He calmed my mother, reassured Michelle, tended to Sara's invisible bruises, made sure everyone was breathing normally. Eventually, the house fell silent, grew dark.

"Are you all right?" Larry asked later, climbing into bed beside me.

I lay on my side, staring at the fuzzy glow from the moon through the bedroom curtains. "No," I said.

It was as simple as that.

Chapter
26

Don't feel guilty," Larry advised me often over the course of the next few days.

But, of course, I did feel guilty. How could I not? I'd hit my child, not once, but repeatedly. I'd used my fists on her back and shoulders, my open palm on her face. That beautiful face, I thought. How could I have slapped it?

"You were provoked. She had it coming," Larry said.

And that was true. I was provoked; she did have it coming.

That still didn't make it right.

"You taught her that she can push people only so far," Larry said.

"The only thing I taught her is that I can't control my temper."

"Stop being so hard on yourself, Kate."

"I'm the adult in this equation."

"She's seventeen," he reminded me. "She's six feet tall."

"I'm her mother."

"You don't call your mother a fucking bitch."

"I hit her."

"She hit you back."

Strangely enough, of all the things that were said and done that night, the fact that Sara had hit me bothered me the least. Maybe because I've always believed that if you hit someone, you have to be prepared to be hit back.

It was something my mother never did.

A torrent of deliberately repressed memories rushed back at me. I heard the front door of my childhood open, saw my stepfather walk through. *Hello, darling,* my mother greeted him. *You're late.*

Are you complaining?

Of course not. I was just worried. Dinner was ready an hour ago.

Dinner is whenever I get home.

It's on the table.

It's cold.

I'll warm it up.

You know I hate warmed-over food. I don't work hard and pay good money for meat to have it warmed over.

Don't get all worked up. I'll make you something else.

You think I have all night to wait until you make something else?

It won't take long.

You don't think I deserve a decent meal when I get home?

Of course you do. That's why I try to make everything nice for you.

Then why isn't *everything nice?*

It is. It's just that you were late.

You're saying it's my fault?

Of course not. These things happen. I understand.

You understand shit.

I'm sorry, Mike. I didn't mean...

You're always sorry. You never mean. You never think, *that's your problem. Why do you do these things?*

Please, Mike, calm down. You'll scare the children.

Fuck the children.

Please watch your language.

My language? Oh, that's right, isn't it? Your first husband, fuck his sainted memory, he never swore, did he? Well, what are you going to do, wash my mouth out with soap? Is that what you're going to do?

Please, Mike.

You know what? That's a damn good idea. That's exactly what I'm going to do. I'm going to wash your mouth out with soap. Then next time you think of getting smart with your husband, you'll think twice.

No, don't, please don't!

What's the matter? Don't you like the taste? I bet it tastes better than that shit you were going to serve me tonight, you stupid bitch.

I closed my eyes, tried not to see the bruises along the side of my mother's mouth the next morning, the red marks on the side of her neck and arms, the angry scratch along her chin.

What did you do to my mother? I demanded on another such occasion.

Ssh, Kate, my mother warned, *it's nothing.*

What are you talking about? I never touched your mother. What lies have you been telling the kid, Helen?

I didn't tell her anything. It's okay, Kate. I tripped on the carpet. I fell against the side of the door.

Clumsy idiot, my stepfather said.

She's not a clumsy idiot, I told him. *You are.*

Even now I can feel the sharp cuff of his hand as it snapped across the back of my head. I'll never do that, I vowed in that instant. I'll never hit a child of mine.

"I'm no better than he was," I told Larry.

"Stop beating yourself up about this," he said.

An interesting choice of words, I thought. "I'm a therapist, for God's sake."

"You're a therapist," he repeated. "Not a saint. Kate, has anything even remotely like this ever happened before? No. It happened once. You were provoked and you lost control."

He's not always this way, I could hear my mother tearfully intone. *There are times when he's gentle and thoughtful and funny. It's only sometimes when he's under a lot of stress. Or I provoke him and he just loses control.*

"It doesn't wash," I told Larry, as I had told her.

Was violence contagious? Was it passed down from one generation to the next, like some dreaded inherited disease? Was there no escape?

I canceled my appointments for the next two days, barely got out of bed. Sara refused to acknowledge my presence. She went to school, came home, stayed in the den until dinner, ate in silence, then returned to the den when dinner was through. I was the invisible woman, a role that was somewhat familiar to me, although this time was different, because this time my invisibility was something that had been deliberately imposed.

"Can I talk to you?" I asked from the doorway several nights later.

"No," Sara said. She opened a book, pretended to read.

"I think it's important that we talk about what happened."

"You beat me up, that's what happened."

"I didn't beat you," I began, then stopped. "I'm so sorry."

"I don't want to talk about it."

"Leave her alone," Larry said gently, coming up behind me and guiding me away from Sara's door. "You have nothing to apologize for."

"She'll start talking to you again as soon as she wants something," Michelle said.

"Is it time to go home?" my mother asked.

"I'm trying to find somewhere nice for you, Mom," I told her, realizing I'd have to make some decisions soon regarding her future. It was increasingly obvious that she couldn't stay here. "But first, we have a doctor's appointment tomorrow, remember?"

Of course she didn't remember. She wouldn't remember two minutes from now or two minutes after that. She had no idea why I was waking her up so early the next morning, or where we were headed as I drove south along Dixie Highway looking for Dr. Wong's office.

"How are you feeling?" I asked her.

"Magnificent," she said. "Where are we going?"

"To the gynecologist. It's just a routine examination."

"That's nice, dear."

It wasn't so nice, as it turned out. It was in Dr. Wong's office that she discovered my twin polyps and promptly removed them.

"I'm sure there's nothing to worry about, but I'll send these off to the lab, just in case," she said, as I struggled to bring my legs together. "Why don't you call my office in two weeks. We should have the results back by then."

I nodded, opened the door to the waiting room to see my mother rifling through the morning newspaper, a photograph of Jo Lynn proudly displaying her self-bought wedding band occupying a prominent spot on the front page. I felt sick, clutched my stomach.

"I'll give you some pills for the cramping," Dr. Wong said. "And no sex for a week," she advised on my way out.

No problem, I thought, thinking of Robert as my mother and I walked slowly toward the parking lot. I fought the urge to curl into a fetal ball in the middle of the warm gray pavement. Good thing Robert and I hadn't made those plans for this afternoon, I thought, and almost laughed.

"How are you feeling, Mom?" I asked, securing her seat belt around her.

"Magnificent. How about you, dear?"

"I've felt better," I confided.

She smiled. "That's good, dear."

I got home, settled my mother in front of the TV in the family room, and crawled into bed. Within minutes, I was asleep, dreams of Sara circling my head, like a plane awaiting permission to land. Mercifully, I don't remember the particulars. I only remember that at some point we got into a horrible fight and began exchanging blows, Sara's right fist catching me square in the groin. I awoke with a start, the pain in my stomach excruciating. I ran toward the bathroom, watched as blood leaked into the toilet bowl from between my legs. "Charming," I said, swallowing another pill, then heading back to bed.

The phone rang. It was Larry. "How'd it go?" he asked, and I told him. "Why didn't you call me? I would have picked you up."

"It wasn't necessary."

"You don't have to deal with everything by yourself, Kate."

"No sex for a week," I said.

He sighed. What else is new? the sigh said.

"I'll try to be home early," he offered.

"No need."

"Don't shut me out, Kate."

"I'm not." I was.

I replaced the receiver, lay back against the pillow, fantasized about sex with Robert. In my fantasy, we were in one of the recently renovated rooms at the Breakers hotel, a large sun-filled room overlooking the ocean, the waves lapping through the floor-to-ceiling windows toward our king-size bed, as we kissed and caressed one another with the utmost tenderness. That's as far as the fantasy went, maybe because of the cramps I was experiencing, or maybe because Sara kept pushing her way into the hotel room, eventually crowding Robert out of our bed, banishing him to one of the older rooms at the front of the hotel, her voice blocking out the soothing sound of the ocean.

I replayed the scene with Sara, reliving every detail of what had happened, the shouts, the sarcasm, the slaps, then played it through again, this time with a different script. In this newly edited version, I kept my cool, refused to take the bait, held my temper firmly in check. Whenever Sara tried to suck me in or drag me down, I stepped aside. I simply explained that we knew the truth about where she'd been, and detailed the consequences of her lies. Ultimately Sara saw the error of her ways and accepted responsibility for her acts. We ended the encounter with a tearful embrace.

How's that for a fantasy?

At three o'clock, the doorbell rang. I pushed myself out of bed, and answered it, thinking it must be Larry and wondering why he didn't use his key. But it wasn't Larry. It was Jo Lynn. Please let this be another dream, I prayed, taking note of her conservative blue pantsuit and tied-back hair.

"I'm in disguise," she said, reading my face. "The reporters are driving me crazy."

"Fancy that," I said, then wished I hadn't. I had nothing to say to my sister. What was she doing here?

"You look awful," she said, stepping inside before I could stop her. "You sick or something?"

"I had some unexpected surgery this morning," I answered. What was the matter with me? Could I never keep my mouth shut?

"Surgery? What kind of surgery?"

"Just minor."

"Yick," she said, not interested in the specifics.

"What are you doing here, Jo Lynn?"

"Uh-oh, you're mad. I can hear it in your voice."

"You're so perceptive."

"You're so sarcastic. Come on, Kate. Surely you're not surprised. I've been telling you my wedding plans for months."

"How could you do it?" I demanded.

"I love Colin. I think he's innocent."

"I'm not talking about your idiot husband," I shouted. "I'm talking about my daughter."

There was silence. "Colin's not an idiot," Jo Lynn said.

I groaned.

"So, you like my new name? Jo Lynn Friendly. Has kind of a nice ring to it, don't you think?"

I said nothing.

"What—you're not going to talk to me?"

"I'd rather not."

"Oh, don't be such a tight-ass, Kate. I needed a maid of honor, you said no, so I asked Sara, and she graciously agreed. It was a joyous occasion, for God's sake. A wedding."

"A wedding that took place behind bars."

"Don't be so melodramatic."

"You expressly went against my wishes."

"You're making a mountain out of a molehill."

I took a deep breath. The last thing I needed now was a fight with my sister. "What are you doing here, Jo Lynn?" I asked again.

"I'm looking for our mother."

I glanced toward the family room. Our mother was sitting in exactly the same position in which I'd left her hours earlier. She hadn't moved, even at the sound of Jo Lynn's voice. "Mom?" I asked, walking quickly toward her.

On the television, an impossibly good-looking young couple were arguing about their father's impending remarriage on one of the daytime soaps. Our mother seemed to be watching, her hands folded neatly in her lap, her feet placed firmly on the floor. Her eyes were open and her jaw slack, a small spittle of drool trickling toward her chin.

"Is she dead?" Jo Lynn asked, leaning over me as I leaned over our mother.

"Mom?" I asked, holding my breath, touching her shoulder.

Her eyes flickered briefly, then closed. The breath in my lungs escaped with a relieved whoosh. I gently wiped the drool from her face, then backed into Jo Lynn's arms. I quickly extricated myself, stepped aside. "She's asleep."

"She sleeps with her eyes open?"

"She drifts in and out."

"Creepy."

I reached for the remote-control unit, about to turn off the TV.

"Don't do that," Jo Lynn squealed. "That's Reese and Antonia. Their father is about to remarry his second wife, who they've always hated because she's a former stripper who once tried to kill them by setting their house on fire. But she's okay now. She went back to school, became a psychiatrist. You got any coffee?"

I flipped off the TV. "No."

"Then make some." Jo Lynn plopped herself down on one of the wicker chairs in the breakfast nook. "You know you're dying for a cup."

She was right. I walked to the kitchen and did as I was told.

"It's amazing what goes on on some of these soaps," Jo Lynn said without a trace of irony. She nodded toward our mother. "So, what's the old girl's prognosis?"

"So far, the doctors haven't found anything physically wrong with her," I said, too weary to do anything but let this visit run its course. "How'd you know she was here?"

"I tried her apartment and was told the number was no longer in service. So I checked with Mrs. Winchell."

"Why the sudden interest in our mother?"

"I can't be interested?"

I shrugged, watched the coffee as it dripped into the glass pot.

"So, aren't you going to ask me what it was like behind the watercooler?" Jo Lynn squirmed in her seat.

"No," I said.

"Come on, you're dying to know."

"No, you're dying to tell me. There's a difference."

"It was fabulous," she said. "Well, maybe not fabulous in the technical sense. I mean, it was pretty cramped behind there and we were pretty rushed, but that made it all the more exciting, in a way. You just know that under the proper circumstances, Colin is a dynamite lover."

What was taking the coffee so long? I wondered, my eyes widening, willing the coffeemaker to pick up speed.

"You think we should wake the old girl up?" Jo Lynn asked.

"What for?"

"I want to talk to her."

"What for?" I repeated.

"Do I need your permission to talk to my own mother?"

"Of course not. It's just that anything anybody says to her goes in one ear and out the other."

"Maybe," Jo Lynn said.

"Not maybe. That's the way it is. I'm the one who's with her all the time. I'm the one who talks to her."

"Maybe you're not saying anything very interesting."

I sighed, shook my head. She was probably right. "Can I ask what it is you want to talk to her about?"

Jo Lynn pursed her lips, twisted her mouth from side to side, as if weighing the pros and cons of taking me into her confidence. "I guess I can tell you since it was your idea in the first place."

"My idea?"

"About going to law school."

"What?"

"I've thought a lot about what you said, and I've decided it might not be such a crazy idea after all."

"You're serious?"

"I *do* listen to what you say, you know," she told me. "Occasionally."

"And you've decided you want to go back to school," I repeated numbly. Surely, this conversation wasn't really taking place. Surely, I was back in bed, the covers up around my ears, my insides cramping to protest the surprise pruning of internal weeds. On Saturday, my sister had married a serial killer; today, she was applying for law school. Fantasies had given way to hallucinations. I was as nutty as the rest of my family.

"I think you were right," Jo Lynn was saying. "It's the only way I can really help Colin, get him out of that terrible place."

"It won't be easy," I warned her.

"I know it won't be easy. First, I have to finish my degree."

"First you have to apply."

"I know that," she said impatiently. "But I'm determined, and you know what I'm like when I'm determined."

"It means at least five years of school."

"Do I have anything better to do?"

"No, I guess not."

"What's your problem?" she asked. "You're the one who suggested it, who made it sound like such a great idea."

"It *is* a great idea."

"I thought you'd be thrilled."

"I am. It's just that…"

"You're still mad at me because of Sara."

"You don't give people a lot of time to catch their breath."

"Part of my charm." Jo Lynn looked toward our mother. "So, think she'll spring for it?"

I reached into the cupboard, grabbed two mugs, filled them with freshly brewed, steaming-hot coffee. "Spring for what?"

"The tuition."

I handed Jo Lynn her mug, sipped gingerly from my own, the steam searing my eyelashes shut.

"What's the matter? You don't think she'll give me the money?"

I opened my eyes. "I'm not sure she has the money to give."

Jo Lynn jumped to her feet, hot coffee from her mug spilling over the back of her hand. She didn't seem to notice. "What are you talking about? Of course she has money."

"Most of what she had is gone," I tried to explain. "Her medical expenses will probably eat up the rest."

"Goddamn her anyway. She couldn't just die?"

"Jo Lynn!"

She was pacing now, turning in small circles between the table and the kitchen counter. "Oh, spare me your righteous indignation. You can't tell me you haven't thought the same thing."

I was about to protest, but didn't. The

truth was that there had been times over the last number of weeks when I thought death might have been kinder, for all of us.

"What about you and Larry?"

"What?"

"You said you'd loan me the money, that I could pay you back when I was *raking in the dough*. Didn't you mean it?"

I hesitated.

She pounced. "You didn't mean it, did you? It was just one of those things you say to make you feel good about yourself, but you have no intention of actually doing."

"That's not true."

"Will you loan me the money or won't you?"

"Hold on a second," I said, trying to slow things down. "Aren't we moving a little fast here? What's the urgency?"

"Why wait? I want to get the ball rolling."

"This is very impulsive," I told her. "Are you sure you've thought it all through?"

"I don't see what the big deal is. It was your suggestion that I go to law school. I'm taking you up on it. I thought you'd be thrilled. I'm finally going to do something with my life. I'm finally going to amount to something. Or is that the problem? Are you so used to being the omnipotent older sister that you don't really want me to succeed?"

I downed the contents of my mug, felt my throat sting. When had this conversation become about me? "Look," I began. "You've caught me off guard, and this probably isn't the best time to be asking for favors in any case.Leave it with me for a few days. I'll discuss it with Larry when I think the time is right."

""Who are you kidding? The time will never be right." In the next second, Jo Lynn was on her way to the front door. "I don't understand," she said, waving her hands in frustration. "I mean, what is it you want from me?"

I stood there helplessly as the door slammed in my face.

Chapter
27

I'm thinking of going to South Carolina next week," Larry said, as we lay side by side on our backs in bed, hands folded across our stomachs, not touching, staring at the ceiling fan whirring gently overhead.

"To see your mother?"

"That, and to play golf. My brother called, invited me up for a few days. Invited us, actually."

"I can't go," I said quickly.

"I told him I didn't think you'd be able to make it."

"It's a bad time," I said. "There's just too much going on."

"That's what I told him."

I heard the disappointment in his voice, ignored it. "But you can go. You haven't seen your family in a while. I'm sure your mother would be thrilled."

"I think I will go," he said, after a pause.

"I think it would be good," I said. "Have you given any thought to Jo Lynn's request?"

"Nope."

"Are you going to?"

"Nope."

"You don't think you're being just a tad short-sighted?"

"Nope."

I took a deep breath, released it slowly, louder than was necessary.

"Look, Kate. After the stunt she pulled, I'm not prepared to give your sister the time of day, let alone the kind of money she's talking about."

"It's not a gift. It's a loan."

"Sure. Like she's actually going to go through with five years of college. Like I'm actually going to see the money again."

"I know we'd be taking a big chance," I agreed, "and, at first, I thought it was ridiculous too, but then I thought about it some more, and I thought that maybe it's not so ridiculous, that maybe this time she might actually pull it off, and I *am* the one who suggested it, who gave her the idea in the first place, who gave it the big buildup, convinced her she could do it."

"That doesn't make you responsible, Kate," Larry said. "You are not your sister's keeper."

"I just think it might be her last chance."

"If she really wants to go to law school, let her get a job and pay for it herself. There are lots of people out there putting themselves through college."

"I know, but..."

"Look, Kate, I know she's your sister, and that you'd like to help her out, and I won't stop you. I mean, if you have the money and you want to give it to her, there's nothing I can do, but don't ask me to contribute. I can't, and I won't."

"Fine," I said. But it wasn't.

"You know what amazes me?"

Larry's question was rhetorical. It didn't require an answer.

"What amazes me is how easily you let yourself get sucked in. She does it to you every time. One minute, you're so mad at her, you never want to see her again; the next minute, you're ready to give her the moon."

"She's my sister."

"She's a flake. She always has been. The difference is that now she's a *dangerous* flake."

"Dangerous?"

"Yes, dangerous. Women who flirt with serial killers are misguided; women who marry them are crazy; women who involve their teenage nieces in their craziness are dangerous."

"I just thought if there was anything I could do to help her..."

"There isn't. You can't." He sat up, leaned on one elbow toward me. "Kate, you know as well as I do that you can never pull people like Jo Lynn up. They can only drag you down."

He leaned over to kiss me. I turned my

head away, flipped over onto my side, faced the window.

"Well, in another week, I'll be out of your hair," he said sadly, flopping back down. "You'll have a few days on your own to decide what you want to do."

He didn't say about what. He didn't have to. We both understood what he meant.

The next day, I picked up the phone and called Robert, told him of Larry's plans. We agreed to meet the following Saturday. At the Breakers, we concurred. A room with an ocean view.

The letter arrived within minutes of Larry leaving for the airport. I stared at it for several seconds without opening it, puzzled by the unfamiliar handwriting, the lack of a return address. I carried it into the kitchen, cutting my finger on the envelope as I carelessly ripped it open, watched as a tiny drop of blood stained the page.

Well, I guess it's official now, *dear Katie*, the letter began. *We're family*. My eyes shot to the bottom of the plain white piece of paper, my hands shaking, my heart pounding. *Love, Colin* was scribbled with obscene clarity across the bottom of the page.

"No!" I cried, eyes returning in growing horror to the main paragraph.

Well, I guess it's official now. We're family, I read again, forcing myself to continue. *Kissing cousins, you might say. I got to admit I like the sound of that. Anyway, I just wanted you to know how sorry I was that you couldn't make the wedding, but wanted to let you know that Sara did you real proud. That older girl of yours is really something. Why, she's as sweet as the first strawberry in spring.*

My eyes filled with angry tears. I wiped them away, continued reading.

I know I'm not one of your favorite people, Katie girl, but you're sure one of mine. One day, I hope to prove that to you. In the meantime, just know I'm thinking about you. Love, Colin

"No, no, no, no!" I shouted with increasing ferocity, ripping the letter into as many pieces as my shaking fingers could manage, watching the tiny scraps of paper fall to the tile floor, like flakes of confetti, realizing only too late what I'd done, immediately down on my hands and knees, trying to gather the pieces together, giving up moments later in disgust. "Great," I moaned. "Just great. That was really smart." I took a deep breath. Talk about destroying the evidence. How could I call the police now? Instead, I called my sister.

"You gave him our address?" I declaimed as soon as I heard her voice.

"He said he wanted to try one more time to make amends," Jo Lynn explained.

I told her what the letter said.

"I think that's so sweet," she said. "What's the matter with you, Kate? He's trying so hard. Can't you give him a chance?"

I hung up the phone, more resigned than surprised. She called right back.

"Have you decided whether or not you're

going to lend me the money for law school?" she asked, as I shook my head in disbelief.

"I haven't talked to Larry yet," I lied.

"Why not?"

Were we actually having this conversation? "He had to go out of town for a few days. He'll be back Monday. I'll talk to him then."

"Monday's too late."

"Too late? What are you talking about?"

This time, she was the one to hang up.

"Figures," I said out loud, although nothing did. I checked my watch, realizing that if I didn't leave for work now, I'd be late for Mrs. Black, a new client I'd scheduled for one o'clock. I'd canceled my morning appointments so that I could drive Larry to the airport, but he'd said there was no need, he'd already arranged for a limo. I headed for the front door, the set of golf clubs I'd bought him for Christmas leaning against the wall of the foyer, like a silent rebuke. He'd taken his old set with him to Carolina. "I'll have better luck with these," he'd said, without kissing me goodbye.

Could I blame him? I'd been dreadful to him for months, closing myself off, freezing him out.

"You should have gone with him," I told myself, unlocking my office door, trying to block out unwanted images of Colin Friendly by imagining how Mrs. Black might look, what her problem would be. So many problems, I thought. So few solutions.

Moments later, I heard the door to my

outer office open and close. I rose to my feet, went out to meet Mrs. Black.

She was standing in the middle of the waiting room, and it took a moment for my brain to register who she was, despite the fact that I recognized her immediately. You know how it is when you meet someone in one set of circumstances, and don't expect to see them in another. Such was the case with the woman who stood before me now, smiling at me from behind layers of blue eye shadow, her too black hair falling into a stiff flip at her shoulders. She was wearing a peach-colored suit with matching peach-colored stockings and pumps. The effect was somewhat startling, like an overripe piece of fruit. "Hello, Kate," she said.

"Brandi," I acknowledged, watching the encounter from somewhere inside my head, struggling to keep my voice its normal timbre. What on earth was she doing here? "How are you?"

"Not so great."

"Oh—I'm sorry to hear that." Actually, I was sorry to hear anything. Brandi Crowe was the last person I wanted to see. Wasn't I planning to sleep with her husband the day after tomorrow?

She smiled, clasped her hands together nervously, then dropped them to her sides. What did she want? Had Robert told her of our plans? Had a reservation clerk from the Breakers phoned her, tipped her off?

"Is there a reason you're here?" I asked reluctantly.

"I need to talk to you."

"To me?"

"Professionally," she said.

"I'm so sorry," I said quickly. "I'm completely booked this afternoon." Had I ever felt so grateful to be so busy?

"I have an appointment."

"You do?" I scanned my memory for mention of her name. Surely, I wasn't so out of it that I wouldn't have noticed the name of my prospective lover's wife in my appointment calendar.

"Mrs. Black," she said, and smiled apologetically. "Not very original, I'm afraid."

Of course. My new client. "Good enough to fool me," I heard myself say.

"I was afraid you wouldn't see me if I gave you my real name. And I didn't want Robert to know I was coming."

I held my breath.

"I apologize for the charade."

"No need." The words slid out as I was forced to exhale. I ushered her inside my inner office, trying to collect the thoughts that were madly scrambling around inside my brain, realizing that she must have called my office weeks ago for this appointment, long before I'd arranged my upcoming Saturday tryst with her husband. There was no way she could know anything about our plans for the weekend. I almost laughed with relief. "Have a seat."

She arranged herself neatly in one of the chairs across from my own, crossed, then uncrossed her peach-tinted legs. "I feel a little self-conscious."

"Are you sure I'm the person you should be seeing?"

"Yes," she said quickly. "You strike me as a good listener. And Robert speaks very highly of you."

Silently, I debated the ethics of counseling my lover's wife. Of course, he wasn't my lover yet, nor had I decided to take his wife on as a client. Brandi's visit would hopefully prove to be only a one-time thing. "It's just that you might feel more comfortable talking to someone you don't know," I ventured, understanding it was I who would feel more comfortable.

"No, really, I'm sure I'll be quite comfortable talking to you."

"Good." I forced a reassuring smile onto my lips, picked up my notebook, readied my pen. "What can I do for you?" It appeared I had no choice but to listen to what she had to say. I could always recommend another therapist later, I rationalized.

Brandi Crowe looked around the room. "I don't know where to start."

"Why don't you begin with whatever it was that brought you here."

She laughed, though her eyes were already filling with tears. There was a long pause, during which she swallowed several times. "God, I'm so embarrassed. It's such a cliché."

"Somebody once said that a cliché is something that's been true too many times. There's no need to be embarrassed."

"Thank you," she said, and smiled, swallowed again. "I don't know who I am anymore." She shrugged helplessly, tears falling toward the collar of her peach jacket.

I grabbed a tissue and handed it to her. She took it gratefully, dabbed at her eyes, careful not to disturb her makeup. "Why don't you start by telling me a little bit about who you *were*," I said.

"You mean my childhood?"

"I know your father owns a string of radio stations," I prompted.

She nodded her head up and down in confirmation. "Fourteen."

""And your mother?"

"She died when I was twenty-one. She committed suicide."

"My God, how awful."

"We weren't very close, but yes, I guess it was pretty awful."

"Do you have any brothers or sisters?"

"Two sisters. Both older. One lives in Maui, the other in New Zealand."

"They couldn't get much farther away."

She laughed. "I guess that's right."

"So, you don't see them very often."

"Almost never."

"How do you feel about that?"

"All right, I guess. We don't have a lot in common."

"How did your mother kill herself?" I asked, genuinely curious. Brandi Crowe was a much more interesting woman than I'd originally imagined.

"She hanged herself in my father's office." Her voice was distant, dispassionate, as if she were talking about a stranger, and not her mother. "I think she was trying to get his attention." She shook her head. "It didn't work. He decided not to go into the office that day. One of the cleaning staff found her."

"Their marriage was obviously not a happy one," I commented.

"My father was happy enough. He had his radio stations, his family, his women."

"His women?" The pen in my hand began to wobble. I laid it down across my notepad.

"My father is one of those larger-than-life characters you see in the movies. Big, brash, demanding. He's not easily satisfied. Oh, he's slowed down a bit now. He's older, can't run around quite as much anymore. Not that he doesn't try."

"And your mother knew he was unfaithful?"

"We all knew. He didn't go out of his way to keep his affairs a secret."

"How did that make you feel?"

Brandi Crowe tilted her head, stared toward the window. "Diminished," she said finally.

An interesting choice of words, I thought. "In what way?"

"I don't know if I can explain it. I guess I took his cheating personally, as if he wasn't just cheating on my mother, but on me too. It made me feel as if I wasn't very important."

"Have you ever talked to him about this?"

She laughed bitterly. "My father's a very busy

417

man. Besides, he's not interested in anything I have to say. He never has been."

"Did he remarry?"

"Several times. Right now, he likes to say he's between ex-wives."

"Sounds like a very selfish man."

"Oh, he is. That's part of his charm." She shook her head, dislodged several fresh tears. "It's funny."

"What is?"

"I swore I'd never get involved with anyone remotely like him, and look what I did."

"What did you do?" I asked, despite my intense desire not to.

"I married Robert," she said simply.

"You think Robert is like your father?"

"He's exactly like my father."

My turn to swallow, tilt my head, look toward the window. "In what way?"

"He's handsome, smart, charming, selfish, self-absorbed, arrogant. Arrogance is a very sexy quality in a man, don't you find?"

"There's a difference between arrogance and confidence," I said, flinching at the reference to sex.

"Robert is both confident and arrogant, wouldn't you agree?"

"I don't know him well enough," I hedged.

"But you knew him in high school," Brandi said quickly. "What was he like then?"

"Handsome, smart, charming, selfish, self-absorbed," I said, parroting her words. "Arrogant," I added truthfully.

She smiled. "And very sexy, right?"

"And very sexy," I admitted, sensing it was pointless to lie.

"I saw him coming a mile away," Brandi continued. "I told myself, whatever you do, stay clear of this one. He's dangerous. But of course, that was part of his appeal. I knew his reputation. Hell, I knew his history with women the minute I laid eyes on him. It was my father all over again. But even though I knew rationally that I'd never change him, something deep inside me must have thought I could. Something inside me obviously was trying to prove that I was not my mother, that I could give the story a happy ending." She laughed. "You see, I've read all the self-help books. I have a pretty clear understanding of my own motivations."

"You're saying that you think Robert is cheating on you?"

"I *know* he's cheating on me."

"How do you know?" I bit down hard on my tongue.

"He's been cheating on me for almost twenty years," she said.

My pen rolled off my lap and onto the floor. I reached down awkwardly to pick it up.

"It started within a year of our wedding. His receptionist, I think it was. It went on for about six months, then it ended."

"He told you about her?"

"Oh no. I said he was arrogant, not stupid."

"How did you find out?"

"I'm not stupid either," she said simply.

"Did you confront him?"

She shook her head. "When you confront something, you have to deal with it. I wasn't ready to do that."

"And now?"

"I love my husband, Kate. I don't want to lose him."

"How do you think I can help you?" I asked finally.

"Tell me what to do," she said.

"I can't do that."

"I knew that's what you were going to say." She tried to laugh, but the sound that emerged was brittle, shattering upon contact with the air. "It's just that I'm running out of ideas. God knows, I've tried everything, turned myself inside out to please him." She pulled at the stiff flip in her hair. "I wear my hair this way because Robert likes long hair. He hates gray, so I have touch-ups every three weeks. I own every anti-wrinkle cream on the market, and I go to exercise class three times a week. But, you know, there's only so much you can do. I'm forty-six years old; I've had four children. My muscle tone is never going to be what it was." She reached up with her right hand, pulled her hair away from her ear. "Four years ago, I had a face-lift. I don't know if you can see the scars."

"No," I said, reluctant to look until it became obvious that she wasn't going to release her hair until I did. "It's a very good job," I muttered.

"It hurt like hell, let me tell you. I felt as if I'd been hit by a truck. My face and neck were covered with bruises for months. They don't tell you that beforehand. They tell you to expect a little discomfort, a little swelling. You might have bruises for a week or two. Hah! I was a mess for months. Although, that was nothing compared to the tummy tuck I had last spring."

"You had a tummy tuck?"

"You name it, I've had it. The face-lift, the tummy tuck, the liposuction, the boob job."

"You had your breasts enlarged?"

"After four children, my breasts weren't quite what they were, and Robert, well, you've seen him, he looks as good as he did thirty years ago. He has that slim, athletic body that never seems to put on a pound, and I looked, well, I looked like a middle-aged woman who'd had four children. I couldn't blame him for looking elsewhere."

"Was it easier to blame yourself?"

"I guess it was. That way, I felt more in control, as if there was something I could do that would make Robert look at me the way he used to. But you know what I've realized?" she asked, then waited.

"What's that?"

"That my husband doesn't want what he's used to. That's precisely the point. It's not a question of my looking younger, or even better. Some of the women Robert's been involved with over the years were older than me. A few weren't even very attractive. What makes them so appealing to him is that they're new, they're something he's never had. They don't have to be young, as long as that's how they make him feel."

I lowered my eyes, counted to ten. "What about your sex life?"

My wife and I haven't made love in three years, I heard Robert say.

"It's fine."

"Fine? What does that mean?"

"It means it's good. It's always been good."

I pulled at the top button of my blouse. "So, you still make love."

"Oh yes, that's never been our problem. You look surprised."

"No." I struggled to make my face a blank. "No," I said again, realizing this was true. "I'm not surprised."

"The frustrating thing is that I honestly thought we'd turned a corner. The kids are getting older. They're more independent. We've been getting along better than we have in a long time. His last affair was almost a year and a half ago. And now this."

"This?"

"It's starting again. He's having an affair. Or he's about to."

"How do you know?"

"All the signs are there. Trust me, I know."

"Do you know with whom?" I held my breath.

"It doesn't matter with whom," she said dismissively.

"What *does* matter?" I asked.

"What matters is that I don't think I can go through it all again. The lies, the deceit, the casual disregard of my feelings. I don't know that I can just sit back and pretend it isn't happening, and that scares me because I've been Mrs. Robert Crowe for so long, I'm not sure I exist on my own anymore. I've done everything I can to make my husband happy. I've turned myself inside out to please him. I've pumped stuff into my body and sucked stuff out so many times that there are days when I look in the mirror and I barely recognize myself. It's like there's nothing left of me anymore." She stood up, walked slowly to the window, stared at the street below. "What does it say about me, that I've tolerated his infidelities for all these years?" She didn't wait for an answer. "You want to know what's really scary?"

"What's that?"

"I'm just like my mother."

Her answer caught me off guard. "What makes you say that?"

"My mother committed suicide," she said, her eyes focused and dry. "In my own way, so have I. It's just taken me a little longer to die."

Chapter
28

"Bastard!" I was screaming, punching the steering wheel as I drove home along I-95. "Lying bastard. *My wife and I haven't made love in three years!* And you believed him." I slapped at the rearview mirror, watched my image tilt, then disappear. "Idiot!"

How could I be so stupid? Was I still as hopelessly naive as I'd been thirty years ago, at least where Robert was concerned? Except that thirty years ago I'd known I wasn't the only one. I'd known all about his visits to Sandra Lyons. And I'd pretended I didn't. Just as his wife had been doing all these years. Pretending that things didn't exist, losing ourselves in the process.

At least she doesn't know it's you, I thought, straightening the rearview mirror, watching my eyes jump into view, widen with alarm. "Or does she?" Perhaps her visit to my office had been calculated well in advance, then executed with the subtle precision one might expect from someone with so much experience in these matters.

"I'm not stupid," I heard Brandi say, sad gray eyes reflecting through mine in the rearview mirror.

Objects in the rearview mirror are closer than they may appear, I knew, feeling Brandi's breath mingling with my own, reexperiencing the touch of her hand in mine as we shook hands goodbye. "I don't think that I need to come back," she'd said as she was leaving my office.

"Beware of women whose names are potable," Robert said. Of course, he'd said a lot of things. Were any of them true?

My wife and I haven't made love in three years.

Well, maybe they hadn't. Maybe it was Brandi, and not Robert, who was the liar in this equation. Maybe Robert had been a good and faithful husband all these years, despite a cold and unloving wife.

"Do you really believe that?" I asked myself out loud.

I glanced at the woman in the car next to mine, also talking to herself. Probably on a speaker phone, I decided, realizing she was likely thinking the same thing about me. All these crazy women driving along America's highways talking to themselves. I laughed. So did she.

Was Brandi laughing as well? Had she left my office chuckling with the knowledge that she'd accomplished her mission, shaken up the competition, stopped her husband's would-be mistress dead in her tracks? Was it possible that *everything* she'd said had been a lie, that she'd concocted the whole story from top to bottom, her father's philandering, her husband's affairs, even her mother's suicide?

I changed lanes without signaling, eliciting a loud horn and a raised middle finger from the driver behind me. I didn't have to make any decisions right now, I told myself. I had till Saturday to decide what to do about Robert. "Your wife came to see me," I rehearsed, afraid to say more.

For the duration of the drive, I concentrated on making my mind a blank. Every time a thought came in, I pushed it out. Every time an image appeared, I wiped it away. By the time I arrived home some fifteen minutes later, I was exhausted from all the pushing and wiping, and I felt a bad headache lying in wait behind my eyes. All I wanted to do was climb into a hot Jacuzzi, then crawl into bed.

The beat-up red car was parked in the middle of my driveway, leaving me no room on either side to get in. "Great. Just what I need." I backed up, found a spot on the street. "What are you doing here, Jo Lynn?" I asked the growing darkness.

The front door opened as I approached the house. Michelle stepped outside, a veritable poster girl for The Gap, in light khaki pants and cropped moss-green sweater. She closed the door behind her, met me halfway down the front walk. "I thought I better warn you," she said.

"What's going on?"

"Jo Lynn's here."

"I can see that. Where's Grandma?"

"She's asleep."

"What's Jo Lynn doing?"

"She's cooking dinner."

"She's cooking dinner?"

Michelle shrugged. She's *your* sister, the shrug said.

"When did she get here?"

"About an hour ago."

I checked my watch. It was almost seven o'clock. "Is Sara home?"

"She's helping Jo Lynn."

"She's helping?"

"I'll taste your food first," Michelle said.

426

I laughed, though the laugh was bitter-sweet. "I don't think that will be necessary." I leaned over, kissed her on the cheek. "But thanks for the offer."

"I think that whatever happens," Michelle advised as we approached the front door, "the important thing is for you to stay calm."

"Nothing's going to happen," I said. Was I seeking to reassure my daughter or myself?

"Well, you know what Jo Lynn is like. For sure she'll say something to upset you. Just don't let yourself get sucked in."

I stared at my younger daughter in absolute wonderment. Where had this wise little creature come from? At the same time, I felt ineffably sad. My fourteen-year-old child was trying to protect me. Protecting me wasn't her job. It was *my* job to protect *her*. "I'll be fine, doll," I said.

Michelle smiled. "Chin up," she said as I pushed open the door.

"Jo Lynn?" I stepped into the foyer. Honey, I'm home, I thought, but didn't say.

"I'm making stir-fry," she called from the kitchen. Her voice resonated warmth, intimacy. What are families for? it said.

"Smells good." I forced my shoulders back, my feet forward. Michelle was right behind me.

Jo Lynn stood in front of the stovetop, stirring a large pan filled with vegetables and small pieces of chicken. She was wearing white jeans and a loose-fitting black V-necked sweater. Sara was standing beside her in blue jeans and a skimpy denim shirt, tending to a steaming pot of white rice. As soon as Sara saw me, she dropped the cover on the pot, spun on her heels, and left the room. "You didn't set the table for dinner," Jo Lynn called after her.

"I'll do it later."

"Now, please," Jo Lynn said.

Amazingly, Sara turned around and came back. Jo Lynn gave me an easy smile. See how simple that was, the smile said, as Sara quickly set the table for five.

"Larry's out of town, right?" Jo Lynn asked.

"Till Monday." Was that why she was here—to check up on my story?

"Anything else you want me to do?" Sara asked her aunt, as if I weren't there, as if I didn't exist.

"Not at the moment."

"Then I can go?"

"Sure. I'll call you when dinner's ready. And thanks."

Sara nodded, refusing to look my way as she walked from the room.

"Why'd you kick Sara out of her room?" Jo Lynn asked immediately. "You could have given our mother the den."

The muscles in my stomach tensed. I looked over at Michelle, who was leaning against the family-room sofa, carefully monitoring the scene. "Smile," she mouthed silently, pushing her lips up with her fingers, as if to underline the word.

"It won't be for much longer," I said.

"A girl's room is pretty sacred ground,"

Jo Lynn continued, speaking to me as if I'd never been a teenage girl. "You have to learn to respect a kid's privacy, you know, if you want the kid to have any respect for you."

"Is that so?"

Michelle cleared her throat, the forced smile tightening on her lips, her eyes bulging with the effort.

"I just remember how I hated for anyone to go into my room, that's all," Jo Lynn said, then: "Wait until you taste this stir-fry. It's the best. I've become quite the cook, you know."

"Great."

"It's practice more than anything else. I mean, anybody who can read, can cook. At least that's what Mom used to say."

"Since when did you listen to anything Mom had to say?"

"I've been trying out all these recipes lately," she continued, as if I hadn't spoken, "for when Colin gets out."

"Great," I said again. It seemed like the only thing I could say that wouldn't get me into trouble. I was wrong.

"Why do you keep saying "great'? You know you don't mean it. You know that the last thing you want is for Colin to get out of jail."

"It's great that you're enjoying cooking so much," I said.

"I didn't say I was enjoying it."

Again, I glanced over at Michelle. She lifted her chin with the back of her hand. I followed her silent instructions and pushed my chin up.

"Something wrong with your neck?" Jo Lynn asked.

"It's a bit stiff," I said quickly.

"That's because you don't know how to relax. You've never learned to roll with the punches. Stop trying to be so perfect all the time."

"I'm not trying to be perfect."

"You know what your problem is?" Jo Lynn laid down the fork she was using to stir the vegetables. "You bring your work home with you."

"That's probably true," I agreed.

"You're so used to telling people how to run their lives, and I'm not saying there's anything wrong with that, don't get me wrong, it's part of your job, but it's easy to forget that not everybody back home is interested in your opinion."

I pulled a large platter out of the cupboard and handed it to my sister. What I really wanted to do was break it over her head. "What are you doing here, Jo Lynn?"

"Cooking you dinner."

"Why?"

"I guess it's my way of saying "I'm sorry.' "

I almost laughed. My sister had a unique way of apologizing. "That's the only reason you're here?"

She shrugged, as if what was about to follow was incidental, unimportant. "I need to talk to Mom."

"About what?"

"Dinner's ready," Jo Lynn called out, transferring the stir-fry and the rice from the stove to the platter, depositing the steaming platter on the table in the breakfast nook. "Come and get it."

"I just don't think you should say anything to upset her," I said before anyone came back.

"This is really none of your business." Jo Lynn punctuated her rebuke with a sweet smile.

Sara was the first one at the table. She filled her plate and was already eating before anyone else had a chance to sit down.

"Don't you think you should wait till everybody gets here?" I asked.

"Go ahead—eat," Jo Lynn said, pouring water into everyone's glass. "Since when do we stand on ceremony here? You too, Kate—help yourself."

"I'll wait for the others."

"Suit yourself. But it tastes better hot." Jo Lynn began heaping the stir-fry chicken and vegetables onto her plate.

"What's this?" my mother asked, Michelle guiding her into the room. "A party?"

She was wearing a pale pink shirtdress, her gray curls slightly flattened from sleep. She looks just like my mother, I thought.

"Yes, Mom," Jo Lynn answered. "It's your party, you can cry if you want to."

"Cry?" my mother asked, oblivious to the reference to the old Lesley Gore hit.

"Eat," my sister said.

"Something smells wonderful."

"It tastes even better," Sara offered, as Michelle helped my mother into a chair.

"Yes, Kate is a wonderful cook," my mother said.

Jo Lynn scooped up an enormous helping of chicken and vegetables and dumped them onto our mother's plate. "*I* made the dinner," she said.

"Did you, dear? Good for you."

Jo Lynn lifted her water glass into the air. "I'd like to propose a toast." She waited, a smile forming, then freezing on her lips, while we raised our glasses. "To new beginnings." We clicked glasses.

"Is this a party?" my mother asked.

"Yes, Grandma," Michelle answered.

My mother took a few tentative bites of her food. "You don't have to be afraid of it," Jo Lynn said. "It's not going to bite back."

"It's delicious," our mother pronounced. "Kate is a wonderful cook."

"Jo Lynn made the dinner, Grandma," Sara said.

"Of course, dear."

The rest of the meal passed in merciful silence. When it was over, my mother complimented me on the delicious dinner. "It was a lovely party."

"Party's not over yet," Jo Lynn said as Sara and Michelle cleared the table and stacked the dishes in the dishwasher. "We have a little business to discuss."

"Business, dear?"

"Jo Lynn, please…"

"Kate, butt out. This doesn't concern you."

"Would you like to watch some TV, Grandma?" Michelle asked from the kitchen.

Jo Lynn's eyes flashed daggers toward my younger child. "Call off the dogs, Kate."

"You know she's not going to understand anything you say," I said.

"So, what else is new?"

"And even if she does understand, she won't remember it."

"She doesn't have to remember it. And you don't have to stay."

"I'm not going anywhere."

"Suit yourself. But stay out of it." Jo Lynn twisted our mother's chair around so that it faced hers. "Mom, listen to me. This is no big deal. I just need some money."

"Money?"

"Yeah, you know, that evil green stuff you've been hoarding away for years."

"Jo Lynn, please…"

"Shut up, Kate."

"She doesn't have any money."

Our mother glanced warily toward me. "That was a lovely dinner, Kate."

"*I* made the dinner," Jo Lynn said, her hands on the sides of our mother's chair, her face mere inches from our mother's. "Thank me, not Kate."

"Kate is a wonderful cook."

Angry tears filled Jo Lynn's eyes. "Kate is wonderful at everything she does. We all know that. But Kate is not part of this discussion. Now, do you remember what I just said?"

"Of course, dear."

"Good. Because this is very important to me. I've decided to go back to college, to become a lawyer. What do you think about that?"

"I think that's wonderful, dear."

"And in order to do that, I'd need money. Money that I don't have. So I'm asking you to lend me some."

Our mother smiled.

"It's not a lot of money. A few thousand dollars is all I need right now."

"Right now?" My voice was sharp, like the crack of a whip.

"I asked you to stay out of it, Kate," Jo Lynn warned.

"But why do you need a few thousand dollars right now? You haven't been accepted anywhere yet. You haven't even applied."

"You have to send in a check with your application."

"Not for a few thousand dollars, you don't."

"Times have changed since you went to school, Kate," she reminded me.

"Not that much, they haven't. Why do you need two thousand dollars?"

"Correct me if I'm wrong," Jo Lynn said, "but isn't this conversation between Mom and me? Didn't you already renege on your promise to loan me the money?"

"What's really going on here, Jo Lynn?" I demanded.

"That was a lovely dinner, Kate," our mother said, eyes flitting nervously between her two daughters. "I think I'd like to go to my room now."

"Sure, Mom," I said quickly. "Michelle, why don't you help Grandma...?"

"Michelle, stay right where you are," Jo Lynn said. "Grandma isn't going anywhere until this is settled."

"For God's sake, what's the point?" I asked, "You can see you're just upsetting her."

"*You're* the one who's upsetting her. I was doing fine."

"She doesn't understand what's going on."

"She understands plenty. Don't you, Mom?"

"Of course, dear." Our mother shifted uneasily in her chair.

"You heard her."

"That's her answer for everything," I tried to explain.

"What's the matter, Kate?" Jo Lynn snapped. "Afraid there won't be as much left for you to inherit?"

"Inherit? What are you talking about? There's not going to be any money to inherit."

"All I need is two thousand dollars, Mom. Surely you can spare that much. It's not like I've asked you for anything before."

"That was a delicious dinner," our mother said, her voice thin, her hands flitting nervously about her lap.

"You're scaring her," I said.

"Is Kate right?" Jo Lynn asked. "Am I scaring you?"

"I think I'd like to go to my room now."

"You can go anywhere you like as soon as

we get this settled."

"For God's sake, Jo Lynn, enough is enough. I think it's time you went home."

"Is the party over?" our mother asked.

"Yes, Mom, the party's over."

"The party's still going strong," Jo Lynn stated, her voice harsh, strangely desperate. "Look, I don't think that any of you realize how important this is to me. It could be my last chance. You wouldn't want to deprive me of that, would you? I mean, think how proud you'd be, Mom. You could tell all your friends about your daughter the lawyer."

"Of course, dear."

"If you tell me where you've hidden your checkbook, I can get it for you."

"My checkbook," our mother repeated, looking at me.

"Don't look at her. Look at me. Just tell me where it is, and I'll get it for you. I'll fill it all out. All you have to do is sign it."

"Of course, dear."

"Where is it? Is it in your purse?" Jo Lynn was on her feet, hurrying toward Sara's bedroom.

"What's all this about?" Sara asked warily, the first words she'd said to me since our altercation.

"I'm not sure," I answered truthfully.

Jo Lynn returned with our mother's purse. "I can't find your checkbook. Where do you keep it?"

"I have her checkbook," I said, preparing myself for the fireworks that were sure to follow.

"What do you mean, you have it? What are you doing with it?"

"There's no money, Jo Lynn. And there's no point in arguing about it."

"Goddamnit, who put you in charge?"

"Why don't we all calm down," Michelle ventured.

"Shut up, Michelle. This is none of your business."

"Don't tell her to shut up," Sara said, taking the words out of my mouth.

Jo Lynn threw her hands into the air. "Oh, great. Gang up on me, why don't you?"

"I'll make you a deal," I offered. "Bring me the application. I'll write out a check for the application fee, and we'll take it one step at a time."

"That's not good enough."

"What do you mean, it's not good enough?"

"Stop treating me like a child."

"How is that treating you like a child?"

"You want to see the application; you want to write the check. You always have to be in control."

"Do you want the money or don't you?"

She ignored me, fell to her knees in front of our mother. "Please, Mom, this is really embarrassing for me. Can't you just lend me the money. Don't make me beg."

Tears filled our mother's eyes. "That was a lovely party."

"Don't do this, Mom," Jo Lynn said. "Please don't do this."

"She can't help it," I said.

"She *can* help it." Jo Lynn pushed herself off her knees, began pacing back and forth in front of our mother's chair, a caged tiger in a small cell, claws extended, ready to leap, go for the jugular. "You're not going to do this, Mom. This time you're not going to get away with it."

"Get away with what?" I demanded. "What has she ever done to you?"

"Nothing!" Jo Lynn shouted. "She does absolutely nothing! Isn't that right, Mom? Isn't that right? You do nothing!"

"I do nothing," our mother repeated, a faint glimmer of understanding creeping into her eyes.

"You just sit there, and do nothing. Just like you've always done."

"I do nothing," our mother agreed.

"When your husband comes home and screams at you, you do nothing. When he hits you and washes your mouth out with soap, you do nothing."

"Nothing."

"When he terrorizes your children, you do nothing."

"I do nothing."

"Jo Lynn, what's the point of bringing this up now?" My voice was a painful whisper. It literally hurt to speak.

"The point is that she did nothing! All those years, she did nothing."

"And she paid for it. God knows, she paid for it."

"No—*I* paid for it! *I'm* the one who paid for it." Tears began falling the length of Jo Lynn's cheeks.

"What are you talking about? You were his favorite. He never touched you." The second the words were out of my mouth, I knew they were wrong. "Oh no," I said. "Please, no."

"Welcome to the real world, Ms. Therapist," my sister said.

"I did nothing," our mother said, rising slowly to her feet.

"That's right, Mom. You did nothing." Jo Lynn looked toward the back window, as if the past were projected on the glass, like a movie on a screen. "All those nights he came into my room to "kiss me good night,' all those times he left your bed to come into mine, all those rides in the country on Sunday afternoon. "You see those cows over there?' he'd say, while his hand was pushing its way between my legs. "When all the cows are standing up, it means it's going to be sunny, and when all the cows are lying down, that means it's going to rain.' "

"Oh God," I said, feeling weak, gutted. "I had no idea."

"No, but *she* did." Jo Lynn glared at our mother, whose eyes were fixed on the back window, watching the same old movie as my sister. "And she did nothing."

"I didn't know," our mother whispered. "I didn't know."

"Don't tell me you didn't know," my sister shouted. "You knew. You knew. You just pretended it wasn't happening. What did you think, that if you ignored it, it would go away? Is that what you thought?"

"I didn't know."

"How could you let him get away with it? How could you let him do the things he did to me? You're my mother. You were supposed to take care of me. You were supposed to protect me."

"He was always so kind to you," our mother said, crying now. "So loving."

"Oh, he was loving, all right."

"I was so envious. I used to think, if only he would be so kind, so gentle, with me."

"You knew," Jo Lynn insisted. "Don't try to tell me you didn't know."

"It wasn't until you were almost thirteen years old that I began to suspect there was something more."

"What was your first clue, Mom? The nightmares I kept having, my poor grades, the blood on my sheets?"

For a moment, the silence was absolute. Sara reached over to Michelle, drew her into her arms.

"It was the way he looked at you," our mother said finally. "You were bending over to pick something up, and I caught the look in his eyes, and suddenly I knew. I left him the next day."

"It was too late by then." Jo Lynn wiped her nose with the back of her hand. "It was too late."

Our mother sank back down into her chair, burying her head in her hands.

"But you went to see him," I reminded my sister. "After he got sick, you went to the hospital. You cried when he died."

"He was my father," Jo Lynn said simply.

No one said another word.

Chapter
29

That night I dreamed I was running through a large open field. The sky was mauve, threatening rain, the grass dry and yellow. In the distance, Jo Lynn was singing: *You can't catch me. You can't catch me.* I raced toward the sound, tripping over a large black-and-white cow that was lying on the ground. As I scrambled to my feet, I saw Sara sitting on the back of another cow. She was crying. I ran toward her, my path suddenly blocked by two rows of thick barbed wire that sprang up between us.

Colin Friendly stood in a high tower, the long rifle in his hands pointed at my daughter's head. "Don't worry," he told me. "I'll take care of her."

"All the cows are lying down," a voice said from somewhere behind me.

I spun around. My stepfather was leaning against the side of a massive banyan tree. In one hand, he held a bottle of beer; in the other, he held Michelle.

"That means it's going to rain," Michelle said, as my stepfather's hand tightened across her chest.

I bolted up in bed, my heart pounding, my body soaked in sweat. In the next instant, I was on my knees in the bathroom, throwing up into the toilet. "Son of a bitch," I whispered between heaves. "Goddamn son of a bitch."

How could I not have known? How could I not have suspected? My sister had been dropping hints for years. The pieces were all there. All I'd had to do was find them, gather them together, arrange them into a cohesive whole. Had I been blind or just stupid? And what of my mother? Had she known all along, as Jo Lynn had accused, or had she left as soon as her suspicions were aroused? Did it matter anymore? The damage had been done.

I thought of calling Larry and decided against it. It was almost two in the morning. I'd wake up the whole house, scare his mother half to death. And why? So that I could share this latest bulletin about my increasingly demented family? What did I expect him to do? What could any of us do now?

It had taken over an hour to get everyone settled after Jo Lynn raced from the house in a torrent of tears, her body doubled over in pain, rubbery legs threatening to collapse under her. "Please stay," I begged as she hurled herself into her car. "You can sleep in my bed. Please, Jo Lynn, you shouldn't be driving. You shouldn't be alone."

Her answer was to lock the car doors and bolt backward out of the driveway, narrowly missing my car parked on the darkened street.

I tried phoning her ten minutes later, got her answering machine. "Hi, this is Jo Lynn," her voice purred seductively. "Tell me everything."

"Please call me as soon as you get home," I told her, calling back ten minutes later, leaving another such message, calling every ten minutes until I finally gave up just after midnight. Clearly, she didn't want to talk to me. What more, after all, was there to say?

"Do you think she's all right?" Michelle asked.

"I don't know," I said.

"Do you think Grandma knew?"

"I don't know."

"Why didn't Jo Lynn ever say anything to anyone?"

"I don't know."

Did I know anything?

"Why couldn't you just give her the money?" Sara demanded. "It's not like you can't afford it."

"That's not the point," I said.

"The point is that she asked you for help and you wouldn't give it to her."

"I've tried to help her."

"Yeah, some therapist *you* are."

I didn't argue. She was right.

Somehow I managed to guide my mother into Sara's room, get her out of her clothes and into her nightgown. I tucked her into bed, leaned forward to kiss her soft, tear-stained cheek. "Are you okay, Mom?" I asked, but she made no reply, simply lay there, her eyes open, tears continuing to fall. When I looked in on her again half an hour later, she hadn't moved.

The next morning, I drove to Jo Lynn's apartment.

"Can you let me into her apartment?" I asked the superintendent, a tall man with a long, angular face and dark, sunken eyes. "She was pretty upset last night. I just want to make sure she's okay."

"How do I know you're her sister?" he asked, viewing me skeptically.

"Who else would I be?"

"Reporter," he replied lazily, not bothering to pronounce the *t*. "You guys been hounding her pretty good since the wedding."

"I'm not a reporter."

"You don't look like her sister."

"Look, I'm just afraid she might have done something to hurt herself." I broke off, too tired to argue, then turned, about to walk away.

"Wait," he called after me. "Guess I can let you in."

"What changed your mind?" I asked as he unlocked the door to my sister's second-floor apartment.

"If you were a reporter," he said, standing aside to let me enter, "there's no way you would have given up so easily."

"Jo Lynn," I called from the doorway, then held my breath. "Jo Lynn, are you here?" I pushed one foot in front of the other, afraid to linger, to look too closely, in case I saw something my mind was unprepared to accept. "Jo Lynn," I repeated, inching forward, the

444

superintendent fast on my heels, like an overly friendly puppy.

In typical Jo Lynn fashion, her apartment was both organized and chaotic. Organized chaos, I thought, my eyes flitting across the well-worn blue-green carpeting, the fading floral-print sofa and matching armchair, the coffee table whose glass top was completely hidden by stacks of old newspapers and the latest tabloids. More discarded newspapers lay scattered across the top of a black Formica bar. A stained white sweater was draped over one of two barstools, while a pair of cerise sandals, one with a broken strap, lay on the floor, one on top of the other.

"Doesn't look like she's here." The superintendent peered over my shoulder as I peeked into the kitchen. More newspapers stretched across the top of the kitchen table, a pair of large scissors beside them, along with an open scrapbook and an empty container of glue. I glanced at the scrapbook, saw Colin Friendly winking at me from the open page, and turned away quickly, noting the row of old cereal boxes that stood in a line on the countertop, along with an empty milk carton. A young girl's picture stared at me from the side of the milk carton. MISSING, it read above her gap-toothed smile. I ran from the room, my eyes filling with tears.

"You all right?" the super asked.

I shook my head, images of Jo Lynn suddenly dropping before my eyes, like a succession of grisly snapshots from the morgue. There she

445

was in the bathtub, her wrists slashed and dripping blood onto the white tile floor; or over there, hanging from the shower stall, an oversized, gaily colored beach towel for a noose; or there, lying on her bed, skin ashen, mouth open, hands folded primly across her ample bosom, dead from an overdose of sleeping pills.

"Would you do me a favor?" I asked. "Would you please check the other rooms for me?"

He hesitated, swayed, ultimately left my side.

"You better come in here," he said several seconds later.

My knees buckled, almost gave way. "Oh God," I said, grabbing the side of the bar, knocking over several sections of newspaper, watching them fall to the floor by my feet. Colin Friendly stared up at me, eyes directed up my skirt. "Oh God," I said again, kicking at his head, watching his face split in two, as the paper ripped apart. "Is she...?"

"She's not here," the superintendent answered. "Doesn't look like she slept here last night."

The laugh that escaped my mouth was one of relief. It quickly turned into a sob that caught in my throat and died as I approached my sister's bedroom, staring toward her queen-size bed, which was neatly made and covered with a childlike blue gingham comforter. A stuffed apricot-colored teddy bear sat on top of a ruffled gingham pillow.

"Looks like a little girl's room," the super said, stealing my thoughts, as I caught my reflection in the mirror atop Jo Lynn's dresser, across from her bed. Pictures of Colin Friendly lined the sides of the mirror, poking out at all angles from the metal frame, forcing themselves into my world, my reality. Wherever I looked, he was there. Laughing at me.

"Her clothes are gone," the super said.

"What?"

He motioned toward the closet. "She say anything to you about taking a vacation?"

I shook my head, my hands slapping against her empty hangers, running across deserted shelves, pulling open abandoned dresser drawers. But aside from a few old blouses and scarves, there was nothing.

"Doesn't look like she's coming back," the super said, once again usurping the thoughts swirling around my brain, like fallen leaves in the wind.

Where could she have gone? Why had she taken all her clothes?

"Her rent's due next Wednesday," the super said.

"I'm sure she'll be back by then," I muttered, anxious now to be on my way. "She goes away every weekend," I reminded us both, trying to fit the pieces of this latest puzzle together, to determine what Jo Lynn was up to. Had she decided to find an apartment closer to the penitentiary? Was she moving in this weekend? Was that why her clothes were gone? Was that why she needed money? First and last months' rent, a security deposit, I listed silently, as the super followed me out of Jo Lynn's apartment and locked the door after us. These things add up, I told myself. It was expensive to start a whole new life. "If you see my sister, would you tell her I was here, and that I need to talk to her? It's urgent."

"Doesn't look like she's coming back," the super repeated ominously as I headed to my car.

"Where are you, damnit?" I shouted into the empty interior of my car.

"She went to visit Colin," Larry assured me when I phoned him in South Carolina. "Stop worrying about her, Kate. She's in Raiford, surrounded by armed guards and police officers. She couldn't be in a safer place."

"You think so?"

"I know so."

"Thanks," I told him. "I'm glad I called."

"So am I."

"How's the family?"

"Terrific."

"And the golf?"

"Great."

"Great," I repeated. "Terrific."

"Everybody sends their love."

Send it back, I heard Jo Lynn say. "Say hi to everyone," I said instead.

"I will," he said, then: "I miss you. I love you very much. You know that."

"I know that," I told him. "I love you too."

On Saturday, I went to the Breakers to meet Robert.

I told myself I was going because I needed

448

to know the truth, that unless I confronted Robert, I would never know for sure if the things Brandi had told me were true, and then I would spend the rest of my life wondering and regretting. I'd been wondering for too long as it was, and my whole life was rapidly degenerating into one huge regret.

"Have you heard from Jo Lynn?" Sara asked, coming into my bathroom as I was applying a coat of newly purchased deep coral lipstick.

I jumped, dropped the lipstick to the countertop, watched it leave a large orange circle on the almond-colored marble. Death row orange, I thought, quickly wiping the stain off the counter with a damp cloth, then tossing the lipstick into my purse, trying to appear casual, matter-of-fact. "No, she hasn't called."

"What are you going to do?"

"What *can* I do?"

Sara shrugged, leaned against the wall. She was wearing cut off jeans and one of those loose-fitting Indian blouses she used to favor.

"Look, I have to go out for a few hours," I said, determined not to think about my sister for the balance of the afternoon. When she was ready, she would resurface. She always did.

"You look nice."

"Thank you." I tried not to sound too surprised by the compliment, wondering if Sara could somehow see through my beige Armani pantsuit and ivory silk shirt to the delicate pink French lace bra and panties beneath.

"Where are you going?" Sara asked.

449

"I'm looking at some places for Grandma," I lied, hating myself.

"I thought you were doing that tomorrow."

"Tomorrow too," I said, thinking that we hadn't had such a long conversation in months, wondering why it was taking place now.

"Do you think you'll find something?"

"I hope so," I told her, my heels clicking on the marble floor as I exited the bathroom.

"Where'd you get those shoes?"

God, she didn't miss a thing. "I bought them a few weeks ago. What do you think?"

"They're kind of high," she said. "I've never seen you wear such high heels."

"I thought I'd try them. For a change."

"When will you be back?" she asked.

"Soon. A few hours. Maybe less," I said. Maybe more, I added silently. "Why?"

"Just wondered." Again, she shrugged, didn't move.

"Is everything all right?" I asked reluctantly, guiltily. Normally, I would have jumped at the opportunity to reopen the lines of communication between us, especially since it was Sara making the overtures. But why did it have to be *now*? "Is there something you want to talk about?"

"Like what?"

"I don't know. You seem kind of at loose ends."

"What does that mean?" Her body tensed, ready to take offense at any possible slight.

"It doesn't mean anything." I didn't have the time, or the patience, to deal with this now.

"I really have to get going."

"Maybe we could go to a movie later," Sara said, following me to the front door.

"You want to go to the movies? With me?"

"Well, I don't have any money, and you won't let me go out with my friends," she said logically.

"Right," I said, understanding the situation somewhat better now. "We'll see when I get back."

"Don't be long," she said as I climbed into my car.

They must have some kind of built-in radar, I thought as I backed out of the driveway, some subtle warning device that signals when their world is about to shift. Don't we all? I wondered, realizing how often I'd ignored mine.

Twenty minutes later, the twin towers of the Breakers Golf and Beach Club shot into view. Immediately I thought of the new Palm Beach County Courthouse, whose vaulted roofs had been designed as an architectural echo. God, why was I thinking of that now? This was hardly the time to be thinking about my sister or her lousy taste in men.

An uncomfortable thought squeezed its way into my brain, like an earthworm through wet soil. My sister and I weren't so different after all, it said. We were both pining for undesirable men. My sister was ruining her life for one. Was I about to do the same thing for another?

I found a parking space at the front of the hotel between a black Rolls-Royce and a chocolate-brown Mercedes and walked briskly along the U-shaped driveway, past the large fountain of sculpted water nymphs, to the entrance of the grand old hotel, a magnificent structure that fairly shouted old money. I hurried past the valets and bellhops with their crisp white shirts and navy epaulets, noting the many luggage carts, golf clubs, and potted palms lined up along the portico as I followed the red carpet through the tall Ionic columns and glass doors into the long expanse of lobby, its vaulted fresco ceiling dotted at regular intervals by huge crystal chandeliers, the marble floor all but covered by richly textured area rugs. There were tapestries on the walls, enormous floral arrangements on tall marble stands, comfortable groupings of sofas and chairs, even small tables set up for chess and checkers. I walked toward the long counter of the registration desk, my feet cramping inside my high heels.

I was early, I knew without having to check my watch. Robert wouldn't be here yet. Even so, I glanced furtively around, careful not to make direct eye contact with any of the hotel's many other visitors. I could spend the next half hour browsing through the exclusive boutiques that were located just off the lobby, or I could stroll around the grounds, visit the bar at the back, off the main dining room. Larry and I had come here for dinner once, not long after we'd moved to Palm Beach. Over the years, we'd occasionally talked of checking ourselves in for a weekend. We never had. Now, here I was, about to check in with another man.

I lowered myself into a nearby antique chair, my body immediately obliterated by a hulking hydrangea plant whose bright pink flowers all but leapt into my lap. I heard laughter, turned sharply, the pointed end of a narrow green leaf catching the side of my eye. A young couple was standing not more than six feet away from me, wrapped in each other's arms, their lips pressed tightly together, their bodies swaying to imaginary breezes, as bemused onlookers tiptoed gingerly around them, careful not to disturb their passion. Next to the registration desk, a young boy of about six was standing beside his mother, pointing at the couple and laughing. His mother admonished him not to point, then looked away, although seconds later I noticed she looked back, sad eyes lingering.

That's what I want, I thought, knowing she was thinking the same thing. To be young and desperately in love, to need someone's arms around me so badly it hurt, to literally ache for the feel of his lips on mine, to be that desired, that carried away, that oblivious to the rest of the world. To be seventeen again.

This was my fantasy: Robert and I in each other's arms, his eyes gazing lovingly into mine, his lips delicately kissing the sides of my mouth, the bend in my neck, my fluttering eyelashes, my cheeks, the tip of my nose, his hands cupping my face, his fingers twisting through my hair as his tongue twisted gently around mine, our kisses growing deeper, yet softer, always softer.

The reality would be different. It always was. Oh, there might be deep tender kisses, but they would be mere preamble to the main event, and they could only linger so long, time being of the essence. Sara was waiting for me at home; Robert, no doubt, had plans with his wife. We couldn't be gone too long without arousing suspicions. And so, soft lingering kisses would give way to increasingly insistent caresses. Clothes would be unbuttoned, shed, and discarded. Limbs would entwine, flesh merge. A different flesh than I was used to, a different way of being touched. And it would be wonderful. I knew it would be wonderful. And when it was over, we would lie in each other's arms, mindful of the moments ticking away, trying to avoid the growing reality of the wet spot beneath us.

That was the difference between fantasy and reality. A fantasy contained no consequences, no mess. When it was over, you felt great, not guilt. Fantasies didn't leave wet spots.

That's what I wanted. I wanted the fantasy.

I didn't need any more reality. I had too much as it was.

I pictured Robert and me sitting on opposite sides of the bed, not speaking, no longer touching, struggling to get back into our clothes. I knew I'd feel awful. I felt awful enough now.

"What am I doing here?" I whispered, catching a long leaf in my mouth, feeling it slither across my tounge. And then I saw him.

He walked through the front door with a comfortable stride, long arms swinging casually at his sides. He was wearing navy pants and a white polo shirt, muscles impressively on display. His hair fell roguishly across his forehead. His lips curled into a natural smile. Could he look more beautiful? I wondered, as every muscle in my body cramped. Was it possible to want someone so much and like him so little?

I gasped, quickly covering my mouth to prevent the sound from escaping, as the truth of my latent observation hit me square in the gut, like a boxer's fist. And the truth was that I really didn't like Robert very much, that I never had, and that was the reason I hadn't slept with him thirty years ago. It was why I couldn't sleep with him now.

Robert strode confidently across the lobby, eyes straight ahead, looking neither right nor left. He didn't see me. I wasn't surprised. The truth was that I was invisible to Robert, that I'd always been invisible. How could you see someone, after all, when the only thing you saw when you gazed into their eyes was the glory of your own reflection?

That was the truth. That was the reality.

I watched Robert speak easily to the clerk behind the registration counter, then glance carelessly around the large lobby. Get up, I told myself. Get up and announce your presence, tell him you've had a change of heart. Instead, I burrowed in deeper behind the potted plant, knowing I was being silly, that even if I wasn't going to go upstairs with him, at least I owed him the courtesy of an explanation.

Except that something kept me rooted to that antique seat as surely as if I'd been potted myself. For despite my recent epiphany and newfound resolve, I knew that if I left that chair, if I confronted Robert, then I was lost, it was game over, I was as good as naked and lying smack in the middle of the wet spot. And so I remained in my chair, hidden by the giant hydrangea, watching as my would-be lover signed the register and took possession of the room key, smiling securely as he headed for the elevators.

And then I raced for the front entrance of the hotel as if someone were after me, as if my life depended on it.

Perhaps it did.

Chapter
30

I phoned Jo Lynn as soon as I got home. Her machine was still picking up, so I called the motel in Starke where she usually stayed. The manager informed me that she hadn't seen Jo Lynn in several weeks, then hung up before I could ask her the names of other motels in the area. "Great," I muttered, debating whether or not to call the police, maybe the penitentiary, deciding against both alternatives. What would I say after all? What could they do?

"I take it she didn't call?" I asked my daughters.

They shook their heads.

I thought of Robert, wondered if he was still waiting for me at the hotel, if he'd ordered champagne, if he was growing restless, bored, worried, angry. "Did anybody else phone?" I asked.

"Like who?" Sara said.

"Nobody in particular." I noticed she'd washed her hair, changed into a pair of surprisingly presentable beige pants and matching sweater. "Still want to go to the movies?"

"I guess so." Sara's voice strained for indifference, almost succeeded.

"How about you, Michelle? Feel like a movie?"

"Can't," she said. "I'm going over to Brooke's, remember?"

"That's right. I forgot." I looked around. "Where's Grandma? Is she sleeping?"

"She's in her room," Sara said. "She's been acting kind of funny."

"What do you mean, funny?"

"Hi, darling," my mother said, as if she'd been standing in the wings, waiting for her turn to resume center stage. She shuffled into the kitchen, purse in hand. "Did I hear you say we're going to the movies?"

Sara selected a popular movie, and the theater, at barely four o'clock in the afternoon on a beautiful sunny day, was almost full. We managed to find three seats together near the front. "Is this okay for you, Mom?" I asked.

She said nothing. She hadn't spoken a word since we left the house.

"Was she this quiet while I was gone?"

Sara nodded. "Except for every so often, when she suddenly screams."

"She screams?"

"Every so often."

"Why didn't you tell me this before?"

"I *did* tell you."

"You said she was acting funny. You didn't say anything about screaming."

"Sshh!" someone said, as the houselights dimmed.

She screamed the first time during one of the previews. It was a piercing wail, like a siren, and it scared me half to death, not to mention the people around us, all of whom literally jumped out of their seats.

"Mom, what's the matter?!"

"Is everything all right?" the woman directly in front of us asked.

"Mom, are you all right?"

Wide eyes stared at the screen. She gave no reply.

"She's fine," I assured those around us.

She screamed again about ten minutes into the feature presentation, once again scaring those people in our immediate vicinity half out of their wits, and causing a general outbreak of nervous giggles in the surrounding rows, not to mention a pronounced smattering of "sshh's." Two people at the end of our row got up and moved.

"I'm sorry," I whispered into the general darkness. "I'm very sorry. Mom, what's the matter? Does something hurt you? Do you want to leave?"

"Sshh!" someone hissed loudly.

My mother said nothing, settled back in her seat, her demeanor outwardly calm, her demons seemingly exorcised. I tried to relax, to pay attention to what was happening on the screen, but it was a bit like waiting for the other shoe to drop. I sat stiffly, my body on full alert, poised to whisk my mother out of the theater at the next outburst. It never came. Instead, she drifted off to sleep, awoke as the final credits were rolling.

"How are you?" I asked her as the lights went up.

"Magnificent," she said.

At least she'd kept my mind off Robert, I realized, as we walked up the aisle. I wondered how long he'd stayed at the hotel, and whether he'd tried calling my house to see if I was there, if everything was all right. Had he checked the hospitals, called the police, contacted station WKEY for the latest in accident reports?

As soon as we reached the pay phone in the lobby, I checked my answering machine for messages. There weren't any.

We went to a tiny Italian eatery in the same plaza as the movie theater. The restaurant was brightly lit and decorated in the colors of the Italian flag—red, white, and green. We ordered a large pizza with everything on it, and a Gorgonzola salad to share. "So, did you find

459

a place for Grandma?" Sara asked as we waited for our food to arrive.

"What?" I was staring out the front window
into the parking lot, wondering where Robert
was now, and what he was doing. I wasn't really surprised he hadn't called. Nor, I realized
with no small measure of relief, was I especially
disappointed.

"I asked if you found a place for Grandma
to live."

"No," I said, staring across the table at the
stranger who used to be my mother. The
harsh light in the small room accentuated
the blankness in her eyes, and gave the rest of
her features an eerie glow. She looked almost
otherworldly, an alien creature dropped into
our midst. I recalled the promo line from an
old horror movie: *First they come for your body,
then they come back for your mind*. Except that,
in this case anyway, reality seemed to work in
reverse. It was my mother's mind that had been
taken, while her body remained reasonably
intact. No, I thought, staring at the woman
who'd given me life almost a half century
ago, staring *through* her, this woman was not
my mother. The porcelain-skinned creature
with the empty, cavernous eyes bore no rela-
tion to my mother at all.

We ate in silence, listening to a man at the
next table loudly critique the movie we'd just
seen. An interesting concept but a mediocre
script, he pronounced, probably the result
of too many writers and too much studio
meddling. The actors were adequate, but no

more; the direction lacked focus. There were too many weird camera angles, no real vision. Decidedly, a minor effort. Rating: C+.

Sara made a face, took another bite of her pizza, dripped tomato sauce and cheese down her chin. "What did you think of the movie, Grandma?" she asked.

"I didn't know," my mother replied, eyes growing fearful.

"You don't know if you liked the movie?"

"I didn't know," my mother repeated, her hands leaving her pizza to scratch at the air.

I reached across the table, clasped my mother's hands in mine, brought them back down. "It's okay, Mom. It's okay now."

"What's happening?" Sara asked.

"I tried to protect you," my mother said. "I always tried to protect you." She rose halfway out of her seat.

"I know that, Mom."

"It's a mother's job to protect her child."

"It's okay, Mom. It's okay."

"I would never let anyone hurt my babies."

"I know that, Mom. Sit down. Please, sit down." My hands guided her back into her chair.

"I had to have a cesarean section, you know," she said. "I had an allergic reaction to the surgical tape. My skin is very sensitive."

"I know."

Her hands began frantically pawing at her stomach. "I'm horribly itchy. I'm not supposed to scratch."

"I'm scared," Sara said.

"It's all right, honey. Grandma's just a little confused."

"Don't be scared, Jo Lynn," my mother whispered, her hand leaving her stomach to caress Sara's cheek. "Mommy's here. I'll protect you."

After dinner, we guided my mother back to the car and strapped her into the rear seat. As soon as I started the engine, the radio came on, the sound of country music immediately filling the air. "How can you listen to this garbage?" Sara said, flipping through the various channels, eliciting a beat here, a chord there, each gone before anything had a chance to register on my brain. What difference did it make? I thought, catching a stray fragment of spoken word.

He apparently escaped...

Sara punched in another channel. The sound of heavy metal assaulted my ears. She quickly switched to another station. *You can take my heart, my achy breaky heart...*

She switched again.

"Wait a minute, what was that?"

"Mom, please don't make me listen to Billy Ray Cyrus."

"Not that. Before. The news."

"I don't want to listen to the news."

"Sara..."

"Okay, okay."

It took several seconds before we relocated the news, and by that time, the announcer had moved on to the weather. *Another beautiful sunny day for South Florida.*

"Find another channel."

"What are you looking for?" Sara asked.

"I thought I heard something."

"What?"

"Just find the news."

We found it, then listened in stunned silence as the story unfolded. *A dramatic escape took place earlier today at the Florida State Prison in Raiford. Colin Friendly, the convicted killer of thirteen women and the suspected killer of many more, escaped while being transferred to the neighboring Union Correctional Institution.*

"Oh God."

Officials are remaining tight-lipped about what exactly happened, but it appears that the notorious death row inmate was aided in his daring daytime escape by his wife, the former Jo Lynn Baker of Palm Beach.

"Oh God, no. Please, no."

"Jo Lynn helped him escape?" Sara asked incredulously.

Apparently, Colin Friendly was able to overpower one of his guards with a knife that had been smuggled into the prison. Police have issued an all-points bulletin for the getaway car, a 1987 red Toyota, license plate number YZT642, that belongs to the killer's wife. If anyone sees this vehicle, you are urged to call the police immediately. Under no circumstances should you approach the vehicle directly. Colin Friendly is armed and considered extremely dangerous.

"I don't understand," Sara said. "Why

would Jo Lynn do such a thing?"

"Because she's a moron," I shouted, slamming the steering wheel with my fists, accidentally connecting with the horn, feeling its sharp blast like a stab to my heart.

Once again: Colin Friendly has escaped from the Florida State Prison and is believed to be in the company of his wife, the former Jo Lynn Baker, who married Friendly in a recent jailhouse ceremony. They fled in the bride's 1987 red Toyota, license plate YZT642, and were last seen heading northwest. Police have set up roadblocks throughout the state, and are advising that should you see the couple, you call them immediately. They are considered armed and very dangerous. Under no circumstances approach them directly. And now, in other news…

"What's going to happen now?" Sara asked.

"I don't know."

"Do you think that's why she wanted the money so badly, so that she could help him escape?"

"It looks that way."

"Where do you think they're going?"

"I don't know. Northwest, the announcer said. Alabama, maybe. Georgia. I don't know."

"Do you think she'll try to get in touch with us?"

"I don't know." God, I was getting sick of saying that.

"You don't think there's any chance they'll come back here, do you?" Sara asked.

"No," I said, because I knew that's what she wanted to hear.

From the back seat, my mother started screaming.

As soon as we walked in the front door, I called Brooke's house and asked to speak to Michelle. I was going to tell her to take a cab home, or better yet, to spend the night with Brooke.

"She's not here," Brooke's brother told me, his voice nasal and bored, barely audible above the television blaring in the background.

"What do you mean, she's not there?"

"They went out a while ago."

"Do you know where they went?"

"I heard them say something about a party."

"Whose party? Where?"

"I don't know."

"Can I speak to your mother?" It was more demand than question. Stay calm, I tried to tell myself. There was nothing to worry about. Colin Friendly was headed northwest, not southeast. He wasn't crazy enough to come back to Palm Beach. There was nothing for me to worry about.

"There's nobody home but me," the boy said. I pictured him sprawled out lazily on the family-room sofa, a bowl of potato chips at his side.

I hung up the phone, not sure what to do next.

"Don't worry, Mom," Sara said. "You know Michelle. She'll be home by curfew."

I checked my watch. It was barely eight o'clock. Michelle's curfew was almost four hours

465

away. Could I last that long? I checked my answering machine for messages. No one had called.

"What are you so worried about?" Sara asked, eyes growing fearful.

"I'd just feel better if I knew where she was."

My mother began crying, swaying unsteadily from side to side. "I think I'd like to go home now," she said.

"It's okay, Mom. Everything's okay."

I asked Sara to get my mother ready for bed, and stay with her until she fell asleep. Then I marched into the family room and quietly placed a call to the police.

"My name is Kate Sinclair," I began, my voice a whisper so as not to alarm my older daughter.

"I'm sorry," said the officer who answered the phone. "You'll have to speak up."

I repeated my name, more loudly this time, then spelled it. "My sister is Jo Lynn Baker," I told him. "Jo Lynn *Friendly*," I immediately corrected, picturing the officer snap to attention on the other end of the line.

"Your sister is Jo Lynn Friendly?" There was a slight chuckle in his voice that told me he didn't quite believe me.

"Yes, and I'm concerned that Colin Friendly might be headed this way."

"And which way is that?" Again, the annoying chuckle wrapped around each word.

I gave him my address. "I'm not making this

up," I told him.

"What makes you think Colin Friendly might be heading back to Palm Beach?"

I told them about Colin's phone call, his letter.

"Did you report these things to the police?" he asked.

"No. I guess I should have."

"You have the letter?"

"I tore it up," I said sheepishly.

"Can you hold on a minute?" He put me on hold before I could object.

I grabbed the remote-control unit, flipped on the TV. Immediately, Colin Friendly's murderous face filled the screen, alternating with video footage of my sister at the courthouse. "Where are you?" I hissed at the screen. "Where the hell are you?"

The officer came back on the line. "We're sending someone over to talk to you," he said.

At 1 A.M., I was still sitting in front of the television, listening to tales of Colin's horrible exploits and staring at his killer smile. The police had come and gone. And Michelle still wasn't home.

★ ★ ★

By one-thirty, I was pacing the floor of the living room, and debating whether or not to call Larry in South Carolina. By two o'clock I was in tears, and wondering whether to check back with the police. They'd promised to patrol the neighborhood, despite the fact they were convinced Colin Friendly was heading in the opposite direction. So far, I hadn't seen one police car drive by.

By two-thirty, when I finally heard Michelle's key twisting in the front lock, I was such a mess that I didn't know whether to hug her or yell at her. So I did both.

I ran toward her, arms extended, tears streaming the length of my face. "Where the hell have you been?" I was hugging her so tightly she couldn't answer. "Do you know how late you are?"

Immediately, she began to whimper. "I'm sorry, Mom. We were at a party, and I had to wait until someone could give me a lift home."

"You could have taken a taxi. Or called me. I would have picked you up."

"It was so late. I thought you'd be asleep. I didn't want to wake you."

"Do you have any idea how frantic I've been?"

"I'm sorry, Mom. I'm so sorry."

"It's two-thirty in the morning."

"It'll never happen again."

"You're damn right it'll never happen again."

"What are you going to do?"

"I don't know." A familiar whiff reached my nostrils. "Have you been smoking?"

"No," she said immediately, backing out of my reach.

"You reek of cigarettes."

"Lots of kids at the party were smoking."

"But not you."

"Not me. Honestly."

I closed my eyes, rubbed my forehead. Was I crazy? Only minutes ago I'd been frantic that something might have happened to her; now I was upset that she might have been smoking. I was too old for this, I thought, double-locking the front door. Menopause and teenage girls—they definitely didn't mix. "Go to bed," I said. "We'll deal with this in the morning."

"I'm really sorry, Mom."

"I know."

"I love you."

"I love you too. More than anything in the world." Once again, I hugged her tightly against my breast. "Now get some sleep."

I watched her walk away, wiping tears from sleepy eyes. Sooner or later, I thought, heading into the kitchen for a glass of ice water, they're gonna get you.

I stared out the back window at the kaleidoscope of stars sprinkled across the black sky, finding the brightest one, making a wish. "I wish everything would go back to normal," I said, walking back toward the living room, past the spot by the breakfast nook that, less than eight hours later, would be covered in blood.

Chapter
31

I undressed, washed my face, brushed my teeth, and crawled into bed, exhaustion coating me like a layer of heavy dust. It filled my nose and mouth, crawled inside my pores, sank beneath the layers of my skin, inhabited my insides, like a tapeworm, growing fat even as its host withers and dies.

Surprisingly, I slept very well.

There were no dreams, no disturbances, no waking up in the middle of the night, agonizing over bad choices or bad memories. I thought of nothing and no one—not Larry or Robert or Colin Friendly, not Sara or Michelle or Jo Lynn, not my mother or my father or my stepfather. No one. As soon as my head hit the pillow, my mind went totally, mercifully blank.

When I opened my eyes, it was eight o'clock the next morning, and the sun was pushing through my bedroom curtains, like a large fist. "Just another day in Paradise," I said, swinging my legs out of bed and heading for the bathroom, fending off the intrusion of serious thought as I showered, dressed, and fiddled with my hair until it gave up and went totally limp. Only reluctantly did I leave the confines of my bedroom, stepping trepidly over the threshold into the main living space, hands crossed protectively over my chest, as if guarding my heart.

I stared at the front door. On the other side, the morning newspaper lay waiting, my sister no doubt featured prominently on the front page. I staggered, closed my eyes, turned away from the door. "Not before I've had my coffee," I said, extending my arms, as if I could physically keep reality a comfortable distance away.

I'm not sure what I was thinking as I prepared the morning coffee. Probably I was trying very hard not to think, which only made things worse. Had my sister really had anything to do with Colin Friendly's escape? How far was she prepared to go to help him? What would happen to her once Colin Friendly was apprehended, as no doubt, sooner or later, he would be? Would the police file criminal charges against her? Would she go to jail? Or would they judge her to be unstable, force her to seek psychiatric help? Was there even the slightest possibility that something good might come of this fiasco?

I glanced toward the TV in the family room. Maybe my sister and Colin Friendly had already been apprehended. How long could they hide, after all? They weren't the most inconspicuous of couples, and would have attracted attention even if their faces hadn't been plastered across the front pages of newspapers for months. Jo Lynn's weathered red Toyota was hardly the ideal choice of a getaway car. Surely, by now, someone had spotted them. "So turn on the TV and find out," I said, but didn't move. Whatever the news was, it wouldn't be good.

Instead I reached for a coffee mug, selecting one with a pink flamingo etched into its side, china tail feathers serving as a handle, and *Beautiful Palm Beach* scribbled in black along its side. I filled the oversized mug with steaming coffee and carried it into the family room, where I lowered myself gently into the sofa and sat staring out the large expanse of floor-to-ceiling windows at the backyard. Another one of those magic days, I thought, where the blue of the sky is so intense, it almost hurts the eyes. "Wouldn't you just love a sweater in that shade?" I heard Jo Lynn ask, and felt the mug in my hands about to slide through my fingers.

I gripped the flamingo's tail tighter, almost snapped it off. "Relax," I told myself. "The day has yet to begin."

"Who are you talking to?" a voice behind me asked, and I jumped, the coffee flying out of the mug and into the air, as if it were lava erupting from a volcano. It burned my hands and slashed across the front of my yellow T-shirt like a knife, the resultant brown stain bearing an uncomfortable resemblance to dried blood. "Are you all right?" Sara asked, rushing forward, taking the mug from my hands, depositing it on the coffee table. "I'm sorry. I didn't mean to scare you."

"I'm okay," I told her. "I just need a wet cloth."

"I'll get it." Sara was instantly in the kitchen, at the sink, back at my side, swatting at the front of my T-shirt with the wet dishrag. "I'm really sorry," she said, tears forming in the corners of already swollen eyes.

"It's okay, Sara. Really, I'm fine."

"You're sure?"

"I'm sure."

"I'm really sorry."

I studied her face, still beautiful despite the swollen eyes and lack of sleep. I knew she was apologizing for more than the coffee.

"I know," I said. "I'm sorry too."

"I don't know what comes over me sometimes. I just get so angry."

I said nothing.

"I love you," she said.

"I love you too."

"Do you?" she asked plaintively.

"Always."

Sara bit down on her bottom lip. It quivered beneath her teeth, broke free of her grasp. "How can you love me when I'm such an awful person?"

"You're not an awful person, Sara."

"Michelle never acts the way I do."

"Michelle's different than you are."

"She's so together. She knows who she is. She knows what she wants."

"What do you want?"

"I don't know. I don't know anything. I'm so stupid."

"You're anything but stupid."

"Then why do I do these things?"

"I don't know," I told her honestly. "Maybe it would help to talk to a therapist."

"You *are* a therapist."

"I'm also your mother. The two don't seem to mix."

Sara tried to smile, though her lips refused to hang on to it, and it slid off the side of her face. "Is there any news about Jo Lynn?"

I shook my head. "I don't know. I've been afraid to find out."

Sara quickly scooped up the remote-control

unit from the coffee table and turned on the TV, flipping through a number of Sunday morning sermons before finding the news. I listened absently as a boyishly handsome announcer filled me in on the latest in global politics, then began a detailed report on the environment. With the flick of a button, he was gone, replaced by another boyishly handsome announcer. A major late-winter storm was about to hit sections of the Northeast, threatening to dump a possible three feet of snow on the area, he intoned, as images of high winds and swirling snow filled the screen.

And suddenly the snow disappeared into the Florida sunshine, and I found myself staring at a dilapidated old red Toyota, parked in front of a seedy-looking motel and surrounded by a virtual horde of state troopers. "My God," I said, holding my breath, inching forward, my hands digging into the back of the sofa.

"Police report that they have located the vehicle they believe was used to aid in the escape of Colin Friendly from the Union Correctional Institution in Florida yesterday afternoon," the announcement began. "A 1987 red Toyota, believed to belong to Jo Lynn Baker, recent bride of the convicted serial killer, was found parked in a wooded area near the family-owned and -operated Wayfarer's Motel just outside of Jacksonville, Florida, early this morning."

"Jacksonville?" Sara asked, echoing my thoughts. "They only got as far as Jacksonville?"

"Police are refusing to speculate whether the

474

fugitive couple are still in the Jacksonville area," the announcer continued, as pictures of Colin Friendly and my sister filled the screen. "They wish to remind the public that both Colin Friendly and his wife should be considered armed and extremely dangerous. If you see them, or have any information as to their whereabouts, contact the police immediately. Under no circumstances should they be approached."

"How could she do this?" I muttered, sinking onto the arm of the sofa.

"Do you think they'll get away?"

"No."

"What's going to happen to her?" Sara asked.

"I don't know."

"This just in," the announcer continued, unable to disguise the excitement in his voice. He's probably been waiting his whole life to say, "This just in," I thought, as once again my breath constricted in my chest. "Police have confirmed that the body of a man matching Colin Friendly's description has been found in the wooded area behind the Wayfarer's Motel near Jacksonville."

"My God."

"What about Jo Lynn?" Sara asked.

"I repeat: police say they have recovered the body of a man believed to be Colin Friendly in a wooded area behind the Wayfarer's Motel on the outskirts of Jacksonville, close to where the red Toyota belonging to his wife, the former Jo Lynn Baker, was spotted earlier this

475

morning. Police are refusing further comment at this time, but promise to have a statement later in the day. Stay tuned for further developments as they occur. In other news…"

"He's dead?" Sara asked. "Colin Friendly is dead?"

"I can't believe it."

"Do you think Jo Lynn killed him?"

"Jo Lynn couldn't kill a bee if it were getting ready to sting her."

"Then where is she? What's happened to her?"

"I don't know." I stood up, sat back down again. "I don't know what to do."

"What to do about what?" Michelle asked, coming into the room, neatly dressed in denim shorts and a lime-green shirt. "What's happening?"

"Colin Friendly's dead and nobody knows what's happened to Jo Lynn," Sara told her.

"What?!"

"Maybe there's something in the morning paper," Sara said. "Where is it?"

"It's still outside."

"I'll get it," Sara volunteered, heading for the front door.

The phone rang. Michelle ran into the kitchen and answered it. It was Larry.

"You've heard?" he asked as Michelle handed me the phone.

"Just now—on the news."

"Any word about Jo Lynn?"

"Nothing."

"Okay, listen, hang tight. I'm on my way to

the airport. I'm on standby for an earlier flight. I'll be home as soon as I can. Don't try to talk me out of it."

"Hurry," was all I said.

"Colin Friendly's dead?" Michelle repeated.

"Apparently."

"Good." The front door opened and closed. "What's it say in the paper?" Michelle called out.

There was no answer.

"Didn't they deliver the paper?" I asked, rounding the corner into the breakfast nook.

What I saw next is carved deeply into my brain, like ancient hieroglyphics on the inside of a cave: my older daughter, in white sloppy shirt and boxer shorts, the newspaper dangling from her limp hand, uncombed multihued hair falling into wide, swollen eyes, tears falling into her open mouth, head thrust back, a long jagged-edged knife held across her throat.

"Oh, they delivered the paper, all right," Colin Friendly said, smiling face pressing against Sara's tear-stained cheek, one arm snaked around her waist, holding her firmly in place, the other around her neck, his hand pressing the knife to her jugular. "But you know how newspapers are. They never get anything right."

For a moment, everything stopped—the humming of the refrigerator, the birds singing in the backyard, the blood running through my veins, my very breath. In the artificial silence, I registered Colin Friendly's startling blue eyes, his wavy hair and twisted smile, the oddly conservative blue shirt and black linen pants that hung loosely on his wiry frame, the powerful hands that escaped from under cuffs a shade too long, the long slender fingers that were curled around the black handle of a long serrated knife, the jagged edge of which was pressed against my daughter's tender flesh.

"Who's here?" Michelle asked from the kitchen, coming into the breakfast nook, freezing momentarily when she saw the nightmarish tableau, then abruptly bolting for the sliding glass door at the back of the family room.

"Stop!" Colin Friendly called out. "Or I'll slit her throat right here and now. Don't think I won't."

Michelle came to an immediate halt.

"That's a good girl," Colin said. "Now, come on back here. Join your mama. Thatta girl."

Michelle walked slowly back to my side, pushing one foot in front of the other with great difficulty, as if she were walking through mud. I grabbed her to me, held on tight, too numb to speak, the sight of my older daughter with a knife at her throat rendering me as helpless as if I'd been bound and gagged. Where were the police? Was it possible that the patrol car had spotted Colin Friendly hiding in the bushes and was, even now, radioing for backup?

"We thought you were dead," Michelle

said to Colin Friendly.

He laughed. "Yeah, well, I was kind of hopin' you'd think that."

A small squeal escaped Sara's mouth. Fresh tears fell the length of her cheeks.

"Please let her go," I said, finding my voice, weak and cowering in a corner of my throat, pushing it out.

"Let her go?" he asked incredulously. "Hell no. She's one of the reasons I came back here."

"I'm sorry, Mommy," Sara cried, although her lips never moved.

Colin Friendly tightened his grip around her waist. "Isn't that cute? The way all little girls cry for their mommy when they're in trouble? Wendy Sabatello cried for her mommy, and Tammy Fisher, she did too. Oh, and that little girl you were so interested in, Amy Lokash, she cried for her mommy. It always gives me kind of a little thrill, you know."

"You're a monster," I whispered.

"Yeah, well, you always knew that, didn't you, Mommy?" he said. "Lucky for me your sister never believed you."

"Where is Jo Lynn?"

"Back in Jacksonville. She didn't feel up to making the trip back here."

"Is she all right?"

He smiled. "You think I'd hurt the one woman who stood by me, who believed in me, who helped me escape?"

"You killed Mrs. Ketchum," I said, remembering the neighbor who'd tried to help him.

The smile grew into a laugh. "Yeah, I did, didn't I?"

Sara squirmed in the killer's arms. He pressed the knife harder against her throat, drawing a small bead of blood.

"Oh God," I moaned.

"Yeah, he's a big favorite too," Colin said. "I hear his name a lot. God and Mommy—they run kind of neck and neck."

"Why are you here?" Michelle demanded. "What do you want from us?"

"Feisty little thing, isn't she?" Colin winked at me, grinned widely. "It's going to be fun doing you, sweetheart. Bet I'll be your first," he continued, as I fought the urge to throw up. "And your last." He laughed, clearly enjoying his power over us. He hasn't stuttered once, I realized. "That's why I'm here, darlin'," he went on. "That's what I want from you. From all of you, even Mommy here." His voice was like a lasso, encircling us, tying us together, pulling us toward him. "I've been thinking of little else since I went to prison. You all been my nourishment, what's been keeping me going. Plus, of course, I missed my goody box."

"Your goody box," I repeated, wondering if the police were anywhere in the vicinity, trying to stall for time.

"Yeah, the box where I keep all my little souvenirs: Tammy Fisher's ankle bracelet, Marie Postelwaite's panties, Amy Lokash's plastic red barrette. Lots of interesting stuff. I got it buried in the backyard of my old apartment building in Lantana. Shouldn't be too hard to find, especially with the police convinced I'm heading north."

"How did you get here?"

"Well, I couldn't very well drive your sister's fire-engine red piece of shit, now could I? So I borrowed some guy's car. He didn't mind. What does a dead guy need with a car anyway?" He smiled widely. "That's the guy they found in the woods. The one they think is me. Probably because I didn't leave him much of a face. He was nice enough to swap clothes with me before he died."

A soft whine filled the air as Sara slumped in Colin's arms.

"Don't faint on me, girl," he said. "Not yet." He drew the knife up toward the underside of her chin, as if he were a barber giving a shave. A faint sound, somewhere between a gasp and a sigh, escaped Sara's lips. "You hear that?" Colin asked. "That cute little sound? It must run in the family. Your sister made that same little sound," he told me. "Right before I smashed her nose in."

"Oh God."

"There's that name again."

"You killed my sister?" Tears filled my eyes, temporarily blinding me. I tried wiping them away, but the room remained blurred, one object bleeding into the next, like ink on a wet piece of paper. I saw Colin Friendly, his wavy dark hair disappearing into Sara's dark roots, the whiteness of his skin merging with the whiteness of her shirt, the knife dancing unsteadily at her throat, so that it seemed as if there were many knives, many throats. The room lost focus, perspective, balance. It threatened to overturn, crumble, disappear.

"Now, I didn't say I killed her," he said evenly. "I just said I broke her nose."

"What have you done to her?"

"It's funny how some people react when they know they're going to die," he said, ignoring my question. "Some people get all panicky, and they yell and cry and carry on. Then there are others who try to reason with you. You kind of play along with them for a while, make them think like they might be getting through to you, and they relax a little bit, get all hopeful, and then there's that wonderful moment when they realize you're going to kill them anyway, and you watch the hope sink in their eyes, kind of like a ship going down in the ocean. That's usually when they start pleading." He laughed, a kind of manic cackle that hacked at the air, like a machete. "I think I like that part the best of all." He swayed, eyes dreamy, as if savoring the memory. "They give you all these reasons not to kill them— they want to live, they're young and they got their whole lives ahead of them, they got their children or their widowed mothers to look after. Shit like that. Janet McMillan, she was cryin' about her two little kids, and your friend Amy Lokash, she worried about her mother. Hey, you still want to know where to find her?" he asked suddenly, continuing before I had a chance to speak. "Remember when I sent

482

you off on that wild-goose chase to Lake Osborne?"

I nodded.

"Well, it really wasn't such a wild-goose chase after all. Amy's there, all right. Just not in the water. I buried her beside that little building they have there for the kids' summer camp. You must have seen it."

"I saw it," I acknowledged, picturing the squat wooden cabin surrounded by trees.

"Couple of months from now, kids'll be dancing on her grave."

Once again, my eyes filled with tears—for Amy, her mother, my daughters, myself. Jo Lynn. "Did you kill my sister?" I asked.

"If I did, she deserved it. She couldn't do nothing right. She didn't bring me one dime of the money she said was lyin' around here, money I know you'll be kind enough to provide me with before I go."

"Did you kill my sister?" I repeated.

"Yeah, I did," he said easily. "And you know, she didn't beg or plead or try to talk me out of it or anything. She just gave that cute little sound and looked at me with those big green eyes like she'd kind of known what was going to happen all along. She wasn't nearly as much fun to kill as you all are gonna be." Without loosening his grip on my daughter, he managed to reach into the pocket of his pants and pull out the wedding band my sister had purchased for herself and worn with such proud defiance. "For my goody box," he said.

I tried to contain my growing panic, to figure out what I could do to protect my daughters from this monster. It was obvious the police weren't going to help us. But there were three of us, I told myself, and only one of him. And even though he held a knife to my daughter's jugular, we were only steps away from the kitchen and knives of our own. Perhaps there was some way to distract him, overtake him, surprise him before he had time to react, before he could plunge the knife into Sara's throat.

And then I saw her. She first appeared in the corner of my eye, like a speck of dust, and then grew, like a shadow, assuming shape and form and three dimensions, her gray curls flat and uncombed, her nightgown falling loosely from her shoulders, her slippered feet making no sound as she crept along the tile floor behind Colin Friendly, her brown eyes clear and focused.

"Grandma!" Michelle gasped before she could stop herself.

"What?" Colin Friendly asked, spinning around.

And then everything exploded.

I didn't actually see the golf club in my mother's hands until it came slicing through the air at Colin Friendly's skull. It connected with bone-shattering fury, pushing one cheekbone into the other, almost tearing the hair from his scalp, blood spilling copiously from his right ear. I lunged toward Sara, pulled her screaming from Colin Friendly's grasp as he staggered sideways, the knife dropping from his hand as the club swooped down again, this time with even greater ferocity, slicing across his jaw, shattering his teeth, so that they flew from his mouth, like niblets of corn, blood gushing down his chin as if from a fountain. The club came down yet again, this time with hammerlike precision across the center of his face, bringing him to his knees in a pool of his own blood, his nose shattered. He looked over to where I stood huddling with my girls, and tried to laugh, although instead of sound, there was only blood. And then he fell forward at our feet.

I ran to my mother, as the club dropped from her hands, kissed her, hugged her tightly to my chest. "I'll protect you," she whispered, as Michelle and Sara joined in our embrace, their bodies surrounding us, clinging to our sides like plastic wrap. "I'll protect you."

By the time the police arrived, her eyes had clouded over. She greeted the officers with a polite smile, and dozed against my shoulder as I tried to tell them what happened.

Chapter
32

The media had a field day. For the next several weeks, we were literally besieged by hordes of reporters from around the world. TV cameras took root on our front lawn, grew like ivy around the house, scaling the windows, burrowing into every nook and cranny of the cream-colored exterior. Everywhere we went, microphones were pushed toward our mouths, strobe lights exploded in our faces, people whispered behind our backs. We issued terse "no comments" to the hundreds of questions posed. It was easier than trying to explain we didn't have any answers.

Even now, four months later, I have no answers. I'm still struggling to understand what happened.

The only thing I know for certain is that my sister is dead.

At first, I tried to deny it. I told myself that Colin Friendly was lying, that once again he'd been playing with me, enjoying my torment, and that, in reality, Jo Lynn was alive and well, that she'd sneaked away from his bed in the middle of the night, was even now hiding out in the wooded area behind the Wayfarer's Motel near Jacksonville. Even if Colin Friendly was telling the truth, I rationalized further, Jo Lynn was a strong woman, and somehow she'd managed to survive his brutal attack. She might have to spend a few weeks in a hospital, recovering from her wounds, but she'd get better. Even after the police reported finding a woman's body in Room 16 of the now-infamous lodging, I told myself that it wasn't Jo Lynn. The police had been wrong about the body of the man they'd initially identified as Colin Friendly. They were wrong now, or so I tried to convince myself. Until such denials became impossible.

I went to the medical examiner's office, but they wouldn't let me see her body, wouldn't even show me a photograph. There was significant trauma to the face, the police officer explained, even though I was no longer listening, having heard it all before. Did they remember me? I wondered absently, recalling my visit with Donna Lokash, at the time never dreaming, as I glanced reluctantly at the photograph of the teenage girl lying dead on a steel slab in the back room, that one day my sister would be lying on that same slab. Or was I lying to myself about that as well? Had I somehow known all along?

What else had I known all along? I ask myself now. Had I known, somewhere deep down in my gut, the things that happened between my stepfather and Jo Lynn all those years ago? Certainly the clues were there, all the missing pieces of the puzzle that was my sister. Looking back on it now, it seems inconceivable that I could have missed them. Jo Lynn was always dropping hints. All I had to do was bend down and pick them up. Was it possible I'd deliberately ignored them?

Some therapist you are, Sara shouted at me, and maybe she was right. As a therapist, I should have known. Had Jo Lynn been a client, and not my sister, I would have at least suspected the truth, but, like the shoemaker's children who go without shoes, this was simply too close to home.

Ultimately, they identified my sister from her fingerprints, and her body was cremated. Ashes to ashes. Dust to dust. For a while, it felt as if she'd never existed, that there'd never been this exotic creature named Jo Lynn. And maybe this is as close to the truth as I'm likely ever to get. Because from the time my stepfather first laid his perverted hands on her, the real Jo Lynn, the Joanne Linda she was born, ceased to be. In her place grew a disturbed young woman with a penchant for high drama and low self-esteem, a woman who'd learned from childhood that to be abused meant to be loved.

The fact was that Jo Lynn had never known safety from a man. Not from her father, not from husbands one through three, all of whom had only underlined the concepts she learned in childhood: that it was acceptable to hurt the ones you love, that dangerous men are often the most attractive, that hard fists are more persuasive than soft words. Colin Friendly was merely an extension of the men who'd preceded him. It could be argued that my sister's marriage to Colin Friendly was as logical a move as any she'd ever made.

Is this sufficient to explain why she would willingly throw herself at a man who would, quite literally, just as soon kill her as look at her? Was she, as the tabloids have proclaimed, that desperate for attention? For publicity? For love?

I don't think so. I think this is too simple an explanation for her behavior, and that somehow it misses the point.

I think that, strange as it may seem, Colin Friendly was someone my sister thought she could control. He was in prison, after all, sentenced to die in the electric chair. Even if he managed to escape death, he would spend the rest of his life behind bars. In a subtle, but very real way, this fact rendered the vicious serial killer one of the safest men my sister had ever known.

Or perhaps she thought she could save him, that if she loved him hard enough, believed in him strongly enough, supported him ardently enough, she would be his salvation, and that by saving him, she could somehow save herself as well.

Could anything have saved her? Could I?

I don't think so, but then, that's always been part of my problem. I think too much. What about how I feel? Isn't that what I'm always asking my clients—how do you *feel*?

Well, how *do* I feel?

I feel like pulling all the dishes from the cupboards and hurling them against the tile floor, watching them smash into a million pieces. I feel like standing in the middle of the road and screaming at the top of my lungs, daring cars to hit me. I feel like running as fast as I can, as far as I can, until my legs give out and my body cries for mercy, and then screaming some more. I feel helpless. I feel angry. I feel frustrated. I feel sad. So sad. Sadness fills my lungs, like water. I feel as if I'm drowning. I'm scared. Jo Lynn has abandoned me. She was wild and reckless and just a little bit crazy. And as long as she was those things, I didn't have to be. I could play it safe, be the good girl, the common sense to her imagination. And now she's gone, and I feel as if a wild animal has torn a huge chunk of flesh out of my side.

Part of me is missing.

I never told my sister that I loved her. And she never told me.

How could two sisters have so much insight into each other, and so little into themselves?

I don't have the answer. The lady with all the answers doesn't have any. What will my clients think?

Actually, I don't have any clients. I've decided to take some time off, maybe a year, maybe more. Reconsidering my options, I believe is the phrase most commonly used. I've been working since I graduated from university, and I need a break, although, to be perfectly truthful, this sabbatical is as much a result of outside forces as inner convictions. Within days of the story breaking in the papers, most of my clients called to cancel their scheduled appointments. I don't blame them. It's hard to entrust your life to a therapist who can't control her own.

Of course, my projected radio show came to naught. Robert called to say that the powers that be at the station had decided that, in light of all the recent publicity, now was probably not the best time for me to be launching such a high-profile career. He talked about the need for credibility in broadcasting, without actually saying that mine had been seriously undermined. He never said a word about what happened—what *hadn't* happened—at the

Breakers. He wished me all the best; I wished him the same.

Yesterday, I was flipping through the channels on my car radio, and I caught the end of Faith Hill's bloodless rendition of *Piece of My Heart*, immediately followed by a husky, and strangely familiar, voice: "We're talking about heartache today on WKEY-FM's Country Counselor. The call lines are now open. If there's anything you want to tell me about the last time you lost a piece of your heart, or you need some advice on finding it again, or you just want to hear a song about it, then call me right now. I'm Melanie Rogers, and I'm here to help."

I recalled the honey-voiced redhead with the emerald-green eyes I'd met in Robert's office. "Let me introduce you to an old friend," Robert had said by way of introduction. "Melanie Rogers, this is Kate Sinclair. We go back a very long way." All the way back to high school and Sandra Lyons, I thought, understanding that some things never change.

It seems almost inconceivable to me now that I could have seriously considered jeopardizing my marriage to Larry for someone like Robert. The truth is that I love my husband, that I always have. I can't imagine life without him. Lately, Larry and I have been talking about leaving Florida, going back to Pittsburgh. We've never made any real friends here, and Larry says he misses the change in seasons. His golf game is the pits, he claims, and besides, he can no longer look at a golf club without thinking of my mother and Colin Friendly.

It's still amazing to me that Colin Friendly survived the attack, although I really shouldn't be surprised. People like Colin Friendly always survive. It's the innocent who perish. I read in the paper the other day that the Florida Supreme Court turned down his latest request for a stay of execution. If I remember correctly the things Jo Lynn told me, that would leave the federal district court, the U.S. Eleventh Court of Appeals in Atlanta, and the U.S. Supreme Court. It's a long process. It could drag on for years.

My mother is in a nursing home now, and something of a celebrity, although she doesn't seem to understand what all the fuss is about. She hasn't spoken since that morning she took a club to Colin Friendly's head, and I'm pretty sure she has no memory of the incident. I'm not even sure she knows who I am anymore, although she always looks pleased to see me when I visit.

Sara and Michelle often accompany me on these visits. Sara's hair is back to basic brown, her wardrobe an eccentric combination of hooker and hippie. Michelle has discovered black. They've been staying pretty close to my side these days, which is normal considering what we've been through. I confess to loving this renewed closeness. I savor every minute, partly because I know it won't last much longer. Several times lately, I've caught the whiff of cigarettes on Michelle's breath, and heard the hint of impatience in Sara's voice. I know they're getting ready to resume their lives. I'm bracing myself, trying to prepare for this eventuality, knowing that whatever course they choose, it is out of my control. I can't protect them forever. I can only tell them how much I love them.

Therapy has helped. Sometimes we all go together; sometimes we go individually. After years of listening to everyone else's problems, I've rediscovered the joys of talking about my own. But it's a long road back to normalcy, and I know it'll take time. I'm only grateful we have that time. For people like Donna Lokash, that time is gone forever.

The police found Amy Lokash's remains buried beside the day camp center in John Prince Park, exactly where Colin Friendly said they'd be, and they located his so-called goody box, filled with items belonging to each of his victims, all neatly labeled with the victim's name and date of death. Nineteen in all, including a hair curler belonging to his mother and a silver cross that once hung around Rita Ketchum's neck.

And so the police can now indisputably link Colin Friendly to the disappearances of six more women. Six more cases closed.

Incidentally, I just heard on the news that Millie Potton was found limping along the shoreline of Riviera Beach in her underwear, sunburnt and confused, but otherwise seemingly healthy. I'm glad. I was worried about her.

I think that's everything. I'll probably edit out some of the more personal revelations before I hand this over to the police. I'm not sure that any of this is what they were expecting. But I've tried to provide substance, context, explanations. I've searched my memory and bared my soul. I'm sure there are still some pieces missing. But I've done my best. Hopefully, it will be of some use.

At any rate, it's time to pick up the pieces. And go on.